SCARS OF YESTERDAY

Sons of Templar Book Eight

ANNE MALCOM

For Ember Rose Urruela.

Cover Design: Simply Defined Art
Editing: Kim BookJunkie

Prologue

This story doesn't have a happy ending.

It's better I tell you that now.

I'm a sucker for happy endings, there's a romantic inside of me that has refused to die, even after all these years. Even after being married to a man who was patched in to one of the deadliest MCs in the country. There was nothing romantic about it, despite what popular culture likes to tell you.

Especially during those bloody years. Before the club steered in a more legitimate direction.

There were losses. Deep cuts that left me with my scars of my own. Wounds I helped my husband tend to. The husband who wore a Sons of Templar MC cut.

He was buried in that cut.

But that's jumping to the end of the story before hearing about the beginning. Which is good. Because now you know what's waiting for you at the end of this story.

You can make the choice to escape all of this pain, loss and grief. The choice I couldn't make.

Part I

Before

Chapter 1

"Can I carry your books for you?"

I looked up and lost my breath.

He was standing there staring at me like such a request was commonplace. Like it was normal for *Cody flipping Derrick* to ask me, Lizzie Kirkpatrick, to carry her books.

And he didn't even give me time to answer—like my answer would be anything but a dreamy yes once I regained the ability to speak. He just leaned forward, smelling like body spray and hair gel, and took them out of my arms.

Took my books out of my arms.

Our bare skin brushed for half a second, and my whole face warmed as I blushed. My whole body seemed to blush.

He grinned, flashing teeth that were white and almost straight if not for one crooked tooth making that smile something other than perfect.

Something beautiful.

"English next, right?" he asked.

Again, he didn't give me time to answer, he just turned and walked in the direction of my English classroom. I was so shocked I just stood there, like an idiot, watching him walk away with an armful—and he had more than capable arms—of my books. He didn't look back, of course. He was *Cody flipping Derrick*. He didn't need to look back. Not with those burnt caramel eyes, those muscled arms, broad shoulders, and five o'clock shadow that he'd had for the past year. Though we were only a couple of months into his last year of school, he'd already turned eighteen.

I slammed my locker shut and jogged to catch up with him. Because of my slow reaction, we were already halfway to my English class which meant I'd wasted precious time.

Cody grinned at me as I fell into step with him. That grin. It was cheeky, genuine and hot as balls. Everything about him was hot as balls. He had really freaking good genes. He hadn't gone through that awkward, teenage phase, all gangly limbs and acne. I knew that because I'd known Cody all my life, and I'd crushed on him since I could remember.

We were friends, even though he was one grade above me. Amber was a small town, and there were few kids our age, so most parties were a mishmash of about three different grades. There wasn't exactly a hierarchy at our high school either. No 'popular' kids, jocks or nerds. No cliques. People were raised different here, maybe.

"You look pretty today," Cody said as I walked beside him mutely, trying to figure out something to say.

His words hit me almost as hard as the sideways glance he sent me. The one that made my insides all melty. A good quarter of the girl's hearts at this school were his because of that melty look. The other three quarters were spread amongst Cade Fletcher, Brock and Zane—despite the fact that Zane and Laurie had been going steady since *forever*.

They were all in my grade, and Laurie was one of my closest friends, which meant I was around Zane, Brock and Cade a lot.

Zane only had eyes for Laurie, but Brock and Cade had eyes for everyone.

They did not seem like they had any interest in going steady with anyone, working their way through the beautiful girls in our school.

I'd never really considered myself beautiful. Cute? Sure. But my boobs hadn't seemed to have gotten the memo that I was a young woman, I had too many freckles, and my hair was a dirty kind of blonde that couldn't be described as anything but plain.

I was good with makeup. Skilled at adding a light touch that emphasized my eyes and lips, my two best features. I loved fashion, and I'd gone through all sorts of phases in high school, usually inspired by movies or books I was reading at the time. I was currently in my Edie Sedgwick phase, so today I was wearing a swing dress and over the knee boots. My earrings almost touched my shoulders.

Suffice it to say, my father had raised his brows at breakfast this morning, but as was his way, he left it to my mother to say something. Luckily, she had long given up on trying to make me into a little pastel wearing daughter.

She had just sighed, handed me coffee and complimented my earrings.

I looked kick-ass.

And I knew it. Sure, I might not have been the prettiest girl in the school, but I had the best style. The kind other girls complimented but guys definitely didn't understand.

But here was Cody Derrick, calling me pretty. Which, in my opinion, was much better than calling someone 'hot'.

A flush crawled to my forehead. "Ah, thank you," I said awkwardly.

He grinned wider, his eyes flickering up and down my body. "Like the boots."

Something about the way he said that electrified me. His

words travelled all the way up my legs and... *right there*. Most of my girlfriends had already lost their virginity. I wanted to. Had no illusions about the first time being special or romantic. I was well aware that it was going to be sloppy, painful and awkward, no matter who I was doing with it. And there had been plenty of chances. Parties where I was drunk enough to make out with some guy who would've jumped at the chance to get laid.

But I was never drunk enough to let stuff go past second base.

Because I was waiting. Like an idiot. I was waiting for Cody Derrick to notice me, really notice me. I was waiting even though I knew I'd never get what I wanted but wasn't ready to give up the fantasy just yet. It happened in the romance novels I'd been devouring since I was fourteen. Yes, they were just books—trash if you listened to my mother, which I didn't since she considered *Good Housekeeping* to be fine literature—but they had to be based on something, right?

"Why are you walking me to class?" I asked instead of addressing the comment about my boots and the fact that his eyes had caressed my legs as he did so.

He stopped just shy of my English classroom, not making a move to give me my books back. I glanced toward the classroom where Laurie and Zane were making out right in front of the doorway, not seeming to notice that there was anyone else in their vicinity, or anyone else in the world, maybe. That was typical of those two. They belonged in a romance novel. It was hard to believe what they had—that kind of love wasn't meant for teenagers. It felt adult, forever. And that was just based on what I saw from the sidelines.

My gaze moved from them because my head moved. Cody's thumb and finger were gently touching my chin, moving it so I was looking at him again.

Every inch of my skin flamed with that single, gentle touch.

He was doing it casually, like he touched me every day, like it was natural.

"Because in those boots, someone else is gonna to try and do a lot more than just walk you to class," he said, voice rough. "And then I'll have to do something like pick a fight with a guy who I have no problem with beyond the fact that he's stupid enough to think he can walk you to class."

I blinked. Cody wasn't exactly a man of few words like Cade was. He was boisterous, funny, loud and conversational. Confident. But he had never spoken to me like *that* before.

"Okay, that is not an answer. Nor does it make sense. Like, not even for a second," I said. "My boots are cute, for sure. But not *that* cute." I waved my hands between us then glanced at the class that was slowly filling up, not wanting to be late. I wasn't exactly the 'good girl', but I didn't like getting in trouble either. I'd tried to balance out going to parties and getting drunk while telling my mother that I was at a sleepover by keeping my grades up and not getting in trouble at school. I still wanted to go to college, after all. I *had* to go to college. My parents never let me forget that they'd worked hard and sacrificed many things in order to get my college fund to its current balance. And as much as my mom pissed me off, I didn't want to disappoint her. Or my father. Especially my father.

Cody grinned. "*That* cute?" he repeated, waving his free hand between us, still holding my books hostage. And he was holding *me* hostage with that smile.

I bit my lip. I would definitely be the last one in class now. It bothered me. Slightly. But not enough to move. Not enough to actually do anything about it. No, I would stay right here, feeling awkward, excited, happy and aroused for as long as Cody was grinning at me.

I scowled, or at least tried to. Wasn't I meant to play hard to get? Willow, my best friend, had assured me that such things were vital in getting a guy interested, and most importantly, to get a guy to stay interested. She should know. She was never single for longer than twenty-four-hours, and in a town as small as ours, that was impressive.

"You know what I mean," I replied, folding my arms.

To my annoyance, he smiled even wider at my tone which was meant to sound snotty and superior. Then again, I didn't exactly have much experience being snotty or superior. I was—I liked to believe—a nice person.

"I do know what you mean," he agreed.

He didn't say anything else.

Maybe this was some kind of game of emotional chicken. Whoever spoke first would lose the upper hand. Willow always talked about the upper hand.

So I waited. It was uncomfortable. Cody was just standing there, staring at me, acting like the situation wasn't weird at all. I tried not to fidget, but it was hard when the guy you've been crushing on since forever stares at you like *that*.

The halls were empty now, no stragglers, no giggling, laughing, shoving or hurrying to class. Even Zane and Laurie had detached. Aside from the slight murmur coming from my soft-spoken English teacher, nothing could be heard. Other than that, dead silence. Although Cody's presence had a sound. His smile echoed through the halls of my mind.

I swallowed roughly, my palms starting to get clammy. That was not cute. No matter how important it was to play hard to get, to win at emotional chicken—or whatever the heck this was —I wasn't going to get a tardy slip and turn into a sweating mess in front of Cody.

"Are you going to give me back my books?" I asked, unable to stand the silence any longer.

His smile went away. He looked more serious now, as serious

as I'd ever seen Cody Derrick look, at least. "Only if you promise I'm gonna carry them from now on."

I blinked. Slowly. Just to make sure I wasn't hallucinating. But no, Cody was still here. "Why would you want to carry my books around?"

"Because, babe, I want you. And in this high school, me carrying your books is just one of the ways I can communicate that you're mine. I'll be doing that in other ways too. Especially if you've got more of those boots."

Holy. Crap.

He just said all of that. No one talked like that in real life, did they? Sure, they did in books, but most of those books were written by women putting their wishes of how they wanted men to talk to them down on paper.

Before I could figure how to get my breath back, how to reply to such a statement, my books were back in my arms, my arms grasping them on reflex more than anything. Cody got close enough to smell, proving that he wore the same body spray that most of the boys in his grade wore, but mixed with something that smelled different and uniquely him.

"I'll be waiting for you outside class," he said. "We'll go get shakes. Then I'll take you home. Talk to your dad if he's home. If not, I can do that tomorrow night. But for now, I don't want you getting in trouble for being late."

"Why do you want to talk to my dad?" I asked, grasping on to one thread of what he'd just said because I didn't think I was capable of handling the rest in one sitting.

"Plan on doin' this the right way, Lizzie," he replied. "Your dad will likely respect his daughter's first boyfriend more if I come up, shake his hand and promise him I'll take care of his daughter. Your dad gotta shotgun?"

I slowly shook my head. My dad was large, gruff man of few words. He was also a pacifist who did not believe in violence.

My mother, on the other hand, owned a gun. I wasn't about to tell him that, though.

"Good, wouldn't wanna get shot before I can even take you on a date," he smirked, guiding me toward the door to the class I was incredibly late to.

I followed, on instinct maybe or because I already couldn't stand to be away from him.

"I'll see you, babe," he said with a wink followed by a lingering glance to my boots before he walked away. I watched him for too long, making me even later to class. But the disapproving look from my teacher nor the curious ones from my classmates didn't affect me.

I was too busy reliving that entire interaction in my head. The one where Cody said the word *boyfriend*.

***

IT WASN'T COMPLICATED.

Not at first.

It was almost like my romance books. Cody treated me with respect, like I was the most precious thing in his world. Like Zane treated Laurie.

Cody was true to his word. He came to my house and spoke to my father with no visible nerves. Then again, it wasn't my mild mannered, quiet and kind father he had to worry about. It was my constantly disapproving, not at all quiet, judgmental mother.

Somehow, he handled both with ease. My father looked to me when they started speaking, as if searching for my silent happiness. Which there was a lot of, it was just buried underneath the pile of nerves that I had been living with the entire afternoon.

After seeing whatever he saw on my face, my father nodded, shook Cody's hand, and that was that.

Things with my mother were not as simple. She drilled him about his parents—the only part of the interaction where he seemed even the slightest bit uncomfortable. Everyone knew that he was raised by a single mother who worked as a nurse at the hospital in the next town over. I'd seen her in the grocery store a couple of times, and she had a kind smile, sad eyes and always looked tired. She was pretty, though, kind of ageless. I hadn't heard of her having a boyfriend since she'd moved here with Cody. And if there was one, my mother would've pounced on gossip like that. In our small town, , a woman moving with her son without a father was gossip worthy. At least to my mom it was.

She already knew everything there was to know about his mother, and there was nothing to know about his father. As far I as I knew, Cody never talked about him, and he wasn't in the picture.

Cody handled it well, though, with manners that my mother —in my opinion—didn't deserve.

"It's just me and my mom, ma'am. She works hard and is the only parent I need." He said this with such firmness that it moved even my mother off the subject, which earned a look of approval from my father who had been trying to master that art their entire marriage.

Of course, it didn't mean he was completely off the hook. Mom continued to drill him about his grades—good but nothing special—about his college prospects—none as of yet— his part time job working at the Sons of Templar MC garage— yeah, my mom got a *real* kick out of that—and her demand that he get me home by curfew.

Pretty mild for my mom.

Cody made all the promises, and he kept them all.

He took me for a picnic on the beach for our first date. Yeah, he organized a picnic on the beach. The eighteen-year-old, mini badass organized something so romantic I cried inside.

He kissed me at sunset.

It wasn't my first kiss, but it felt like it was. Everything with Cody felt like a first.

I think I fell in love with him during that kiss. Or maybe it was when he complimented my boots in the hallway. Or when he handled my mother so well. Or when he brushed my hair from my face and whispered to me how beautiful I was.

Yeah, it was probably all of those.

And he was acting like he felt the same way. Like this was something natural, like he'd been feeling this way for as long as I had, but Willow warned me not to be fooled.

"If there's one thing men are good at, it's pretending they feel the same way about you until they get into your pants. That shit should be an Olympic sport for them."

She was too young to be such a cynic about men and love in general, but then again, she had divorced parents and a rotating door of stepfathers, the latest of whom had tried to sneak into her room while she was sleeping. Willow had woken up and, of course, punched him in the face. Her mother had immediately kicked him out. She might've had bad taste in men, but she loved her daughter.

I, on the other hand, had two parents who at least pretended to love each other and a stable home life where I didn't have to wake up with my right fist ready in case some creep is trying to touch me in my sleep.

I read romance novels and had a quiet, caring father, a brash, casserole making mother, and no real traumas in my life. So I found it hard to believe that Cody was just putting this on in order to get into my pants. If he wanted to get into a girl's pants, there would be a line around the block of girls volunteering for that.

Nonetheless, I heeded Willow's words. Or tried to. It was hard to be a cynic when the guy I'd crushed on my entire high school life was carrying my books for me, holding my hand and making out with me in my bedroom with the music turned all the way up.

He'd had plenty of dinners at my place, having won my mother over, plus she knew that his own mother was working nights and was absolutely aghast at the idea of a teenage boy having to fend for himself.

She'd never admit it, of course, but she was really starting to like my first boyfriend.

I'd officially met his mom as his girlfriend. She was soft spoken with a slight rasp to her voice, had Cody's eyes and loved her son. They didn't have a lot of money. Not something I had ever had to think about, but it was apparent in their small, one story, two-bedroom home on the outskirts of town. She'd put a lot of effort and love into it, though. Flowers in the front yard, a greenhouse full of vegetables and herbs in the backyard, bright, vintage sofas with cozy looking throws. It was definitely a feminine home.

With the exception of Cody's room, of course. A room I'd spent a lot of time in. Since his mother worked nights, that meant we had an entire house to ourselves. There were many nights I lied and said I was studying at Willow's, because no matter how much she liked Cody, no way was my mom going to approve of me being there without an adult present.

But I was.

We'd been boyfriend and girlfriend for four months.

It felt like forever and a brief moment at the same time.

Up until now, there had been heavy make out sessions. Over and under the bra action. His hand resting comfortably and possessively on my butt at parties we attended as a couple. He never left my side at those, and if he did, his eyes were always on me.

But tonight was different.

Not because he was pressuring me. He was so respectful it was almost getting annoying.

I was under no illusion that he was a virgin. He must have wanted more, second base at least. In fact, the hardness I'd felt against my leg during a few of our heavy make out sessions was evidence of that. And the tight way he held himself when he decided he had to stop... Yes, he wanted more, but he didn't pressure me.

The problem was, I wanted more. I was terrified and worried I'd do it wrong, wouldn't know how to be sexy and embarrass myself.

But it was getting out of control. That need. For him. For more than just making out and heavy petting.

Willow had already informed me that the guy usually lasted a minute. Tops. But I didn't care about that. However it would be, I wanted it with Cody. Wanted everything.

"Don't stop," I whispered when things had started to get hotter than normal. My shirt was on the floor, and I was wearing a plain, pink cotton bra. Not sexy. Cody was also shirtless. He had a lean, muscled body that was most definitely sexy.

Cody had tried to pull that muscled, sexy torso away from me when the telltale hardness between his legs brushed against the thin fabric of my shorts. The mere friction of it caused me to gasp in pleasure. Cody, always attuned to my body and sounds, obviously mistook this for pain or fear, so he tried to stop.

I was quicker, for once. Need was hot in my blood, making me grip the back of his neck with both of my hands so he couldn't move, his body still pressed against mine.

"Lizzie," he gritted out.

"I want this," I begged. "I want you. Please."

His eyes searched mine then lowered down to my bra that suddenly felt like the sexiest thing in the world. He let out a harsh hiss of air.

Then the pressure against my hands released as he moved to press his lips against mine.

I kissed him back hungrily, desperately.

He stopped it as if he was trying to torture me. "I'm gonna give you something," he murmured against my lips. "I'm gonna make today all about you. Because you may think you're ready now, but I don't want you to have any regrets. I don't want it to be in my bedroom on a night my mom is gone. I want it to be... more special for you." He brushed the back of his hand against my cheek. "But I'm going to be your first, Lizzie. I want to be your last, but I'm not stupid enough to think you'll be with me forever, no matter how much I want that." His hand moved quickly, unlatching my bra and pulling it free. No matter how naïve some might say it was to think it, I knew he was my forever.

"But I'm gonna make the most of every moment I have with you," he continued, lips firm and hard against mine once more.

Then he moved.

Downward.

First to my exposed breasts.

Then to my bellybutton.

His tongue teased me with what was going to happen, moving across my stomach.

Then *much* lower.

Suffice it to say, the need I was feeling was sated. Twice.

Chapter 2

Five Months Later

"Well," I said, closing the door to Cody's room. "You're officially no longer shackled to the institution known as high school."

There was a low thump coming from the living room, we'd left the music on. Everyone had left the graduation party that Cody's mom, Olive, had given permission for him to throw as long as they stuck to beer and everyone was out by midnight.

My mother would never leave me alone in a house to have a party; she'd never trust a bunch of teenagers to abide by such rules. But Cody adored and respected Olive, so it was five after midnight and we were the only ones here.

My mother was out of town, and I'd told my father I was sleeping over at Willow's. He was far too smart and observant to believe me, but he also trusted me.

So he'd told me to, "be careful" and kissed me on the head.

This wasn't the first night I'd be sleeping curled up with my boyfriend. We didn't get many of these since there were only so many sleepovers my mother would believe I was having, and Olive rotated night shifts. Although she never said anything when I was sitting at her breakfast table when she came home from work. She'd just smile, kiss me on the cheek and sit with me and Cody while we ate.

She was the mother I wished I had. I knew it was a nasty and a cruel thing for me to think considering my mother didn't beat me or verbally abuse me and bought me whatever clothes I'd decided fit my vision at the time. I was into more rock chick, Bridget Bardot these days, growing my hair longer, wearing winged eyeliner, tight black jeans and band tees. My mother hated it, but she still bought me the clothes.

She was a good mother.

But she didn't kiss my cheek in the morning. Didn't sit at the table with me and just talk about life. Her version of talking was gossiping, pressuring me about college, grades, the future. Lecturing my dad about whatever he'd done wrong that week.

Olive asked me what my dreams were. What was my favorite book? Movie. Who inspired me? What countries I wanted to visit.

She'd taken me in as the daughter she'd never had, and it made me feel warm and accepted.

My mother didn't have that in her.

Which was fine, because I had Olive. I had her for as long as I had Cody in my life, and I planned on having him in my life forever. I knew it was a stupid, naïve thought to have about my very first boyfriend—my very first *everything*—especially when he had just graduated high school and I had another year.

But it didn't matter.

We were different.

Cody was different.

He loved me.

Beyond that, he didn't have big dreams of leaving Amber,

going to fancy colleges. He'd told me what he wanted to the night I gave him my virginity.

━━

PROM NIGHT...

"It's cliché, but I wanted to give you that."

We had rented a hotel room the next town over. Mom thought we were all staying together for a girl's sleepover, and each of us had carefully coordinated this 'sleepover' since out of the three of us involved, we all had boyfriends who booked hotel rooms.

I was afraid.

Tipsy, because I'd wanted to loosen up and not act like some virgin. I was only a virgin in the most technical of terms. Cody and I had done everything but. And sure, I might've been nervous or awkward at first, but my need, my desire had always clouded such feelings. Everything thus far had been awesome. Had made me feel different. Like a woman. More loved. Worshipped. Confident.

So sex was going to be good. After the first painful part.

And it was painful. Despite the nice hotel room that Cody had put overtime in to pay for. The candles, the lingerie that I'd bought on a shopping trip with Willow and had hidden in the back of my closet.

He'd been gentle, reverent and loving, but it didn't make a difference. It hurt like a bitch. Unlike every heroine in the romance books I read, I didn't enjoy it. I gritted my teeth through it and counted it as a victory that I didn't cry.

Cody felt bad.

Terrible. Tortured even. It was written all over his face, hatred for himself because he'd caused me pain. He'd taken me to the shower and cleaned me meticulously, with such tenderness that I fell even more in love with him in that moment.

He'd then taken me to bed, taking his time to cover every inch of my body with his mouth, then moved to the important and tender parts, coaxing me back to the edge.

Suffice it to say, the second time was much better.

And the third.

We spent every moment we could naked after that. Willow joked about Cody turning me into a nympho, but it was really just that we were obsessed with each other. To an unhealthy extent, some would say. Some being my mother.

Despite her reservations about the time I spent with him, mom was still enamored by Cody. In fact, she thought it was my fault for becoming a lovestruck girl, letting my grades and therefore losing college prospects because of a guy of all things.

She wasn't wrong. I was lovestruck by Cody. I was obsessed with him. With what our lives would be.

Which was what we talked about that night, the first night. And again after the second time, when I felt sated, satisfied and sore. Above all, happy.

I'd let him know that sure, I'd like to go to college maybe major in English lit with a business minor just so my mom would be happy. Find a job doing something I loved after graduating. Something to do with books maybe. That wasn't really the goal, though. My real goal, the one I didn't say out loud, was to marry Cody, have lots of babies and live an extraordinary but peaceful life.

Cody had listened intently, as he did with anything I had to say. He'd even watched *Factory Girl* with me despite the fact it was a chick flick and that I'd already seen it about five times. He sat at vintage stores with me while I found faded Levi's to cut into jean shorts. That he probably didn't mind so much since he loved those shorts and enjoyed watching me change.

"I want to patch into the Sons of Templar MC," he said quietly, arms tight around me.

It shouldn't have surprised me, considering he'd been working at the garage since he was sixteen and talked about each of the members with reverence.

I didn't have any experience with the MC. Or I had about the same experience as the average citizen of Amber. They were a large presence, casting a shadow over the town, but they were also respected. Almost a land-mark. They did charity rides, they volunteered around town. But they were also criminals, and everyone knew that.

I'd always thought they were kind of interesting, exciting even. The lifestyle fascinated me. Not enough to be brave the parties at the clubhouse Willow had begged me to sneak into with her that she got kicked out of—they were well known for not letting in underage girls.

"You've been quiet for a long time," Cody said, unease in his voice. When I looked to him, his face looked different than it did at school, parties, even with his mom. He'd let his walls down. He was vulnerable with me and only me. It was a kind of trea-sure I'd never imagined getting.

"I was just thinking," I shrugged.

"You wouldn't stay with me if I patched in?" he asked, a slight tremor to his voice.

The insecurity in his voice had me moving. Pushed him flat on the bed and moved to straddle him, his cock pressed against my beautifully tender parts.

I moved so my hands clasped his neck, his gaze held in mine. "I will be with you no matter what, Cody. Nothing will change the way I feel about you." I laid my lips gently on his. "And the fact that this news will mean you're going to stay in Amber makes me even happier."

He frowned. "But you're going to go to college. You have to go to college."

I rolled my eyes. "You sound like my mother."

He didn't smile. In fact, he moved us again, so I was now on my back and his naked body was pressed against mine. "I'm serious, Lizzie," he continued. "You're smart. All you know is this town, you deserve to see something more. You need to go to college. I'm not going to let you jeopardize your future for me."

I didn't like his tone. The way his eyes looked when he said this scared me. "*You're* my future, Cody. Losing you is the only thing that could jeopardize my future. I've never wanted to leave Amber. You're just giving me another reason to stay."

The look stayed on his face, but he didn't say anything.

"What does your mom say about your plan to patch in?" I asked, deciding to change the subject because it scared me in ways I didn't want to admit.

As progressive and laid back as Olive was, I couldn't see her wanting her only son to patch in to the town's resident motor-cycle gang. Especially if it put him in any kind of danger. Now and then there were funerals for members and they'd all died violently. The mere thought of something happening to Cody made my stomach clench and my heart climb up to my throat.

He winced ever so slightly. "Yeah, I told her," he replied. "She took it about as well as I thought she would. At first, she thought I'd change my mind, that it was a phase. Then she got pissed. Now she's just accepted it. I've let her down. But I just can't... see anything else for me. I'm not worth anything else."

My blood turned cold. He really meant what he'd said. I'd caught things like this every now and then, a self-deprecating remark about himself peppered into our conversations. It had been enough to bother me, but he glossed over them so quickly that I'd never had a chance to address them.

"Cody," I whispered. "You're worth everything. You are the

kindest person I know. You are the most special person I know. What makes you even think such things?"

He paled ever so slightly, his eyes darkening.

I got the feeling that he was going to tell me something. Something that explained those comments, that undercurrent of darkness that I sensed in him from time to time.

But then it went away. He put on a mask, and the Cody I recognized returned. "I don't know, guess it's shit from not havin' my Old Man in my life. But I don't wanna talk about that." He pressed his lips against my neck. "Actually, I don't want to talk at all. I want to make love to my Old Lady."

Something moved inside me. Grew. Something good. "Old Lady?" I repeated.

"Yes," he growled, his lips moving down my neck. "If I'm going to patch in to the Sons of Templar, then you're gonna be my Old Lady. You okay with that

I didn't hesitate.

"Yeah, I'm more than okay with that," I murmured.

So our future was laid out in front of us. Just like a romance novel.

Too bad romance novels were fiction.

⊏⊐

"SO WHAT HAPPENS NOW?" I asked after closing the door to Cody's room on graduation night, starting to unbutton my shirt. The act of undressing in front of Cody was still novel to me. It was so intimate, so grown up, so precious. Mostly, we'd been ripping each other's clothes off with desperate need. Though I liked that a lot, this was special too. I couldn't wait until I could undress for him every night. He was going to save up to get a rental, move in before I graduated then I'd move in with him. My mother would have a cow, but I'd legally be an adult so she wouldn't be able to do anything about it. Plus, I'd be going to a college forty minutes' drive away, commuting daily, so she couldn't complain.

I was anxious to get my senior year started. An entire year of school ahead of me seemed like torture, especially knowing that Cody would be living on his own and prospecting with the Sons of Templar MC, likely being exposed to all kinds of very attractive, very experienced women.

Not that I didn't trust Cody, but my obsession made my thoughts ugly.

"Do you like drive your motorcycle into their compound and then they test you for worthiness or macho-ness? Or do you have to like rob a bank or something to show you're willing to do anything for the MC?" I continued. "As much as I support you doing this, I really don't think you should rob a bank. I know that movies make it seem like bank robberies have a high success rate, but they really don't. It's not a feasible way to steal money."

Cody didn't laugh or even crack a smile, which really didn't reassure me about the whole bank robbery thing. In addition to the silence, there was the look. That look. The cold, tortured one from our first night together.

"Cody?" I asked, getting worried.

"I was your first," Cody said, his voice dead.

I was scared. No, terrified. Because I didn't recognize his voice. I didn't recognize the way he looked at me. I suddenly felt too exposed with my shirt half unbuttoned. Like I needed a barrier because I had the feeling something was going to cut up my bare skin.

"I was your first," he repeated.

The way he said those words to me gave me pause. There was something in his eyes. Something detached from us.

So I didn't speak, just nodded.

"You weren't mine."

I flinched at his tone, though, the truth stung a little too. "I'm aware that you weren't living in a convent prior to us getting together," I teased, trying to joke but not succeeding.

"No, I didn't have my first sexual experience with some fuckin' cheerleader," he scowled. There was violence in voice. In every cell of his body. My relaxed and charming boyfriend was nowhere to be seen. This was the dark side of him that I'd sometimes seen snippets of. Flashes. Things that had told me I hadn't yet seen all of him. Didn't know all of him.

"Without going into detail that neither of us need, my first sexual experience was not consensual, happened when I was too fuckin' young to understand what was going on, and the fact that my uncle was the one doing the... shit, I wasn't brave enough to stand up to him. To say no." He ran his hand through his hair, looking anywhere but me.

My heart thumped between my ears, a dull roar. The beer I drank earlier tonight curdled in my stomach, and it took effort to keep from throwing up. Hearing the pain and shame in Cody's voice was sickening.

"He did it more than once," he continued. "Told me it was a secret, that I'd get in trouble if I told anyone." He laughed, but it was a bitter, ugly sound. "Stupid kid that I was, I believed him."

I stepped forward, intending on touching him, comforting him, doing anything to take the suffering, pain and self-hatred from his body. He was coated with it.

Cody stepped back from my touch. Recoiled. His rejection hit me in the chest, but I got it.

"You weren't stupid," I said. "You were a *child*. And he was a monster." Tears blurred my vision, and I tried to force them from falling. I couldn't be weak in the face of this. Couldn't show him an emotion he might construe as pity.

"Ah, no, he was just a man," he said. "One that has to die."
My blood went cold. "What?"

"He ruined me, Lizzie," Cody hissed, finally looking at me. "He ruined what I might've had with you. Stole it from me. Ripped me up inside so self-hatred is all I know. When I told my dad, you know what he did? He smacked me around and called me a faggot." Another one of those cold laughs spilled from him. "My mom would've believed me. But it also would've broken her heart, I knew that even then. Was protecting her even then. My dad beat me so bad that it made her leave him. When she saw what he did to me, she ran. With me. As far away as she could get." He looked away. "Here," he murmured. "She wanted Amber to be a fresh start. Clean slate. Something good. I didn't want to tarnish our good thing with the rancid truth, so I buried it. With the promise to myself that when I was older, stronger, I'd go back there. I'd find him, and I'd kill him."

A tear rolled down my cheek. I couldn't stop it. "Cody..." I stepped forward, but the way his body tensed made me pause. It wasn't even tensing, it was a recoil. An emotional slap to the face and knife to the soul.

"You need to leave," he said in that cold, disembodied voice.

"Leave?" I repeated, my voice shaking. "No. I'm not going anywhere." Something told me if I left right then, I'd never see Cody again. It would be over in a scary, permanent way. "I can't lose you."

"You never really had me, Lizzie," he countered. "Not all of me. I can't give you that. fuck, you're in fucking high school. This is not the kind of shit we should be dealing with. That *you* should be dealing with. We need to grow up. Both of us." He stared at me. Like I was a stranger. "You need to leave."

I knew him, so in that moment I knew nothing was going to change his mind. And he was right. We were too young for this intensity. He'd just told me something that he'd been hiding, his greatest shame. The secret had obviously been cutting him up from the inside out. And I didn't know how to handle something like this. Even if I did, Cody was telling me he didn't want my help. Even though I wanted to be there for him, maybe Cody could tackle his demons alone. Maybe he needed to focus on himself, because when we were together, all his thoughts, effort and love went to me. And how was he meant to repair what had been broken without time for himself?

But the selfish part of me didn't care. I didn't care about all of that. About all the possible repercussions. I just wanted my boyfriend. I wanted to undress and go to bed with him. Sleep with his arms around me. I wanted to find a way to fix his pain, show him that it didn't make me love him any less. That it didn't make him any less. But he wouldn't believe me. It wouldn't sink in. I didn't have any experience with this kind of horror, and I had no idea how to help him. Worse, I was terrified I'd hurt him.

"I'm going to leave," I whispered, tears streaming down my face, "even though I know this decision is going to be painful for the two of us. I hate that you're forcing me to go. I don't want to. I don't want to be without you. I don't want you to think horrible things about yourself that aren't true. But I can't control that. Just please, carry this with you." I undid the heart necklace he'd bought me for Christmas. The one that caused him to take a month longer to finish his motorcycle than it should've.

I didn't trust myself to move closer and physically hand it to him, so I laid it gently on his nightstand.

"Carry me with you," I pleaded, looking at him, another tear rolling down my cheek. "Just remember, there's nothing you can do that will make me stop loving you. No matter what you think. However long it takes, I'll be waiting for you. No matter what."

I turned and walked out.

Part of me thought he'd chase after me, kiss me and promise everything was going to be okay.

But he didn't.

Because everything wasn't going to be okay.

Unfortunately, that's not the way this story goes.

Chapter 3

Five Years Later

"I'll call you tomorrow, I promise!" I yelled to Laurie and Bull as I got out of their car, my words only the slightest bit slurred from the margaritas we'd had. Well, Laurie and I had been having margaritas Zane, I mean Bull, wouldn't do anything to impair his judgement or motor skills when he was driving Laurie around. He'd turned into a full on badass since patching into the Sons of Templar MC, complete with the macho man nickname. There was something about him now that made him seem like he'd be able to handle anything bad from happening. That he'd be able to save Laurie from a fricking plane crash.

Nonetheless, he didn't drink and drive. Not with her in the car.

It hurt to be around them, so relentlessly in love, so devoted to each other when I was just an empty space where a human used to be.

Okay, that was maybe a little dramatic. But heartbreak kind of did that to you. Especially when paired with tequila.

It took me a second to fumble for the door handle. I hadn't expected to be out this late, or else I would've left the porch light on.

I was still getting used to being alone. Living alone. I'd gone from my parent's house to my college dorm to a shitty apartment off campus with a few friends to this little bungalow in my hometown. I'd just gotten a job at the bookstore on Main Street, helping the owner, Evan, with accounting and business management. I'd been one of his best customers for years, and when I mentioned I was moving home, he'd offered me the job. The pay wasn't great, but it was more than enough to pay rent and have enough money for tacos and margaritas. Or it would've been if Bull wasn't caveman who didn't let Laurie and I pay for anything.

Sure, I could've gone away, could've headed to a city somewhere where I worked my way up in the publishing business since college had made me fall even more in love with the literary arts. But that wasn't what I wanted out of life. I'd never had big dreams of leaving my small town and living some fabulous life. No, I'd been happy with the idea of settling down again. Working somewhere close to Amber. Getting married, having kids.

With Cody.

I'd been so sure that it would happen with Cody.

He'd talked about wanting to patch in to the Sons of Templar MC. It had made me nervous, but I'd understood why he'd wanted to, and I'd accepted it.

But then he'd left.

Almost five years ago. Hadn't heard a single thing from him. Not one single thing. In romance novels, there was always something big and dramatic that separated the two young lovers. It was necessary.

There would be pain, longing, but ultimately a happy ending.

There was plenty of the first two, but none of the latter.

I should've hated him. I *wanted* to hate him. I wanted to throw myself into college life, college boys and forget him. Find someone new and stop pining over my high school boyfriend like a pathetic teenager.

Best laid plans and all that.

Willow tried to help. She had wanted to make a puppet of him—Wicca was one of the many things she'd studied during her four years at college where she'd gotten a lot of experience but not much else—and curse him. Among other things. She wanted me to party with her every night and find a new guy to forget the old one. But I didn't work that way. Willow had eventually accepted that, since I'd always accepted who she was. She was the girl who'd decided to drop out of her last year of college to drive around the country with a guy she'd just met. She sent postcards sometimes. I'd always known that's all I'd get from her. Postcards and stories from travels that never landed her back here. She felt suffocated in our small, quiet town. Amber wasn't her dream.

It was mine.

I'd had relationships, of course. Mostly because I wanted to try to prove to myself that I was over Cody, but also because I was lonely.

It hadn't worked. Some of the guys were nice, others were assholes. Neither type helped. So I'd decided I'd forever be the slightly jealous third wheel to my friend and her seriously smitten boyfriend.

"You didn't lock the door," a voice stated as I stepped into my bungalow.

If I could've crawled up the wall in fear, I would've. As it was, I just scuttled back, hit the door and let out a girly scream.

I didn't go for a weapon or try to run or anything. Didn't do any of the things women were meant to do when there was a man in their house nearing midnight.

But I knew that voice.

I used to, at least.

My hands fumbled for the light switch.

"Cody," I whispered, my eyes running over the man standing in front of me. That's what he was, a fully-grown *man*. Sure, he'd been pretty damn manly the last time I saw him, but he'd packed on muscle now. A lot of it. The sleeves on his Henley were straining with the muscles he'd covered it with. His shoulders, broad before, were huge. His midnight hair was closely cropped now, making the angles of his face that much sharper.

It was his eyes that had changed the most, though. They were colder. Scarier. But there was still something in there. Something him.

I moved forward, to go to him, smell him, taste him, but his hands on my shoulders stopped me.

"Why wasn't your door looked, Lizzie?" he asked, voice flat.

I blinked at the inane question considering everything. His hands burned at my shoulders, my body sucking up the contact like a drug. "Um, the door?" I repeated, still swimming through tequila even though his presence was enough to almost entirely sober me up.

"Yes, Lizzie, the fuckin' door." The grip on my shoulders bordered on pain now.

Cody had never hurt me. He was always gentle. Too gentle almost. I'd ached for him to press me against walls, to ravage me like I'd read about in all those books.

That was a good word for him right now. *Ravaged*. With something.

"This is Amber," I said in response. "Nothing happens here."

This, apparently, was the wrong thing to say. His face twisted into something resembling fury, his grip tightening even farther.

"Something can happen anywhere. You're *alone*." His eyes ran over my body, my body immediately responding. "You're fuckin' beautiful. Something will happen. It's just a matter of time."

"Maybe I'm not alone anymore?" I wondered out loud, looking up at him. "Are you back, Cody?" I swallowed roughly, his presence, his anger, his scent doing things to me. Awakening things that had lain dormant for four fucking years. But I had to pause. I forced myself to take a slow, deep breath even though all I wanted to do was pounce on him. Taste him.

"Have you come back to me?" My question came out softer than I'd intended. Weaker. I was supposed to be stronger now. Harder. Supposed to prove what these four years had done to my independence. Supposed to torture him, make him pay for the way his absence had tortured me. Make him work to get me back. But I couldn't help it. I couldn't lie to Cody, couldn't put on any kind of mask. All I wanted was him. I didn't want games. I'd already forgiven him the second I walked out of his bedroom four years ago.

Something moved on his face again. It wasn't fury. No, this was something else. Something softer. Something that resembled the Cody I had once known. The one I dreamed about.

"You're not going to yell at me? Tell me how much you hate me for breaking your heart? Tell me to get the fuck outta your house?" He sounded different. Confused. Lost some of that fierce bravado that was foreign yet attractive.

"You did break my heart," I explained. "But you broke your own too. You hurt yourself because you thought it was the best thing for me." I moved my arm to cradle his jaw. When we were together, he'd let his stubble grow because he'd known I liked the roughness against my skin. Loved the marks I'd get on my inner thighs. He'd grown a full beard now. It was rough against my palm. He smelled different too. Leather and smoke.

"You've tortured yourself more than enough by the looks of it," I whispered, my heart breaking all over again as I took in everything that was different about him. "And I'm not going to waste the precious time I have with you yelling. Now, I repeat my question, have you come back to me?"

Pain clouded his eyes, his body still tense under my touch. "It's not that simple."

I tilted my head. "Oh, of course there're a lot of complicated things that we'll have to work through. But the one thing that is simple is whether you're going to let me in or not. If we're going to work on them together. I want to tell you right now, wherever you've been, whatever you've done that I'm sure you've convinced yourself that I can't handle," I narrowed my eyes, "I can handle it. I can handle you. So are you here to stay?"

There was a pause. A long one. One that frayed the nerves I was trying so hard to hide from my voice.

Then he moved. His mouth crashed onto mine, and I surrendered, submitted easily. There was no point fighting this. No reason to struggle about the years between us. The things that had changed. And many things had changed, that much was obvious.

But what hadn't changed was the magic between us. The fire.

It was hotter than ever before.

It was an inferno.

And I let it devour me.

Let Cody devour me.

WE WERE NAKED on my bedroom floor.

After fucking against the wall, we'd moved to the bed. Fucked some more. That's what this was. *Fucking.* It was primal. Urgent. Desperate. Carnal. Maybe there was still love in there somewhere, but this wasn't making love. It was something else entirely. It was like I was losing my virginity to him all over again. No one had ever touched me like this. Cody had never touched me like this. It awoke something different inside of me.

We ended up tangled in blankets on the floor

Well, *Cody* was on the floor. I was mostly on top of him, relishing the feel of my skin on his. The need I had to be close to him was bordering on desperate. Like I had to make sure he wasn't going anywhere. At least not without me attached to him.

We'd been quiet for a long time. He wasn't asleep, though. I knew that because of how tight he was gripping me. Bordering on pain. Hinting at that same desperate need I had to have him close.

He'd missed me too.

Sure, I'd had my moments when I'd convinced myself it had all been fake. That Cody had never really loved me and that he was never coming back.

Those moments usually involved some kind of liquor or a romance movie.

But for the most part, I'd had hope. Maybe not hope that he was coming back, but that wherever he was, he was thinking of me. Missing me. Yearning for me like I was him.

And four orgasms had totally proven that.

Was this the part where I asked him about where he'd been? Who'd he been with? If he'd made good on his promise to murder the man who had ruined his childhood?

Maybe it was. Maybe a strong, independent woman would demand those kinds of answers, those kinds of specifics.

But I already knew the answer to a lot of those questions. Knew that Cody would not have spoken of murder lightly. And he wouldn't have come back if he hadn't done what he'd promised himself he was going to do.

He'd killed.

Perhaps done other things to change the core of him.

But I didn't care.

However right or wrong that was. I didn't care. He was still Cody. To me, at least.

"So I'm going to need you to do something if you're really here for good," I said, my voice raspy from crying out his name the past few hours.

His arms flexed around me before his fingers moved in lazy circles across my bare back.

"Anything, baby," he murmured.

My heart jumped with that. With those two words. A promise.

"I'm going to need you to marry me," I said.

His hands froze, his entire body going stiff. "Come again?"

I moved so my forearms rested on his pecs and my eyes locked in on his. "I know you've been gone these past years because you needed to be gone. I hated every moment of it, and sure, I wanted to hate you too. But the problem is, I just love you too much." My eyes ran hungrily over his face then his neck where a heart hung from a chain. My heart. The one I'd given him five years ago.

"I want to make sure it's harder for you to leave," I said. "Now, I know that marriage isn't a guarantee that you're not going to leave, but I also know that you're a man of honor. Of your word. So if you give me your word on forever, I'd be much happier."

Cody stared at me for a long time, his eyes moving over me with hunger, with reverence, with a love that hadn't dimmed over four years.

"Just to clarify, you're askin' me to marry you?" he asked.

I nodded.

Suddenly I was then I was no longer on top of him, Cody moving so I was entirely on the floor, and his body was entirely on mine. He didn't give me his full weight, though. If he'd done that with all his new muscles, my ribcage might've been crushed.

His hand moved to push my hair from my face then he cupped my cheek. "You know I'm meant to do that, right? With some kinda fanfare. A ring?"

"You can give me all of that after. I just need your word. Just need you to give me forever," I whispered.

His hand moved to the back of my neck. "If there's one thing in this world I can promise you, it's forever."

Then he landed his lips on mine.

And there was a lot of fanfare.

"YOU'RE TAKING HIM BACK." My mother's voice was flat but the sounds of the pans clanging together and hitting the counter harder than they needed to told me how she really felt.

Cody leaving me had broken my heart. Though that sounded cliché, too common for what I'd gone through, it was true. I hadn't been able to get out of bed for a week. Barely ate. Was in what Willow coined my "zombie chic status" for three months.

Naturally, this had worried my parents. My father, definitely. More than anything, it had pissed my mom off. Mostly she'd ranted about how this period of my life seriously jeopardized my college prospects, furious at Cody for doing this to me. But even I saw that it was more than that with my mother.

Once I'd gotten myself out of that funk, gotten myself good enough grades to go to college and had made a really good show of getting on with my life, my mother had decided not to mention Cody's name again, pretty much pretending he didn't exist.

So, despite my overwhelming sense of happiness and relief that Cody was back, I'd been dreading telling her. Telling her that I felt whole again.

"I'm not taking him back," I told her, sipping my coffee as I watched her bang around in the kitchen from my spot at the breakfast bar. "He was always mine, and I was always his."

Mom turned, a scowl already firmly in place. "Elizabeth, you're too old for such idiotic romantic thoughts. He almost ruined your future. He *will* ruin your future if you don't get smart about this."

"He won't ruin my future, mom, he *is* my future," I tried to explain. "I'm not asking for your permission or your blessing. I'm an adult now. But I do want you in my life. I want you in our lives. In our children's. And we are planning to have them." I held my hand up as the vein in Mom's head looked like it was about to explode. "You're not going to change my mind on that, even if you think what I'm doing is idiotic. And I know you had bigger dreams for me, but they weren't ever my dreams for me. They were ones that you lost. But mom, I'm not losing anything. I'm gaining everything." I stood up, figuring I might as well peel off the entire Band-Aid. "And he's patching in to the Sons of Templar MC. I'm going to support him."

My mother no longer looked furious. She no longer looked anything. Defeated might've been a word for it, although that's never a word I'd ever used to describe my mother.

"You're giving yourself a harder life than you deserve," she

ANNE MALCOM

said quietly, shaking her head. "That club is going to poison what you have. It's going to ruin your life. And it will take him from you. One way or another."

Her words chilled me to the bone. Were they some kind of cold premonition? Or just the most logical outcome of the life I was choosing to live? It didn't much matter, did it?

I straightened my spine. "Well, I'd rather be ruined with him than have to survive without him."

⊏══⊐

"ARE you sure you want to do this?" Cody asked, his expression stoic.

We were both sober despite the fact that we'd been indulging heavily at the engagement party thrown by the Sons of Templar.

Cody still had another ten months of prospecting as did Gage, the man who had appeared in Amber the same time as Cody. I didn't know where or how they'd met, but my guess was it was somewhere dark. I hadn't asked Cody much about his time away. Where he'd been, what he'd been doing. I knew a lot of women wouldn't be able to handle that. Would need to know what had happened. Why he'd left. Why he'd come back. How he'd encountered the tall, foreboding handsome man with ribbons of scars moving from his wrist to shoulder.

Parts of me were desperate for the details. To know where Gage had got his scars, where Cody got the ones I saw behind his eyes. But those scars were from their darkest of yesterdays. Healed as much as they would ever be. I didn't want to rip them back open for selfish reasons.

Cody had said Gage saved his life, that the man had been near death himself, would've met the reaper if he'd left him where he was—wherever that was. I saw the death in Gage's

40

eyes, he made no effort to hide it. I hoped one day, there would be something, someone for him to live for.

For now, the club was something to guarantee he'd exist tomorrow. A purpose. Even if it was shrouded in criminal acts and bloodshed.

Cody been a friend of the club since he'd started working in their garage at sixteen. Beyond that, Cade and Bull were two of his closest friends, and they were already patched in.

Cody already considered their Prez, Steg, to be a father figure, a mentor of sorts. A mentor who was in charge of a deadly chapter of the notorious one percenter MC, who looked scarier than all hell and always carried a gun.

There had been no question where the party was going to be held. Evie, the matriarch and wife of the president of the MC, had decided it would be at the clubhouse, since she always made the decision with things like this.

"It's a reason to celebrate," she'd countered when I'd tried to argue that it was too much. "Fuck knows we need to hold on to those. So we're havin' it here. Don't want to hear more shit about it."

So I gave her no more shit.

To say my mother was horrified was an understatement.

We didn't talk for three weeks after I'd announced my engagement. She'd invited both Cody and I over for dinner, though, I got the feeling that the dinner was not at all her idea. My father rarely tried to tell my mother what to do about much, but when it came to me, he always put his foot down.

I was sure he wasn't exactly thrilled that I was staying in Amber and marrying Cody, especially with him prospecting. My father likely wanted a steadier life for me. Safer. But he wouldn't say anything.

"Don't you want to know?" Cody asked, jerking me back to the moment. The moment consisting of us standing in our bedroom in my bungalow. Cody had moved in. It hadn't been stated officially, but there was no question about that. There were plenty of questions and arguments about were regarding him taking over the rent. I knew he wasn't going to earn anything being a prospect, which would take up most of his time. He'd work part-time at the garage, but I didn't want him spending all his money on the rent when I had enough for it. Cody had alpha maled his way out of the argument, telling me about money he'd earned the past five years. He didn't say how he'd gotten the money, and I didn't ask.

I frowned at him. "Do I want to know what?"

"All the terrible things I did when I was gone," he said. "Horrific. Monstrous. That's what I am now, Lizzie. Especially since I did all of those things, became this person, then I came back to you. Couldn't even do you the honor of leaving you alone, letting you live a life that isn't tainted."

My eyes watered, my heart shattered. He was still like this from time to time. Full of self-hatred. Full of anger at himself. I tried my best to fight against it, even if my best was just loving him. But it hurt. It killed me to see him like this, knowing there was nothing I could really do. Just wait and hope his wounds would heal. Scab over. Turn into scars.

I reached up to cup his face. He still had the beard. He'd trimmed it a little for the wedding, but he'd kept it. Like it was part of the mask he'd been wearing since he got back because he was afraid I'd run away from what he'd turned into.

"You can tell me all the monstrous things you've done if you'd like," I said. "If it will feel better for you to say them out loud. To give them another home that isn't the inside of your head. You tell me every detail that you think I can't handle, and I'll continue to love you. More, if anything. Because you've shown me new spaces, parts of you to love. I'm not afraid of you. Of what you've done. Who you are. What you've had to do to come back to me. All that matters is that you came. And I promise you right now, if you hadn't come back, if you'd tried to be that man of honor and stayed away, that's the only thing I wouldn't be able to forgive. To love. I'm not going anywhere. I'm not some scared teenage girl. I'm tougher than I look. I can handle you."

He searched my face, his eyes filled with love, reverence. Emotion that hit every nerve in my body. It was unlike anything to be loved this much. Adored this much. Especially by a man with all the demons Cody had. Demons I had no idea how to slay but hoped to learn to tame. To love.

"Fuck, baby. It might be wrong of me, but I'm never letting you go," he murmured, lips on my neck.

"We're getting married tomorrow," I replied. "You're never letting me go."

"Promise," he murmured.

He kept that promise.

Until he couldn't.

Chapter 4

One week into prospecting, Cody became Ranger. One of the crazy rites of passage that went with being patched in to the Sons of Templar MC was that you either had to have a seriously badass name—like Cade who was such a badass he was born with it—or someone decided to give you one.

Of course, Cody didn't tell me he'd gotten one of his own, I heard it at one of the first MC barbeques I attended. It was nerve wracking. I knew the Sons of Templar and everyone connected to them my whole life, but this was different. I was attending as an Old Lady of a prospect. I knew that meant something. Especially since there were very few prospects, or patched members for that matter, with Old Ladies.

There were plenty of beautiful, scantily clad women around, making it so most of the brothers didn't feel the need to have a relationship. Why would they want that complication when there were loose women ready to suck their cocks at a moment's notice?

I'd handled it well, I thought.

Evie hadn't done anything like rip my face off. She'd just sat down beside me, chain smoking and chatting.

Though, her version of chatter was every curse word known to man and letting me know what I was in for.

"He's going to come home late," she said, inhaling. "Or he's not gonna come home at all. He'll have to leave in the middle of the night, not tell you where he's going. You're gonna have to deal with that, if you want him."

She nodded to one of the women leaning just a little too fucking close to my husband for my liking. "You're going to have to deal with them too. Now, you can show them what's yours. And you can show him what happens if he decides he wants to indulge in that shit. A lot of the time it might feel like you don't have power or control over this shit. That you have to embody a role that feels like a time in the past where you don't have a vote." She sucked on her smoke. "But you don't. Not in there, at least," she nodded toward the clubhouse. "Which can piss you off until you figure out the ways to get what you want. Not the same ways as women who have men who don't wear that cut, but the same process. Every woman learns the tricks to get her way. Ours is just a little different." She glanced to me. "And you've got a family behind you now. Hold you over during the tough times. There's gonna be some of those, I can feel it. You love him?"

I nodded. "More than anything."

"Well, buckle in, honey. It's gonna get rough."

And it did.

Get rough.

Everything Evie said came to pass. The late nights. Unreturned phone calls. The not coming home at all. Blood stains on his shirts. Something changing about him, in his eyes, his mannerisms. The way he touched me. Fucked me.

That's what it was. Fucking. Not making love. Not gentle.

No, it was desperate, furious, like he was trying to lose himself inside of me. Like it was the last time he was going to touch me.

I changed too.

There was no choice. I was an Old Lady. I'd made that choice, so I leaned into it. I learned how to deal with the uncertainty, the fear, the long nights alone. The club girls.

Evie was my lifeline. An unconventional one, to be sure, but she held me steady, poured me drinks. Invited me over to her place for dinner when the men were out doing... whatever they were doing.

Rosie, Lucy and Ashley were always around too. They were only a little younger than me and definitely bat shit crazy, Rosie the self-proclaimed leader of the trio. I liked being around them, even if they scared me just the littlest bit. Cade tried his best to rein his sister Rosie in, but that was like trying to use an umbrella in a hurricane.

Fucking useless.

There were many nights at Rosie's place with cocktails and all sorts of plans made, butI always crept home before those plans were executed.

Laurie was there too. Of course she was. She was my best friend. But it was different with her because she was different now. We were in this together, of course, because we'd been friends all our lives..

It didn't touch her. Zane—he was Bull now, to everyone except Laurie—didn't let it touch her. His duty was to the club, like the rest of the members, but Laurie was always his first priority. Protecting her was what he was put on this earth for.

I liked that for my friend. Loved it. But I was also jealous. Cody would protect me from anything in this world, except the Sons of Templar. He couldn't protect me from the MC or their lifestyle.

The first year of Cody prospecting was hard. On me. On

him. On us. I'd thought I knew what I was getting into. The club had been a presence in Amber since before I could remember. My mother respected them, but she didn't approve. She'd raised me bedtime stories about the big, bad bikers and what would happen to me if I found myself embroiled in their world.

Which was exactly where I was.

Despite the fear, the danger, the loneliness, I liked our lifestyle. Loved the family we had. Loved that Cody seemed to have found his peace.

But to find that peace, Cody had left himself behind. He was no longer Cody. He was Ranger. First to the club, then to himself, then to me.

Five Years Later

I stared at the two lines on the stick in my shaking hand.

Were my hands shaking out of happiness or fear?

We'd agreed that we didn't want kids until Ranger had patched in, been in the club for a good amount of time. We were going to wait for the chaos to settle down, until things weren't so dark for the club. Until we could save enough money to afford a baby. Ranger had enough money to buy us a small bungalow with a view of the beach, near Cade's newly purchased house. Cade and Brock were already members when Ranger got back from… wherever he'd been. Five years married and he still hadn't told me where he'd been or how he'd come across Gage.

Gage was broken in ways that Ranger wasn't. There was a violence to him that should've scared me, but instead, I wanted to protect him. I made him come over to the house for dinner at least twice a week and didn't force him to speak if he didn't want to. I didn't want him to be alone.

I didn't ask him about his past, just like I didn't ask Ranger where he'd been or how he had the money to buy us the beach-front bungalow. I wanted to know, but I wanted him to have peace more. As much as I wanted him to share all of his dark-ness with me, I trusted him to tell me if he needed to, and I wouldn't push it if it meant that whatever had brought him back to me would go away.

It was naïve maybe, but I was just happy to have him back. To sleep beside me every night. To whisper to him in the dark-ness, telling me things about himself that made tears stream down my face. He was still healing from wounds I would never be about to stitch up, erase, but I tended to them best I could. Loved him exactly as he was.

I even loved the Sons of Templar. It was hard at times, but mostly it was a life that I felt like I belonged in. There was danger. Uncertainty. Late nights. Lonely nights. Blood-soaked clothing. Bloody knuckles. But there were also full dinner tables. Barbeques. A sense of safety. Brotherhood for Ranger. Family like I never would've had otherwise.

My mom never came around to the house, but she at least attended our small wedding. On dad's insistence, no doubt. We had dinner with them once a month. It was always strained.

But I had Ranger.

The club.

And now, a positive pregnancy test in my hands.

"YOU HAVEN'T TOLD RANGER?" Evie asked.

She was sitting out on our patio with a glass of whisky. I had wine that she'd urged me to at least sip to take the edge off.

Though I desperately needed something to take the edge off, I hadn't touched it.

"He's still on a run," I said. "And I didn't want to call him with this type of news. Especially..." I trailed off.

"Especially if you're not sure if you wanna keep it," Evie finished for me, no judgement in her voice.

I flinched anyway, hating the words being spoken out loud. Why should it make any difference? I'd been thinking those same words since I'd seen the result of the test.

"It doesn't make you a bad person or bad wife if you don't want it," Evie continued.

"I want it," I whispered, placing my hand on my still flat stomach. Hearing it out loud, actually thinking of a reality where I did something to the life Ranger and I had created with our love, I was suddenly sickened by the idea.

"Ranger doesn't?"

I smiled. "No, he does. He's wanted one since he got the patch. I just, I don't know if this is the right time. With everything going on."

I said everything as though I knew what that entailed. I didn't completely. Ranger didn't like to bring that shit home, said he didn't want to pollute our alone time with the worries of the club. The dangers. I knew enough about some of it, though. The guns. The rival clubs. I knew things were tense right now.

"There's never a right time to have a kid, sweetie. And honestly, if there was, right now would be the time. With everything going on, the club needs this. Ranger needs this. Some light in the middle of this shit. Something beautiful and pure. Something to fight for." She sipped her whisky. "In saying that, it's only beautiful if it's right for you. There's no shame in saying it's not. No one will judge you."

She was wrong. I would judge myself if I did what my mind whispered was best. Was safest. It would make me a coward. It would create cracks in my soul and in my marriage, eventually tearing it apart.

"You're right," I said after a beat. "This is what the club needs. What Ranger needs." I looked down to my stomach. "A family."

Eight Months Later

"We need to go to the hospital now," Ranger clipped, glaring at me as I descended the stairs of our new home. He'd decided a beachside bungalow, while beautiful, was not practical for a baby. It was too small. Too unprotected.

Initially, I hadn't known what he truly meant when he said "unprotected". We had enemies, I knew this, but they were face-less to me. I hadn't put any thought to whatever the club was doing finding us at home, Old Ladies and families were off limits, in the rules of outlaw war. But things were turning. Men were getting tense, you could feel it in the air. It scared me, but not enough as it probably should've. I trusted Ranger to protect me. Us.

So we'd moved into town, onto a quiet street, into a beau-tiful house paid with money I knew was somehow stained with blood.

"We don't need to go yet," I said, pausing in the middle of the staircase. I inhaled sharply and clutched the railing as another contraction took hold.

Ranger watched, obviously furious at me for not listening to his alpha commands. He was also furious because he had to watch his wife go through pain, and there was nothing he could do about it. He was committed to protecting me from anything and everything, and right now, there was a lot to protect me from. He could do plenty about the outside influences, just not our son making his arrival known my ripping apart his mother's womb.

He must've moved at some point because he was no longer glaring at me from the bottom of the stairs, I was in his arms as he descended them.

"Cody!" I snapped. "You can't carry me. I'm an elephant, and you'll pull something. Plus, I'm totally capable of walking."

He put me down but did not let me go. One of his hands went to the large swell of my stomach, the other to the back of my neck. "Not going to apologize for not letting my pregnant wife go through fucking contractions on the middle of the staircase," he gritted out. "You can be the strong, independent woman all you want in every other aspect of your life. But not this part. Not when my whole world is possibly in danger. When I can't do a damn thing but take you to the hospital. So let me take you to the fucking hospital."

Long story short, I let him take me to the fucking hospital.

Jack Cody Derrick was born fifteen hours later.

The entire club took over the waiting room during that time, showing their support. Showing me my son would always have family.

———

I CLOSED THE DOOR, quietly.

Not that I needed to, Jack slept like the dead. He had since we'd brought him home from the hospital.

Quiet.

Too quiet.

It had me checking on him every five minutes to make sure he was still breathing. Olive stayed with us for the first two weeks of Jack's life. She might not have approved of the life her son had chosen, but she loved him and supported him no matter what. She supported me no matter what too.

My own mother warmed up with the birth of her first grandchild, but that wasn't really saying much considering she was my mother. It was like saying hell had gotten itself a space heater.

She wouldn't be the favorite grandmother, that title was reserved for Olive. My father, on the other hand, would most definitely be the favorite grandfather, and not just because he was the only one Jack would have.

Along with his grandparents and parents, Jack had an entire club of uncles ready to fight for him, to protect him. He even had a Sons of Templar onesie already. He was born into the club, and most likely would patch in to it when he was older. Of course he would have a choice, and I could be wrong about the kind of man he'd turn out to be; he may not want anything to do with the club, but I didn't think so. I had the feeling he would grow up to idolize his dad and the men in the club. He would be surrounded by family, by Harleys, the idea of a life lived free and wild.

The thought was bittersweet. I loved the club, loved the idea of my son wearing a patch and having brothers. But not the way the club was now. Not with the idea that my baby boy could either end up behind bars or in an early grave if the club continued on the way it was going.

It would kill me if something happened to my son because of the club. It would kill all the love and loyalty I had for the club. I shouldn't have been thinking of such morbid things when my son was still decades away from such a choice, but I couldn't help it. My mind forced me to think of every single danger to my boy so I could protect him from it.

Including the club.

Yet I couldn't protect him from that.

"He sleeping?" Ranger asked, handing me a glass of wine.

I took it, thankful for the fact that my husband was cooking me dinner and had wine ready for me after putting our son to bed.

"Yeah," I said taking the first sip. It was cold, sweet and cheap. The only wine I really drank. I wasn't cultured in my drinking habits and was happy with a beer most of the time. But dealing with a baby required wine. Ideally some mood stabilizers too.

Ranger lowered the burner on the stove, put down his beer —he was not a wine guy—and moved to kiss me. Long. Slow. Enough to make my stomach dip beautifully.

"Good," he murmured. "As much as I love our son, and I do, more than anything in the world, I do need some alone time with his mother." His hands trailed along my hips—much wider than they had been before Jack. Fortunately, Ranger hadn't made me feel self-conscious about that one bit.

"You're not allowed to do that," I murmured. "We still have two more weeks before the doctor said we're allowed to do anything that involves what you're insinuating."

Now, physically, there was *no way* I was ready for sex down there. Things were tender, healing but tender. Having a child was exactly as painful as everyone said, and anyone who said different was on a serious amount of drugs or was a huge fucking liar.

But inside of me, my hormones, my soul… yeah, it wanted my husband. Really fucking bad.

He kissed me again before pulling back, his eyes running over my body with hunger. "Yes, my love. I am all too painfully aware of the stretch of time that's passed since I was inside my wife," he smirked, his eyes lingering, almost tempting me to forget about my ruined vagina in order to let him make good on all his promises.

Ranger stepped back farther and picked up his beer. "I'm not exactly a patient man, but it does stand to reason that I should wait for you to be completely healed for what I have in store for you."

Another stomach dip as Ranger turned back to the stove. My eyes moved across his back, memorizing the vision of my husband in our kitchen while our son slept.

"I need you to make me a promise," I said.

Ranger obviously heard something in my voice because he turned off the stove again and came back to stand in front of me, giving me all of his attention.

"Anything."

I took a sip of wine. A big one. "I need you to live to be an old man," I said. "I want your hair to turn gray, I want you to complain about your knees, refuse to get hearing aids even though you need me to repeat myself a thousand times. Although that might not have to do with medical hearing impairment, just male hearing in general." I smiled weakly.

"I want you to hold our first grandchild in your arms. Then the second. I want you to be the old biker who reminisces about the ol' days over whisky. I want to grow old beside you. But to do that, you have to live through these days. I'm not asking you to give up your patch, though, sometimes I wish I could ask, wishing you'd say yes. But that's not how it works. So you keep that patch on. Keep it on now and keep it on as the Old Man I need you to be." I stepped forward to clutch his neck. "Please, Cody," I whispered. "Please live to be an old man."

He didn't answer straight away. His eyes searched mine, running over my body as if he was imprinting every part of me into his mind. I knew the look because I had the same one on my face every time he left the house lately.

"I'd never leave you in this world without me. I'll do everything in my power to keep me here, right here," he murmured, his lips close to mine.

"Promise?"

His eyes flickered with a danger that had become so common. "Promise."

Chapter 5

One Year Later

We didn't speak as we left the hospital.

Ranger held my hand, though, I didn't want him to touch me. I just didn't have enough energy to try to pull my hand out of his iron grip. Didn't have the strength to look him in the eye and tell him his hand on my skin made acid from my heart crawl up my throat.

He needed this. Some form of support. Of love. Because this was the only thing he could do. The only thing he had control over was the grip he had on my hand. He couldn't save me, couldn't save the baby we'd lost at fourteen weeks.

So he held my hand.

And I tried to handle it.

The entire club was there when Jack was born.

There was no one there when my second baby died. This was not something to celebrate. People did not want to be around this. Have to face the ugliness.

Even Ranger didn't want to be around this. Around me. He

wanted to escape. I didn't blame him. If I could've escaped my body, I would have.

He wordlessly opened the door for me, helped me in then closed it. I held my breath, trying to prepare myself for being in an enclosed space with him. My husband. The man I knew better than myself. The man who knew everything about me. I winced when he got in the car. The air felt stifling, I couldn't breathe around him.

Ranger went to start the car then paused, looking over at me. I saw all of this through my peripheral vision, no way could I look straight at him.

"I don't know what to say," he choked out, voice broken.

I continued to stare ahead of me. As cruel as it was, I couldn't control it.

"Don't say anything," I replied, my voice emotionless. "Just take me home."

I DIDN'T HAVE SHOES.

If the check-in clerk at the only slightly cheesy, Hawaiian themed motel two hours out of town thought that a woman checking in with no shoes and luggage consisting of two paper bags full of vodka was odd, he didn't show it. He simply handed me a plastic key card and told me to enjoy my stay.

I didn't reply, but I don't think that bothered him either. He just went back to his crinkled Playboy.

It must've hurt, walking with bare feet along the rough ground. But I didn't feel it. I was numb. Except between my legs and in my stomach, which felt painfully empty and ruined. The vodka would surely help that.

It would help me forget that I'd walked out of my house, the one where my husband was bathing our child, and stolen the first car I could, stopping only to get vodka, then drove myself out of town without a word to anyone.

Yes, I needed to forget that too. Even now, the shame and guilt crawled up the back of my neck and threatened to paralyze me.

My hand was shaking when I put the keycard in. Still shaking when I unscrewed the first bottle of vodka. It was steadier when I opened the second one.

———

SOMETHING BLOCKED OUT MY SUN.

There had been a bright warmth at the back of my closed eyelids, one that I was trying to get to burn away all my shame—in addition to the vodka I'd ingested—and put me to sleep.

I'd managed to get some—sleep, that was—the night before, but that was only because of the sheer amount of vodka I'd consumed on an empty stomach.

My head was still pounding, and the candy bar I'd choked down from the vending machine hadn't exactly soaked up much alcohol.

I was still wearing my clothes from yesterday as I hadn't had the sense to pack a bikini for this trip. Which was fine, since the pool looked like it hadn't been cleaned in the past month. Or year, maybe.

As it was, I was doing my best to soak up the sun on this crappy lounger, trying to forget about what a terrible person I was.

It had been almost working until someone decided to block out the sun.

I kept my eyes closed for a full minute, hoping whoever was there would get bored and leave me alone. No such luck. With a frustrated groan, I succumbed to the fact that I'd have to go through the painful process of opening my eyes.

The figure was blurry at first, but familiar. Wearing a Sons of Templar cut. Should I have been surprised?

"I thought it might take you a little longer to track me down," I muttered, my words thick.

Gage stared down at me for a beat, probably deciding whether he was going to try and talk to me—not exactly his strong suit—or just do the alpha male thing and throw me over his shoulder then drag me back to Amber.

He surprised me when he moved to sit on the lounger next to me, taking the bottle from beside me, taking a hearty swig without flinching. An impressive feat since it was warm, cheap vodka at... I didn't know the exact time, but it was still morning.

"Is Ranger too mad at me to come and get me himself?" I asked. "Does he hate me?" The last part was said in a small, vulnerable, terrified voice. That pissed me off. People were already going to treat me different now. Smaller. More breakable. I didn't have to sound that way too.

He had every right to hate me. What I'd done was unforgivable. Abandoning him and our son in a time when they needed me most.

"Sweetheart, no one on this earth and no one wearing this cut has the capacity to hate you," he replied. "Most especially your husband. You know that."

I stared at the dirt in the pool. "I don't know anything anymore."

"You do. You just can't see anything through the pain you're going through," Gage countered.

"What do you know about it?" I snapped, suddenly furious at his presence, his kindness.

Neither of us spoke, a vodka-infused silence lingering for a long time. "I had a kid." he finally said, his voice the softest I'd ever heard it. "A daughter. I lost her. It was a pain unlike anything I can explain. I wanted to rip off my skin just so I wouldn't have to feel the pain of her loss slowly killin' me. So I know about the pain."

His words, the loss etched into his voice, carved a hole in my chest.

I turned my head, Gage was staring at the pool, clutching the vodka bottle. His arms were covered in scars, ones that I'd always wondered about but never questioned. No one had. He'd had the misfortune to wear the scars of his past on his arms, like his insides had run out of room. I'd always known it must've been bad, his past, but I never imagined it could be something like this. Because I couldn't fathom the idea of walking, breathing, having a heartbeat if I lost Jack.

I was doing all of those things now, though, even though I'd lost a baby who didn't have a name.

I didn't say I was sorry, though twenty-four hours ago I would've. Would've told him I was sorry for his loss and tried to hug him, given him some kind of support. I would've been deluded enough into thinking that there was a point in doing such things. Like they would make any kind of difference.

"That's why you patched in?" I asked. "Because you were hoping the club might kill you?"

He shrugged. "Wouldn't have been mad if it did. But no, wasn't exactly looking to die. Just looking to hurt in a different way. Ranger is the reason I found the club. He was going through his own kind of pain, somehow convinced me to come back here with him. To the club. I went because I had nowhere else to go. He went because it was the only place for him to go. To be with you." He took a swig. "You took him back when he came back because that's who you are. Knew that he needed to be gone. He knows you need to be gone now too."

"And he just let you come to retrieve me?" I asked.

Gage grinned. Or at least his version of a grin, a slight twitch of his mouth. "Oh, fuck no. He doesn't know you're here."

I stared at Gage. "You didn't tell him?"

"Figured you were gone for a reason. That you needed to be away for a reason. Shit you went through isn't simple. You need time to sit at a crappy motel in the middle of nowhere and drink crappy vodka, that's fine. Won't force you to say shit. Just gonna sit here and make sure no opportunistic asshole tries to hurt you while you're going through this."

And he did exactly that.

He sat beside me for six hours, leaving only to get water and a greasy hamburger that he forced me to eat. Eventually, the bottle was empty, and I was ready to go home.

Ranger was waiting for me.

With no hatred. No judgement. Only love.

It was enough to get me through it all.

Not unscathed, of course. We were both scarred now. Our marriage too. Things would be hard. I'd be distant for months, and Ranger would be frustrated that I wouldn't talk, that he couldn't help, that he didn't know how to handle his own pain.

But we survived.

Chapter 6

"Evie, to what do I owe the pleasure?" I asked, jostling Jack on my hip. He immediately reached for the leather clad woman who smelled of cigarettes and expensive perfume.

She took the baby from me before pushing the sunglasses on her head. "You got vodka?"

"Is everyone okay?" I asked immediately, letting her in.

If my husband was dead, would they send the matriarch, or would they send a member? Like soldiers informing the family of their loss.

"Everyone is breathing and whole," she reassured me. "But you'll still need the vodka."

I'd known Evie for a good amount of time now, so I knew to trust her if she thought I needed vodka.

She kept Jack occupied while I poured two drinks.

"Take a sip first," she instructed, nodding to my glass.

I did as she said.

"There was a raid on the clubhouse earlier today," she explained. "Picked up Steg, Ranger, Brock and Bull."

I inhaled sharply, thankful for the vodka in my hand. "For what?"

She sipped her own drink. "Bullshit, most likely. I don't think the ATF has anything concrete. Probably enough to justify the raid, the warrant. Keep them for a couple of nights. Beyond that, no. We have expensive lawyers on retainer for this very case."

I took a steadying breath. This wasn't the first time something like this had happened; the club had been the subject of these kinds of things since Ranger patched in. Nothing ever really stuck, though. The chief of police was in their pocket on the proviso that nothing related to the Sons' business affected Amber. Hell, that was why the town respected them so much, they were protected from them.

I had accepted this as part of the status quo, but that was before Jack. Before my son wouldn't have his father to tuck him in because he was in prison.

Evie narrowed her eyes as if she was reading my mind. "This is what you signed up for, honey. This is what being married to this club is."

I sighed. "I know. And I love the club. But—"

"No buts," she cut in. "You love the club. You love your Old Man. You weather this shit. We get through it. There is no other way to survive this. Don't fight it, don't take it out on your man, and don't carry resentments. This is just the way shit is." She squeezed Jack. "We'll get through this. It'll calm down."

I sipped the vodka.

I hoped she was right.

Two Months Later

I was struggling to keep my breakfast down when the bikes rolled in. Jack apparently sensed my unease and was struggling in my grasp. The rest of the club, prospects, club girls and various girlfriends were gathered, waiting for the homecoming.

Despite the expensive lawyers, the ATF had managed to hold them on pending charges. Those charges eventually fell through, but not before my husband and half of the club was behind bars for two months.

It was the longest Ranger and I had been apart since that separation all those years ago. And definitely the longest since we'd had Jack. But Evie had been right. The club rallied.

Laurie was over at our place often, being lost without her own true north. This had been the longest the two of them had been apart *ever*. She'd been lost, but had held it together. She stayed over a lot of nights, not liking to be alone in an empty house. Also because she adored Jack.

She desperately wanted a baby, and I knew that she'd be an amazing mother. I doubted Bull was one to not give her what she wanted, so I worried for her. She never spoke of dark things, though. She was all sunshine and hope. She believed everything would work out. She always had faith that everything would happen at the right time, that everything happened for a reason.

Evie was a constant presence too. Rosie, Lucy and Ashley were also over a lot, usually arriving with the makings of some kind of cocktail and stories of their latest dating dramas.

Gage came around. Lucky. Asher. There was never a moment when my house felt empty. Until nighttime. When I lay in bed trying to find sleep, wondering where my husband was sleeping, if he was safe. For all I knew, he was at even more risk while locked up with rival gangs inside the prison. And there was always the uncertainty. They were surely guilty of something. Something that could put them away for years. Years of my son's life. My life.

I held fast to hope.

And to fear.

When I looked at those two lines three weeks ago, fear and dread swam in the bottom of my stomach. Just a shadow of what I'd felt after we lost our second, but enough to bring me to my knees.

I'd lost our baby when we were happy. Safe. When everything was going well. Yet we'd still lost it. Despite what doctors had said about it not being in our control, about it being inevitable, I'd harbored the toxic thought that it was my fault. That my doubts at the beginning had caused it.

Now, I was in the middle of not knowing when my husband would get home, not knowing if he'd even come home, yet I was going to have to be strong enough to grow a baby and take care of a toddler?

I couldn't.

There was a certainty inside of me that I'd lose this one too. So I told no one. Didn't mention a thing when I called Ranger —he wouldn't let us visit—and told none of the women.

What was the point in telling anyone when I was going to lose it anyway? I'd gone to the doctor's office, heard the heartbeat, listened to her tell me that my baby was healthy. But she'd said all of that before. I didn't want to know the sex because I didn't want to think of it as real. Didn't want it to become something other than what I'd lose.

It was healthy enough to make me violently ill every morning. Lunchtime. Dinner. There was barely a respite from the nausea, and it was hell trying to hide it from constant visitors. The way Evie looked at me told me she knew, but she said nothing because she wasn't a woman to try to make me talk about something I'd made a point to be silent about.

When the men pulled in, I decided I wasn't going to tell Ranger either. Not yet. I couldn't. I just wanted to be happy that my husband was getting off his bike and damn near sprinting toward us.

He gathered both me and Jack into his arms, and my entire body relaxed with his warmth, strength and scent. He didn't say anything, neither did I, we just held each other silently. My family was complete again.

⸺

"I HAVE SOMETHING TO TELL YOU," I said, my voice shaking.

All of the promises I'd made to myself shattered with him home, with our son, in our bed. I couldn't keep secrets from Ranger. Especially not one this big, even though it scared me as much it did.

Ranger looked up from his book. I took in the vision of him laying in our bed, glasses on, low light illuminating every ridge of his toned body, leaving shadows on his ink. His son's name on his heart, next to mine. His name was on my right wrist. Jack's on my left.

"If it's that you've taken another husband in my stead, can you tell me tomorrow?" he asked, dog earing his book and placing it on his nightstand. "I have plans for you."

His words made my thighs clench and my nipples pushed through the thin fabric of my nightgown.

Ranger hissed between his teeth. "Come here. Now."

"No, I need to tell you something first."

He threw the covers back and was in front of me in a blur. "Well, you can tell me from bed," he said, lifting me into his arms and carrying me.

When your shirtless, tattooed, muscled and horny husband carries you to bed, you tend to forget things. Very important things. Like you were planning on telling him you were pregnant.

I was only human.

It wasn't until his hard-on was grinding against my panties

and my shirt was gone that I remembered what I was meant to be doing. And I only remembered because of Ranger's sharp intake of breath when his eyes went to my boobs.

"What the fuck, babe?" he growled, kneading them, causing me to flinch ever so slightly in pain.

He stopped immediately, far too in tune with my body for his own good. "Lizzie?" he asked, voice still.

Yeah, what was I thinking trying to keep this from my husband? My boobs hadn't changed a whole lot, it was still early, and Jack had done a number on them with breastfeeding. I liked to think they bounced back well, all things considering, but there was no mistaking the increased size or the fact that my nipples were much larger and tender.

"I'm pregnant," I whispered, fear coating my words.

He stilled when he heard those words. "Pregnant?" he repeated in an unreadable tone.

I nodded. "It's still early. Thirteen weeks. I don't want to tell anyone. Don't want us to get our hopes up."

Ranger obviously wasn't listening to this, because while one hand stayed at my breast, the other moved down to settle on my stomach. Flat but peppered with stretchmarks, the evidence of carrying our son. Marks that Ranger worshipped.

"Baby, I spent two months with only one hope," he murmured. "To get home. Be with my family. So all my hopes and dreams have been fulfilled no matter what." His eyes moved to mine. "Know why you want to take it slow. I know that you don't wanna expect anything but the worst because life's given you the worst. Hate that there's nothing I can do about that. But I'm here. No matter what. You aren't alone going through this shit. But just know, I cannot wait to meet our baby girl."

I blinked through tears. "How do you know it's a girl?"

He grinned. "Just know."

Just under six months later, Lily Olive Derrick came into the world.

EVERYONE REMEMBERS where they were when they got terrible news. News that hit them right in their core, ruining everything they knew about the world. Hoped about the world. Tearing out their insides.

I was at the hair salon when I found out.

It seemed like an impossibility that one could get that type of news at such a mundane place. There was a sense of safety here, with glossy magazines neatly stacked, mirrors, glam décor, the scent of hair dye and the sound of blow-dryers.

I knew something bad had happened when Ranger walked into the salon. There was nothing that would force my macho man into the den of femininity unless it was bad. Well, that was a lie. He had when I'd forced him to drop me off a coffee.

But with no coffee in his hand and the grim, tight expression on his face… yeah, it was bad.

The chatter quieted with his entry. The salon was full of women I knew and had known for most of my life. Women who knew who Ranger was, knew about the club, and sensed the tension rippling off my man.

"Babe?" I asked, pulling off the cape I was wearing.

"We need to go," he commanded, his voice flat. He was forcing the emotion out of it. This was bad.

My stomach dropped. "The kids?"

Something moved across his face as his hand reached for mine. "No, baby. The kids are fine. They are with my mom at the clubhouse. We need to get there now."

Something inside of me, the primal mother inside of me, relaxed. But tension still coursed through the rest of my body.

My children were the most important thing in my world, but I'd also been blessed to have many other precious people in my world. Many other people who could be the reason for the look on my husband's face.

"You need to tell me what's going on," I urged, planting my feet firmly in place as if the tiled floor of the hairdresser's was going to make the news any different. Was going to make my reaction to it any different.

"Lizzie," he murmured, glancing around. "You need to come with me."

I let him lead me out of the salon. I hadn't paid, but no one said anything. Guessed they could read the room.

As soon as we were outside and away from any prying ears, I stopped letting Ranger lead me. He turned, brows narrowing.

"You need to tell me," I demanded. "Now."

He frowned, his forehead creasing into deep lines. "We need to go, I'll tell you when we get to the club."

Most of the time when Ranger spoke in that 'alpha male, hear me roar' tone, I listened. Not because I was a female who listened to a man's every command, but because he usually only used that tone in the bedroom, and it was super-hot.

"No," I said, arms crossed. "I am not going to get on that bike and wonder what horrible thing awaits me. I need to know *right now*." I used an alpha female tone of my own.

Ranger took in a sharp breath, seemingly measuring my words, assessing his ability to be able to convince me otherwise. Beyond that, there wasturmoil in his eyes. This was hurting him. Killing him. Not just whatever the news was, but the fact that he knew it would hurt me. This was a man who'd spent the entire time we've been together trying to protect me from harm. He was battling with the knowledge that he had no power over this, and that he was going to have to deliver the news.

His hands settled firmly on my hips, as if he thought I'd need help standing.

"It's Laurie, baby. And it's bad."

———

RANGER HADN'T SPOKEN since the funeral.

There was a lot going on. Members from chapters all over the country had attended in a show of solidarity. In a show of force.

I'd been with the Sons of Templar long enough to know what this meant. War.

We'd been through several skirmishes. There were plenty of other MCs, gangs, criminals, police FBI… there were countless organizations looking to take the Sons of Templar down. We were always fighting some kind of war.

But this was different.

This was like a wall had been erected between us. Some time when I hadn't been paying attention. When I'd been too busy trying to fathom that I'd lost my best friend. That she'd suffered some of the most horrific things a human can go through at the end of her life.

She was light, love, laughter.

Yet she'd died in an ugly, violent, brutal and bloody way.

We'd waited at the hospital knowing it was bad. Bull had become nothing but a human shaped ghost. Everything about him was empty. Dark.

The air was toxic with the truth.

That there was no way Laurie would survive what had been done to her. She wouldn't want to survive because there was no way that any woman would be able to live with what had been done to her.

I'd prepared myself for her death. Sitting in the hospital

waiting room with Ranger beside me, his hand in mine, I'd gone through the motions. Thought I had, at least.

But when we got the news, I broke. Completely. Ranger took me home. He put me to bed, held me close. I didn't feel the change in him then because in that moment, I only felt pain.

Then I became distracted. I forced myself to be distracted with funeral arrangements and with helping Evie with the logistics of having multiple chapters arriving in Amber to show support.

Ranger was around. Of course he was. He was there to check on me. The kids. To make sure someone was with us at all times.

Old Ladies had always been off limits, even to the most ruthless of criminals.

Until Laurie.

I was clutched with fear, thinking about how ugly this war could get, how it would only get uglier now.

I thought what I felt was grief. And fear that something would happen to me or the kids. I was too deep in my own head to realize it was something else. Something much worse. Something that might completely end us.

Chapter 7

"You can't go again," I said, crossing my arms over my chest.

Ranger didn't even look me in the eye. He hadn't in weeks. Not since the funeral. My best friend's funeral.

It still didn't seem real. But she was buried. She was gone.

Things had been getting ugly since then.

Since she'd died because of the club, we were at war. Jack, Lily and I were never alone, and there would be a lockdown soon. The club was gearing up for vengeance. The whole town felt it. The air was quiet, like one big exhale. The calm before a storm.

Yet things were everything but calm in our house.

"It's club business. I got no choice," Ranger replied. He did have a choice, he just didn't want to be at home with his wife. And his children who couldn't understand what was going on but knew something was wrong.

"We need you here," I pleaded, my voice small. It had taken me too long to understand the extent of the chasm between us. Too long to recognize how hard Ranger was working to distance himself from me. Now I didn't know what to do. How to act. I was scared. He was like a stranger.

"Lucky will be outside," he said. "You don't have to let him in the house."

"Of course, I'll have him in the house," I snapped. "He's not a dog."

Beyond that, I liked Lucky. Some of his light has been dimmed throughout this, but he worked hard at keeping everyone together. He always had a smile and a joke for Jack, a hug and kind word for me.

"Well, you won't be alone."

I glared at Ranger. "This isn't about being alone. This about my husband taking every chance he can get to escape his wife. His family. I don't know if you've noticed, but we exist."

"Of course, I've fucking noticed!" he roared.

I flinched at his outburst.

"I've got shit to do," he said, quieter now.

"Yeah," I agreed. "First and foremost, you're taking a long look in the mirror to see if you can recognize the man standing in front of you, because I sure as fuck don't."

Then I turned away from him, hoping he wouldn't leave like this.

But the door closed and I was alone with my thoughts. With the truth of what my marriage had turned into.

⸻

I WAS STILL AWAKE when he got home. As much as I wanted to be the kind of woman who could sleep soundly in an empty bed, the fight with her husband hot on her skin, I was not. I didn't work that way. Words circulated around my head. I'd let myself fantasize about the ways he might come back, how we'd sort it out, and it would end in epic making up.

I still thought this, no matter the fact that I'd been with my husband for over a decade, and we'd been through many fights, none of them ever working out like that.

Despite the fact that we'd had many fights, this one felt different. Scarier. The cracks that had emerged after we lost the baby had found their way into the foundation of us, damaging the entire structure of our relationship. Add to that the pressures everyone felt around the club. Things were escalating.

It was ugly of me to stand at Laurie's funeral feeling grateful that it wasn't my husband being buried, but that's what I'd done. Truly, there was no use feeling grateful about anything because this wasn't over. There would be more funerals, something told me that. It was in the way Ranger acted. The fact that we had increased security, that I had to text Ranger anytime me, Lily and Jack were leaving the house, and he had to know where we were at all times.

Yeah, things were bad with the club and bad with us.

So I was awake because I was afraid something had happened to him. Afraid something happened with him and one of the many women who offered an easy fuck without expecting anything in return.

The roar of his bike alerted me to his arrival, followed by a thump as he took off his boots at the front door. He didn't come into our room immediately. Murmured voices carried to where I laid as he likely said goodbye to Lucky, who'd been watching *Charmed* in our living room.

The front door closed.

Lucky left.

Still no footsteps heading to our bedroom.

A clang of glasses and bottles told me what he was doing.

I should've stayed in bed. Should've squeezed my eyes shut and pretended to be asleep until he stumbled in here or until I woke up to an empty bed and my husband sleeping on the couch.

Instead, I pulled back the covers and got out of bed. I did not go for my robe or my slippers because I worried that would make me look like the cliché shrew of a wife. Then again, he was coming home late, reaching for the whisky bottle, so he was swimming in clichés too.

I checked on Jack first, placed my hand on his little chest, pulled up his covers and closed his door quietly. Then I did the same to our sleeping toddler. She had been a good sleeper since the beginning, and I was thankful for that now. I had a feeling this was going to get loud, and despite Jack being a heavy sleeper, I did not want his early memories being his parents screaming at each other.

Ranger was standing at the kitchen counter when I walked in. There was only a dim light on in the corner, cloaking him in shadow.

He knew I was there, but he didn't look up. His shoulders were slumped. Everything about his posture screamed defeat. I sighed, forgetting my anger because my love for my husband would always trump that. My heart would always hurt seeing him look like this, knowing how much he carried on his shoulders.

He needed comfort. Our marriage needed repairing, sure, but nothing would get fixed if my first instinct was to give him anger instead of understanding.

I stopped abruptly when I got close enough to smell it. It was so strong that I thankfully didn't need to get any closer to him for it to blanket my skin.

Perfume. Cheap. Fruity. Not the kind I wore, but definitely on brand for a woman who hung out at a biker club trying to fuck anyone in a cut.

The only reason I didn't double over in pain was because I

was pretty well versed in how to cope with it. I'd gone through childbirth. Losing a baby. Burying my best friend. I knew how to feel bone wrenching pain and still stand.

My hand was shaking when it found the light switch. He did not deserve to get to hide in the shadows and down whisky right now.

No, the mother fucker needed all the harsh light in the world to shine on him right now.

Still, he didn't look at me. His gaze stayed firmly fixed on his glass of whisky.

"Yeah, I wouldn't look at me either," I whispered.

He picked up the glass and downed it, immediately pouring another. "I don't know what you want me to say."

My blood boiled. "I don't want you to say anything. I want my husband to come home not smelling like a whore. But then again, we obviously don't all get what we want."

He shuddered ever so slightly at my words but still didn't look at me.

"Did you fuck her?" I asked, making sure to make my voice as flat and cold as I could. I needed to prepare for the answer. Needed to shield myself against the truth I already knew.

Ranger didn't have the arrogance to look shocked or offended. He didn't have the compassion to look sorry either. Not now, not in the middle of this ugly situation. This horrible period of our relationship.

"I kissed her," he said, in the same cold, flat tone I'd adopted.

I nodded once, even though the pain was blinding, all consuming. A knife through my belly, tearing through the skin so my insides hit the floor. The kind of wound that killed you slowly, but not before you'd been through the worst pain you could ever imagine.

"Once?"

He narrowed his eyes, his mask faltering as uniquely male rage filtered in. "What the fuck difference does it make how many times I did it? I did it."

He hated himself. I saw that, beneath all the anger he was trying to use to cover it up. He might not have been sorry—in this moment, at least—but he was neck deep in self-loathing.

Ranger was an honorable man. Lived by his own code. All the Sons did. Now, a lot of those Sons, the ones with Old Ladies, they had different kind of codes when it came to fidelity. Like, if you were in a different state it didn't count. If she didn't find out. If you didn't take off your cut. You get the gist.

Ranger did not have those kinds of codes. Because of the kind of man he was, sure, but also because I'd made it clear that cheating was a dealbreaker for me.

Once I'd firmly immersed myself in the Sons of Templar universe, I'd understood what manwhores they all were. How easy it was for each of them to get laid. There were always women around, clinging to the club, waiting for their moment.

I'd never thought less of those women; they were just doing what they could to get through their lives. Find adventure, whatever. Even the most calculating of them—I didn't like them, that was sure—but there was no equation without a man's involvement. It takes two to tango and all that.

Ranger had made his promises that he would never touch another woman. Those promises were made, of course, back when he couldn't keep his hands off me. When we were gripped by the throat with our intense young love.

We hadn't loved each other any less over the years since.

But our love had changed with the seasons. We had moments of that intensity. Weeks, months where we were both like horny teenagers. But there were other times that were quieter, when we used the bed to sleep only. To watch movies with our kids.

Pressures of life, the club.

The realities of marriage.

We were going through one of those seasons. A bare one. We had sex, but it wasn't for passion, more out of routine, obligation. Even the worst sex between us was better than what a lot of people got in a lifetime. But still... It wasn't anything like what a young woman with fake tits, blowjob lips and legs to her neck could offer.

I hadn't been stupid enough to think Ranger wouldn't ever be tempted, he was a man. But I had expected him to show restraint. Loyalty. Honor.

"It matters," I said on a rough swallow. "Because more than once constitutes a habit. An affair. A continuing deception. Once is different. It's no less despicable, but it's different." I sucked in a breath, preparing myself. "So how many times was it, Cody?"

He flinched.

I never called him Cody unless I was mad. Even then, I hadn't been mad enough to hit him with the name of the boy who had died when he put on the Sons of Templar cut in years.

I was glad about that flinch. A small shred of evidence that I'd caused him pain. Sure, I wanted to cause him more. I wanted to step forward and kick him squarely in the balls that had tempted him to try to ruin our marriage.

But then again, if it wasn't just his balls, if it had been his head—the one on his shoulders, that is—that had caused him to do this, then there wasn't a marriage left to ruin.

Ranger eyed me, a hard stare. Was he considering lying? Was he measuring whether the truth would get him what he wanted?

"Once," he gritted out.

"Do you care about her?" I asked, unable to stop.

"Care about her?" he scoffed. "Of course I don't fucking

care about her. She's a hot body at the club. I was drunk off my ass. Fucked up in my head, and I kissed her. I don't even remember her fucking name."

"Ah, well that makes it so much better," I muttered.

His hand curled around the edge of the kitchen counter, knuckles going white from the force he was holding onto it.

"Why didn't you fuck her?" I asked. "If you were going to see what the inside of another woman's mouth tasted like, why didn't you stick your dick in her too?

I was being crass. Vulgar. Cruel. But I didn't care. Couldn't care.

"Because I couldn't," Ranger bit out. "I could barely stomach kissing her. Hated every second of it, hated myself for doing it. Because touching any woman that isn't you is a fucking betrayal of everything I am."

The words would've been nice if he wasn't saying them with the same mouth he'd cheated on me with tonight.

"Why did you do it then?" I asked.

"I'm trying to get rid of you!" he exploded, his roar echoing over the corners of my brain. We'd fought plenty in our marriage, but he'd always spoken in aggressive, sharp and quiet tones. He'd never raised his voice.

Which is why I was struck dumb.

Plus, it wasn't the volume in which he said the words, it was the words themselves.

Ranger started pacing.

He never did that either. The man had always been annoyingly free of most nervous tics.

"Fuck, Lizzie, the club..." he trailed off. Stopped pacing. Stared at me.

I'd been married to this man for years. Known him for longer. I was an expert in Cody, an expert in Ranger. I knew every movement on his face, every expression.

But this man standing in front of me was a stranger.

"The way things are going, it's darker than I ever thought we would go. I'm in deep. Even if I wanted to get out, I couldn't. Not now. And I don't want to. That's not the right thing to say as a husband and a father——" his voice broke and he sucked in a sharp inhale. "But fuck, it's the only thing I have to say. I hate myself. But the club is me. It's my blood. And those men are my brothers. It's not inside me to walk away... even if I could. I do love you. More than anything. And I don't want you hurt. But I also don't want to find you broken and half dead on the side of the road."

Laurie. He was talking about my beautiful friend, raped, tortured and abandoned like garbage just because she'd loved a man who wore a Sons of Templar cut.

That's all it had taken... a little bit of love pointed in the wrong direction. It became a death sentence. Not just for Laurie, who I'd known almost all my life, but for Bull. He was gone now. Just an empty shell wearing a cut, breathing, not existing.

That would be Ranger. That's what this was. A glimpse of what he'd look like if the club got me killed.

"I don't forgive you," I said. "I understand why you're doing this. Why you did what you did. I wish I didn't. Wish I could blindly hate you for what you've done, throw you out of this house, giving you what you want. But I can't. I won't. So I'll hate you with my eyes open. For as long as it takes for me to resolve you. I'll stay right here, by your side, because I'll always love you more than I could ever hate you."

I stepped back. "But you're sleeping in the guest room. Tonight for sure. Maybe when I've slept on it, I'll figure out how to share a bed with this stranger you've turned yourself into." I ran my eyes over the man that looked exactly like my husband.

Then my gaze went to our living room cloaked in shadow, always warm, full of love, laughter and safety.

It was cold and dangerous now.

"Maybe I'll need a few nights, but I'm not leaving," I said, voice soft. "I'm not raising our son without you teaching him how to be a man. Even though you're not acting like one now, I know you have him inside."

My voice cracked a little and I angrily swiped a tear from my cheek.

"I'm going to stay so you can show your daughter how all women should be treated. I hope what you've done haunts you with the thought of how she'd feel if some cowardly asshole did this to her. I'm staying for our kids. For you. Remember that."

I turned on my heel and walked calmly to our bedroom, closing the door gently behind me. Didn't slam it. Then I leaned my back against it, sank down until my butt hit the floor. And I sobbed. Soundlessly.

I didn't want to stay.

I wanted to be strong enough—or was it weak enough—to pack up the kids, drain our savings and leave. Disappear into the night and start a new life. Tell my parents, of course, but not where.

It was so intoxicating, the thought of escaping from this dark and scary point in my life. In our marriage.

But I couldn't.

Wouldn't.

I'd made a vow.

'Til death do us part.

I intended to keep that vow.

So did Ranger. I knew that. He wouldn't leave me until the reaper took him.

And I found myself wondering how long that would be.

Five Years Later

"I've got a bad feeling about this," I whispered, watching Ranger strap on his holster, checking the clip of his gun before sliding it in.

He turned to me. "Yeah, babe. You should have a bad feeling about this. It's gonna be bad. Gonna be bloody."

I scowled at him. "Way to make me feel better," I snapped.

He shrugged his cut on and made his way over to me. As pissed as I was at my husband—and I was—there was no way I couldn't appreciate him sauntering over to me in his cut. Even after all these years, after kids, losses, fights, cracks in our marriage, deaths... I still had the same reaction to him that I'd had when I was a teenager.

We'd worked hard on it. On this feeling. This love. After that horrible, terrible night when his lips had touched someone else's, we'd worked harder than ever.

He treated us all with reverence. With adoration. Still carried his guilt around, but we'd worked through it. Worked through that and all the other obstacles we came across.

And I loved him more and more every day.

His hands clutched my neck, then he pulled me in so our foreheads touched. "I'm not gonna be able to make you feel better this time," he said. "I've been married to you long enough to know that no matter what I say, it's not going to stop you worrying anyway. Though you'll hide it well in front of the rest of the women because that's who you are. You don't want them to worry, wanna take care of them. The kids. You'll take it all on so nobody else has to." He stroked my cheek. "One of the many things that infuriates me about you. I hate thinking of you in pain, clutched by that much worry. But I also love you for your damn heart. Soul." His eyes searched mine. "We both know that there is no way around this. No way outta this or around it.

There's only through. And, baby, we've been through a lot before. We'll get through this too."

"We've never been through *this* before," I whispered.

We'd been through a lot. So much ugliness. Risk. But I couldn't put my finger on why this felt different. It was as though there was a certainty hanging in the air, painted on the men's faces, telling me that not all of them were coming out of this.

"Ah, but you forget, baby. I made you a promise," Ranger mused, his gaze searching my face with his head cocked to the side. "I promised that I'd grow old with you. That I'd meet our grandkids. That I'd scare the absolute shit out of Lily's first boyfriend. Walk her down the aisle. Throughout the years, I've done a lot of shit wrong, haven't been the best husband, father, but one thing has always been true: I'm going to keep that promise."

He laid his lips on mine. It was meant to be light. They were about to ride out, after all. But I grasped on. Made the kiss harder, more violent. I needed to imprint myself onto his lips so he'd feel me until he came back to me. I needed to taste him on my tongue, a reminder that he was alive. That he was coming back.

"Baby," he hissed, pulling back ever so slightly. "I've gotta go."

I didn't reply, just put my hands to his belt and started unbuttoning. "Well, then you'd better be quick. Because you're not leaving here until you've fucked me so hard, I forget how scared I am."

His eyes flared with a desire that had never dimmed all these years. "I'll make you forget everything but the feeling of me inside of you," he growled.

I didn't forget about everything.

But I did still feel him inside me when I found out he was dead.

Part II

After.

Chapter 1

I didn't sink down to my knees and scream when Brock told me Ranger was dead.

I'd thought such news was meant to bring you to your knees. That's what I'd imagined I might do. And I'd imagined this moment many times. Sure, a regular person might have horrible fantasies every now and again about how it would feel to lose their husband. It was human to dwell on our fears. To a certain extent. It was also human to brush them aside, burying them, because we couldn't very well go dwelling on how we would feel if the love of our lives was killed.

Unless the love of your life was in a line of work where he faced the very real possibility of death every single day.

Like a police officer.

Firefighter.

Member of the Sons of Templar MC.

Though the Sons wasn't a line of work. It wasn't even a lifestyle. It was a marriage. One you couldn't divorce yourself from. It was for life.

I'd married Ranger knowing that meant I was marrying the

club. I'd grown up with the club. Loved it. Hated it. Resented it. Counted my blessings to have it. Raised my children within it.

All of it.

And his death was a moment I'd been preparing for.

After Laurie, when there was more blood than usual, I'd prepared. Knew it might be my husband soon. I'd accepted it because I'd had no other option. I'd just prayed to whatever god was listening that my husband would come home.

And he did.

Sometimes covered in blood that wasn't his own.

Sometimes needing me to tend to wounds.

Other times with ghosts in his eyes, with a stranger residing in his soul.

He would wake me with his hands, with his mouth, desperate to feel something. Feel alive. Or he'd just held me. The worst of times were when he'd come to bed smelling of whisky and turn his back to me, erecting a cold shield between us.

But we'd gotten through it all.

The club was legit now, so I'd let myself lapse into a false sense of safety. Stopped preparing myself for the prospect of my children growing up without their father.

Silly me.

It hurt.

Brock's eyes had sucked everything out of me. Everything good, everything bad, everything in between. I was a hollowed-out shell, drained of life and hope in one sentence.

I stared at something Brock was holding in his outstretched hand. It caught the light. Sparkled.

Ranger's wedding ring.

The one he'd worn on his finger for years, even through the toughest of times.

Now it was laying lifeless in Brock's palm. Shiny. Too shiny.

Ranger had always taken good care of himself. But he spent a good amount of time in a garage working on cars, and no matter how much he scrubbed, the dirt and oil stained. Blood was much easier to wash off.

"I want to see him." I was surprised at how normal my voice sounded. How could it sound the same when I had no insides? When there was nothing left of who I was moments ago?

Brock's face tightened. "I don't think that's a good idea, Lizzie."

I regarded him. He was the same age as me. We'd gone to high school together, but he'd always seemed older. Even though he was a joker, smiling easier and talking a lot more than his president, he was born to wear this cut. Though most of the time he was approachable, kind and funny, there was something that changed in Brock when need be.

And there was a need for him to change then.

Cade was in the hospital.

It was bad.

Half of the club crowded the hospital waiting room while the half that wasn't here was at the clubhouse, holding a wake. Brock was taking over as president, because there wasn't a guarantee that Cade would pull through.

Though I'd known all of these men before they'd put on the cut, I'd always gotten a little bit scared when they put on their masks.

But I wasn't scared anymore.

And I sure as hell wasn't about to bow down.

"Brock, I'm not sure I give *a fuck* about what you think is a good idea," I replied. "I'm not asking your permission. I'm telling you to take me to my goddamned husband."

Brock's eyes flickered to the side, to his wife who stood beside me, holding my hand so tight that the bones could've been broken for all I knew. I didn't feel anything.

Something passed between them. Something secret. Something that they only shared, not for the world.

I didn't have that anymore.

Not another raise of my brows that Ranger would know meant I needed him to rescue me from a conversation I didn't want to have. No furrowing of Ranger's brows that I knew meant he needed me to wrap my arms around him.

No more messages.

I couldn't talk to the dead.

Amy must've silently told him something. Given him permission maybe.

Brock stepped aside. "He doesn't look——"

"He's dead, Brock," I said. "I don't expect him to look any other way."

⊏━━⊐

I WAS WRONG. He didn't look dead. That was the worst part. Maybe if the bullet had gone through his forehead, ruining his face, it might've been different. I might've been able to hold on to that.

But it wasn't one bullet. It was three. They'd hit him in the stomach, shoulder and heart.

I knew that because I undressed him. He was still wearing the clothes I'd watched him put on this morning. I couldn't bear to look at my dead husband wearing the clothes he'd put on. So I'd undressed him. I touched the single chain around his neck. He'd had to replace it from the one he originally gave me all those years ago, the one I gave back to him as I reminder I was always there. Always waiting. He'd never taken it off. Never, even in the hardest of times. It had blood on it now. My hands were steady as I unclasped it and shoved it in my pocket.

Then I'd looked at the bullet holes. The blood staining his body. The one I knew so well.

His face didn't have any blood on it. No marks to show his violent end. Nothing but the faint lines from our years together and a slight tan since we'd taken a day at the beach with the kids last weekend. Someone had closed his eyes.

His lips were stained a faint pink. They were cold. He was cold. Not as cold as a dead person should be. I guessed it hadn't been long enough.

I brushed the hair from his face then leaned in to smell it. A faint trace of smoke lingered, but mostly it was the shampoo that still sat in our shower.

How could the shampoo bottle still be full when he wasn't going to be around to empty it?

I leaned back, continuing to stare at him. Made myself stare at those bullet holes. At the blood.

I stared for a long while until there was a gentle knock at the door.

Evie.

Had they drawn straws? Seen who'd got the job of coming in here to rip the hysterical widow away from her husband's bloody corpse?

No.

Evie would've wanted to be here. It was her job. Despite the fact that her husband no longer held the gavel, she was and always would be the matriarch of the club.

She had no soft, pitying look in her eyes. She was too accustomed to the reality of this life for that.

"I need water," I spoke before she could. "Warm. Soapy. And a cloth."

She nodded once, not questioning my request. When she looked to Ranger, she didn't flinch, didn't look away from his body. She looked at him a long time. Like he was still alive. I was thankful to her for that. For not looking away from my husband like he didn't exist anymore, even though he really didn't.

She left, coming back quickly with what I needed.

I thanked her with my eyes when she set everything down beside me.

She didn't offer me any words of support, there weren't any. Smelling of smokes and whisky, she just gave me a firm squeeze of my shoulder, a soft kiss on my cheek. Then she left. Gave me the last of the moments alone I'd ever have with my husband.

I dipped the cloth into the water then carefully began to clean the blood from Ranger's body.

I couldn't have the last memory of him being dirty. Being stained with blood. Blood washed off.

I could do that.

Wash off the blood.

That came off.

This memory of day would be like dirt and oil, though. I'd never be able to scrub it from my memory. It would always be a stain.

THE FUNERAL WAS AN EVENT.

As it should've been. The Sons did a few things big. Weddings, patch parties, funerals. It was maybe a show to the newer members that yes, there was a chance of you dying, but you'd get sent off like a king. An important if not attractive quality to the MC life when you were young and looking to become a badass.

I didn't want this funeral. I didn't want to see my son in a little suit. Didn't want my daughter in a black dress. I didn't want to have to make myself presentable for the world. In truth,

I wanted to stay in bed, cuddle my babies close and inhale the faint scent of Ranger that remained on the sheets.

But I hadn't done that.

Because that's not what a Sons of Templar widow did. So I got out of bed in the mornings. I welcomed the women who came into my home in a show of support. I made the guest room up for Olive, because I didn't want her to be alone during what was most definitely the most horrible moment in her life.

I'd been the one who told her. Brock had offered to do it, after I'd emerged from the room where I'd cleaned my dead husband.

I'd refused his offer, as much as I'd been tempted to take it. No way was I letting Olive learn about her son's death from someone other than me. It was my responsibility. That's what Ranger would've wanted. It's what a strong Old Lady did.

And I did it.

I told the strongest, kindest women I knew that her only son was dead. And doing that caused me to die a little more inside.

She was taking it well. Or as well as could be expected. She hadn't really spoken, merely cooked, drank wine and hugged the kids. I knew she was drained. Emptied. It was in her eyes. And as horrific as losing my husband, the love of my life was, the thought of losing my children made my want to rip out my insides. I would not survive that.

I was barely surviving this.

In my darkest of moments—and life was just a series of dark moments these days—I'd wished that Ranger and Cade had swapped places. Cade had been seriously injured in the battle, was discharged from the ICU against doctor's recommendations so he could attend the funeral today.

It was cruel and ugly of me to wish my loss on one of my closest friends, but I couldn't help it. This reality was terrible, unthinkable. I would've made a deal with the devil to get out of it. But even the devil wasn't listening to me.

Lucky had broken his leg.

Steg had lost an eye.

Only Ranger was gone forever.

"Mommy, is Daddy going to heaven today?" Lily asked me as I tied a ribbon in her hair.

My stomach clenched, acid running through my veins. Lily was still young, and she understood the concept of death since we'd buried hamsters, goldfish and now her father.

But she hadn't yet truly fathomed what her father dying meant. She was a little girl who had had a wonderful, loving dad who treated her like a princess. She had not experienced horror and was not expecting a world where her dad didn't read to her at night or do her hair in the morning. Or maybe she was regressing back into a baby-like state in order to deal with the trauma. I'd read about that online. Since I wasn't sleeping, couldn't sleep since the night it all happened, I'd taken to reading all sorts of articles about how children dealt with the death of a parent and how it affected them later in life.

Jack was three years older, therefore he got the fact that his father was dead. He'd cried the entire first night, but then he'd changed. He was grief stricken for sure. Hadn't smiled, laughed or played, just stared at the TV when it was on or sat on the swing set in the back yard. But he hadn't cried since that first night. He'd begun insisting on looking after everything by himself, including me.

"Daddy is already in heaven, honey," I replied, using all the strength I had in order to sound stable, not letting it show that I was in mind numbing pain. "We're just having a... party for him so we can say goodbye." I looked at her in the mirror. "Do you get that, honey? That we're saying goodbye to your Daddy today? You're not going to see him again."

She stared at me in the mirror and scrunched up her nose, deep in thought. "Do I get to see him in my dreams? Because I dreamed about him last night. Will he leave them too?"

I swallowed razor blades, my eyes watering ever so slightly as I shook my head. "No, baby. He will always be in your dreams."

Lily nodded then looked at her reflection. "I think you need to get much better at doing my hair then, if Daddy isn't here to do it."

I choked out a laugh at her no-nonsense tone. She smiled at me, sad yet comforting, and that beautiful smile scraped against the wounds of my soul.

I redid Lily's here then left her to check on Jack.

He was sitting on his bed, fully dressed. He would've looked adorable in his black suit if not for the fact that he was wearing it to bury his father.

"You almost ready to go, baby?" I asked him.

He jerked, looking up, so deep in thought he hadn't even realized I was there.

My son was too young to be staring into space with such intensity. To have that ravaged, jaded look in his face.

"Are you ready?" he asked instead, standing.

"You don't need to worry about me, sweetie," I answered.

He furrowed his brows. "I'm the man of the house now, mom," Jack said, as he adjusted his tie. "It's my job to take care of you."

I stared at him, the boy with Ranger's eyes who looked more and more like his father every day. I couldn't decide whether this would be torture or a blessing, watching my son grow into a man without my husband there to steer him.

I cupped his cheek. "No, sweet boy. You will become a man one day. A wonderful one. One that your father would have been so very proud of. But not yet. Not now. Right now, you're going to be a kid. I'm going to take care of you. That's my job."

95

Jack stared at me with far too much seriousness and worry. "But Mom, you had Dad to help you with that job. He told me that I had to be the man of the house when he wasn't here." His voice was starting to wobble now, cracks in my little man's façade spreading. "He's not here. He's dead, so I need to take care of you and Lily. Because he's dead, mom." Tears began to trail down his cheeks, and I pulled him into my chest, if only so he couldn't see his mother crying too.

⊏⊐

I DIDN'T SHED a tear during the funeral. Not a single one. I didn't cling to the coffin as they lowered it to the ground. No falling to my knees this time either. That wasn't becoming of an Old Lady. Or a mother.

I wasn't really an Old Lady anymore, though, was I? I didn't have to play the part, be strong and ready to kick some bitch's ass if she didn't know her place. I didn't have to handle my husband coming home late or covered in blood.

Because I didn't have a husband anymore.

But still, for my kids, I held on. They were already going to have memories of their father's funeral, they sure as shit weren't going to have memories of their mother losing her shit.

All of the women, the Old Ladies, my friends, stood in the front row. Their husbands, wearing cuts and dark glasses of their own stood behind them. The cemetery was drowned in a sea of leather.

It was a massive show of support.

But I'd never felt more alone.

I wish I could say that the day passed by in a blur. Amy had given me a Valium before the service which I took gratefully. I'd take whatever pills or do whatever it took to help numb the pain.

Though the Valium worked on the edges, softening them, it

didn't reach down to the core of me which was bleeding and dying.

So the funeral was not a blur. I remembered every single. Horrible. Detail.

The only thing I was thankful for that entire day was that everyone went to the club after the funeral. I couldn't stand having people in my house, which was already full of casseroles and death flowers, none of which were able to hide the absence of Ranger.

I didn't want to go to the club.

Not one fucking bit.

But I went anyway.

The kids stayed close to me the entire time, all but clinging to my dress. Lily stuck to my side because she didn't know what to do with herself other than cling to her one remaining parent. Jack was near because he was still convinced that he had to protect me.

As much as I wanted my kids to be nearby, to be within touching distance, I needed space. I needed to breathe. Needed to down three tequila shots.

So I found Gwen, gave her the look, the one that got her distracting the kids, all but prying Lily away from me.

It was a bad move on my part, but I just needed a second.

Just one.

That's all I got.

Because Ranger was dead, I could die inside but I had to continue.

Had to endure.

Chapter 2

One Year Later

New members had been patched in.

It made sense.

The club had taken losses. There were holes that made the club vulnerable, even if they were walking closer to the right side of the law these days. Any rivals, enemies who smelled blood in the water, would strike. And we had plenty of those.

Steg had died six months ago.

It was sudden. Unexpected.

A brain bleed that was connected to the injury he'd sustained that took his eye. So we'd had another funeral. Evie handled it the way Evie handled everything, with strength and whisky, didn't wear the label of widow like I did.

Despite what she'd lost, she was more of a support system to me than I was to her. To be honest, I was jealous of her. She had longer with Steg. An entire lifetime. Which didn't make it any better. Maybe it even made it worse. What did I know?

So new patches. Members from other charters had moved to

Amber too. I knew this because Evie kept me updated during her weekly visits. She had started off coming by daily, but now that time had passed, I was meant to be somewhat of a functioning human being. There was never any pressure in my interactions with her. She didn't expect me to reply in a certain way. I didn't even reply to her at all in the beginning, yet she wasn't at all bothered. She continued to come, bringing food and booze, smiling at the kids. Updating me on the club that killed my husband.

The one that killed hers, too, if you thought about it.

The club was moving on now. As they should. As they needed to. Steg and Ranger's deaths would be a wound that didn't heal quite right, but the club had many of those wounds.

I'd declined any and all offers to be at any kind of club function. Hadn't stepped foot in the clubhouse since I'd washed my husband's body clean of blood, since we'd held his wake there.

It wasn't because of the bad memories the place held, there was no escaping those. It was the good memories. It was the fact that I'd walk in there and expect to see my husband, expect to be the person I was before, and I couldn't handle that.

I couldn't handle people eying me with pity, tiptoeing around me, just like I couldn't handle seeing those who had moved on. I didn't need to see how things had changed when I felt the exact same I had the night he died. They could move on, but I couldn't.

Hence me avoiding everybody. Slowly, at first, because it was kind of hard to avoid the people who'd took up residence at my home every day and night, working in shifts to make sure I was never alone with my thoughts.

But eventually, I managed to distance myself. Made sure to decline any and all invitations to cocktail nights, girl's nights and any kind of shopping trip. I couldn't stop them from turning up at the house, but I made sure to communicate I didn't want to be part of the group anymore.

These women were good friends. The best. But they also had lives. Children. They couldn't dedicate their entire lives to watching over me, trying to bring me back to the person I had been before.

I'd never be her again. Never even resemble her. She was buried in the soil right under my feet.

"I don't even know why I'm here," I grumbled, looking down. "This is just a rock with a name and a birthdate carved into it. Beneath that it's just wood, holding the decaying bones of the man this headstone is claiming him to be." I looked up at the sky, the cloudless blue taunting me with the fact that the sun still shone, even in cemeteries. The world still moved on.

I laid my hand on the rock. "I guess I'm here because I think this is what I'm supposed to do. I'm supposed to visit your grave. Put flowers on it so they can die too. Go through all the motions. The routine." I scoffed. "Which is kind of ironic, since we've lived our life in opposition to routine. But I guess death wins everything."

The words made me angry. The stone made me angry. The fact that grass was growing over my husband's body made me furious.

A tear trailed down my cheek. "I'm not coming back," I said. "I'm not going to make your death routine. Not going to make it okay. Because it's not. And I'm so angry at you. I'm not even angry at you for dying. I'm angry at you for coming up to me in the halls. For making me fall in love with you then leaving. Most of all, I'm angry at you for coming back for me. For patching in and giving me no choice but to live a happy life with you."

I wiped away my tears, standing to leave.

"And I can't even wish I'd never met you, because I wouldn't have our children. Wishing for that would make me a wicked, selfish person, yet I feel like that all the time. I hate you for dying. For living. For everything."

⸻

"THANKS FOR TAKING CARE OF THEM," I said to my mom, watching the kids from the window.

"You don't need to thank me, they're my grandchildren," my mother replied, an edge to her voice.

It was nice that she wasn't treating me with care. Even though it should've upset me, it actually reassured me. I didn't need her to treat me like the moms at school were, like everyone I encountered at the grocery store did. Like the whole fucking town did. Like I was wounded, like I was surrounded by eggshells, that one must tread lightly when interacting with me. Even a year later.

I nodded, continuing to watch the kids outside. They played together well. Brothers and sisters were meant to hate each other, or that's what I thought. But ever since Lily was born, Jack had taken it upon himself to make her his best friend, and that hadn't changed over all of these years.

"They seem to be doing well," Mom commented.

"Yeah, kids are resilient." I replied. "Our kids, especially."

"This is going to follow them around, no matter what," my mom proclaimed.

I turned my attention to her. She was focusing on me with anger in her eyes.

"You're going to be affected for life."

I flinched. "I'm well aware of that."

"I told you," she hissed. "I told you that this would happen, marrying that boy. Staying with him through all of that. I told you that you would lose him." She slung the words sloppily, her voice shaking with emotion, but they were missiles and they hit their mark.

"Yeah, Mom, you told me," I agreed. "And you were right. I did lose him. Are you happy you're right? What would you like from me in order to show you that you were right? Because I can't give you anything right now. I don't have anything."

Her face drained of color as she fully realized what she'd said. My mother was a harsh woman. She'd never really have that maternal gene, no softness to her. But she was never intentionally cruel. Just like she didn't have that motherly kind of love inside her, she didn't have hatred either.

She didn't know how to deal with this. With me, seeing this pain she couldn't repair. Despite what she was, she was my mother, and she loved me in her own way. She didn't want to hurt me.

"Elizabeth, I'm so sorry," she whispered.

"I know, Mom," I replied.

———

"GOOD NIGHT, MY SWEET GIRL," I said, kissing Lily on the forehead, wondering how much longer I had to tuck her in. "Say hi to Daddy in your dreams."

She snuggled close to the worn stuffed rabbit she hadn't slept with in years. "I always do," she murmured sleepily.

I left the door open a crack so the light from the hall filtered in. Again, something I hadn't done in years, but if a stuffed bunny and a halfway light did anything to make my fatherless daughter feel better, then that was okay with me.

Light from Jack's room and the low hum of the TV told me he was still awake. Ranger and I didn't usually let him watch TV in bed this late, but again, I didn't really give a shit about the way things used to be. I had a feeling that the movies made him feel less alone, distracted him from his grief and helped him sleep without the quiet that would remind him he'd never hear the roar of his father's motorcycle ever again.

I checked on him throughout the night—I checked on them both—and he was always asleep with some movie playing.

"What's on tonight, my friend?" I asked, moving into his room.

He glanced to me. "*Lost Boys*".

I raised my brows. "A classic. Not too scary, though?"

Jack gave me a 'mom, really?' type look. "No, Mom."

I held my hands up in surrender. "Okay, okay. You're a fearless dude, I get it. Don't stay up too late."

"Okay, Mom."

I leaned in to kiss his head. He made a face typical for a twelve-year-old being shown affection by his mother, but he let me.

"Love you," I whispered.

"Love you more," he whispered back.

I walked through the house, past the photos I didn't look at anymore, straightening pillows, putting away shoes. It was the routine I had every night. One that Ranger had always helped with. Then we'd go to bed. Not always together. But since the club had settled, that had been more and more common. I'd read. He'd read. We'd watch a movie. He'd make love to me. Or fuck me. Usually a combination of both. Not every night. Sometimes twice a night.

Our marriage was stronger after we got through those hard years. But we had valleys. Peaks. Though the lows were far lower, more like potholes really, the highs were higher, more constant.

Now I wasn't just in a valley. I was in the basement of my life.

I poured myself a whisky and walked outside. It was Saturday. I was allowed hard whisky on Saturdays.

A few years ago, Ranger had spent an entire month working whenever he could to completely redo our backyard. He'd wanted me and the kids to have an oasis. He built a greenhouse similar to the one Olive had. We had all sorts of vegetables in it, and Olive came over once a week to make sure I wasn't killing anything.

He'd built a large deck jutting off from our French doors, complete with fancy wicker furniture, a small dining area, a hammock. Pavers led to our built-in barbeque area and a corner where we could pitch a tent and have campouts with the kids. Solar lights that automatically came on and lit up the entire area when the sun went down were strung across the entire area. It was my favorite place to be no matter the weather. The kids loved being outside too.

I hated it now, with all its memories. But it wasn't as loud in its silence as the house was. So I came out here, for respite. For... something.

"I don't really know that much about astrology, but I know there's power in a full moon," I said, looking up to the sky. "I might've liked to learn more about it all, but kids and all." I trailed off, embarrassed that I was talking to the moon like it was some old high school friend I'd ran into at the grocery store. "I know there's probably a lot of people out here doing the same thing as I am right now, looking for some strength, asking for something. Surely those people need it more than I do. But I'm not asking for a lot. Anything you can spare. I just need a little..." I trailed off as my voice cracked.

It was a large crack, resounding evidence of how damaged I was. How close to falling apart I'd become. But I wouldn't let myself break completely. I had to stay strong because I had two children inside that house who needed their mother whole. Who at least needed to believe that she was.

So that's why I was out here looking to the moon for help. For strength.

"I just need something," I continued. "Whatever I can get, whatever you can give. I just need it. To get through this night. I just need to get through this night. I think I'll be able to figure out tomorrow when it gets here. I just. Tonight..."

I stayed out there for a long time. Maybe too long. The moon didn't answer. No one did. I was alone.

Chapter 3

There were a plethora of women who I could trust with my children. I was aware that there were a lot of mothers out there who couldn't say the same, so I knew what a blessing it was to be surrounded by women who would protect my children as if they were their own. Who loved them.

Adored them.

Cared about me.

For years that was great. Ranger and had been able to have date nights, even weekends away. But these were not regular circumstances. I didn't want to let my children out of my sight, and I surely didn't want my well-meaning, strong, loving and overbearing friends trying to make things better.

A lot of other people's friends would've given up. Not because they were bad people, but because there was a limit of someone else's suffering most people could handle.

Most people didn't do well at witnessing grief so close to home, being assaulted with the knowledge of just how close they were to that kind of pain. That kind of loss.

But these women were not most people.

They had certainly proven that throughout the years.

I'd been proud to call them friends, that the club finally had Old Ladies who inspired the men to head in a more legitimate direction.

Not that that had mattered for me, of course.

But I also resented them. That was the prickly, ugly truth of it all. I resented that they got to witness my pain and then go back to their homes, to their husbands, and they didn't have an empty bed or broken heart.

It was unfair of me.

But life wasn't fair lately, so whatever.

And one day, on a Tuesday afternoon after I'd picked Jack and Lily from school, I fully shattered. There was no other word for it. I didn't snap. No, there was no room in my life for 'snapping' under the weight of everything. Before now, there were hairline fractures on the surface of my soul, ones that small children thankfully couldn't perceive.

But the thing about cracks was that they usually got bigger. Made things more fragile. And that Tuesday after school, I realized how fragile I had become.

So I carefully, calmly bundled my kids into our car and drove them to one of the many women who would take care of them. One that would look at me, not ask questions, and take my kids without a word without expecting me to call and tell her when I was coming back. One who would understand if I didn't come back for a while.

Amy opened the door looking movie star perfect, as always. She smiled when she saw me. A genuine smile. Not full of worry or pity.

"Hey! I was just about to blow my brains out watching Peppa Pig. You saved me. I'll get the wine."

"Can you take care of the kids?" I asked, my mask starting to slip, unable to hide the tremor in my voice.

Amy's smile faltered ever so slightly before she winked at Jack then leaned forward to take the bag I had packed from them. "I have brownies that Gwen made on the counter," she rolled her eyes at Lily before continuing. "She is an evil witch, trying to get me to binge on sugar. Luckily, I now have you tiny humans to do that."

Lily needed no more urging, passing me to run through the house. Jack glanced up at me, worried. He looked at me like that a lot these days. I ruffled his hair. "I'll be fine, dude. Just need to go and take care of some things. Go and consume terrible amounts of sugar."

He frowned for a beat. "Love you," he said uncharacteristically, especially in front of an audience.

"I love you more," I whispered as I gave him a squeeze.

Jack moved inside the house he'd been in many times.

"I'll be back..." I trailed off, not wanting to lie, but afraid to tell the truth and become the world's worst mother.

"You'll be back when you feel like you can be back," Amy finished for me. "We're good here. Brock will be home soon, and I've got wine. I'm really good at keeping kids alive. I've babysat Mia's kids before and managed to survive that." She winked. "It'll all be okay here. Take care of you, okay? You need this."

I nodded once, not trusting myself to speak in fear of bursting into tears that I wouldn't be able to stop.

So I turned my back on them all and got in my car. Drove away. Not knowing where I was going or when I'd be back.

───

I HADN'T MADE the conscious decision to pull into Sunset Lodge. To drive in that direction. But it didn't exactly surprise me either. That's where I'd found myself during my last episode of hopeless sorrow. It was the place that had sucked in all my pain. Didn't take it away exactly, but the air felt lighter there. It didn't make any sense, but I guess it didn't need to. What mattered is that being there helped.

So did the vodka I'd brought with me.

I was wearing shoes this time, so I called that a win. And my earbuds so I could lay out by the pool listening to earsplitting rock. The anger and hate in the music helped me. I resonated with it. I'd never understood why people listened to music like this, but right then I got it.

It was nice to hear someone screaming at the top of their lungs when I wasn't brave or strong enough to do it myself.

So that's what I did. I listened to heavy metal while drinking vodka by the pool on a Tuesday. Didn't go to grief counseling, didn't go to any circle jerk in a church basement, both of which were most likely much healthier and would've set a better example for my children.

At some point, I stumbled to my room, managed to drink some water, choke down two aspirin then fell into a dreamless sleep.

⊏▭⊐

I WAS hungover the next morning. Not surprising and not a negative. The throbbing in my head and the acid in my stomach was enough to distract me from reality for most of the morning. Enough to make me almost entirely focus on bad TV and not the fact that my kids were waking up without me. Waking up without their father and the fact that I was quite possibly the worst mother to ever exist.

That's when I started drinking again.

When even my headache couldn't drown out those thoughts.

The pool was abandoned as it was yesterday. I could've been the only person in the entire motel. In the entire world.

It was nice, feeling so alone. To be miserable in such an all-consuming way. I hadn't been able to grieve properly with so many people around watching, wanting to help, trying to show me they cared. What they'd really been was an audience.

I think I'd played my part well enough. Grieving mother, in pain but still managing to hold it together. That's what people wanted, wasn't it? They wanted to support you, make casseroles or what the fuck ever, feeling good about themselves and then moving on. Well, that wasn't exactly what the women of Sons of Templar had done.

I'd taunted myself with how each of them would act if they were in my shoes. Each of them loved their husband with a ferocity, each couple had a lifetime love. Any one of them would've been shattered if she lost her man. But they were also strong. The strongest women I knew. They'd crumble. They'd wallow. Then they'd figure it out. Put on heels, lipstick and find a way to face the world again.

So why couldn't I do that? It had been a year, yet I couldn't even face myself. I hadn't even been to his club. Our club. I'd hidden myself away in our home, said no to every invitation, doing my best to shut away the world.

No, I hadn't faced anything.

So I sat there and drank. Tried to drown the misery, poison the pain and get all the ugly out. Tried to do all my despicable grieving in one shot so I could go home and be the Old Lady that I needed to be. The mother I needed to be.

Unfortunately, my plan didn't work that way.

I didn't open my eyes. Not for a long time. I kept them squeezed shut and the music blasting.

Gage was sitting on a chair, regarding the pool when I pulled out my earbuds and opened my eyes.

He wasn't the same man who had sat in the same spot years

ago. He still had the same scars, the same cut, but he was not the same man.

There was something about the way he held himself, about his energy that was different now, his wedding ring glinting in the sunlight. He wasn't any less dark, he would always be a dark, tortured man. But he'd become more at peace with life now. There was more substance to him, which was in large part because of his wife and son. He'd managed to move on from the terrors of his life before. To rebuild. To become more than he had been before.

I was so glad he'd gotten that. The second chance at a life that he deserved. But I knew I wouldn't get that. Even if I did deserve it. I wasn't a bad person. I was a good friend—before all of this, at least. And a good mother—also before all this.

Yes, maybe I deserved something else. But I'd never get it. Something in my bones told me that. I'd had it, one shot at love, happiness and everything else that comes with a happy marriage.. Maybe I'd had too much. That was it. We'd had too much. My allotted happiness had been depleted, all used up. Whatever love I was meant to have in my lifetime had been stretched too thin over the years, and it was now gone.

"You come to take me back again?" I asked.

He shrugged. "Depends on if you wanna go," he said. "Not gonna force you to do anything. You need this."

I raised a brow at him. "I need to sit in a shithole motel drinking vodka all day while someone else looks after my kids?"

"You need to grieve," he said, raking a tatted hand through his hair. "Hate that word. Always fucking hated that word. I avoided it for years. Thought that violence and pain was the way to treat my loss. To get over it. But it only prolonged it. Made me more fucked up. There's no right way to deal with this shit. You're facin' it, that's all that matters. I'll stay with you for as long as you need."

He would. Gage was a man of few words, and the ones he used he meant. He would sit here all day. All night.

We had a morbid connection, him and I. We had death between us. Darkness. He had a duty to Ranger. One he'd take seriously for the rest of his life.

Beyond that, he was my friend.

One who didn't expect words, didn't expect anything from me.

So I just sat there with my vodka, my friend and my grief.

Chapter 4

I'd just finished cleaning the house top to bottom. That's what I did on Saturdays. Every Saturday. Though I'd made it a point to make sure I was the exact opposite of my mother in almost every way, I had picked up a few habits from her that had served to be valuable. Like the fact that she'd told me I should always carry tampons, moisturize twice a day, always take off makeup before bed, make my bed as soon as you got out of it, and keep a tidy house for a tidy mind.

Though tidy was a bit of a stretch with two kids, especially Jack who loved to explore and trek mud through the house after aforementioned exploring.

I settled for clean in the early days, accepting that tidy was a pipe dream. Now that they were a little older and slightly more well behaved—freakishly more since their father died—they actually listened when I told them not to draw on walls with lipstick or trek mud in from the backyard.

Routines and keeping busy were essential for me to stay sane. To prevent a repeat of the twenty-four hours I'd spent at a shitty motel drinking vodka, being a bad mother.

As expected, neither Amy or Brock had mentioned the fact that I'd dropped my kids off and disappeared for a day, coming back sunburned and likely looking like hell. Of course they hadn't. That's what happened with true friends. They let you have your complete break from reality, didn't hold it against you, didn't ask questions and didn't look at you any different after.

I felt different now. Not better, but different. Did people ever really feel better after a complete breakdown? After hitting bottom? No. But there had been a release of pressure. I'd let go of something. The film covering my vision that had allowed me to pretend that I was somehow going to be able to handle life without any kind of dramatic event, that film was gone. I had needed something. And a twenty-four-hour bender at a crappy motel wasn't nearly as dramatic as I could've gone.

Turns out that after hitting rock bottom, there was a lot of climbing to do. And I'd been climbing since I'd returned, peeling my fucking fingernails off trying to get up out of this well of grief.

Two kids who needed school drop-offs and pickups, rides to games, playdates, help with homework, distracting trips to the beach, who needed to be fed, cleaned and clothed—yeah that helped a lot. I found myself barely having a moment to actually think about what the fuck I was going to do with my life.

Like continuing to feed and clothe the kids, for example. Ranger had made good money when the club was breaking the law, earning big from gun running and murder for hire. Enough for us to own this house with a mortgage so small we'd paid it off by the time Jack entered elementary school. Enough for me to be a stay-at-home mom, puttering away at ideas and stories that, of course, wouldn't ever see the light of day.

Sure, we hadn't had enough for me to buy designer handbags like Amy and Gwen, but that was fine with me. I considered luxury to be having a home that I loved, one that my children could grow up in, and the college funds that had been accumulating throughout the years. To me, luxury was the fact that we'd never worried about bills, had two cars in addition to Ranger's Harley, and we could even take a few vacations a year, with and without the kids.

There were some lean years, of course, but those were time I'd budgeted for. Being an Old Lady for as long as I had been, I'd known that we'd need a little buffer. Working as an outlaw in a motorcycle club wasn't exactly steady, reliable money.

So through the lean years, the buffer depleted. But once the garage started earning good money and the club started to work on more legitimate ventures, the buffer got large and healthy again.

We'd taken the kids camping and to Disneyland, though, Ranger fucking hated it. He did it for his little girl, who was obsessed with princesses, and he'd made sure to treat her like one every day.

We'd had a trip to Hawaii planned for later this week. Of course, we weren't going now since there was no *we*.

Ranger's funeral expenses had been covered by the club. They had funds allocated for those kinds of things. Of course they did. Not that they'd had to dip into them for a while. And then there was the fact that as a widow, I got a small cut of whatever they made. For life.

They looked out for the families of their fallen members.

I wasn't about to turn it down—not that anyone would let me—not if it helped put my kids through college or be able to backpack through Europe if they didn't want to go to college. Not if I could use it for all the expenses that came with having a growing girl and boy who wouldn't have a father. No. I wasn't about to turn down anything. My pride was cheap.

But even with all that, covering our finances would be a stretch. Technically, I could make things work the way they were, but only if I wanted to constantly worry about money and have my kids go without things like holidays and school trips. Since they were already going to have to be without their father for the rest of their lives, I wasn't about to deny them anything else.

I had enough to cover what I estimated would be another year at the very most. Six months would be ideal, so I'd still have a good buffer for the worst-case scenario. I'd need to find a job.

I was focusing on one thing at a time, though, and today I was focusing on the fact that the house was clean and my kids were happily playing in the backyard together. I'd only had to breakup one squabble, which was some kind of record. As well as Jack and Lily got along, they were still brother and sister with very different personalities.

Eventually they'd come in, needing to be bathed and fed. But it was Saturday and one of our routines was having takeout every Saturday night. Tonight was Lily's turn to choose, so we'd likely be having Indian. My little girl was obsessed with trying as many different foods as she could. Amber was small, but it had a surprising variety of different restaurants, consistently growing as our small corner of paradise continued to get discovered my tourists and people looking to relocate to a town in California with affordable houses.

It was almost three in the afternoon, probably another hour until I could crack open a beer or bottle of wine and not hate myself.

I'd limited how much I drank while the kids were awake but indulged slightly more once they were asleep. Saturday was also the night I routinely let myself get a little bit tipsy. That combined with some Valium made it so I was able to get a small amount of sleep at least once a week.

Only Saturdays, though. I couldn't really make a habit of

getting drunk and taking mood stabilizers every night if I wanted my children to be even vaguely well adjusted.

My friends invited me over for wine and food almost daily. Despite the fact I always said no, they kept asking.

I wasn't ready for that yet. To go back to the life I had inhabited before Ranger died.

Sometimes, I craved all of that. Felt guilty for not giving my kids back some normalcy.

But I couldn't do it. Even for the kids. Not now, not that I was still processing my rock bottom, who I was down here.

So, after fixing the kids a snack and throwing a ball with Jack for twenty minutes, I settled myself on the sofa with a candle burning and a cup of tea that I wished was beer. My laptop was nestled on my legs as I typed away at the document I wasn't letting myself call a book. It was an escape. A period of time when I could imagine life was easy with happily ever afters, hot sex and romance with no bumps in the road.

I couldn't read romance books anymore. None of them were *right*. They made me mad. I couldn't relate to anything. Couldn't escape into anything. So I just wrote what I needed to read. Nothing else. It wouldn't go anywhere.

I got so into this 'not' book, that I lost awareness of my surroundings. Which meant that I didn't notice someone standing in my living room, watching me for who knew who long before she cleared her throat.

I jumped, turning to see Amy standing behind me, purse in the crook of her elbow, a smile on her face.

"What you doing there?" she asked with faux innocence, the tone telling me she'd been peeking over my shoulder.

Heat crept up my neck, and a little annoyance. This writing and this not book were private. It wasn't even something I'd talked to Ranger about. He'd see me on my laptop typing things, but he hadn't asked about it. Not because he didn't care, but because he knew if I wanted him to know what I was doing I would've talked to him about it. We shared almost everything, he supported me in whatever made me happy. I wasn't sure writing my stories made me happy. They made me... feel whole. It was nice to have something that didn't have anything to do with being a mother or an Old Lady. Something that was just mine.

And right now, I needed something just mine more than ever.

"Nothing," I said to Amy, slamming the laptop shut. "What are you doing here?"

She moved to sit on the chair opposite me, placing her purse down beside her and crossing her legs. Every movement was graceful, elegant, sexy down to her snakeskin boots that I would've stolen right off her feet if we were the same size. Unfortunately we weren't. But both her and Gwen knew my weakness for shoes—and Ranger's liking for them—so every year, for my birthday and Christmas, they bought me shoes that were far too expensive, physically forcing me to take them.

"Jack let me in," Amy said. "Him and Lily are getting ready, so you should probably stop doing '*nothing*' and get ready too. You're totally hot in any outfit, but I don't know if that shirt with all the holes is the look you want for the party."

Being Saturday night, the only party she could've been talking about was the weekly barbeque the club hosted. Friday nights were party nights, too, but not the child friendly kind. Although I would hazard a guess and say more than a few children were conceived on those nights.

I narrowed my eyes. "I'm not going to a party. Neither are the kids. And I don't appreciate you telling them they were without talking to me."

Amy didn't even blink at my tone, which was rather practiced at being sharp. I was an Old Lady, after all. But the problem was, so was Amy. Beyond that, she'd grown up in upper class social circles that I had come to understand had made her all but immune to any kind of bitchy tone. And somewhat of an expert in them.

"Babe, I'd totally be respecting that concept if I didn't know better," she explained crossing her arms. "The time on your self-induced club isolation is up. I get you wanting to hide forever. I do. Well, kind of. I don't think I'll ever really get it because I'm not you. Not inside your head. Not in your shoes. But I get losing someone you love. Someone you'll always love. I understand that pain. The need to shut out the entire world and just linger in your pain because you don't know what else to do. Maybe being too scared to do anything to distract yourself from that pain because that might take you even further away from him..." she trailed off, her voice softer and more vulnerable now.

I knew she was thinking about Gwen's brother, Ian, the man she'd been in love with when she moved here. The one who had died and broken both of their hearts.

She still wore that, her grief for him. Still palpable and fresh even though it had been years. Even though she was madly in love with her husband, had a family, a beautiful life.

That scared the shit out of me. Especially since I didn't have a husband or a beautiful life right now. So how would I look in a few years? Would sorrow and pain be etched into me like carvings in stone?

"You're going to come to the party," she stated, her tone a little more familiar and commanding. "You can totally be mad at me for turning up here and forcing you to go. I can handle it. I'll actually respect it. But I think you know how stubborn I can be. If I can convince my biker husband to engage in a four-step skincare routine, I can get you to this party." She raised her brow, inviting me to even try to challenge her.

I was tempted.

Very fricking tempted.

In any other situation, there was no way I would go head to head with Amy Abrams. Only a few people in the world were brave enough to do so, one of those people being her husband, the next her best friend. And... okay, there were actually only two people I could think of. Which was saying something considering all the badasses in cuts that we knew.

But this was not just any situation, and I didn't really have enough self-preservation to fear going head to head with her. I wasn't afraid of anything anymore, and if I was honest with myself, I was unconsciously trying to sabotage the life I'd had before and any relationships I'd had in that life. If I pushed away the Sons of Templar and everyone connected to them, I'd have less reminders of my husband and that I'd lost him.

So yeah, I was tempted to fight Amy on it. To get ugly. But then I thought of my kids getting ready to go to the club, both of them likely excited about the prospect of seeing people I hadn't let into their lives for months. People who loved them. Who only wanted to protect them.

Fuck.

I got up from the sofa. "You can be a real bitch, you know?"

She smiled sweetly. "I'm well aware. Do you need me to pick you out an outfit while you do your makeup?"

I scowled. "Yes," I snapped, wishing I could deny her, but the bitch had impeccable style. If I was going to go to this fucking party, I was going to do it looking good.

Chapter 5

It wasn't great.

Being at the club again. Being around everyone. Being the sad, lonely widow and not the content, in love Old Lady. Despite the fact that no one made me feel like the widow.

I didn't *need* anyone to make me feel like the widow. That's who I was. What I was now. It was all but tattooed on my forehead, etched into my soul.

That fact was all the more prevalent at the party because Ranger wasn't there, shooting me looks every now and then. Grilling with Jack. Catching me leaving the bathroom and pushing me against the wall for a make out session. Getting me drunk while staying sober, driving us home, carrying our sleeping kids to their beds and then fucking me on the kitchen counter.

None of that.

He had been my anchor, so without him, I was floating around this place. Of course, all of the women in attendance made it their mission to make sure I was never left alone, not for a second. You would've thought they'd coordinated it. They probably had.

But the kids were happy.

More than happy. They were ecstatic at the welcome they got, at seeing all of their friends in one place. A place bursting with memories of their father. I had been worried and watchful at first, thinking being there might trigger them, that going might somehow be a huge step back. But it was easy to forget just how resilient kids were. They were so fragile in so many ways, yet they healed quicker than us. They played. Ate. Played some more.

They were currently cuddled up on the huge sofa in the common room of the clubhouse watching *Moana* with all the kids. And Lucky who was also in there because it was his favorite movie.

Me on the other hand?

Yeah, I did not handle the night well.

Better than I thought I would, though.

But not well.

"You look like you need this."

I glanced up from where I'd been staring into space. Somehow, I'd managed to go off on my own, staying for an extended amount of time without some worried friend coming to make sure I wasn't too deep in the well of grief after being back at the club for the first time since my husband died.

Until now.

The owner of the voice was wearing a cut and was extending a muscled arm to me with a beer in hand.

I took the beer because I did really need it. Vodka would've been more welcome, but I was thinking I'd probably find myself in the middle of an intervention if I started drinking that. Everyone here was totally on board with drinking to solve problems, to celebrate, and to drown sorrows. But straight from the bottle might be construed as a cry for help, even with this crowd.

"Thanks," I said, not smiling or letting my tone sound friendly or inviting.

Not something that I'd usually done, prior to Ranger's death, at least. I used to be the welcoming committee for the Sons of Templar. Evie was the one who did all the intimidating, she was great at it, using her practiced eye to measure each new patch or new girlfriend entering through the gates. If you passed Evie's inspection, you'd have her loyalty for life. And it could be pretty damn daunting going through all of that, and being one of the few women who had been with the club for as long as I had, I knew that for sure. Rosie had been with the club since birth, so she could also speak to how intimidating Evie could be. And Rosie, she wasn't exactly the welcoming committee either. She was the party girl usually looking to cause more trouble than all of the members combined. Which she usually succeeded in doing.

So yeah, there was me. I wasn't intimidating nor was I the party girl looking to cause trouble. No, I was just the girl who fell in love with a guy who ended up patching into one of the most notorious clubs in the country. And most of the guys were just... guys at the end of the day. Guys who more than likely had killed people, who broke the law on an almost daily basis and had no problem talking with their fists.

Those guys had also been my family for a long, long time. But now my family was broken. Severed. Like someone had taken a hacksaw to an arm, the cuts jagged, messy and ones that would never heal. It was still bleeding, and I didn't yet know how to function without that missing part of me. I didn't know who I was to the club now that my Old Man was buried and rotting.

So I didn't smile at the unfamiliar face who was offering me a beer and smiling.

He had a nice smile too. Genuine. Something that only came with youth. And he was young for sure. Maybe five, even ten years younger than me. As hard as these guys lived, their age never really showed on their faces. The assholes. Then again, it didn't really show on us women either, thanks to all sorts of expensive face creams, Botox and a lot of orgasms.

The man in question did not take my not so subtle hint that I didn't want company and sat down across from me.

I pursed my lips in annoyance and lifted my beer, purposefully taking a long sip so he didn't try to talk to me.

Apparently, this did not dissuade him as he casually sipped his own beer, watching me in a way that didn't feel uncomfortable.

He was hot.

That was a given.

It seemed the Sons of Templar liked to patch in badasses who could also make a mint in male modeling. Though none of them would do such a thing for any kind of money. Except maybe Lucky. He wouldn't do it for the money, though. He'd do it for the attention.

My beer fairy was no different. He was tall, although not as tall as someone like Bull, but you'd have to be a basketball player to have that honor. Muscular in a bulky way, everything sculpted, including his biceps straining the fabric of his tee.

One of his arms was covered in tattoos travelling all the way up to his neck, the other completely bare. His hair was a light blond, mussed at the top of his head in that artful way that surely took longer than it had for me to do mine. Granted, I'd just thrown mine up into a messy bun because with two kids, you get the choice of doing your hair or makeup, never both. Unless you were superheroes like Gwen and Amy. Or weren't a single mother like me.

Which was what I was. A widowed single mother. The title burned on my chest like a scarlet letter.

This man with the artfully mussed hair, tattoos, muscles, piercing blue eyes and a slightly crooked nose hadn't noticed this label, somehow.

He had an open face. I didn't know how to explain it other than that. Sure, he had all the ingredients to a biker badass, but something about his face—wrinkle free and young—was open and friendly.

I narrowed my eyes. "Why are you sitting here?" I asked, a bite to my tone.

Now, many of these men were well practiced in menacing glares, in deadly threats and general airs of danger. But us women were also well versed at ways in which to make even them go back on a motorcycle boot.

Not this guy, though. No. In the face of my scathing tone he just grinned.

Grinned.

Showing straight, white teeth, showing me that he was definitely a man who smiled often.

"Why wouldn't I sit here?" he quirked a brow. "You look like you need company. I'm new here, haven't seen you around. Wanted to introduce myself."

"I don't want company," I shot back, taking another sip of my beer. Even though I had the whole dead husband pass, a part of me recoiled at being so rude to a perfectly nice and perfectly attractive stranger.

"Because you lost your husband a while back, and this is your first time back at the club, so you wanted to escape all the well-meaning women and men currently watching us both like hawks?" he asked conversationally.

I blinked at him. The man with the eyes, the open face and easy smile. I was used to people tiptoeing around me. That's what you did with widows. You treated them with care, even though there was no point because there was no way to care for broken things. All I craved was for people to treat me like my husband wasn't dead so maybe I could pretend he wasn't for a hot minute.

But here was this guy, coming and saying all this shit within a minute of meeting me.

"Yeah, because of all that," I murmured.

My eyes flickered to the large group of partygoers, and like the man had said, more than a few eyes were pointed in my direction.

"So you know all of that, and you still decided to come over here?" I continued.

"I did."

I waited for more. There was nothing more. Just him sipping his beer and sitting in what looked like content silence.

That annoyed me. For whatever reason.

"You can leave now," I grumbled.

"I haven't even introduced myself," he replied, not reacting to the ice in my tone.

I frowned. Wasn't it the duty of all the men who had welcomed me in their alpha male way earlier tonight to seize any—seemingly unattached—member of the opposite sex communicating with me and tell him that I was off limits?

Or at least for one of my friends to come and try to protect me. Although their eyes kept flickering, no one moved toward us.

"Yes, well you do seem to have me at a disadvantage since you know not just my name but all of my tragedies," I said, suddenly curious about the young, attractive, far too friendly young man who had decided to chat with me despite his chances of getting a shiner—at best—for even talking to me.

"You're right," he nodded, taking a pull of his beer. "It's only fair I share some tragedies with you."

He put his beer on a table then turned his body, giving me his full attention. It was oddly unnerving. "My dad left the second my mom got pregnant with me. He wasn't into commitment. Or fatherhood. Or a life that wasn't lived completely on his terms."

He shrugged. "Or at least that's what I remember my mom telling me. She died when I was six, so I don't have a bunch of memories. She didn't have extended family that wanted to take on a six-year-old, so I went into the system. Just missed being attractive enough for a rich, barren couple looking to adopt. So I bounced around foster homes for the next ten years. I'd say I ran away, but running makes it sound like someone was chasing me. No one cared enough to chase me. Fell into the crowds that got me fast money and the prospect of prison time. But I didn't get caught. I was lucky. More than that, I found a talent in the underworld. Many talents. Got enough of a reputation that I ran in the same circles as the Sons of Templar MC. Liked the idea. I was eighteen years old. Riding bikes, livin' free. Yeah. Liked the idea. Liked the life. The brotherhood. Family." He paused, rubbing a hand down his handsome face. "Went fine for a long time. Better than fine. I was a kid who didn't know shit about brotherhood, certainly not freedom. Not to mention the money that we made. More than I'd ever seen."

He glanced back at the clubhouse. "Didn't bother me at first. The illegal shit. I wasn't scared of prison. Sure as fuck wasn't scared of death. And I liked breaking the rules. The law. Sticking it to the man. See, I'd spent my whole life taking orders. Got no say in where I went, who I lived with. So yeah, had enough anger at the world to feel like I was doing some good.

Probably wouldn't have even left the charter if Gunner, my best friend, hadn't died. His Old Lady too. Drugs. Bad shit." He ran his hand through his hair. "Woke me up. Made me question shit. Look at the future. I'd like an Old Lady. Kids. Never want to let go of the patch, the club is my life. I was already considering requesting a transfer someplace new when I heard what this chapter was doin'. . But Washington charter had been my family for over a decade. Didn't have it in me to just leave. Then the war happened, the one that took your Old Man. Saw it as my opportunity to help rebuild. And here I am."

"Here you are," I agreed, slightly dumfounded by all the information he'd dumped on me.

All of the men in the club had pasts, some uglier than others, but all dark enough to push them toward this life. If you'd been here as long as I had, you might know about some of it, maybe even most of it. But never all of it. That was reserved for each man's Old Lady. And it took a lot to get them into the sharing kind of mood.

Yet here was this guy, laying out his past honestly to a complete stranger.

"Kace," he said.

I blinked.

"My name. Kace. Figured I should've said that first, but then again, I'm not exactly a man who's known to do what he should." He winked, got up and walked away.

Just like that.

Okay. That just happened.

He just came over and spilled his entire life story, unfiltered and completely honestly. Purely because he thought that him knowing my history—only the facts, definitely not with any of the personal details he'd told me—and he thought it was unfair for us to be on uneven ground.

Who the actual fuck was this guy?

I didn't have time to think about that, because I was already watching the women leave their respective Old Men to converge on me and demand to know why I was talking to a man. A single, hot, younger man at that.

Not that it was like that. But it didn't matter. I couldn't have that conversation. That attention. I was emotionally tapped out.

So I did what any sensible, adult woman would do in my situation. I ran away. I walked quickly, avoiding all their meaningful looks and 'come here' gestures. The kids were still glued to the movie, Lucky included. I kissed Lily's head on the way past and winked at Jack, doing my best to look like I was holding it together.

I wasn't even sure where I was going. The bathroom was out. There was at least a ninety percent chance that one of the women, if not more, would follow me in there, thinking I was either having some kind of breakdown or needed to talk about the interaction with... Kace.

The hallway was empty, thankfully, most of the doors to the rooms closed. Ranger had never had one of those rooms, not with us being back together when he patched in. He never lived that bachelor life that so many of the men had, the life a few were still living.

But there were plenty of nights when we'd utilized an empty room.

Which was what I was looking for. An empty room where I could get my bearings. Could take a breath and decompress.

"Oh shit, sorry!" I squeaked, opening a door and not finding an empty room.

Nope.

I found Ashley, pressed up against the wall, half dressed. Wire, who had been pressing her up against the wall, was also half dressed.

They both detached as soon as I opened the door. Although I felt bad for interrupting, I couldn't control the smile that spread across my face.

Ashley was the only one in our group who had not been claimed by an alpha male biker. Many had tried. They'd be mad not to. She was beautiful, in an original, unique way. Ashley favored the sixties, always dressing like she'd just stepped out of that decade. Hair always perfect, makeup... perfection. I'd never seen her look anything less than perfect.

Until now.

She'd told us all that she was not interested in being with a biker. Not interested in a relationship.

But she was most definitely interested in being with partic-ular a biker.

"I'll just... leave you to it," I chuckled, realizing I was still standing there, and neither of them had said anything. "As you were." I nodded my head, backing out.

The door closed quietly behind me, then I returned the way I came. No way was I going to risk opening any other doors. At least my head had cleared some from that shock.

Wire had been with the club for years now, but he was different than most of the other patches. Sure, he was just as badass as everyone else, could handle himself in any situation, but his battleground was mostly in the virtual world. He'd emerged at parties every now and then, shared a beer and a burger, maybe even engaged in a conversation or two, but mostly he was working on computers, doing what, half the time the club didn't know.

He'd been the topic of many cocktail nights, each of us wondering when he'd find a woman. If he'd ever find one. Everyone had agreed he wasn't gay, since we'd heard he enter-tained club girls on a somewhat regular basis.

Ashley had been present for many of those discussions, and I realized now, she had stayed rather quiet.

"Lizzie!"

I turned toward the familiar voice. Ashley was rushing down

the hallway, buttoning up her dress. She always looked impeccable, pressed and perfect. Right now, however, her lipstick was smudged, she was rumpled, disheveled and definitely had make out hair going on.

I liked that for her.

I stopped just short of the corner that would lead us back to the common room.

"Hey, you didn't have to get dressed on my account," I grinned. It was fake, but I wanted it to be real.

She did not return the grin. Her pretty face was painted with worry.

"Do you think you could keep that," she nodded her head backward, "between us?" There was a twinge of panic to her voice.

I tilted my head, curious as to why she was so desperate to keep this under wraps. But it wasn't my business. She wanted it kept quiet for a reason. And in a group that knew everyone's business, I could understand her wanting... whatever that was with Wire without having to label it.

"Of course, sweetie," I replied.

Her shoulders sagged in relief. "Thank you," she murmured.

"For what it's worth, you two are super cute together."

Her eyes flared. "We aren't together," she snapped.

Oh, yes they were. She obviously wasn't ready to admit that. but this totally had the makings of a Sons of Templar courtship. Their story was going to come out sooner rather than later.

I held up my hands in surrender. "Okay, I won't say anything else. You can trust me."

She smiled weakly. "Thanks. I definitely can't trust myself."

"Oh sure you can, babe. You're just a little scared of what your instincts have to say. I get it." I leaned in to kiss her cheek before walking back to the common room. It was time to take my babies home.

Chapter 6

One Week Later

I was exhausted, frustrated and covered in sweat. So, of course, that's when a Harley pulled into my driveway.

Not just any Harley.

One with *Kace* on the back.

No, it couldn't have been one of my very married, very committed to their wives, friendly neighborhood bikers. It had to be the young man who'd made somewhat of an impression on me.

It wasn't like I'd spent the whole week thinking about him or that we'd had some kind of spark. That's probably how it would've gone in a romance novel—that's what I was writing in my 'not' book, at least. But in this life, all I could think about every moment of the day was how much I missed my husband. Trying to figure out how I could act like I wasn't in total and utter agony. How I could hide that I was absolutely terrified that I hadn't healed, not one bit. So I hadn't been thinking about any kind of spark or connection between Kace and I. We didn't have one.

Seeing him get off his bike, take off his shades and tuck them in the front of his tee didn't do anything to me either. Except piss me off. Because I was exhausted, frustrated and sweaty.

My tank was covered in paint stains from this morning, when the kids and I had decided Lily's room needed a 'feature wall'. Well, it was Lily who'd decided that, Jack and I'd just been roped into actually doing the painting. I was also covered in sweat since it was the middle of the afternoon, the middle of the summer and the middle of a heatwave in California.

I was wearing a pair of Ranger's shorts I'd cut to not look ridiculously long on me. Most of the things I wore around the house belonged to my dead husband. Most I hadn't even washed, though barely anything still smelled like him. The healthy thing to do would've been to burn or donate all of his clothes, but I wasn't healthy. I was sick with grief, and if getting rid of all of the reminders of my husband was some kind of cure, I didn't want it.

"What are you doing here?" I demanded, wiping the sweat from my forehead and glaring at Kace.

He glanced to me, his forest green eyes flickering up and down my body before he surveyed the yard and then the lawn mower I would've hurled across the street if I'd had the upper body strength.

"Well, I was just driving by at first, then I saw all of this," he waved his hand at me, the lawn mower and the grass. "I figured it was my duty for your grass, your lawnmower and most likely your entire neighbourhood, if I offer my services."

"Your services?" I repeated, my foot tapping impatiently.

"Well, my day job involves fixing cars... among other things. But I am known to be a expert at mowing lawns. And..." he moved forward, knelt down, opened a cap, moved the lawn mower slightly then looked up at me. "I'm also an expert at knowing when it's run out of gas."

I bit my lip. Heat flushed my cheeks, but this time it had nothing to do with the heat of the day and everything to do with the fact that I was seconds away from driving to Home Depot to buy a new lawn mower because ours was 'broken' when all it really needed was gas.

Kace stood up. "I'm guessin' you got some gas cans in there." He nodded his head toward the garage.

I pursed my lips. "I'm guessing we do," I replied, not exactly sure whether we did or not. But it was highly likely, since Ranger was an orderly, organized kind of guy when it came to the garage and maintaining the house.

No matter what was going on with the club, he'd mowed the lawn once a week. Took out the garbage. Cleaned the gutters. Changed lightbulbs. He took care of all of the 'man' jobs. Despite how sexist it sounded, that was the way it had been because I couldn't do that shit. He'd changed the oil in my car. He'd taken pride in our home. In giving me small things.

Hence me deciding to mow the lawn.

While I'd been in my... funk these past few months, the lawn had been mowed. I hadn't been the one doing the mowing, which meant someone had been doing it. I hadn't even noticed. When I did start to notice, I realized a Prospect came once a week to do the job my husband could no longer do. I'd scared him off earlier this morning, which didn't say much about his potential for getting patched in. You had to be able to survive a lot more than the wrath of an Old Lady. Okay, maybe not a lot more, but close.

Since I was paying attention now, deciding to try to figure out how to live my life without my husband, I thought it was beyond time for me to learn to do things like mow the lawn. No way was I going to be the woman who had the club take care of all of this shit. Like some kind of burden. A charity case.

Fuck that.

How hard was it to mow a lawn?

After an hour, an inner temper tantrum and a crying jag in our garage, I'd deduced it was very fucking hard if you had no idea how to operate a lawn mower. Which I realized was totally fucking pathetic. I was a single mom raising two kids, I should be able to teach them every life skill. Ranger should've taught me every 'man job'. He should've fucking known there was a possibility I'd be right here, alone, unable to mow the goddamn lawn without someone on a Harley feeling obligated to save the day.

"I'll go and grab some, fill 'er up and finish this job. For you, but mostly for the lawn that's just trying to survive," Kace smirked.

Friendly. Funny. Who the fuck *was* this guy?

"That's not necessary," I argued, not hiding the irritation in my voice. "I'm more than capable."

"I'm sure you are," he agreed, lying expertly. "This isn't some alpha crap where I don't think a woman can do the work. It's just I know for a fact that Cade would reem me out for driving past, seeing you doing this shit and taking no for an answer. Especially when my Sunday afternoon plans include a cold beer, a football game and not much else." He paused and I took the time to drink him in.

He was taller than me, though that wasn't hard since most of these men were over six foot and I was only five six. Muscles, but of course. Vibrant tattoos covering one of his sinewy arms. Hair long enough to almost brush his shoulders if it were down. But he'd slung it back into a messy bun at the nape of his neck.

I was not a fan of the man bun. At least, not before this moment.

"Now I can see you're rearing up to argue with me," Kace said. "I bet you're damn good at it too. But I'll let you in on a secret." He leaned in, and I held my breath, not wanting to smell him, and I could only imagine what he was smelling on me. "I'm damn good at it too. And as I mentioned before, I don't have any plans, so I've got all the time in the world to stand here and argue with you."

I stared at him. This man I'd met *once*. Who had shared personal information with me because he felt it was only fair since he knew my shit. Who'd stopped his bike on his way home to drink and do nothing in order to argue with me about mowing some lawn.

The nerve.

Seriously. Who did he think he was?

I'd been geared up to argue with him. I really had. On principle mostly, and also because I couldn't face the fact that I'd failed at being two parents before I'd even really began. Fighting back was what I should've done. Should've straightened my spine, jutted out my chin and assumed the female battle stance.

But I was tired. Tired in every way a person could be tired. I did not feel like fighting this stranger in the middle of my half—okay, quarter—mowed yard in the ninety-degree heat. Nor did I particularly want to finish mowing this lawn after a fight with this stranger.

So I sighed and stepped back. "Whatever. If you want to waste your Sunday, be my guest." I paused, wiping sweat from my brow. "Just know this is not me approving a male coming in to take over a job that I'm totally capable of finishing. It's me realizing that my children have been far too quiet, which worries me, and I fucking hate mowing the grass."

I shouldn't have relented, but I was tired. To my bones. And I didn't have the energy to fight this man, especially when it was clear he was up for a fight.

"Not putting any strings on it, just bein' a good neighbor," he responded.

I raised my brow. "Uh huh."

He chuckled. "Go on in, and give yourself a break, investigate those all too quiet children."

I stared at him for a beat longer, trying to understand his motivations for doing this. For talking to me that night at the club. There was no way he was doing it out of the goodness of his heart.

"I'm not sleeping with you," I blurted.

His eyes bugged out ever so slightly. "Well, I didn't offer it, so stand down. I'm not here for you to sexually objectify me. I'm just tryin' to do a good deed."

"No man ever just tries to do a good deed," I returned.

"Well, I guess I'm gonna have to prove you wrong. For now, I'm gonna mow your grass."

I didn't believe him. But I also didn't want to stand out there arguing with him. So I didn't. Instead, I turned on my heel and walked back into my house.

⸻

"MOM, who is the man mowing our grass?" Lily asked as I emerged from my room, freshly showered and in a light sundress. Not because Kace was here, but because I didn't want to look pathetic wearing Ranger's tees when I encountered him again. Didn't want him to look at me in pity.

"He's wearing a cut," Jack observed, peering out the window like his sister was, although his gaze was slightly more guarded. My son had only seen one man in a Sons of Templar cut mow his front lawn. His father. And he hadn't actually worn his cut while mowing, but whatever.

"He's a... friend from the club," I replied, deciding a slight lie was better than saying I barely knew him, and he'd strong armed his way into letting him do that. "I wasn't having the best luck with the lawn mower cooperating, and he was driving by and offered to help."

"I could've mowed the lawns, Mom," Jack said, a frown curling his lips.

I sighed, smiling although my heart cracked at Jack's words, his tone. "I'm well aware you could have, my boy," I smiled, moving forward to ruffle his hair. "And once you turn thirteen, I'll definitely be roping you in to doing all sorts of household chores. For now, you can enjoy not having to do them. Trust me, you'll thank me for this moment when you're older." I winked.

He did not wink back, just kept a suspicious eye on Kace. "This guy is new. I don't know him."

Oh, my little boy was being protective.

"He has nice hair," Lily chimed in.

I bit my lip, ignoring her comment. "Yes, he's new. He moved from a chapter in Washington. But he's been in the club for years. Cade wouldn't have let him come in here if he didn't think he was a good guy." I met my son's eyes. "You like all the guys at the club, right?"

He nodded slowly.

"Well, that's because you've had a lot of time to get used to them. To get to know them. I bet once you get used to Kace, you'll like him too."

"Kace is a cool name," Lily offered.

"It's a weird name," Jack corrected.

"Really?" I asked, hands on my hips. "You have uncles named Bull, Cade, Brock, Gage, Lucky, Asher and Wire, but you think that *Kace* is a weird name?"

Jack stared at me, maintaining a serious, straight face for a moment, then the corner of his lips twitched .

"Oh, I think I see a smile," I sang, bending down to take a closer look. "Lily, help me pull it out, get on the other side."

My dutiful daughter jumped from her spot at the window and got on her brother's other side. We both began 'pulling' at the air beside Jack's face.

He folded his arms. "I'm not a baby. You can't get me with that," he proclaimed, his tone serious but his mouth twitched again.

"I see it, Lily!" I yelled. "It's in there. We've just got to put in some elbow grease."

My daughter played her part well, screwing up her face with effort, pulling her little arms.

Jack kept up his 'I'm too old for this' routine for about another five seconds before he flat out grinned, staring at us both. "You two are goofs."

I smiled at my son. "Ah, but you're related to us by blood. You can't escape us. In fact you *have* to love us." I glanced to Lily, giving her a wink. "And kiss us!"

"No!" he protested, but Lily and I were already laying smooches on either one of his cheeks.

He made a big show of wiping his cheeks when we were done, rolling his eyes and everything.

My heart healed up just a little in that moment. The stitches were crooked, ragged, and they'd left a mark when they came out, but it didn't matter. My kids still laughed. They still loved. They had a future. I had to hold on to that.

⊏⊐

KACE KNOCKED on the door not long after that. I didn't want to answer. Wanted to pretend we had all disappeared. Too bad my car was in the driveway, which he would've noticed.

So I opened the door.

Kace was covered in sweat. He'd kept his cut on, which would've only made it hotter, but apparently, he was old school and wasn't about to put the leather down just anywhere. Ranger was like that too.

His shirt was clinging to his abs, his body, hair slicked back with sweat.

I cursed myself for not offering him water or lemonade. That was the polite thing to do.

"All done," Kace grinned. His eyes flickered to my dress and legs, but returned to my eyes quickly.

"Thank you," I grated out, the words coming out like sand-paper. "For interrupting your day to do something I could've done myself," I added, because for some reason, I couldn't control my bitch around him. I'd always been soft, kind. Sure, I threw attitude when needed, but I hadn't found the need very often. Flies with honey and all that.

But something about this guy... pushed my buttons.

He smirked, still not bothered by my bitchiness. "Not a problem. Glad to do it."

I stared at him then peered around him to my lawn, noticing the blaring sun that had been bearing down on him all after-noon. "Can I offer you a beer?"

He tilted his head slightly, regarding me. "You really don't want to offer me a beer, do you?"

I swore a muscle in my brow twitched with the effort to keep a borderline pleasant expression in place. "I just did," I gritted out.

"But you don't want to."

My hands fisted at my sides. "It's the polite thing to do," I answered, instead of admitting he was right.

No, I did not want to offer this man a beer. I did not want him to come into my home, likely charming my daughter, maybe my son. I did not want him continuing to piss me off.

I wanted him to leave so I could shut the blinds, snuggle up on the sofa with my kids, watch a movie and forget the rest of the world existed.

He chuckled. "I'm not going to force you do to the polite thing, Lizzie. I'm an outlaw. Don't need manners, just honesty."

Something about his chuckle and the way he said my name pissed me off too. "Okay, honestly, I don't want to offer you a beer. I want to hang out with my kids for the rest of the afternoon, because on Sundays, we have movie and junk food evening. It's our routine, and offering you a beer would screw with our routine, and it's..." I trailed off, not about to tell him routines were all that held me together. "Important," I finished instead. "So I feel incredibly rude for not wanting to offer you a beer, since you did a really nice thing for me, and I'm normally a nice person, but—"

"You don't have to explain yourself, Lizzie," Kace interrupted. "You don't have to be nice to me either. I didn't do this expecting anything in return. In fact, if you'll remember, I was kind of an asshole about it. So how about you spend time with your kids? I've got beer at home."

I pursed my lips. Despite not wanting to, I was starting to like this guy. But I wasn't about to show that. To him or myself. Denial was best.

"Thank you," I said.

"I'll be here next week," he replied with a wink, and before I could argue, he turned on his motorcycle boot and walked away. I watched him walk away, because it was a damn fine sight and I couldn't help myself.

Fuck.

KACE WAS a man of his word.

He turned up after lunch the next Sunday. Didn't knock or anything, just parked his bike in the driveway, let himself into the garage and started mowing. Thankfully, the kids were out. Jack was two towns over playing in a soccer game. It was one of the other mothers in the team's turn to carpool. If I was a good mother, I might've gone anyway, but it was bad enough that I had to sit through all the home games and have all of the mothers' staring at me with pity, or worse coming up and trying to talk to me. That didn't happen when I had Bex or Amy with me—they were far too intimidated by them to try it then—to ask me 'how I was doing'. So I skipped away games when I could.

Lily was having a 'spa day' at Amy's house with the rest of the Sons of Templar girls. It was still difficult for me to let the kids out of my sight. Though I knew that they'd be safe, that they'd come home to me, I still breathed a sigh of relief the second they returned home.

Despite how much I wished I could constantly hold them close, never let them go and try to protect them from the world, I couldn't do that to them. I had to let them grow. Somehow had to figure out how to survive through their absences, with the truth that it would only get worse once they got older. Jack had already started turning into the man I knew he was going to be. Strong. Passionate. Stubborn. Determined to patch in to his father's club.

Then there was Lily. Beautiful. Kind. Romantic. She was just like me. And she was growing up around many mini badasses. Yeah, I was in trouble.

Which was probably why Gwen came knocking at the door with two coffees and a paper bag filled with muffins, presumably it was her shift to make sure I was handling everything okay on my own. Now that I'd opened the floodgates by attending the party, it seemed like my self-imposed isolation was over.

The timing could not have been worse, considering she couldn't have missed the man mowing my lawn.

Maybe she wouldn't mention it.

Or maybe I was completely fucking delusional.

"I brought coffee and muffins, but the drive over here was long, and it's hot, so if you've got anything cold and alcoholic, I wouldn't say no," Gwen chirped, walking through the door.

"I think I have something," I mumbled.

"What is Kace doing here?" Gwen asked the second she sat down on a bar stool.

To be fair, I was expecting her to ask that question before she'd even got in the door, so she was showing restraint.

"He's mowing my lawn," I replied, ignoring the coffee and pouring rosé into two glasses. It was after three on a Sunday, plus I wasn't alone. It was allowed.

"I see that," she replied, grinning in approval. "But *why* is he mowing it?"

"Because he got first-hand knowledge of how terrible I am at doing outdoor chores and took it upon himself to save our lawn," I quipped.

Gwen raised her brows as she took her glass. "He did that out of the goodness of his heart?"

I shrugged. "Guess so."

"Honey, these guys are a lot of things. Good isn't one. I'm not saying they're bad, there's just no black and white with them. You know better than anyone."

I bit my lip. "Well, maybe he feels guilty that the only reason he's here is because my husband is dead."

Gwen flinched ever so slightly. My tone was harsh. Cruel.

"I'm sorry," I said immediately.

"Don't you dare apologize," she snapped, her eyes tiny slits. "I see you holding all this stuff in. It isn't healthy. You're trying so hard to keep it together when this is the one time in life when you can fall apart. You have to. What happened broke you. There's no hiding that. You don't have to. Especially around your friends."

My throat thickened with Gwen's words, the kindness and love in her eyes. "Okay," I choked out. "But for now, can we just drink wine and talk about something else?"

"Always," she agreed, clinking her glass with mine. "And I'm here," she added. "We all are."

I smiled at her like her words made a difference.

They really, really didn't.

Chapter 7

Two Weeks Later

"You're a little dressed up for a movie night," I said, looking Amy up and down. She looked how she always looked... fabulous. I had yet to see the woman in sweatpants or anything stained with spit up or any other stains that served as evidence that you're a mother.

I was pretty sure she was a very powerful witch.

But the skintight, white dress—showing no evidence she'd ever had a child—and six-inch green heels with ties that crawled up her legs was dressy, even for her. She also had on what I was pretty sure was a real emerald choker and matching earrings. Her hair was teased into a messy bun, with just the right amount of red curls escaping.

"We're not having a movie night," she replied, leaning in to the mirror to apply her lipstick.

My kids had already run into their large family room, where Brock was with their son Hendrix. Jack and Lily loved all of their 'cousins' equally and all of their 'uncles', but they definitely loved being at Brock and Amy's, hanging out with Hendrix. Mostly because Amy let them run wild, do whatever they liked, and Brock had boundless energy to play with them. They also loved going to Gwen and Cade's by the ocean to play with their kids. Isabella was a few years younger than Lily, but they were still friends. Kingston younger still, but he was impossible not to love. Jack considered himself their protector, and I wondered what might happen when they all grew into young adults. With all the kids and their excellent genes, there was bound to be some romances that each of the respective fathers would likely hate.

"The kids are staying here with the hubby. We are having a girl's night," Amy declared.

Her eyes flickered to my outfit. I'd dressed for a movie night. Granted, a movie night with Amy, but still.

Earlier, I'd decided I to mask all my sadness and sorrow with a biker babe chic style somewhat inspired by Evie. I'd kind of been a biker babe before, but biker babe lite. I'd decided to really going to lean into it now, even though my biker husband was gone. My jeans were tight, faded and distressed. I was wearing low-heeled, black ankle boots, a wide belt with a silver hammered buckle, and a faded Harley Davidson tee. Various necklaces were slung around my neck, the one tucked under my shirt holding Ranger's wedding ring. I still wore mine on my finger. I figured I'd take it off when Lily was old enough and I'd give it to her. If she wanted it. Maybe I'd do a crappy job raising her, she'd grow up to hate me and refuse to wear the ring her father—the one she most likely wasn't going to remember—gave me as a symbol of our love.

My hair was up in a bun like Amy's, but mine was messy and didn't exactly have the same effect. I had some makeup on, if only to cover up the sleepless nights and general grief that was imprinted into my skin, making it look sallow, pale and lackluster.

Definitely not enough glam for a girl's night with some of the most beautiful women in Amber, if not the country.

"I'm really dressed for a girl's night," I hedged. Amy was well aware of the fact that I'd been absent to all girl's nights the past year, including the one with world famous actress Anastasia Edwards in attendance. The very same one where she'd been kidnapped.

I'd heard all this after the fact, since Mia was at my house the very next day with coffee, donuts and all the gossip. Thankfully, she hadn't come with her two boys, since I usually needed an hour to prepare the house and remove all possibly dangerous objects in order for those hellions to visit. And needed to have at least three fire extinguishers on hand.

So yeah, life hadn't stopped since my husband died, the crazy continued.

"You look amazing, actually," Amy countered, looking me up and down. "Which isn't really a surprise since you're a stone-cold hottie. But you've also lost your husband, your heart has been broken and your world has pretty much imploded. That shit is bound to show up on a girl's complexion." She moved to cup my cheek, smiling sadly. "But you still look beautiful. A different kind of beautiful, a sad one which breaks my heart. I wish I knew a dark magic to make this all go away, but the only magic I know can make it hurt a little less and comes in a cocktail glass."

She let go of my face and stepped back before I did something insane like cry in the face of Amy's unique form of comfort.

"Do you really think girl's night is a good idea?" I asked, nervous to be around everyone, wondering if they'd be mad at me for avoiding them and ignoring all of their calls. Even though that wasn't how our group worked.

"No."

That answer didn't come from Amy but from behind her.

Brock was leaning against the wall, watching his wife primp with heat in his eyes.

Amy frowned and whirled around to face her husband.

"Ah, even after all these years of marriage you still think you have any kind of say in where I go or what I do. How adorable," she cooed with saccharine sweetness. "Shouldn't you be watching the children, honey?"

I bit back a smile.

"Girl's nights don't really have the best track record lately," Brock replied, eying his wife while smartly not commenting on her statement. There was a warning in his tone and a danger in his gaze. The kind of danger that most men and women would blanche at and go off running, no matter how much Brock resembled a chill surfer dude.

Amy merely rolled her eyes. Old Ladies were immune to all the intimidating and scary glares. Which was mostly why they were Old Ladies. These men didn't want women who scared easily; they needed women who could weather their alpha bullshit and throw them sass right back. Or be gentle in the face of it.

Amy wasn't about being gentle right now, though.

"Well, the last one doesn't even count because Rosie totally *planned* on Anastasia being kidnapped," she snapped.

"And the rest?" he asked, a whisper of a grin teasing at the corner of his mouth.

She waved her hand. "All part of the Sons of Templar mating process."

He blinked. "Sons of Templar mating process?"

She raised her brow. "Oh, come on, don't play dumb. We've

only been through this like..." she trailed off, counting on her fingers. "Eight times. Give or take. You know that once a man in a leather cut sets his sights on a woman, that woman most likely gets involved in trouble. Usually through no fault of her own."

Brock was flat out grinning now. "No fault of her own?"

She scowled. "Are you trying to tell me that Gwen *wanted* to be kidnapped by those creepy Spider dudes? That *I* wanted to be kidnapped by an arguably creepier crime lord type dude? That Mia wanted to be kidnapped by her gross, asshole ex-husband? And that Lily, Bex, Lauren, Macy and Caroline wanted all the shit that happened?"

Brock looked suitably chastised. His grin disappeared, most likely from the memory of his now wife's kidnapping and all the dramas and near-death experiences that came after it. "I'm not saying that at all."

She put her hand on her hip. "Well, you should stop saying anything at all if you want to get lucky tonight." She hitched her purse onto her shoulder, one that I was pretty sure was worth as much as my first car, though, I was used to her pricey accessories by now. "Now, Lizzie and I and the rest of the girls are going for a quiet drink, to shoot the shit with Laura Maye. No drama. And even if there is, we're all more than capable of handling it." She winked, leaned in to kiss her husband then left.

━━━

THE TABLE that was always reserved for us at Laura Maye's bar was almost entirely full of glamorous women, laughing, drinking cocktails and commanding the attention of everyone in the bar when we arrived.

Everyone stopped talking when Amy and I approached.

It had been a long time since I'd attended a girl's night, the night at the club taking more than enough out of me. Sure, since then there had been coffee dates with Gwen, Mia, Lauren. Each had gently—except Mia, who wasn't really the type to beat around the bush—asked about my conversation with Kace. It was clear they were not only curious but hopeful.

For what exactly, I didn't know. For some kind of romance? A fling? Distraction? For some kind of second chance at a happily ever after? They were all hopeful women, insulated by their own happiness. It was sweet of them, but too simple. As cliché as it was, you couldn't put a Band-Aid over a bullet wound. And that's what any kind of romance would've been right now. Despite the subtle pull I felt toward the man, he wasn't a cure. Or a salve. A distraction at best.

But I didn't need to distract myself from the pain. I had to face it head on, figure out how to live with it so I could eventually move on.

In about ten years or so. Maybe longer, when the kids had moved out of the house, not having memories of their father tainted by some strange man their mother brought in because she was lonely.

So I told the women, and myself, that it was nothing. That he was just being friendly. I definitely did not tell them about him mowing my lawn. Gwen thankfully kept her mouth shut too.

"You look amazing!" Gwen squealed, getting up to hug me.

"I'll have to second her on that one," Mia winked, giving me her own hug, followed by the rest of the group.

Laura Maye placed a drink in front of me as soon as my ass hit the stool, squeezing my shoulder.

"There you go, honey. That'll solve all your problems. For the time bein' at least," she joked in her trademark country twang.

Laura Maye had been in Amber for over ten years. Maybe longer. It was hard to remember what life was like without the beautiful, buxom, Southern woman who wore leopard print, faux fur and leather and hair *out to there.*

I'd known her for years and had yet to see her without perfectly applied makeup. I knew she had a sad story, but she'd never told any of us. You could see it in her eyes sometimes. In the wisdom she always shared with women when they were going through hell. The kind of wisdom that only people who had made that journey could give.

We'd all gently tried to pry it out of her, but she was as stubborn as she was strong, intent on keeping her past where it was.

I got that. In fact, I envied that. There was no option for me to do that here in Amber. Not with everyone knowing my story. I couldn't erase it. Couldn't ignore it. Just had to find a way to live with it,

Laura Maye's cocktails certainly helped.

IT WAS BOUND TO HAPPEN.

As kind and understanding as my friends were, they were also pushy bitches. They were not going to let me sit down and bleed quietly without helping.

Or at least trying to.

"How are you, Lizzie?" Mia asked. "Really. Before you say fine or give us some other bullshit. We know you're not fine. Your husband is dead, and your world is nothing like it should be. Like you deserve. So how the fudge are you?"

My first instinct would've still been to lie. To pretend to be brave and strong and act as though I'd been handling life with a semblance of sanity.

As it was, Laura Maye's cocktails didn't just soften the edges, they loosened my tongue.

"I used to tell myself all kinds of stories about what would happen if I lost him," I mused, swirling my drink. "Not that I wanted to invite those kinds of things in, but with Ranger being involved in the things he was, me loving him as much as I did, there wasn't really a way not to think about the worst happening."

The women around the circle nodded, their eyes dark with the possibility of how easily they could've been me. How they still could be one day.

"I figured I'd be a mess," I continued, taking a sip. "That I wouldn't get out of bed for months. I wouldn't brush my hair or eat or breathe without crying." I took another sip. Amy was right about one thing, Laura Maye's cocktails were definitely strong enough to dull most of my feelings.

"But that's not how it's gone," I continued. "I've been brushing my hair, getting out of bed, eating every meal, going about life." I paused. "But I'm not okay. Not by a long stretch. But I'm also not broken how I thought I'd be. And that scares me."

"Oh sweetie," Lily frowned, moving to squeeze my hand.

"We all like to tell ourselves stories about how life's gonna turn out," Laura Maye said, sipping her own cocktail. She'd long shut down the bar and kicked out the rest of the patrons in honor of girl's night. And also to "reduce the risk of kidnappings."

"But the thing is, we're not the ones writing our stories, not really," she continued. "Yeah, Ranger's story is over. He got his end, however premature it was. But your story is far from finished. You, my dear, are not someone to be broken and battered down by even the most horrible of things." Her eyes moved around the table, at the women who had been through hell yet managed to carry own. Still managing to create beautiful lives.

"You, my dears, are far more complex than a simple love

story, as amazing as those stories may be. Yes, without that great love, your story feels a lot darker, sometimes even hopeless, but that's not all you have. Not all you are. You have your children. You have your kickass girlfriends. Most of all, you have yourself. You still have endless things to discover about who you are. About what you're capable of." Her eyes were soft as they pinned me, even with all her harsh—but totally epic—makeup around them. "And, my darling, you might not be ready to hear this right now, but you may have another love in your story. One that you deserve. One that will be nothing like what you've had, one that won't erase anything you've felt before. You're still young. Look at that face. You look like that... without Botox!"

I chuckled under the weight of her words, especially the love comment. It sat like a stone in the bottom of my stomach. It was tempting to dismiss such a notion verbally, but I stayed quiet. I couldn't ever love another man. Not now, not ever.

"Wait!" Gwen exclaimed. "You've never had Botox?" She squinted at my forehead with a practiced gaze, here own not moving with the gesture. "How is that even possible?"

I shrugged, happy for one of my friends to break the moment, stopping me from having to respond to what Laura Maye said. My eyes touched on Laura Maye, hopefully communicating all of my feelings about everything she'd said. She smiled at me, like the sage in pleather she was.

After that, the discussion melted away from my trauma, thankfully moving on to wrinkle lines.

Which was totally fucking fine with me.

⊏⊐

"WHAT IS *HE* DOING HERE?" I snapped, my eyes zeroing in on the cluster of men entering the bar.

One man stood out from that cluster. The one who had

mowed my lawn and given me kindness that I hadn't exactly returned.

Bex's eyes followed mine, much sharper than the rest of the women since she was sober. Despite her past issues with drugs, she enjoyed many cocktail nights with us, though, she was a lot more conservative with the amount she consumed. I figured losing control might bring her too close to demons of the past that were only sleeping, never dead.

Plus, she was still breastfeeding. Ember was just over six months old, as cute as a button, and the light of Lucky's life. Though a lot of people might not expect it—on face value, at least—Bex was a wonderful mother, surprising herself most of all, I thought.

Babies weren't cures for problems, but they surely made the prospect of tomorrow a lot more hopeful.

"Well, considering the sheer number of women well over the legal limit, you included, I'm guessing he's here to help with the sober driving effort. There was probably some kind of pool tonight, and he drew the short straw." Her eyes darted between the both of us. Or at least I thought they did. I had not been conservative in my cocktail consumption tonight, so I wasn't positive.

"Or maybe he pulled the long straw," she continued, her eyes narrowing and some kind of knowing in her voice.

I frowned up at her, planning on asking her what the heck she meant by that, but it was too late. The men in leather had approached our table.

"I'm delighted to see there hasn't been a single kidnapping, bar fight or drive by shooting." Brock announced, winking at his wife.

"Speak for yourself," Amy replied.

He grinned at her, yanking her forward for a kiss.

Asher moved to Lily, her arms wrapping around him easily while he murmured something in her ear.

My stomach clenched at my utter aloneness. All of these women had men to pick them up or men waiting at home. Someone to fall asleep with tonight, someone who would bring them Advil and coffee in the morning.

Against my control, my eyes flickered to Kace. His were already settled on me, as if he'd been staring at me the entire time. Which, of course, was insane. Why would he want to stare at me?

More aptly, why did I want to stare at him? That was not an appropriate thing to do. Staring. Appreciating how sculpted his arms looked in that tee. Thinking his hair looked good in a delightfully messy way. Wondering what it might be like to run my fingers through it.

It was the cocktails.

It had to be the cocktails. Laura Maye put something in them to cause these thoughts.

While I was thinking about all of this, apparently the drivers and passengers had been divvied up.

"Lizzie. You good to go with Kace?" Brock asked.

I blinked. This was not happening. I was already having weird feelings about his hair, no way should I be riding with him. But I definitely did not want to cause a scene about it. I couldn't complain about the man giving up his Saturday night in order to drive the poor drunk widow home.

Plus, it's not like it would be just us. And whoever else went in the car was going to sit in the front seat, of course, so she could do all the talking.

"Sure," I shrugged, trying to force a smile or at least seem more sober than I was. The kids were having a sleepover at Amy's now; she had asked me if it was okay earlier in the night. I'd said yes, then proceeded to down the cocktails. Since Ranger had died, I hadn't spent a single night without my babies—not counting my breakdown night. Nor had they said anything about wanting to be away from me.

Both of them were understandably afraid of having their one remaining parent away from them for an entire night. They had the memory of their father putting them to bed then waking up to the news that they'd never see him again.

So this was a big step for them. I'd had to say yes, support my children in growing, healing, despite the thought of being alone in my house making me physically sick.

I went through the motions with everyone started hugging, kissing and making plans for hangover brunches.

"Do you want me to come and have a sleepover with you tonight?" Ashley offered once she let me go.

My throat clenched at the offer, at the softness in her eyes. The kindness. The pity. "No, sweetie. I'm good. Promise. I might even be able to sleep past six in the morning." I winked.

She furrowed her brows ever so slightly, obviously not believing me but not going to push me on it.

"Ready?" Kace asked me once the obligatory, drunken goodbyes had been made.

It seemed he was only talking to me. "Wait, what? No one else is coming with us?" I looked around me for help, momentarily tempted to grab onto the nearest body, refusing to let go until I found a suitable buffer for the ride.

"Well, everyone whose husband isn't here lives on the other side of town, Asher's taking them. You alright with that?" Somehow, there was a challenge in his gaze, his tone. Or was I imagining that too?

On the off chance I wasn't, there was no way was I about to back down, admitting any kind of weakness, especially where Kace was concerned.

"Of course," I snapped. "Let's go." I stormed forward so I

didn't have to risk falling into step with him and to make my point. I think the point might've been made a little better if I hadn't stumbled so much.

The air outside was balmy and thick compared to the air-conditioned bar. Especially when I stopped on the sidewalk because I had no idea which car I was meant to be getting into. That, of course, gave Kace time to catch up to me and get close enough for me to smell his cologne.

"It's the red one. On the right." There was poorly hidden amusement in his tone.

I looked to my right, where a Camaro was parked in front of Asher's SUV.

"Really?" I scoffed.

He shrugged. "I like cars."

It hit me then. The vast majority of the Sons of Templar men were married with children. They drove Harley's, of course. But their second vehicles were SUVs or manly trucks capable of hauling furniture their wives bought, bikes their kids rode or the charred remains of a playhouse that Mia and Zane's boys had set on fire.

But Kace didn't have children or a wife to worry about. He was a young, single man in a motorcycle club with a decent amount of disposable income.

I was getting in the car with an unattached man with nice muscles, I was drunk, and hadn't had a warm body beside me in over a year.

This was dangerous.

But I had no other choice.

I got in the car.

Chapter 8

The ride wasn't awkward.

I wanted it to be.

Somehow, it would've been easier if it was awkward. It would've been good. It would've helped if whatever I thought I felt toward this man was imagined or brought on by the strong cocktails. Sure, the fact that I was tipsy helped make things less awkward. But mostly it was just... Kace.

We didn't speak. He seemed content with that. Then again, we'd done plenty of speaking the first time we'd met.

I stared out the window and thought about nothing but the rumble of the engine and how pretty the town looked at night. I was thinking about how clean his car was. How much I enjoyed the ride. The comfortable silence between us. It was like I was insulated from all responsibility. All of my pain.

This was a magical car. It stole away everything I'd been feeling and replaced it with... nothing.

But the problem was, Kace was driving me home from a bar that was ten minutes away at most. There was no traffic and Kace liked to speed. So we were in my driveway in five.

Everything in my body tightened with the proximity to my home, my empty home. Not counting the torturous memories lurking there.

I was bracing for impact.

And right now, I was far too scared to do something insane like go inside my house.

So after he parked in my driveway, I stayed where I was. Seatbelt on and all.

Kace kept the car idling, not commenting on the fact that I hadn't spoken or made a move to leave the car.

"Do you believe in moving on?" I asked him, staring at the porch light I'd left on. Ranger would do that on the rare nights I was out and he wasn't on the list for picking me up.

More often than not, he'd be waiting up with whisky and a book, and he'd hear the car, at the door waiting for me before I even made it to the porch.

He'd never wait for me again.

I'd never meet him at the door again.

"Moving on from what exactly?" Kace replied. "Because moving on from a cheating girlfriend? For fucking sure. From a terrible past? Also for sure. From some really bad bleached tips in high school? Definitely. But I figure you're not talking about any of those things."

I bit my lip. "No, I'm talking about from death. Do you think there is such a thing as moving on after your whole life was ripped apart? Do you think there's a chance of... something else?"

Kace didn't answer me straight away. Didn't automatically try to reassure me with false placations like 'time can heal every-thing'. Kace was a lot of things, but he wasn't a liar. Despite barely knowing him, I knew that.

"I definitely think there is a possibility for something else," he answered finally. "Maybe not what you would expect. Definitely not what you have ever had before. Because you're a different person now, right?" He didn't wait for me to answer. He was looking at my porch light in a way that told me he wasn't really seeing it.

"Yeah, I'm a different person," I agreed.

We didn't say anything else. Not for almost ten minutes. We just sat, looking at that porch light. Then I got out of the car. Without a goodbye. Without an acknowledgement of what the fuck this was. Because doing that would be far too terrifying.

Even more terrifying than walking into that empty house.

Which I did.

WHAT DID you buy a girl who had everything?

Isabella was Gwen's first girl and first child. Gwen was a self-confessed shopping addict; she'd even opened a store here in Amber which did amazing considering how often she bought her own products. Her closet was the size of a small apartment, the contents of it likely costing the same as a car or the deposit on a home. She came from money, had a lot of it, dressed like it, but never acted like it. She was not the type of person to look down her nose at anyone. She was kind, generous and loved giving people gifts.

I'd even taken to slipping money into the cash register at the store when she wasn't looking because of the discounts she gave me on some of the pricier items.

So it stood to reason that Isabella wanted for nothing. She had a bedroom to die for, nicer clothes than me. All the best toys. Despite this, she was not a spoiled child. Not bratty or whiny.

She was quiet. Kind. More like her father than her mother.

Her large, gray eyes watched everything intently, with a concentration that a child shouldn't have.

Of course, her brother, Kingston was a hellion—though such a word lost its meaning once Mia and Bull's sons were born —to balance it all out. I was sure Kingston could've been a nightmare for a young girl without patience or empathy. But Isabella adored her younger brother, ignoring him when he tried to get a rise out of her.

I'd settled on a beautiful, illustrated version of *The Secret Garden,* one of my favorite books, one already sitting on Lily's bookshelf. One of many.

It was somewhat of a tradition for me to get books as gifts for all of my friend's children. Of course, I usually included some cheap plastic toy to appease them since most kids weren't that excited about a book when they were young. Isabella, on the other hand, was quite like my Lily. Intense. Soulful. So she always loved the books I gave her.

This birthday was no different. She gave me a beautiful smile, a heartfelt thank you and a hug after opening it. Even with all the things she had, the way she was spoiled and adored, she had been raised by two parents who were already ensuring that she would turn her into a remarkable young woman.

The party was, of course, extravagant. Tables were piled with beautiful food with fresh flowers everywhere. The entire place was decorated in a butterfly theme, but not the kind of plastic butterfly tablecloths or paper plates that most kid birthday parties would have.

No, this looked like what I imagined a Kardashian would do for their child's birthday party. Everything was tastefully decorated, ornately designed, wooden and crystal butterflies scattered around the house. The party spilled outdoors, onto the patio where the theme continued. It was like some kind of garden party, but not the stuffy, pretentious kind where the kids were hushed quiet and not allowed to have fun or get dirty.

No, the kids roared around, playing various games that Gwen had set up. There was a rotation of parents watching over them, mostly just to make sure Zane and Mia's kids didn't try to set anything on fire or blow anything up.

This party was full of light and love and happiness. My kids had run off in two different directions as soon as we'd arrived, And I probably wouldn't see them for the rest of the afternoon.

I could make it through this. All of the birthdays, parties and gatherings. The happiness. Surely, I'd be able to really feel the smile plastered on my face instead of just faking it. Eventually.

"FANCY SEEING YOU HERE."

I had just grabbed another beer from a tray set up beside a table full of cupcakes, definitely needing it. I looked up, even though I knew the owner of the voice. I shouldn't have recognized it after only a couple of interactions. And I sure as shit should not have had any kind of reaction to the voice. It was the alcohol. It had to be. Even though I'd only had a few beers. I hadn't eaten lunch, though. Yes, that was it. It was the beers today, and it had been those fucking cocktails last week. I'd imagined whatever feelings I thought I'd felt. I'd convinced myself of that.

I didn't smile at him. That would send the wrong message. To the both of us. And to everyone at this party. Most importantly, to the women with eagle eyes and romantic hearts.

"Why did you come and talk to me at the club that day?" I asked, toying with the label of my beer.

His eyes went first to my fingers then to my eyes. "You were alone, figured you might want someone to talk to."

I stared at him. "I'm pretty sure I remember that everything about me that day communicated that I did not want or need anyone to talk to."

He smiled. In that easy way of his.

"Ah, but you most likely didn't want or need anyone to talk to that knew you. Anyone who had expectations, for better or for worse, of you. Sometimes it's nice to talk to a stranger, someone who has no idea who you are so you have no pressure on who you're meant to be."

I blinked. He'd spoken the words in the same way he smiled. Easily. He was all alpha male, there was no doubt about that, that was all but a requirement to patch in. But most of the alpha males I knew found it hard if not annoying to speak in complete sentences. Especially to women they barely knew.

The words themselves were something else. Emotionally perceptive.

"How old are you?" I demanded, leveling him with a steady gaze.

"What does that have to do with anything?" he asked, a twinkle in his eyes.

"Because I'd barely put you over thirty. And if I'm right, then you must be some kind of warlock or demon. Men in their twenties, and men with all those muscles, rarely have emotional intelligence like that. It wouldn't be fair to the rest of the male race. God doesn't give with both hands."

"God, warlocks and demons in a sentence about emotional intelligence. Don't think I've heard that before," his brow crinkling and his tone too close to familiar and teasing for someone that was meant to be a stranger.

"You didn't answer my question." I made sure there was no teasing or anything familiar in my tone.

He smiled. "I'm thirty."

Yeah. Younger than me. By ten years. That was a lot. Too much. Not that it should've mattered since there was no reason we were going to have any kind of relationship where his age would matter.

He was a new member in the club, trying to do good by the widow of the member he'd replaced. Trying to make a good impression on the rest of his brothers. He had a nice smile. A nice body and a presence about himself that was purely and utterly unique. He was good with kids—I knew this because I'd been watching him all afternoon—and he seemed to get along with everyone in the club.

But he was just another member. I should've treated him as such.

"Do I pass?" he asked when I didn't say anything.

"What?"

"Whatever test it was that had to do with my age?"

I was far too aware that we were having this conversation in full view of everyone at this party. And despite the fact that it had been over a year since Ranger died, people were still watching me carefully, making sure I wasn't going to break down. Wasn't going to fall apart. I was doing both, I had just become an expert on doing it all on the inside.

"There was no test," I replied. "You just confirmed what I already knew. You're young. Much younger than me. So you should be talking to someone your own age."

"I don't want to talk to anyone my own age. I want to talk to you. I like you."

I scowled at him. "You don't know me," I snapped.

He wasn't bothered by my tone. "Well, I would like to get to know you. Be your friend."

Who the fuck was this guy?

"I've got enough friends," I scorned. "And you do too. Your

brothers. You want a lady friend, there's plenty of them hanging out at the club for you to choose from. Now, if you'll excuse me, I'm going to talk to my friends. You should go talk to yours."

I didn't move. Wasn't going to walk away. He was the one who had come and interrupted my solitude.

The look I was giving him communicated 'fuck off' pretty darn well.

"Okay, I'll leave you be. But just to let you know, you haven't scared me away. I'm a lot tougher to scare than that." Then he winked and walked away.

I did not watch him walk away. Instead, I turned to look at the beach in the distance, longing to run from the party and all the people who loved me just so I could have a moment without wearing a mask.

But it didn't work that way.

Especially when you had friends like mine.

I knew the second he left that it was only a matter of time before someone pounced on me. It was just a matter of who was closest.

"Did I just see you talking to the hot, new member of the Sons of Templar?" Mia asked, slightly breathless and spilling her margarita as she sat down with force. "Of course, he's not as hot as my husband, just in case he's in the vicinity and is gonna get all alpha male jealous," she said, glancing around.

"I think he followed the boys inside, most likely to foil some kind of plan," I replied with a smirk. Mia and Bull's boys were a full-time job. It was a forgone conclusion that they'd patch in and they'd likely be the craziest members the Sons had ever seen, which was saying something considering Gage and Lucky.

"Perfect," she said, eyes flaring. "Now, I repeat, was that some flirting I spotted?"

Before I could answer—more accurately lie—someone else

popped down on the chair beside her. "Okay, I totally need the skinny on what that interaction just was," Amy demanded.

Mia glanced at her. "Uh, duh, do you think I'm here to discuss a fucking PTA meeting?"

"You're banned from the PTA," I reminded Mia.

She scowled at me. "We don't talk about that. Plus, stop trying to change the subject."

"I wasn't changing the subject," I said, sipping my drink. It took considerable effort to keep my gaze away from the other side of the pool where I'd tracked Kace's journey. He was in some kind of guy huddle. I wondered if they were demanding the 'skinny' on our conversation too. With Cade and Gage in attendance, I suspected there was some kind of deadly warning involved. As far as the men were concerned, I was damaged, vulnerable goods that it was their duty to protect.

Though it sounded like a totally misogynist ideal—I guess it kind of was—it wasn't meant that way. There was a code, a way these kinds of things worked. If some guy decided to come up to me and engage in anything from polite conversation to casual flirting, it was also their job to scare him away. Even if that man in question was part of the club.

"Hello?" Mia called, waving her hand in front of my eyes.

"You're not allowed to pretend to lapse into some kind of waking coma, you're still going to have to tell us," Amy chirped.

"Did I miss it?" Lauren asked, moving to the last available chair.

"Miss what?" I questioned, although I already knew.

She gave me a look. "Don't play dumb. You know exactly what everyone is here for."

"Because I had a conversation with Kace?"

My question is followed by eye rolls all around and looks to show me that I was not fooling anyone.

"Kace, you're calling him *Kace*?" Mia put extra emphasis on his name as if she knew something. Which of course she didn't, because there was nothing to know.

"That's his name, Mia," I replied.

"It's a good name," Lauren commented.

"*Great* name," Amy corrected.

"What does his name have to do with me?" I asked the group, doing my best to sound neutral, if anything sounding slightly pissed off.

"It has everything to do with you," Mia said. "Considering you had the look on your face when you were talking to him.

I frowned. "What look?"

Amy sipped her drink before speaking. "Um, *the look*. The one where you're imagining him naked and also fighting against that image because you're a strong woman and don't want any man, no matter how hot, to have that kind of control over you."

All the women nodded in agreement, and I had to fight to keep my expression neutral so they wouldn't know I agreed. Because that was exactly how I'd felt.

"We've all been there," Lauren added gently.

I drained my drink, standing. "I don't know what you're talking about. I'm going to check on my kids, then getting myself another beer, and I am not having this conversation."

The women let me off the hook. I guessed because they'd already said what they had to say. They'd already planted the seeds. And now they were going to wait. I knew them too well to think anything different.

Which was fine. They could wait for as long as they wanted. Nothing was going to happen with Kace and I.

Nothing at all.

Chapter 9

It was a school day. Lunch had come and gone. I was in town running errands, groceries, pharmacy, buying things so I could make Lily a costume for the school play. Things I'd done for years. Things I would've been doing if Ranger were alive.

Which was what had me walking into a bar before one in the afternoon on a Wednesday.

Amber didn't have much in the way of bars and restaurants, but there were a decent amount considering the size of our small town. And with Mia's bed and breakfast with the spa attached gaining national attention, more and more people were flocking to our town.

Laura Maye's bar was not a dive bar by any stretch of the imagination. It was sleek, trendy and offered a beautiful view of the ocean. If you wanted a dive bar, there were a couple on the outskirts of town where the damned, the lonely and the unemployed drowned their sorrows. I should've gone to one of those bars. That was where I belonged. But there were limits on how much I'd let my grief control me.

Laura Maye's bar wasn't empty, a few people sat along the

windows, taking in the view, having afternoon drinks. Thankfully, I didn't see any familiar faces, just what I assumed were tourists enjoying the excuse to day drink in a nice bar, in a small town on vacation from their responsibilities for a while.

"Hey there, honey," Laura Maye said with a smile when I walked up to the bar.

Her hair was piled in a messy bun at the top of her head, curls hanging down in tendrils with glittered barrettes scattered through it. She had on blue eyeshadow that matched the suede mini dress she wore .

"What brought you here to Amber?" I blurted, suddenly desperate to fill my head with someone else's demons instead of my own.

If she was surprised at the question, she didn't show it. She grinned, taking some bottles from the bar before pouring them into a cocktail shaker. "Ah, if you want to know the answer to that, we're both gonna need a drink in our hands."

"As much as I'd love to say yes, I've got to pick up the kids from school. Even one of your cocktails will make sure that doesn't happen," I said.

She giggled. "Don't you worry, sugar. I'm doin' half strength, and I'll get Donny in the kitchen to whip us up some jalapeno poppers and nachos to soak it all up." She winked, calling out to Donny.

Laura Maye made quick work of making the drinks. She was an expert after all. Though she owned the place, she spent a good amount of time behind the bar. People from three towns over knew about her cocktails. This place got packed on the weekends, so there were other bartenders who helped, but she worked hard and constantly. She'd created all of this herself, and even though she could've relaxed, letting the place rake in the money, that wasn't her style. Not at all.

After taking care of the other customers, she sat down beside me, drinks in front of us.

"Now, you're not the first person to ask me this question," she said. "Not that our girls are pushy or nosy. They're curious. Want to know that they've got shoulders to cry on if that needs to be done. Vaults to keep their secrets in." She sipped her drink. "I've cried enough tears to know that I won't need a shoulder for some time. My secrets don't need to be in vaults exactly, just haven't been ready to come out into the light. Guess I've been waiting for the right time, the right person."

She reached over to squeeze my hand. "Glad I waited, 'cause I get the feeling that this is the absolute right time for that."

She sighed, looking out the window for a beat, a faraway look in her eyes. "I grew up in the South. To a Momma and Daddy who didn't love each other. Barely even liked each other all that much. But they feared God enough to know that divorce was a sin, and they surely didn't want to anger him by getting one. So they stayed together. Made each other angry and bitter. Even my Momma. She was a romantic. A former pageant queen. My God, she was beautiful. Always, absolutely always had her hair done. Makeup on. Heels, outfit, everything matching."

She looked wistful, as if she were imagining her mother.

I was imagining her, too, thinking she might've looked like a different version of Laura Maye. Though that was hard to imagine. There was only one Laura Maye; she was one of a kind.

"We didn't have the money for much, so she had to get creative," she continued. "Would go to thrift shops. Altered things with her rusty old sewing machine, making them look good as new, original. She took so much pride in herself. But her and Daddy's constant fighting, all the money problems, living in an environment she didn't think she'd ever end up in... it chipped away at her. At her beauty. She started to drink to escape from all of it. The life she found herself in. Then she started to go to bars, looking for men who'd treat her like they wanted her. Daddy eventually found out, making things even worse. For all the fear he had about angering God with a divorce, he didn't at all mind beating on his wife."

She sipped her drink, and I did the same because the story was already breaking my heart, and I had a feeling she wasn't even half done.

"My momma loved me. She wanted to give me a life that was different than hers. She told me the dangers of falling in love, taught me the value in looking beautiful. 'No matter what kind of ugliness the world gives you, make sure you face it with your hair did and your lipstick on', that's what she used to say." Laura Maye smiled. A sad smile, full of pain.

"She said that being beautiful was a gift. That it would get me places with men. That I could use it to my advantage, as long as I never got attached. Never let myself end up like her. My daddy wasn't a bad man. Least I don't like to think so. He'd been the same as Momma. Thought the world had more to offer him. Quarterback in high school, meant for big things. Then he blew his knee out, and his future went up in smoke. Momma's too. He had to work in a factory. Back breaking, soul crushing work. Dawn till dusk for crappy pay. He was tired from work, tired from life, angry with everyone, most of all himself. Although he did love me in his own way."

"Here you go, ladies," Donny said with a smile, setting down two amazing looking plates of food. The smell reminded me that I'd had nothing but coffee and a bite of Lily's oatmeal today.

Laura Maye grinned at the man. "Thank you, sweetheart."

He winked at her and made his way back to the kitchen.

"Fried food and booze are the best ways to get through stories of a damaged past," she said with a cheerfulness in her voice that amazed me. It was genuine, as was everything about Laura Maye. Except her nails, and her eyelashes.

I picked at the nachos while she continued.

"I wasn't too great at school, except math. I liked numbers. Numbers are always reliable." She smiled wistfully. "But people didn't see much more than dumb, blonde trailer trash when they looked at me. And if people think that about you long enough, you start to believe them. Especially when the momma who used to tell you how beautiful you were is more concerned with a bottle than anything else."

She popped a chip into her mouth.

I sipped my drink while I waited, watching the beautiful Laura Maye, sitting in the bar she built. The life she'd earned. As if I didn't already have enough respect for the woman.

"I got out at eighteen, only 'cause I had to. 'Cause I knew that I'd fade away just like my momma if I stayed. Me and my boyfriend—I always had one of those—decided to up and leave. Decided to go to Dallas. Figure I'd wait tables while I tried to become an actress or model. Something like that. I hadn't decided. Just needed the world to tell me I was beautiful because I didn't believe it anymore.

That's how it started. Well, it truly started because we didn't have much money to our names, lived in a shitty area and it was hard getting jobs. I waited tables at a shitty bar. The boyfriend didn't do much of anything but get himself tangled up with the wrong crowd. The kind of crowd that made him eventually convince me to work at a strip club. More money for us. Convinced me I was so beautiful that I'd make the most money."

She laughed again.

"It took some convincing on his part. Before her fall from

grace, my mother had taught me how a lady acted, conducted herself. I listened hard about that because I wanted nothing more than to be a lady. Wanted to be one with a nice house, handsome husband, beautiful kids. But I didn't listen hard to her warnings about falling in love. I didn't really know what love was, so when he showed it to me, I was willing to trust him with anything. And if he thought stripping was a good idea, then it must've been.

I earned a lot of money. Good money. But not enough. He worked on me. Quietly. Subtly. Figuring out my weaknesses, how to control me, how to make me listen to him. Sometimes he used his fists, but most of the time, his words worked just fine. So soon I wasn't just stripping. There were private lap dances. There were 'dates'. Nice hotel rooms. Then sleazy motel rooms. My body wasn't mine anymore. It was his. It was up for rent."

She drained her drink, and I did the same, needing it. Although I knew that Laura Maye's life hadn't been easy, I'd known that she carried around demons, I couldn't have imagined this. Especially from Laura Maye, who I'd considered to be so strong, so sure of herself. Confident, like she'd never let anyone take anything from her. But those were rarely qualities a woman was born with. Those were usually qualities a woman acquired after people—usually men—took things from her.

"Nothing crazy happened... beyond what I've already told you," she continued, her voice still carrying the same light, easy tone. "I got used to the occasional beating. To strangers treating my body like it was something that existed only for what they wanted. Then, one day... I just didn't. I saw it for what it was. Saw that my life had turned into something much darker than my momma's, and I realized that it would only get worse if I didn't do anything about it.

"I'd saved what money I could," she said with a sad smile. "My boyfriend took almost all of it. What he thought was all of it, at least. Even in my lowest of moments, I was always thinking of a way out, because on some level, I knew I'd die if I didn't escape. So I pocketed small amounts at first after figuring out how much I could take without him noticing. I managed to keep more as he got further into drugs. Soon I had enough to leave. Not a fortune, but enough to get out, The price of my freedom was priceless. I left in the night, with nothing but the clothes on my back and a purse containing one tube of lipstick."

She glanced to the windows, to the ocean, then back to me.

"Went as far away as I could. Lost myself in L.A. Things didn't immediately get better, of course. I was a young, damaged girl, easy prey for that city. But luckily, I was smart. Knew that I still had the body, the looks. Knew I wouldn't be able to get any nine to five job. So I made friends with girls like me. I've always been good at that, making friends. I found out about the best place to dance in the city, place called Fantasia. Apparently, they paid their dancers well, didn't put up with any kind of pimping and even had health insurance. It was like the gold standard of strip clubs. Girls had been trying to get in there for years. But you remember, I'm smart, friendly. Found myself a way in. And as they say, the rest is history."

She smiled, looking down at her nails. "Well, kind of. A lot happened between then and now. Enough for an entire book. A movie. But I made good money. Saved every cent I could. Always had a dream to go somewhere quiet, somewhere safe. To create something beautiful of my own." She looked around the bar. "Think I've done that."

"You've definitely done that," I whispered, a tear trailing down my cheek.

"Oh, sugar, don't cry for me," she murmured, leaning forward and brushing the tear from my cheek. "I've survived, which is more than a lot of girls in my situation can say. Beyond that, I've thrived. Sure, I've got some scars, but we've all got those. I've got girlfriends, my bar, a life. I'm happy, darlin'."

She was. She really meant that. There was always going to be a darkness to her, but that only made her light shine that much brighter.

"Have you ever found love? Since then?" I asked, marveling even more at this remarkable woman. I yearned for her to find someone who marveled at her too. Who worshipped her. I knew that Laura Maye definitely didn't need a man, she'd proven that. But she deserved one. A good one.

"I have found love," Laura Maye replied, her eyes twinkling. "I've got it all around me here."

"You know what I mean."

She nodded. "I do know what you mean, honey. And I've been close to finding it, a couple of times. Might've even turned into something, if I'd let it. But I haven't got there yet. When it comes to scars on the heart, they take longest to heal. Maybe I'll find love again. Maybe I'll even go looking for it. But I'm okay even if I don't."

"I hope you find it," I offered. "Any man who wins your heart will be the luckiest man in the world."

"You're not wrong on that one, honey, I'm a gosh darn catch."

I laughed, something I hadn't thought would be possible in such close proximity to that story. But that was Laura Maye. She was a little bit magic.

"Thank you, for telling me that," I said.

"Thank you for giving me the opportunity," she replied. "I don't like traveling back into the past much, but it's much easier when I have good company. Glad it was you, sweetie."

"Me too."

We let the silence swim between us for a while, it was nice. It shouldn't have been, now I that knew the truth, the sad truth of Laura Maye's past. But it only made her more beautiful.

"I am sure you came in here for more than listening to my story," Laura Maye said finally.

"I don't even know why I came in here," I admitted, looking out toward the windows. "I'm a little lost, I guess."

Laura Maye laughed, not in a cruel way, she didn't have that in her. "Of course you are, baby. You can't expect to even know what direction is up right now."

"But I should. I'm a mother—"

"A damn good one," Laura Maye interjected. "Doesn't mean you aren't human. And you've had your heart ripped out in the most brutal of ways, forced to try to keep it together for your kids, for your friends, for the club. You're allowed to fall apart now and again. You're allowed to talk to your friends."

"It feels like I'm failing," I whispered. "He's the one in the ground, yet I'm the one rotting. Everything hopeful inside of me, everything romantic, everything that somehow remained untarnished even through the hardest years of our marriage... The things that he nurtured, he grew, they all died. They withered inside of me first. And now I'm just decaying I feel like I'll decompose until all that'll be left are rotten pieces of what I used to be."

"No, baby," Laura Maye said firmly. "You're young and you're strong. Even if you don't want to, you're gonna have a second life. Just you wait."

She said this with such conviction, with such certainty, I actually believed her.

For the afternoon, at least.

Chapter 10

Kace was mowing the lawn again.

Both of the kids were at Asher and Lily's place. Now that I'd almost, kind of let myself back into the Sons' fold once more, our rotation of playdates had resumed. Potluck dinners. Cocktail nights. Pre-gaming before any kind of game or school event.

Shopping.

Trips to L.A. to visit Lucy, Rosie and Polly.

Life was almost normal. Except I never had Ranger at my side. Except I was the only one at all of those events who didn't have a husband anymore.

They didn't treat me any different, though. Of course they didn't.

But I *was* different. There was a reminder in my empty heart every damn day. Walking into houses, bars, stores knowing I'd always be walking in alone. There was no escaping it. The urge to say no to every invitation, wanting to hide at home with wine and my books was overwhelming at times

But I'd done that. For a year, I'd done that. It hadn't

changed anything. Didn't make the hurt any less. It had only made my children suffer.

So I was sucking it up.

It wasn't so bad when I got the house to myself for an afternoon. As much as I'd feared being alone, especially in our home, I realized needed it. Needed the time to just be... me instead of 'mom'.

Ranger used to give me that.

Constant reminders that I was not just a mother. That I was a woman. His and my own. Since I didn't get reminders like that anymore, I didn't feel like anything but a mother and a widow. And it was infuriating. I was sick of my own fucking misery. My own pain.

So I had to find a way to get more familiar with it.

Which meant time alone.

Which also meant reorganizing Lily's dolls—which she hated doing—changing around Jack's room—which he barely noticed—and sorting out my clothes while studiously avoiding Ranger's side of the closet.

Then I'd go into the backyard, picking up the rogue toys. Did a little gardening. Made fresh lemonade for when the kids came home. Scones to go with it.

That was another thing I was getting really good at.

Making sure the kids had some kind of treat waiting for them whenever they came home. Fresh baked scones with homemade jam. Cookies. Bread. Lemonade. A new room layout.

Like I could distract them with baked goods and maybe they wouldn't notice that their dad wasn't coming home.

It was just as I was putting scones in the oven that the lawn mower started. It gave me a fright, since I'd been doing all my tasks in silence. I didn't like music anymore. Too many possible encounters with a song that meant something to me. That had meant something to *us*.

Silence was much safer.

It shouldn't have been surprised that he was there. He'd been doing this every Sunday for almost two months. The kids had even gotten used to him. Last Sunday, Lily had insisted we bring him milk and cookies, despite the fact that the last thing he probably wanted after mowing the lawn in the heat was a glass of milk. Nonetheless, he took them with grace, charming Lily. Like he often did, Jack had just watched the encounter with a stony expression that reminded me of his father so much I'd locked myself in the bathroom and sob for five minutes.

But then the lawn mower broke down. Kace disappeared for a few then came back with a part. By then, Jack was out in the yard, inspecting the mower like he thought it was his job to fix it.

When Kace arrived back, Jack's stony expression returned. But Kace invited him to help, and my young son was just far too curious to just walk away.

So Kace taught Jack about the inner workings of a lawn mower.

Apparently, he'd promised to teach him about cars next— with my permission, of course.

Jack had recounted all of this, since I had made an art of avoiding the man since the girl's night and Isabella's birthday. Avoiding him meant avoiding whatever feelings I had toward him, so that's what I did.

Jack hadn't had a stony expression when he'd begged me to let Kace show him how he was rebuilding a car he had in his garage. I wanted to say no. Really fucking badly. Mostly because my feelings were getting in the way, but mostly because the thought of Kace spending time with my son, charming him further, scared me.

Also a little bit because it made me angry. Furious. That offer. He was practically a stranger, offering my son things his father should've been teaching him. Things he never would.

Which was why I said yes.

Sure, Jack would have plenty of male role models in his life of the badass, alpha male variety. Men able to teach him how to be a badass alpha if he so wished.

But those men also had families of their own.

Who was I to deny Jack one more positive influence?

And, inexplicably, I trusted Kace. It was irresponsible to trust a man I barely knew, especially with my children. Maybe that made me a bad mother, but I had to trust my instincts. I had nothing else.

So, next week, Jack was going over to Kace's to help with the car.

It was after I pretended not to watch him out the window that I decided if I was sending Jack off to spend time with him, it was my responsibility to get to know him a little more. Make sure he wasn't some crazy murderer.

Which probably shouldn't have been my criteria, since most of my son's positive influences were either crazy, murderers or both.

I took a deep breath as I opened the door. Kace's eyes went straight to me, walking back from the garage where he'd stored the mower. It had become somewhat of a routine. He never tried to approach the house, but always interacted with the kids when they came out to talk to him.

I had not come out to talk to him.

So he definitely looked surprised to see me. Probably more so the beers in my hand. But his gaze didn't focus on the beers. No, they lingered on my legs, my denim cutoffs smudged with dirt from the garden suddenly feeling far too short.

This was a bad idea.

A very bad idea.

But it was too late now.

"You dangling those in front of me as a form of torture?" he asked, eyes teasing.

It's too late to back out now, I told myself again. Throwing the bottles at him and sprinting back into my house would totally cement me as the crazy woman.

"No, I think making you mow my lawns without any form of payment other than a glass of milk and some mediocre cookies is torture enough," I replied.

"I'm going to agree to disagree on the cookies," he retorted, walking toward me. He had a confident, easy swagger about him that shouldn't have been attractive. Nor should the thin sheen of sweat clinging to his body. But it was.

"And the milk was a necessity. Cookies without milk is a crime," he continued, taking a beer from my hand, his fingers brushing with mine.

I snatched my hand back in the guise of necking my beer.

Kace watched me drink my beer and sipped his own.

Unfortunately, there was only so long I could have my lips around the bottle without looking like a frat boy or like I was preforming a sex act on an inanimate object.

"Do you want to come in?" I asked, even though I really didn't want that to happen. "I was just about to order pizza that I'd have to consume completely on my own because I can't have any remaining evidence when the kids come home tonight."

Now why did I offer that? I could've suffered through one beer and forced s brief, surface level conversation. One beer was only, what? Five minutes? Ten tops? The pizza thing was more than one beer for sure. And then there was the ordering, waiting for and eating aforementioned pizza.

Way too much time alone with him.

"We got to get one thing straight before I reply to that offer," he said, his eyes pinning me in place.

I swallowed. He'd felt it too. Or he'd noticed that I was acting completely odd around him and staring at him like an insane person while he talked. Me, the older woman with kids and enough emotional baggage to fit a passenger plane front to back.

"Please don't tell me you're one of those psychopaths that thinks pineapple belongs on pizza," he teased with a straight face.

I waited for more. But nothing came. And Kace didn't seem perturbed at how long it took me to answer the question about what toppings I liked on my pizza.

"No, I definitely am not into fruit on my pizza," I replied, trying to sound as casual and amused as he had. "When the kids are in charge of the ordering, which is any other time I ever order pizza, it's usually half barbeque, half every meat on the menu. But in those glorious, rare, kid free pizza nights, I order from the fancy Italian place and go with a delicious, traditional margarita."

Kace raised a brow. "What? Sauce, cheese and basil? That's it?"

I frowned back at him. "Of course that's it. That's how it's meant to be. Americans have butchered traditional Italian foods with all sorts of sacrilegious toppings. It's only meant to be three. Four, at a stretch."

"I'm a smart man. And a hungry one. So I'm not going to even try to argue with you on that. Instead, we're just gonna get two pizzas."

———

WE'D HAD MORE than two beers.

We ate outside. No TV on, no music, no distractions. We talked. About what, I couldn't even remember. Nothing deep. Not the traumas of our past or the scars of our yesterdays. We talked about easy things. Kace led the conversation, but it happened naturally. I even enjoyed myself.

So much so that after we finished the pizzas and cleaned up, I offered him another beer and suggested a movie.

I only suggested this because Asher had texted to say the kids wanted to stay the night. For selfish reasons, I'd agreed to that. Because tonight I was feeling like something more than a widow and a mother.

The movie had barely started when I paused it.

Kace had carefully placed himself on the opposite end of the sofa. He'd been looking at me a certain type of way all evening. Not constantly, but I'd seen it. The slight heat in his eyes when his gaze lingered on my legs. I'd felt something when our fingers brushed trying to pick up a slice of pizza at the same time.

It was a spark. The kind I hadn't expected to ever feel again.. One that had grown. Or maybe one that was there because he was attractive and available, and I needed something to numb the pain.

But I couldn't handle the mundane shit anymore. The ordering of the pizza. The cleaning up. The movie on the sofa. That was entering dangerous territory. Hence me pausing the movie and turning on the sofa so I faced Kace.

"Okay, I know you're super-hot, and it's obviously clear that I'm attracted to you because I am a woman with a libido and a heartbeat, which I'm thinking are the requirements to be attracted to you. So yes, I'm human. But I'm also a total fucking mess. Slightly less of a mess than I was six months ago to be sure, but a mess nonetheless. I'm not ready for any kind of relationship," I blurted.

He grinned, his eyes bugging out ever so slightly at all of the information I'd just laid on him. "Now, I have a good memory. Not the best, but I'm pretty sure I'd remember asking you to be in a relationship with me."

I stared at him. Holy fuck. He was right. He hadn't asked for a relationship. Hadn't even made a move, for that matter. "But you mow my lawn," I said weakly. "You hang out with my kids. You're always going out of your way to talk to me."

"Yeah, I like being around you," he replied. "Like your kids." His eyes flickered over me. It was a quick glance, but I felt it everywhere. "I'm not going to lie and say I don't want to. I fuckin' do. But I know you're not ready. Know you're going through some shit right now. So I'm waiting."

"You're waiting," I repeated.

He nodded. "Yeah, I'm waitin'. Till you're ready. Because no fucking way am I letting any other guy have the chance when you are. I want that chance. So I'm waiting."

I blinked. Several times. My mouth felt dry, and the rest of my body was flaming hot. "Why would you want to wait?"

His eyes did that thing again. My body also did that thing. Again. "Why *wouldn't* I want to wait?" His voice was husky now. Sexy.

Okay, this was not supposed to be going this way. I definitely was not supposed to be reacting this way. All of my sexual urges needed to be muted for at least another year. Two years maybe. That was acceptable. Three years would've been preferable. Even then, I would only allow sexual dalliances two towns over, leaving right after it was done. There was not going to be any men going in and out of my children's lives. No.

So right now, the smart thing would've been to banish this beautiful man from my home and from my life. Then I'd drink the rest of my beer and go to bed, grab the vibrator from my bedside table and think about his voice and the looks he gave me. Which was already bad enough because I should've been thinking about my dead husband.

But what I did instead was place my beer on the coffee table, reached over and did the same to Kace's. Then, I pounced.

Our mouths met in a clash of tongues, teeth and pure need. He kissed me back immediately, though I was pretty sure he was not expecting me to jump on him like a horny hyena.

Before long, we were completely horizontal, me on top of him, grinding my body against his.

"Lizzie," he rasped, pushing at me enough so our mouths detached.

I did not like that. The pause in the frenzy was too stark, too dangerous, potentially giving me time to think and realize the mistake I was making.

"No talking," I ordered, trying to move forward again, before common sense kicked in.

He held fast, but at least it looked like it was a struggle for him. There was fire in his eyes, his entire body taut with what I hoped was restraint.

"Lizzie," he ground out. "Need to know that this isn't me takin' advantage of you."

I groaned, hating that him being this sensitive and considerate turned me on.

"No, *I'm* taking advantage of *you*," I hissed.

He let me kiss him then. Let me take control. Though I didn't feel like I had control. Whatever this was, it wasn't a conscious choice. It was a need. The kiss lasted forever. Hands in my hair. On my ass.

Clothes needed to come off. I needed to feel his skin. In fact, I needed him inside me. More than anything in this moment, that's what I needed. My shirt was already heavy, dragging me down, I wanted to claw it off. But there was no way we could have sex on the couch with the prospect of my kids walking in.

No, couldn't think of them. Couldn't think of anything.

"Bedroom," I murmured, my own voice rough.

He didn't hesitate. In an instant, we were no longer kissing on the sofa. My legs were wrapped around his hips, his hard-on pressing into me, his plump lips still on mine. I didn't pay attention to the fact that we were walking through the house like this, I was too busy with the kissing thing and almost orgasms from kissing and dry humping.

The door to my bedroom closed quietly, that small sound jerking me into somewhat of a coherent state.

"Not the bed," I all but hissed as he began to move across the room.

Panic clutched at my throat with the idea of us doing what I wanted to do in my bed. Our bed. No. I wasn't ready for that.

Kace didn't hesitate either, moving to the bathroom, putting me down on the counter. His mouth went to my neck then down, yanking the fabric of my tank to the side so his lips landed on my nipple.

I tore my hands through his hair, sinking my teeth into my lip to stop from crying out. His teeth grazed my nipple, not gently. My stomach dipped, and an orgasm started to build up.

He'd somehow gotten my shorts off, so caught up in the frenzy I hadn't even noticed. He didn't tease, didn't move slowly, hesitantly. No, his fingers landed there. Right there while his mouth moved against my nipple.

I tasted blood as my lips sank down even farther.

Kace was no longer at my breast. His fingers had stopped moving in those expert circles, instead, they'd plunged right inside.

I let out a hiss of pleasure at his beautiful intrusion.

Kace's eyes were dark. Hard. "You're not gonna try to silence yourself now, baby," he growled. "If you try again, I'll punish you until you got no choice but to scream."

"Punish me?" I repeated, voice scratchy.

His fingers still moved inside me, coaxing me, teasing me, not giving me the full relief I knew he could. He was doing this on purpose.

"Yes," he grated out. "You don't scream my name, you don't moan, cry out like I know you want to, I'll take you to the edge and bring you back so many times you'll get on your knees and beg me to make you come."

Fury settled in my stomach, battling with need. "I will never beg."

He grinned. But it wasn't easy or simple like it had been before. This grin was wicked. Dark. And I fucking loved it.

"Oh, yes you fucking will," he ordered, moving his finger deeper now, brushing against my g-spot, causing my breath to hitch, my body to tense, ready to shatter, burst apart. But then he stopped, lifted his finger between us, put it in his mouth and tasted me.

"Knew you'd be sweet," he murmured.

Fury drowned in the sea of my desire. "Well then, taste me properly," I invited.

His eyes flared, palm moving back between my legs, cupping me. "Let's get one thing straight." His other hand moved to my neck, circling it. There was pressure. A considerable amount of it, but not enough to hurt. I could still breathe.

"I'm the one who gives the orders here," he rasped against my mouth. "You got a problem with that?"

I definitely should have had a problem with that. Kace was a relative stranger. He was ten years my junior. He definitely shouldn't have been ordering me around.

"I don't have a problem with that," I breathed.

He grinned wickedly once more, lips landing on mine. Then his fingers moved inside me again. Slowly. Torturing, showing me that it was up to him if and when I got my release.

His fingers left me and his mouth moved down my neck, skirting over my breasts, moving down my stomach, hovering at my hip bones and finally landing on the place where I needed him to be.

His lips didn't move slowly or gently now. He devoured me like a starving man. Didn't stop as I screamed his name, tore at his hair, exploded under his touch. No, he kept going, relentlessly, until my second orgasm washed over me.

Then his lips were gone. His mouth on mine, tasting like the both of us mixed.

"Condom," he murmured.

I barely registered what he was saying, only realizing it because he wasn't doing what my body craved. He wasn't fucking me.

"Babe, you got a condom?" he asked again against my mouth.

A condom?

I'd been married for well over a decade. No, I didn't have a fucking condom. The mere thought of it started to yank me out of the moment.

That couldn't happen.

"I'm on the pill," I murmured. It was more for the regulation of my cycles than anything these days. I took them out of habit. Because I wanted as many things to stay the same in my daily life as I could. Even the smallest of things.

Kace's eyes were dark. "You sure?"

I let out a frustrated sound at the back of my throat. "I'm fucking sure," I commanded. "Now fuck me."

He moved quickly, freeing himself and thrusting into me. Hard. Brutal. Brilliant.

My eyes squeezed shut under the intensity of it all. My skin felt like it was going to burst open. Like I wouldn't survive another orgasm, even as his cock coaxed another one out of me.

"Open your fucking eyes," Kace demanded, voice guttural.

I obeyed him immediately, without thinking. His eyes were glued to mine, holding me captive as he moved. "You're keeping them here, on me," he grunted.

My hands scraped down his back. He hissed in pleasure.

"Yeah, baby. Fuckin' let your claws out. I can handle it. I won't break." He moved harder. Faster. "Neither will you."

He was wrong.

I could break. I had before.

And he did break me again. Into millions of little pieces I'd scramble to get back after this was done. Pieces he'd managed to steal for himself. Of course I hadn't known this at the time.

―――

WE WERE ON THE FLOOR.

I couldn't quite remember how we'd moved from the bathroom to here, but there were blankets tangled around us, yanked off the bed I wouldn't allow us to use. As if that would've made any difference.

"I meant what I said before," I panted, only starting to get my breath back. I still kind of felt like I was floating five inches above the bed. Id' forgotten what sex could do. What good sex could do.

No, *great* sex.

Which we'd just had.

Three times.

Every single one of my muscles were no longer functional. I was pretty sure I'd never be able to move them or use them again.

And I was totally okay with that. Who needed muscles after sex like that?

"That you believe pizza should only have one topping?" he teased, rubbing my back then moving down to cup my ass.

I winced ever so slightly at the pain that came with that touch. A delightful pain. Kace had helped me discover that I was into pain now. Rough, borderline angry sex. I was more than into it. I fucking loved it. Wanted bruises and marks. Wanted anything but love and tenderness.

"Believe me, I can tell you're very serious about pizza," he murmured.

"No, I meant about the relationship thing," I said, voice raspy. "I'm not ready. Not in any kind of way. Nor are my kids ready for a man in their life whose connected to their mother. Or anyone knowing about this." I waved my hand up and down our naked bodies.

"So you want this to be a one-time thing?" he asked, voice even and not letting me go.

My entire body reacted at the mere thought. It was an unexpectedly dramatic response. I shouldn't have felt such a deep-seated surge of panic about that. Shouldn't feel this attached to this man and all the pain and pleasure he gave me. The escape he'd given me.

"No!" I exclaimed, louder than I should've, a lot of that deep-seated panic saturating my voice.

He moved me so my eyes were glued to his. There was too much amusement there. "So you need this to be secret sex?"

I didn't like the way he said that at all. That he was teasing me about this. "I'm saying that I do not want anyone to know about this, especially anyone in the club." My tone was cold.

Something moved on his face now, the twinkle in his eye receding. "Babe, know that you don't know much about me. But know that I'm not the kind of fuckin' man to take you to bed without knowing this ship is bein' steered by you. I'm following your lead. I want your pussy because it's sweet. Your body because it's hot and hungry and makes my dick sing. Straight up like spending time with you 'cause you're unlike anyone I've ever known. You've got no real proof that I'm a good guy. But I'm telling you right now, it's an insult to even suggest I'd go back to the club and talk about this. Disrespect you in that way. That's not the kind of man I am. No matter what happens with this, you call the shots. Not gonna push you for more 'cause I know that you gave me everything you could just now. And I'm more than fucking happy with that."

I was taken aback by all of that. The passion in which he spoke. It hit me in different places throughout my body. Not just between my legs.

It was too intense. *He* was too intense.

"Okay," I said, moving. His hands tightened around my body for a second, as if he was considering not letting me move from his grasp, but then he slackened and let me go.

Despite what we'd just done, three times, I was uncomfortable with my nakedness. There was something more intimate about moving around our bedroom—my bedroom, everything that was ours was now only mine—not wearing a thing.

I'd had two children. My body hadn't 'bounced back' without effort. I was young when I had Jack. That had been easier. I'd had more energy. Exercised. Ate well, and then didn't have time to eat because I was too busy using all my energy on another human. Lily came when I was older. Bouncing back from her birth took longer. I'd been self-conscious about the fact that it took me longer to return to how I'd looked before, or at least as close as was humanly possible, after having two humans. Pregnancy, birth, motherhood... all that altered a woman's body in unchangeable ways.

Or only in ways that could only be changed with a scalpel.

Not that I judged any mother who went that route. I'd been tempted, looking at myself in the mirror, seeing the evidence of my children like a roadmap of everything we'd gone through. I wouldn't give them up for anything. They were my world. Sometimes, though, selfish vanity whispered.

But I'd had a husband who had worshipped me. Who'd made it very clear he loved the evidence showing I'd carried his children. Who'd left no room for me to be insecure.

And even with what had happened in our darkest of days, I'd never worried about the young club girls with tight asses and fake tits. What he did back then was not about the woman. Was not about sex or desire.

It was about Ranger's demons. His fears. His scars. In so many ways, he was my perfect man. Perfect husband. But humans couldn't be perfect. We were too prone to damage. To self-sabotage. We wore the traumas of the world on our souls. Ranger was damaged in irreversible ways. So I'd had to love the parts of him he hated. Had to forgive the actions that were driven by those parts.

It was hard. It hurt. But we overcame it. We'd had a marriage that I was proud of. A love we worked at. I'd never thought I'd be walking around in our bedroom with my naked body on show for a man who wasn't him.

It made me sick.

What I'd done.

That my husband was no longer the last man to see me naked. To touch me. Fuck me.

I was disgusted with myself as I shrugged on my robe, tying it so tight it hurt. Kace must've felt the energy in the room move, because he got up and dressed quietly. I didn't look at him, just listened to the rustle of his clothes as he put them on. I held my breath so I didn't have to smell his scent, the smell of sex that coated the room.

The silence between us was awkward now. It was harsh. I'd never experienced anything like this. The weirdness that came after sex with someone who was little more than a stranger. Even when Ranger and I had been separated, I'd only had sex with one other man. A boyfriend I'd had for six months before doing that. He'd been kind, gentle and just a nice guy. Nothing more than that. He was nonthreatening because I'd only ever thought of him as a nice guy.

Kace was threatening.

I'd already known that.

I prayed for him to leave without a word. To not try to salvage this moment with words that would only make it more awkward.

His boots thumped on the floor, but the door didn't open. My hair moved from my neck, lips settling over my skin. My body reacted immediately, despite everything swirling in my head. I relaxed a little, sinking back against him.

"Until next time, baby," he murmured. His lips hovered for a moment longer then my hair fell back in place. Boots thumped against the floor, the door opened and closed. I stayed standing where I was for a long time. No tears. No breakdowns. I just stood there. I snapped into action First, I took a shower. Then I stripped the sheets from the bed, took the blanket from the floor and put them in the wash.

Got ready for my kids to come home. Tried to pretend it never happened.

But I dreamed of him that night.

It was the first night in over a year I hadn't dreamed of my husband.

Chapter 11

Three Weeks Later

"I need to go," I groaned, trying to pull myself out of bed.

Strong arms held onto me, yanking me back into bed.

He smelled of leather and sex.

"You need to *come...*" he murmured, his hand moving down my stomach.

My eyes rolled to the back of my head at the thought of yet another orgasm. I was like a teenager. We both were.

Sex was working to be the ultimate distraction. Addiction. We stole moments whenever and wherever we could. Usually at my place when the kids were at school. Or when they were asleep. His place on rare occasions. I didn't like it there, though. Not because it was messy. Not because it was strange, foreign. Because it made it real that I was with another man. A man who had a home that was sparsely decorated but with comfortable, good quality furniture. A man who kept his bathroom clean. Who made his bed every morning. Didn't have a sink full of dishes. Liked scented candles.

I didn't want to learn any of this new stuff about Kace. Didn't want what we were doing to be more intimate than it was. But his place was safer, not as many people could drop by. I could scream as loud as I wanted. Kace liked to make me scream.

Once, when I'd had too many cocktails at the latest Sons' party, we'd slipped into a room in the back.

Yes, I was desperate. Never full of him. And when were together, I felt distracted by pain and pleasure, by the fact that he physically demanded everything from me.

But then came the guilt. Shame. The self-hatred and promises made that I was never going to do it again.

Yet here I was, not exactly fighting him when he yanked me back into the bed.

"I have to go home to change then pick the kids up from school," I said, voice breathy as Kace moved his hand downward with frustrating slowness.

"You don't need to change clothes," he murmured, his mouth running along my neck. "I have it on good authority that you look hot as fuck in those clothes."

I sucked in an uneven breath as Kace trailed his hand across instead of downward, brushing over the small scar from my C-section.

"Those are sex clothes," I argued, though my voice was weak with submission. "I can't wear sex clothes to pick up my children."

His hand paused, and I clenched my teeth in frustration. "Sex clothes?" he repeated. "I distinctly remember ripping those clothes off you *before* I fucked you."

My body shivered at the memory. I distinctly remembered that too.

"Yes, but they are sex clothes by association," I explained. "Plus, I smell of sex. I have sex hair. I have friends who are also going to be picking up their children from school who are like fucking hawks at spotting sex hair. I don't need to answer questions about that. So I need to go."

Although I was supposed to be sounding firm and strong, I barely convinced myself.

Kace's hand moved again. It snaked down. All the way down. His fingers moved expertly, maddeningly coaxing an orgasm from me within minutes.

Then they stopped.

I let out a mewl of protest, hating the sound, hating myself for making it.

"You need to go," he reminded me, pushing me gently up to my feet.

I stood on shaky knees, watching him move his fingers up to his mouth, tasting me while maintaining eye contact.

My eyes didn't move from him, reveling in him tasting me like that.

The corner of his mouth turned up in amusement, his eyes still dark with desire.

"Don't you gotta go, sweetheart?" he asked blandly, not hiding the fact he was checking out my naked body.

I narrowed my eyes at him, a small tickle of irritation helpful in stopping me from forgetting about everything and jumping right back into bed with Kace.

"Yes, I do have to go," I snapped, snatching my panties, shoving them on, then going for my bra. "And this is the last time we're doing this," I added while putting on my jeans.

Kace moved so he was sitting up in bed, not bothering to use a sheet to cover himself. He was proud of his body. His nakedness. As he should've been. His body was nothing short of perfection. Which would've intimidated the fuck out of me if he hadn't constantly showed me how much he worshipped my non-perfect, birthed two children and rapidly approaching forty body.

"Sure thing, babe," he said easily, watching me dress.

He wasn't bothered by me trying to break off... whatever the fuck this was. Not since I said this almost every time. Then, usually less than a few days later, I'd make a fool of myself by ending up naked with Kace again.

"I mean it this time," I declared, pulling my shirt over my head. "This... this isn't good. I shouldn't be doing this."

Kace no longer looked amused. He moved from the bed to stand in front of me, hands firm on my hips. "Lizzie, fuck it hurts to see you like this. Every damn time. Every damn moment I'm not inside you." There was frustration in his voice. Fury.

"What are you talking about?"

"I'm talking about watching you doubt everything you do. Like you're failing some impossible test you've set for yourself. Like somehow you can only live with yourself if you're constantly in pain. Constantly punishing yourself for every single decision you make. Everything you want. I've been keepin' my mouth shut because I know this is something you gotta work through. Even though it's fuckin' torture. But I can't anymore. So I'm not going to let you say this shit out loud. I can't control what you think. Maybe, in time, I'll be able to help change that. Maybe not. But however long I'm fuckin' you, however long I'm in your life, secret or not, it's my mission to make you stop punishing yourself for any second of happiness or pleasure."

His words hit true.

Not just the words but the feeling behind him.

He had feelings. For me. Which was a problem. A big fucking problem. He was too young. This was too soon. He was in the club.

And worse than that, I was getting feelings for him too.

Which was why I walked out of the room without saying another word, without looking him in the eye.

━━━

I WENT through the motions of the afternoon. Picked up the kids. Took them out for ice cream which we ate on the beach.

Took them home. Made them shower off the sand, do their homework and then get ready to go for our weekly dinner at Evie's.

Sometimes it was a huge dinner with everyone from the Sons coming. A dinner that usually turned into a party. Other times it was a mishmash of whoever could arrive. But once a month, it was just us. The two Sons of Templar widows. It sounded pathetic, but with Evie involved, it definitely wasn't pathetic.

The routine consisted of us ordering in whatever we wanted, whatever the kids wanted, with wine or whisky, depending on the mood. It was a night for talking about everything, while usually skirting the subject of our dead husbands.

Evie had taken Steg's death in her typical stride. On the surface, at least. I knew she was suffering. Bleeding. Trying to make sense of a life without the man she'd been next to for decades.

As much as I hated any activities that were born out of my husband's death, I actually looked forward to dinner with Evie. Being around her, I didn't feel like such a broken, weird shell of a person.

"You look different," Evie stated the second she let me through the door, the kids already running toward the 'toy room' Evie had set up for the various Sons of Templar children who visited on a daily basis. Despite being the most unlikely of grandmothers, she sure knew how to entertain.

Shit.

I knew I should've made some excuse to miss this week. The bitch was far too perceptive for her own good. But I'd reasoned that canceling our plans would've only made her more suspicious.

"I got my hair done," I lied, walking into her home.

It was warm. An interesting description, especially when looking at Evie. There were a lot of things that came to mind looking at the biker queen, but warm was nowhere on the list.

For a start, it was huge. There were enough guest bedrooms for the many families that had needed them over the years during lockdowns, wars, weddings funerals.

There were three different living rooms, one with a huge L-shaped sofa in a deep brown. Sitting on that couch was like laying on a cloud. There were pillows. Throws. Candles. Books on the coffee table. A huge TV. Pretty much everything inviting you to stay awhile. Her and Steg had always had two cats, Boris and Nigel who were most likely hanging out with the kids. The two kids who'd named them the oddest cat names in the world.

Photos decorated almost every surface. The Sons of Templar throughout the years. Her and Steg. Wedding photos. Baby photos.

Memories of the legacy she was a part of. The life she'd lived.

I walked into her huge kitchen, where I'd helped cook many Thanksgiving and Christmas dinners, snatching two whisky glasses from a cupboard filled with various types of alcoholic drinkware.

Evie raised her brow at my choice. "You did not just get your hair done," she asserted, grabbing a bottle of whisky from the wet bar off the kitchen.

"Mia treated me to a facial. They just got a new esthetician; she wanted me to try her out."

Not a lie. Though I was pretty sure Mia was lying about the new esthetician in order to trick me into getting some pampering.

I'd long stopped fighting against what I'd thought was pity charity at first but had now realized was just my friends trying to help me in any way they could.

Plus, I wasn't about to turn down a free facial. I was a single mother with a broken heart and a secret sex relationship. I needed a facial. And maybe a lobotomy.

"Your skin looks great, honey, but it's got nothin' to do with a facial," Evie recounted, pouring us each a generous amount of whisky.

I was planning on driving home, so I made a mental note to only drink this one glass, eat a lot of carbs and stick to water for the rest of the night.

There had been a handful of times, in the beginning, when we'd stayed the night because I'd gotten too drunk to drive my children home. Those days needed to be over.

I glanced to the hall, the sounds of my children giggling carrying. The happiness hit my throat.

"We need to go outside," I said to Evie.

She nodded, leading me out the sliding doors that looked out onto their swimming pool, hot tub and barbeque area. There was wicker seating peppered around the property. Flowers everywhere.

It was an oasis that had only grown more beautiful following Steg's death. Evie was not a woman to disappear into a hole of grief and whisky. No, she was a woman of purpose. She gardened. She renovated the kitchen. She organized club rides. I envied her.

"You've been screwing someone," Evie stated matter-offactly the second my ass hit the chair.

I looked to her with narrowed eyes.

"Don't look so shocked. I know what a well fucked woman looks like," she explained, lighting up a cigarette. She'd smoked continuously since I met her, yet the only thing she had to show for it was her husky voice and the faint smell of smoke that mingled with her perfume.

She'd aged with only a few wrinkles that only managed to make her more harshly beautiful. I worried that one day this vice would steal her from us too early. But if there was anyone who seemed too strong and stubborn for death, it was Evie.

Or maybe that was my brain trying to protect me because there was no way in hell I'd be able to manage if something else happened to someone I loved.

I could lie to her.

Rather, I could *try* to lie to her, but there was no way she'd believe me. Or let me get away with it. Plus, I respected her too much to lie to her. Beyond that, I needed someone to talk to about this. Someone who wouldn't judge me. At least not as harshly as I was judging myself.

"Fine, I'm definitely well fucked," I admitted.

She grinned. "I'd say."

I looked at her face, looking for traces of anything to communicate that she thought it was too soon. That I was some kind of whore. Or a bad mother. Not that that was Evie's style. Even if she was having thoughts like that, she wasn't ever going to show that on her face. Being an Old Lady in the Sons of Templar for as long as she had had taught her a lot of things, including the art of having a poker face.

"He's in the Sons," I admitted.

"All the better," Evie replied.

I furrowed my brows, looking to her. "Isn't that a little... I don't know, incestuous or somehow morally wrong? I should be with someone different." I paused, trying to think of someone who would be more sensible to be fucking than a man in my dead husband's MC. "An accountant," I said finally.

Evie stared at me and cackled. "An accountant?" she repeated, still laughing. "Oh, baby, there is no way you'd ever be satisfied with an accountant. With some civilian with a 401k and a day job. We don't work like that. Just because you didn't patch in doesn't mean you're no less of an outlaw. For better or for worse, just like there's no way out for the men wearing ink and leather, there's no way out for you either." She sucked on her cigarette. "There's no way out for any of us."

I pursed my lips. "Apart from death."

She glanced at me then back out to her yard. "Yeah, apart from death."

"And *you're* going to move on to another member?" I questioned, trying to take the focus away from me.

She laughed in that throaty way that communicated she'd been a smoker for longer than I'd been alive. "No, honey. I'm not going to do that. I had a whole lifetime with Steg. As an Old Lady. I'll always be her. I'll always be his. But I get away with sayin' shit like that because I'm old enough that I don't have much of a life to squeeze that in to the few years I've got left."

I scowled at her as the bottom fell out of my stomach. "You've got a lot more than a few years. I'm not letting you die too."

She smiled. "I'm not about to leave the party early, that's not what I'm sayin'. I'm also not sayin' that I'm not gonna get laid."

I smiled back, thinking of everything that had happened these past years. When I was a fifteen-year-old girl, trying to find sleep after finishing a book at two in the morning, I'd write my own versions of my life. Imagining wild things that would happen to me. Wild adventures I'd take with some man who would sweep me off my feet. We'd have struggles because all the best couples did, but we'd also have a story for the ages. It would change me.

All of that happened with Ranger. And not just the things I'd imagined for myself. In so many other good ways.

And then one of the worst.

"I wanted to die," I confessed, looking back at her.

I hadn't talked to anyone about this. Hadn't spilled my ugly grief at anyone's table. Even though any one of my friends would've taken it. Would've wanted to hear it. To help. Maybe because I was trying to forget. Or because I just hadn't wanted to say it out loud.

"Not at first," I continued. "There was too much to be done. The funeral. Telling the kids. All that practical stuff. It sounds insane, but I was distracted enough to forget about what this was going to do to me. But that didn't last long. When life started to get back to normal, the grief hit hard. I didn't let it show on the outside. That's the craziest thing. There was so much normal. The kids went back to school. I had to get them up every morning, make them breakfast, pack them lunch, drive them. I still had to pay the bills, clean the bathrooms, cook dinner. Shower. I had to do all that stuff and then it suddenly became so starkly apparent and so inescapable that Ranger wasn't a part of my normal anymore, I wanted to die. With every part of me I wanted to."

I paused, sitting in companionable silence for a beat. "The parts of me that belonged solely to Ranger wanted me to give up. But I couldn't, of course. Because there are other parts to me. I'm a mother. It is my responsibility to stay alive for my children. It's my duty. So no matter how much I wanted to, I didn't die. I lingered in limbo for a while, of course. But there was a time limit on that. So I had no choice but to live. For them and them only at first. Then, a long time later and much, much slower, for myself." I drained my drink. "Though I don't think I'm fully there yet."

Evie stared at me for a while, really thinking about my words, listening in that way of hers.

"I'm too strong and too stubborn to forfeit my life because my Old Man is in the ground, but I get wanting to die. Thing is, you did die. Parts of you, at least. Parts that are never going to come back to life. Parts that lie in the coffin with Ranger. But you're being reborn. In some ways. Not 'cause of any man you're fucking, though, that surely helps you recognize that life is worth living and worth living well." She sighed. "We've all got seasons of our lives. Your winter was brutal, honey. Not gonna lie. But looks like spring is here. Happy to see you start to bloom, baby."

I blinked back the tears at her words, because you didn't cry drinking whisky with Evie. You ovaried up.

I did that by getting up to pour us another whisky and informing the kids we were having a sleepover.

I suspected Evie might need that too.

Even if she never said it.

Us widows had to stick together.

Chapter 12

I knew from the moment I woke up it was going to be a terrible day. Mostly because I woke up to a tightening in my head and an uneasiness in my stomach. The telltale signs of a migraine. They'd started when I was seventeen.

"Headache episodes", my mother had called them. As if they were something I chose whenever I felt like a leisurely escape from the world when in actuality, it was an agonizing period of time where I had to lay perfectly still in the dark because even breathing too deep was like a rusty knife being inserted into my skull, piercing my brain.

Over the counter painkillers were like a rowboat in a tsunami. Same with most of the stronger medication doctors prescribed.

It only got worse during pregnancy. Luckily, with Jack, it only happened a couple of times. Though those were the worst ones that lasted two days at least and had me recovering for a week. Lily was even rougher. It was only after the morning sickness subsided that the migraines began. It was hard on Ranger seeing me in that much pain, not being able to do anything about it.

Though it wasn't exactly a picnic for me either.

After Lily was born, they subsided some. Hormones settling, whatever. I got them once yearly, on a good year. And I always had Ranger to put me to bed, check on me, take care of our children.

Now it was just me. There was no one else to make my kids breakfast, get them to school, pick them up again. Sure, I could call on Olive. My mom. Gwen. Amy. Laura May. Lily. Or the long list of women and men who would happily take over. Take care of my kids for me.

But that had happened one too many times already. Plus, it was only painful now. Excruciating was around the corner. There was still time. I had to get used to the pain, get used to doing everything despite it.

I got up. Took four Advil. Made the strongest cup of coffee I could. Caffeine technically made migraines worse, or that's what every patronizing doctor tried to tell me. But for me, it was the only thing that chased away the worst of it. For a time, at least.

One cup got me strong enough to get the kids up. Then showered. Dressed. Breakfast consisted of the sugary cereal I kept for special mornings, weekends, sleep-ins and middle of the night cravings.

Jack noticed something was wrong straight away. His eyes caught the strained way I was moving, every step launching pain upward to my skull. The way I didn't look at the overhead light that seemed to be doing its bests to burn my retinas.

A small hand took the milk from me as I attempted to pour milk into bowls.

"I got it, Mom," Jack said gently, low, as if he somehow knew that any kind of noise made my eardrums bleed.

I should've fought him on it, but I didn't have the strength.

So I let my son finish breakfast for him and his sister. Then I thanked myself for being organized enough to have prepared both of their lunches the night before. As it was, getting them packed and into their bags each morning was a mission in itself.

"Mom, you need to go back to bed," Jack said.

I'd sat on a bar stool, head in my hands to close my eyes for just a moment. Now that I opened them, the table was cleared, and Jack was standing in front of me, Lily beside him, her large backpack dwarfing her small frame.

Shit.

"I need to take you to school," I argued.

Jack raised his brow in a very adult kind of way much like his father had done to me many times when I'd tried to argue about something that even I knew was bullshit.

My heart hurt. Screamed, rivaling the pain in my skull.

"I'll call someone," he countered. "Grandma Olive can take us. Or Mrs. Gwen or Grandma Evie. Just not you. You need bed." He said this firmly. In a tone that brokered no argument, again, much like his father.

I sighed, holding back the tears I really, *really* didn't want to shed in front of my children. The ones who were somehow stronger than their mother. Smarter too. As I was about to surrender my phone to my boy's outstretched hand, a knock sounded at the door, making me flinch.

Jack glanced toward the door with his father's face on. "I'll get it."

"No!" My own shout caused me so much pain I almost threw up my four Advil and two cups of coffee all over the carpet. "No, honey," I repeated, softer now, which took quite a bit of effort. "I'm going to answer the door, okay?"

Though Amber was safe and the club was not in any kind of danger anymore, my instincts wouldn't let my son answer the door, no matter how grown up he was acting.

Every step was agony. My vision blurry, the floor was tilting and my brain felt like it was growing while my skull was shrinking.

The sunlight assaulted me when I opened the door, causing me to flinch back on reflex. The person standing in front of me was nothing more than a large, dark, blur.

"What the fuck?"

The voice was familiar. Worried. And much, much too fucking loud.

I was doing my best to get it together so I could answer, but a small person beside me was quicker.

"Mom has a migraine," Jack explained. "She gets them sometimes. Dad used to put her to bed, and we would leave her in the dark until she got better. But..." he trailed off.

My heart hurt once more. No longer did the pain there rival that in my head, it superseded it.

But he was dead now, that's what Jack was going to say. His father was dead, and he wasn't quite sure what to do. All he knew was that he needed to take care of me.

"Okay, I'll get your mom to bed. Make sure she's got everything she needs, then I'll get you to school. Sound rockin'?" It was Kace who spoke.

I was about to argue with him, but he moved past me. My vision was better now since Kace had shut the door before he'd finished speaking. I didn't process how it happened, but suddenly, he was right beside me, his arms around me.

"Can you walk?" he murmured, speaking as softly as possible.

"Yes," I snapped, making the tone loud and grating, trying to sound much stronger than I was.

It didn't work because I swayed as I said it, and Kace's hands tightened to steady me.

"Why don't you go and make sure your sister is ready to go, and I'll get your mom into bed?" Kace asked.

Jack frowned, folding his arms. "I can help her," he argued.

I smiled at my son, at him not being ready to hand over responsibility to someone else. "Sweetie, it'd be so much help if you went to get your sister ready," I pleaded gently.

Jack looked to me, then Kace, then back to me again. He nodded once and walked away.

Kace wasted no time in piling me into his arms as soon as my son's back was turned. The movement was quick and gentle, but I still couldn't hold in my whimper.

"I know, baby," he murmured.

My teeth sank into my lip, drawing blood during the rest of the short journey. Kace moved quickly, depositing me into bed with the utmost care. Then he moved to close the curtains, his footsteps heading to the bathroom followed by the water running. I kept my eyes firmly shut and did my best not to move.

His footsteps came back then something cold and soft settled over my eyes.

"You got any pills, drugs?" Kace asked softly, rubbing my hair.

"Don't work," I murmured. "Just have to ride it out."

"Fuck," he hissed.

"I'll be okay," I whispered. "Just need dark. Sleep. Call Olive. She'll take care of the kids."

"I'll take them," he said.

Fuck. I couldn't think around all this pain. I needed cool darkness. Quiet. But I also couldn't leave my kids in the hands of the man I'd been fucking.

"No, I—"

Hands on my face silenced me. A gentle, barely there touch. His palms were cool and felt almost nice against all of the agony.

"Lizzie, this is not a debate," he murmured. "You're not in any kind of state to argue. Beyond that, arguing is takin' up too much energy. You're in pain. You need to sleep. Need to trust that I'm gonna take care of your kids."

Trust.

He wanted me to trust him.

With everything I had left in this world.

"Okay," I whispered, submitting everything to this man I had promised myself I'd never truly surrender to.

His lips touched mine. "Sleep."

───

"HOW YOU FEELIN', babe?"

The words were spoken softly, gently, as close to a whisper as the husky voice was capable of.

Despite this, I sat upright in bed quickly, yanking the covers up. I'd been awake to hear the door opening and closing, but for some reason, I hadn't computed the silent way in which it was done. I'd just assumed it was one of my children, coming to jump into bed with me. Although it was only really Lily who did that these days. Although he still participated in our movie nights that consisted of all the snacks they weren't usually allowed and more than one fight over which movie would be playing for the night, Jack was getting much too old to snuggle with his mother.

But it wasn't my son or daughter in my room this morning, it was Kace. Carrying a cup of coffee and a plate of what looked like dry toast.

Light was barely peeking through the blinds in my bedroom, which meant he'd either arrived here before dawn or he had slept here.

Although that scared me, I really hoped he had slept here

because my memory of yesterday was spotty at best. There had been changes in the cool compress on my head. Someone feeding me water—someone who must've been Kace upon reflection—small, cool hands in my palm, kisses on my cheek, likely Lily.

But there was no memory of me picking them up from school, fixing them afternoon snacks, helping them with their homework or making them dinner. Of course there weren't memories of that. Because I hadn't done any of that.

"The kids?" I asked Kace, ignoring his question. I felt like shit. But like a human, at least. Not a giant ball of pressure, scared to move an inch.

I'd probably be feeling the effects of this migraine for a few days at the very least, though, more likely a full week due to the severity.

"Fine," he replied, sitting on the bed and pushing the hair from my face. His brow was knitted in worry. I didn't like it. There was a tenderness to it.

"They're worried about their mother, of course, but seem to trust me to take care of them. Though Jack has been watching me like a hawk," he continued. "I think he was waiting for me to slip up in any kind of way." He chuckled. "So I did my best to make sure I didn't. Even cooked them enchiladas. They're famous. With everyone I've ever made them for, at least. And I stuffed a bunch of veggies in them."

I tried to imagine Kace in my kitchen, cooking for my kids. Him driving in the car with them, asking them about their day. A part of me was angry that I'd missed it. I was curious about what Kace looked like in that setting. In my setting.

Then I worried about what they might've thought, having a strange man suddenly taking up duties only their father had done previously.

"Now you didn't answer my question," Kace probed gently.

Instead of replying, I sat up in bed, hiding my slight wince as I did so, reaching for the coffee that would give me the wits I needed to navigate this conversation.

It was hot, perfect, just the way I liked it. Black. Two sugars. I couldn't remember making coffee with Kace, so it made no sense that he knew how I took it, yet he did.

"You need to eat something," he suggested. "Could only get water into you yesterday."

More worry in his voice.

I forced my walls up, the ones that came down with the vision of him eating dinner with my children.

"I know what I need," I said, voice cold. "Thank you, for taking care of me yesterday, for taking care of the kids. I appreciate it. But I can take it from here."

Kace wanted to argue. I could see that, clear as day, even though it was only early morning. He wanted to take care of me. Didn't like to see me in pain and wanted to shoulder responsibilities that weren't his.

But he didn't do any of those things. Instead, he brushed the back of his fingers against my jaw and stood up. "Okay, baby. You win," he said. "But soon, you're gonna get tired of holding that hand up, the one you're usin' to push me away. You're gonna use it to hold on, to pull me in. I'll wait."

Then he left.

———

THE JOB SEARCH wasn't going well.

To be fair, I wasn't exactly putting my whole self into it. I wasn't applying for the positions at the local bank or working as an admin for an accounting firm one town over. Mostly because I feared they'd laugh at my resume and not give me an interview. And on the off chance they did, I'd be terrible, working in positions like those.

Although I hadn't put on a cut, patched into the Sons, I had the same views as they did. I'd always had a little rebel in me, a little outlaw, a desire to stretch outside of the norm. Ranger and the Sons had nurtured that. The thought of having to cram myself into society after living this way for so long made me feel ill. Tempted me to either get creative on how to earn or swallow my pride and talk to Cade about working at one of the Son's more legitimate businesses.

The problem was, my pride was the side of the state of Texas, and it would take me far too long to cut it into small enough pieces. I didn't want to disappoint Ranger, to show that I wasn't strong enough to look after myself and our children on my own.

Even though I knew he would've hated the thought of me working in some office, answering to someone else. That would've made him furious.

But he wasn't here, so it didn't really matter what he thought, did it?

I needed to escape the house. The feelings that came with it. The stress when I thought of how we needed a new fridge or that Jack would need a computer for school soon.

The kids were at Olive's place again; they went almost every week. She made them dinner, they ate ice cream on the beach and sometimes painted the sunset. Other times, they'd make pottery with her in her garage turned studio. They'd come back with stains on their shirts and smiles in their hearts, which gave me hope for them. That they had this ability to utterly enjoy life even without their father. And Olive needed it. Time with her grandchildren so she could see her son wasn't truly gone.

I also needed time with her. Usually, I needed time with

Olive to remind me that I still had different parts of Ranger too. That I still had her.

But today I'd needed a break. Mostly because I couldn't look her in the eye while I was screwing someone else and not grieving over her son.

She had been more than understanding and supportive of me going to Gwen's for the evening. Had even offered to have the kids for the night.

"You need this," she'd urged, reaching out to squeeze my hand.

I almost broke down right there, because of her kindness, love and support. But I'd managed. I was getting good at lying now.

Ryan and Alex had just left Gwen's place. They'd been her for the past week, and we'd already had a large and lively dinner with everyone. They had announced that they were in the process of adopting a child, which meant celebrations all around.

It was hard for me to do that. Celebrate people having good in their lives. Despite the fact they were kind people who deserved all of that kind of stuff. I didn't want to take anything away from them, I just didn't want to be part of it. I didn't need to see it. But that wasn't really going to work unless I shut myself away from the world. People I loved and cared about were going to have milestones, parties, celebrations. I needed to learn how to be okay with that.

Alcohol helped.

Which was what Gwen greeted me with at the door with. Cosmos. Apparently, Cade had made them. I gave him a raised brow while walking past him in the kitchen.

"Not a fuckin' word," he scowled.

I only grinned. Though I didn't really feel like doing it. It was all part of the act.

"Cade is playing bartender and babysitter tonight," Gwen explained, ushering me outside onto her patio. "Though babysitting your own kids is literally just called parenting. Which is what I've told him about one thousand times. He'll still call it babysitting one thousand and one just to piss me off."

"Of course he will," I agreed, sitting down and taking a sip of my drink. It was fabulous, and I made a mental note to somehow leak the information that Cade made a better Cosmo than any of the women in our group.

"Because he loves you. Men who love you, especially these kind of men, take great delight in pissing you off since they like fire in their women," I continued. "And also because such a concept is laughable. He loves those kids more than life."

Gwen's eyes flickered inside with a loving look of contentment I used to have. "He really does." Something darker crossed over her beautiful features, probably the memory of how close she'd come to losing him.

She straightened, refocusing on me. "How are you?" she asked.

She didn't ask it in the way people did when all they wanted was a generic answer that would make them seem nice for asking, not wanting to do any emotional legwork.

No, Gwen asked liked she really wanted to know. Like she needed me to answer honestly. Like I was safe to do that.

I don't know why I answered with the truth. Lying had become so easy. Maybe that was why; maybe I was scared of what would happen if I kept lying to my closest friends. My family.

"I've been sleeping with Kace."

Gwen blinked, her face perfectly blank, cocktail pausing halfway to her mouth. "What?"

It was too late now. I took a huge gulp of my own drink before pressing on. "For a couple of months now. It's just sex."

Just sex that invaded my every waking moment. That stained my body like a sunburn that wouldn't go away. Sex that had made me come to want him in my bed every damn night. That made me let him stay longer and longer those nights.

"Good sex, by that dreamy look on your face," Gwen pointed out. "I knew there was something different about you. I thought you were just trying a new moisturizer that was really working for you."

I raised my brow at her. "Come on."

"No, it's true. You're like glowing or something."

I stared at her. "I'm not fucking pregnant if that's what you're trying to imply.

She laughed. "No, I'm not trying to imply that at all. Plus, for me, pregnancy didn't give me any kind of glow apart from the thin sheen of sweet on my face from all the energy I expended throwing up the first three months."

I winced at the memory. Like Gwen, my early days of pregnancy were miserable. Morning sickness that lasted all day. Heartburn. Headaches. It was only toward the end of the second trimester that I resembled a human again.

"Apparently, good sex can create a whole other glow that even the most expensive of skincare products cannot replicate," Gwen said, sipping her drink.

I didn't respond to her because I couldn't exactly dispute it. She was right. Everyone had noticed something different about me. Lily's teacher. Olive. Lacey at the coffee shop.

It didn't make sense, and it certainly didn't make me feel better about what I was doing. I was lying to everything, screwing another man while my children slept, and hating myself for it. Yet it was somehow making my hair shinier and my skin brighter.

"I haven't spent much time with Kace, but Cade seems to

like him. Likes that he's got a really good, new, legit income stream. Plus, he's hot as balls."

"Who's hot as balls?" Cade asked, walking onto the patio with a jug of cosmos. I had to bite my lip in order not to giggle at the big, bad, menacing biker carrying a pitcher of cocktails he'd made for his wife.

Gwen smiled sweetly at the man in question as he set the pitcher down. "No one important. You're the hottest one out of the entire lot. No competition."

Cade's stare was hard and the littlest bit scary, even though I knew how much he adored Gwen and the fact that he'd cut his own hands off before harm came to her or any woman.

The corner of Cade's mouth twitched in what was widely known as his version of a smile. "Uh huh," he murmured, leaning his head down to kiss his wife's lips. The kiss was quick, casual but intimate. Showing the heat that had never fizzled between them.

"Okay, go now, hubby. We've got girl stuff to talk about," Gwen ordered, a slight blush to her cheeks.

I drained my drink if only to salve some of the burn that I felt watching my friend and her husband like that. The jealousy I felt that I didn't have that. That my version of that was gone. My chest reopened up into one gaping, festering wound as it did every now and then.

"Now he's gone you need to tell me more," Gwen demanded, smiling, unaware of what I was feeling. Which was exactly what I wanted. There was nothing I needed less than for my friends to know I was a massive, fucked up mess.

"I just told you," I said as she poured me another drink, one that was sorely needed.

"How did it happen?" Gwen asked.

"How does anything happen?" I shrugged. "You're right,

he's hot as balls. He doesn't know me. It's nice, you know? Having someone who doesn't know to pity me too much."

Gwen's face fell, and she reached across the table to grasp my hand. "Honey, we do not pity you."

I smiled sadly at her. Of course they did. They hadn't know they were doing it. And if they had known how to stop it, they would.

"I know that," I lied. "But it's just... nice with Kace." I swallowed. "Not that nice is exactly the word I'd use," I muttered. It's easy.

"This is perfect!" Gwen exclaimed, clapping her hands.

I blinked at her. There were many ways I'd expected Gwen to possibly describe my situation, but I'd never thought perfect might be one.

"I was thinking it's more irresponsible, selfish, reckless and vaguely skanky," I replied, draining my drink.

Gwen's expression softened as she poured me more to drink before reaching over to grasp my hand. "I don't think you or what you're doing are any of those things. In fact, if anyone that has ever met you was asked to come up with ten words to describe you, none of those would even factor in. I know as women, especially as mothers, our first instinct when we're doing something purely for ourselves is to feel guilt. Men don't feel it because they're hardwired to be selfish. To see what they want, go out and get it without letting anything get in their way. My husband is an example of that. Though I will say, he definitely isn't selfish inside or outside of the bedroom." She grinned wickedly. "And, based on that glow you have going, I bet Kace is the same way."

Heat crept up my neck at the mere mention of Kace's bedroom skills. I shifted in my chair ever so slightly, the motion slightly uncomfortable in the best way.

"You seriously think this is a good thing?" I asked.

"It's a *great* thing. You need to do more things for yourself. Just don't put any pressure on yourself to make it into something. Or to make it into nothing. It's going to be what it's going to be. If we've learned anything from all of these years, it's that we don't have much control over what will happen when it comes to relationships."

"Relationships?" I repeated. "No, I'm not going to have any kind of relationship. This is just sex. I'm not going to have any kind of relationship in the near future."

"You're still so young, sweetheart. You can still have another life. Another chapter. It wouldn't take anything away from what you had with Ranger."

I knew all of this. In theory. I knew that it was not logical or healthy to suspend myself in perpetual mourning or self-pity. To turn myself into the ever-enduring widow, permanently shutting out all forms of happiness. Though it was so very tempting to do just that. I would've done it already had it not been for the kids. If there weren't two humans relying on me to help them navigate the world. Little humans who took their cues from me, who would be, at least in part, molded from my decisions. From the way I handled this. And if I did it in the way that my heart and soul desired, it would ruin their future relationships. Their views on the world. It would alter them in ways I couldn't repair.

So I wouldn't give in to my darker impulses. My ugly desires. I would continue on.

Or do my very best at pretending that's what I was doing.

Chapter 13

I had decided to take Gwen's advice to heart.

Kind of.

I wasn't going to push myself to make whatever Kace and I had into something. We had sex. Amazing sex. Sex that dark parts of me craved. Something I needed after the sun set on all my other identities and responsibilities. But he still needed to be gone when the sun rose. I was definitely not ready to turn this into anything more.

But I was going to explore my future. Maybe I wanted to rebel against what Evie had told me, about not having a choice in my future.

I was going on a date.

One with someone who didn't wear a cut, didn't carry a gun, didn't drive a Harley. No, Edmond owned the one and only law firm in town. They did not represent the Sons of Templar; the Sons kept a very expensive LA law firm on retainer because if they were being accused of anything, they were already in deep shit. They were obviously good since no one had been prosecuted or even arrested in years.

Edmond had purchased the firm a few years ago, so he was reasonably new to town. Despite that, I was sure he was acquainted with the Sons of Templar, or at least their reputation.

We'd bumped into each other a few times over the past few months, after he'd read me Ranger's will. Yeah, I hadn't thought my husband was sensible enough to have written a will, but then again, it made sense. He'd always been was well aware that his lifestyle could steal him away from us.

It could be construed as totally fucking weird that I was going on a date with the man who my husband had employed to write his will. And it was. But this was my life.

And every time I'd bumped into Edmond, he'd been friendly, respectful. Normal. Attractive in that Brooks Brothers kind of way.

Before last week, our interactions had been entirely platonic. Although I hadn't missed the way his eyes had quickly flickered over my body. He was interested.

And he made that clear when I was buying coffee—the best in the continental United States—after school drop-off last week.

"We've got to stop meeting like this," he joked as I almost ran into him and almost spilled scalding hot coffee over my chest.

"Yes, I would rather not have to visit the ER with third degree burns," I replied, using a napkin to mop up the coffee that had escaped the lid.

"Well, how about we abandon the idea of scolding hot coffee and go for an ice-cold beer. Or wine, if you're into that," he offered with a smile.

It took me a moment to catch his meaning, and when I did, I prolonged my mopping up so I could have some more time to think. And so I didn't have to look him in the eye.

He was asking me on a date. Me. The lawyer in the suit asking out the biker widow wearing leather and lace. That definitely sounded like the plot of a good romance novel. Our 'meet cutes' certainly fit the bill for that.

But my life sure as shit was not a romance novel, and these kinds of things didn't work out that way. This lawyer in a suit would likely be getting visits from men in cuts if they caught wind of this interaction.

A certain biker in particular. One who had left my bed in the middle of the night last night. The reason I needed the extra-large, triple shot coffee I was drinking.

"Or not," Edmond continued when I'd been silent a long time, making a ceremony of wiping coffee from the top of my cup. "I'm not going to be offended if you're not interested or—"

"I'm interested," I blurted out, not entirely of my own volition. "I'm a beer girl mostly, but I won't turn down wine either. Though I'm not entirely sophisticated in my drinking habits, which horrifies some of my more cultured friends. And you definitely look like a guy who knows things about wine. So as long as you don't judge me."

A smile hooked his lips. "Judge you? Never. As long as you don't judge the fact that I'm partial to a glass of rosé as opposed to whisky on the rocks or more masculine drink that is more masculine."

I smiled back. Mine was mostly forced but that didn't matter. "Okay, it's a deal."

"It's a date," he corrected.

I'd thought about cancelling about one hundred times since then. Especially since the night before the date another man had been inside me.

But I didn't cancel. Precisely because of the man who had been inside me last night. It was meant to be just sex. It was meant to be the way I got my needs sated. No strings. Men did this all the time, got younger women, used them for sex and felt nothing.

But I was not a person who felt nothing. I was a woman who felt it all. Even before Ranger took my books from my arms all those years ago. My mother had tried to discipline it out of me, my emotional tendencies. Emotionality didn't become a lady, apparently. But she'd failed. My marriage, my life had been full of all sorts of emotions. Pain. Joy. Love. Heartbreak. Fear. Rage. The feelings weren't always good, but never had I gone a moment without being consumed by feelings.

After losing Ranger, something broke in me. It had needed to. As a sensitive person, I wouldn't have been able to survive if I'd actually let myself feel all of my grief and pain. It would have destroyed me. So my body and mind worked together, entering survival mode. Dulling down the edges of my feelings. It still hurt, of course. I'd have to be dead not to feel this pain, but everything was muted.

Hence me making the decision to take Kace to bed. Yes, I was still fooling myself into thinking that had been a conscious decision within my control. I had figured that with my heart so broken, my insides so torn and gnarled, that there'd be no way my soul would ever let me feel anything again.

But something was growing. In the rotten soil of my heart. And the best way to kill it was to go on this date. Not ending things with Kace, no. But I couldn't get too wrapped up in him. So the date was my plan.

"You sure you're okay to babysit?" I asked Mia, walking into the room, fastening my earrings at the same time.

Her eyes were glued to *The Real Housewives of Beverly Hills*. The kids were in their respective rooms doing their homework, as asked, like aliens had come in and invaded their bodies.

"Okay?" Mia repeated, pausing the episode. "I should be paying you for the opportunity to sit here and watch television

gold without worrying about the men in my house sponta-
neously combusting because I dared to binge reality television.
Any time you need to—"

She stopped speaking when she turned her head to look at
me. Her eyes flared, and she made a low whistling sound.

"Girl. Wow."

I smiled. Though I wasn't usually one to agree with such
statements, considering the caliber of women I was always
around, I thought I looked pretty wow too.

I figured that Edmond wasn't the kind of guy who appreciated leather pants and snakeskin boots.

Not that I was about to change myself for a man, but I
wanted to try him on, so to speak.

I was wearing a beige skirt that Gwen had leant me then
refused to take back, saying it looked better on me. Which was a
total lie, but I'd learned after all these years that you couldn't
argue with Gwen. So I'd kept the skirt, thinking I might have
use for it on some anniversary or occasion when Ranger and I
decided to go fancy. He'd done that for me sometimes.
Surprised me with a dinner at one of the nicest restaurants in
town, or a hotel, a spa. For no special reason.

I'd never gotten to wear the skirt with Ranger. So I was
wearing it for another man. For another life I'd been forced into.

The skirt fit snug around my ass, cupping everything
expertly, forcing me to wear the skimpiest underwear I could
because according to Amy, "visible panty lines should be
a crime".

My tank was loose, edged with cream lace, tucked into the
skirt. I'd gone with studded, spiked heels and various jewelry.
My hair was up in a messy bun, and I was wearing more
makeup than I had in a long while.

"Momma, you look beautiful," Lily said, coming from the
hallway. Her wide eyes trailed over my outfit. I already knew

that I had a little fashionista on my hands. Especially with Gwen and Amy's influence.

A smile stretched my lips. "Thank you, baby."

Jack walked in after his sister, heading for the fridge. "Where are you going again?"

"You know, you should always compliment a woman who's made an effort with her appearance before asking questions," I told my son.

He rolled his eyes, sighing dramatically. "You look very pretty," he retorted.

I smiled wider. "You're just the sweetest, Jack. Thank you."

"Where are you going?" he repeated.

"To dinner with a friend," I replied. No way was I telling my kids I was going on a date. Lily would get the wrong idea, likely getting overly excited. Jack, on the other hand, would not be excited.

As it was, he was already suspicious. "What friend?"

"An old friend from college. Is that okay with you?" I gathered things into my purse, making sure to concentrate on it so I didn't have to look at my son's face while I lied to him.

"I guess," he muttered, pulling a juice box from the refrigerator.

I looked to Mia. "I've got lasagna in the fridge, if you want that?"

She waved her hand. "No, the kids have the cool babysitter tonight. So it's takeout. Loads of it. Whatever they want. And that homework stuff is stopping as soon as your mother leaves, dude," she winked at Jack.

I just grinned.

Even Jack's mouth twitched ever so slightly. No one was immune to Mia's charms.

"I won't be late," I said to Mia.

"You can be as late as you want," she replied. "We're totally good here. Just let me know if there's anything on fire when you drive past my house, won't you?"

"Of course," I said seriously, such a prospect not actually outside the realm of possibility.

EDMOND HAD MADE reservations at Valentines.

We were meeting there, despite him trying to convince me to let him pick me up. He was very old fashioned, it seemed, because I'd had to be pretty damn firm about driving myself. It irritated me in a way it shouldn't have. He was only being polite. Chivalrous. But I had said no once. I'd always thought you shouldn't have to say no to a good man more than once.

Then again, what did I really know about good men?

They didn't exist.

There were only shades of gray.

I arrived exactly on time, which was only because Mia had arrived at my place early

He was already waiting at the table when the hostess led me to it. It was a good one. Tucked away in the corner, romantic lighting, view of the town below, the ocean beyond that.

"Elizabeth, you look beautiful," he said, standing as soon as I approached the table. He leaned in to kiss my cheek, lingering just a bit longer than I'd expected. His cologne smelled expensive and not overpowering. But I didn't like it. My body tensed the second his lips touched my cheek.

If he noticed, he didn't let on.

"You look very handsome yourself," I sat after he pulled out my chair for me.

And he did. He wore a very stylish suit. Expensive but not flashy. Well-tailored. No tie. He was clean shaven, his dark hair gelled to the side, not one strand out of place. There was a very large and pricey looking watch on his wrist. Nice hands. I knew if I looked at his palms that there wouldn't be calluses from working on cars, no oil stains. He most likely got manicures.

"I took the liberty of ordering a bottle of wine for us." He nodded to the bottle in the middle of the table. "So it has time to breathe."

I bit the inside of my lip. It was a nice gesture. A romantic gesture. But what if I didn't like wine? I didn't want some pretentious bottle of wine that needed to breathe. I liked beer, I'd told him that, hadn't I? Sure, wine was great too. But I liked the pink, chilled stuff. A red was great, too, but I usually kept it under fifteen dollars. Ranger and I had always kept a nice selection of faithful bottles in our rotation.

Admittedly, I wasn't really worried about how the alcohol tasted lately, just how well it numbed.

But none of these things were appropriate to say on a first date. Nor was thinking about what Kace would've done for a first date. He'd probably take me on a picnic or stop by a food truck on a ride down the coast. That was definitely more my speed.

"That's perfect," I lied with a painted-on smile.

I tried to push away my irritation, focusing on putting my napkin on my lap, grabbing the menu and studying it.

I wondered if I could hide behind it the entire night.

⸺

"I HAD A GREAT TIME," I voiced through gritted teeth.

It wasn't a lie, exactly.

Okay, it was a total fucking lie. I didn't have a great time. But that had nothing to do with him.

Okay, another lie.

It had a lot to do with him.

Not because he was a bad guy.

Or maybe because he *wasn't* a bad guy. He was too ironed, perfumed, polite. With the wine, with him recommending what I should order that would pair well with the wine. Yuck.

He had asked me questions about myself, about my kids. I might've imagined the slightly snide look on his face when I'd told him I had been a stay-at-home mother all these years.

I'd asked him questions too. Mostly because I wanted to stop talking about myself, not because I really cared about his history.

He grew up in New York state, to what I could gather was a wealthy family. Had what seemed like a trouble-free upbringing. One brother, one sister. Went to college, law school. Worked in the city for years. Divorced. No kids. Always wanted them, apparently.

He came to Amber after his divorce because he needed to slow down. He was adjusting to Amber well, at least that's what he said. Though I got the impression small town life didn't exactly suit him.

There were no awkward silences throughout the date. He seemed genuinely interested in me. Seemed to like me.

"It was an enchanting evening," he responded as he walked me to my car.

Ugh. *Enchanting?* Who said that unsarcastically?

I dug through my purse for my keys, cursing myself for not doing it sooner because now he'd have an excuse to linger by my car. It wasn't exactly late, but there'd been three courses. Then after dinner coffee. So the parking lot was emptying, and there weren't many cars around where I'd parked.

"I'd love to do it again sometime soon, maybe next week?" Edmond asked, hand on the small of my back as it had been since we'd left the restaurant.

I moved so my back faced the car, getting away from his touch, my hands thankfully finding the keys.

"Yeah, I'll have to check the kids' schedule," I hedged, smiling. "The joys of motherhood, my time is not my own."

He smiled back. His teeth were too white. "I'd love to meet them sometime."

No way. "Um, yeah. I'm kind of... protective over them. With everything that happened. It's not personal."

He nodded. "Of course. I'm getting ahead of myself." His eyes flickered over my body before he met my eyes again. "I really do hope that I'll meet them. That we continue this. You're a beautiful woman, Elizabeth."

That was another thing. I'd told him at least three times over all of our interactions to call me Lizzie. He was like my mother who had a strong distaste for Lizzie. For any casual nicknames, really. She'd named me after a regal woman, and regal women were not called Lizzie, apparently.

I swallowed roughly. Crap. He was going in for a kiss. My entire body recoiled from just the thought. Which was insane. He was an attractive, polite and cultured man. So much safer and more responsible than what I was used to. Unlikely to be killed by multiple gunshot wounds.

"Thank you," I said in little more than a whisper. "I've, uh, got to get home." I jangled my keys. "Kids. Early morning soccer game."

Edmond smiled. "Of course." He didn't step back, though. In fact, he stepped forward so our bodies brushed. I held my breath as he leaned in, moving my face at the last minute so his lips found my cheek instead of my mouth.

To his credit, he didn't seem pissed off or offended by the rejection. His lips lingered before he straightened. They were dry, and I fucking hated the way they felt on my skin.

"I'll call you tomorrow?"

He would call me tomorrow too. No games. No waiting three days or whatever it is Ashley told me guys did these days.

"Sure," I said, thinking of how the fuck I was going to let him down gently during tomorrow's phone call. In reality, I'd probably be a coward and send it to voicemail. But tonight, I had higher hopes for myself.

Edmond opened my car door after I beeped it open. Polite. But somehow it felt domineering. And not in the good way.

This would not have been the end of the night if I'd been with Kace.

Who I felt myself longing for.

Chapter 14

I had managed the almost impossible feat of escaping Mia's demands for the 'lowdown' on the date. Though I wasn't exactly sure I even knew how or why I'd done that. Maybe it was the look on my face that wasn't exactly saturated in elation or lust that had her giving me a break. That or the fact that she had ordered takeout from three different places and was in a walking food coma.

Whatever it was, I had respite for the night, at least. I'd muted my phone, too, not ready to even look at all the texts I'd received. Tomorrow was another day.

Tonight was a cheap, pink wine kind of night. I'd done my best to pretend I'd actually liked the bottle he'd chosen, but it was bitter and heavy and totally not something that took the edges off anything.

I was on my second glass, standing at the kitchen counter, staring out the window when I felt it. There was someone in my house. Someone watching me.

Crap.

Ranger's guns were in our bedroom. Because we lived a life

where it was totally plausible that we might need them in a hurry, they were kept where the kids couldn't get them, but close enough for him to grab in a hurry. He'd trained me relentlessly when he first patched in. I'd hated it at first, but once I'd accepted guns as part of our life, I liked them. Knowing that I was capable of defending myself. My family, if need be. As much as I loved my protective, alpha male husband, I did not love the idea of being some damsel that always needed to be saved.

And now that I was the only point of defense in my home, I should've been more aware. There were two humans relying on me to keep them safe.

I turned, ready to throw my wine glass. To attack. Claw off the face of the fucker who would dare to put what remained of my family in danger.

But it wasn't a home invader, murderer or rapist standing in my kitchen. No, it was a man wearing a Sons of Templar cut.

"How did you get in here?" I demanded, glaring at Kace, hating that everything inside of me heated up at his mere presence. All of the things that I'd tried to make myself feel all night, finally making themselves known.

"I'm an outlaw, Lizzie," was his explanation. His voice was off. Cold. Dangerous. Same with his face. There was nothing easy or familiar about the way he was looking at me. No, Kace was giving me a glimpse of the man he was when the Sons needed him to be cold, fierce, deadly.

And I fucking loved it. My thighs pressed together with need.

"Kace, you shouldn't be here," I said, fighting to keep my voice even. Battling to sound convincing.

He raised a brow, a silent challenge of my lie.

"You gave this to another man?" Kace growled, eyes running over me.

232

Fire and ice left a trail in they're wake.

"Kace," I began, not quite sure what I was planning on saying next.

He didn't give me a chance to say anything else because he was there, right *there*. His hands were on my hips first. Then they went their separate ways, one going down, moving to cup my ass firmly. The other went up my ribcage to knead my breasts.

Air hissed from my mouth as my entire body responded to him.

"That's okay," he murmured against my lips. "That you went out with another man, let him think he had a chance of doing anythin'. That you put this on for him." He fisted the fabric of my skirt. "That you got all dolled up like this for him." His hand moved to my hair, tugging at the strands to the point of pain.

My knees were in danger of failing me.

"Because I'm the one who gets this." His hand moved quickly under my skirt. Kace didn't move slow or tenderly once he reached the lace of my underwear, he went right in, coating his fingers with my wetness before plunging them inside.

I let out a muffled cry.

"Yeah," he grumbled, his mouth moving at my neck. "You weren't this wet for that fuck in the suit." His fingers kept moving with expert grace, my orgasm building from the bottom of my stomach.

"You wouldn't let him in," he continued, mouth moving down as his other hand yanked my dress so my nipple was exposed. "No fuckin' bra," he hissed before he landed his mouth on my nipple.

Every nerve ending in my body felt electrified. I made another sound, or tried to. He was commandeering all of my motor skills. I was his.

"You're not gonna let some lawyer fuck you like I do," he informed me, removing his mouth to look me in the eyes.

He pulled out his fingers, and I moaned at the loss. At the orgasm he'd stolen with his retreat.

He stepped back, and it was all I could do not to sink to the floor.

Kace picked up the wine from the counter, draining it without taking his eyes off me. "You think I was going to make it that easy?" he asked, voice guttural. "That you'd get off wearing *that*?" He shook his head. "Get in the bedroom. Now."

Fuck me if I didn't heed his command immediately.

I hurried down the hall, and he trailed me like the predator he was. My skin was hot, heart beating in my throat. I was excited. Nervous. Desperate.

Kace closed the door behind me, and I turned to face him. His face was cold, brutal.

He nodded to the shirt. "Take. It. Off."

My shaking fingers moved to do his bidding with an embarrassing amount of speed. I didn't have it in me to be embarrassed right now. No, I was too desperate. I was near feral with my need for release. For him.

He was punishing me at the same time he was giving me the most erotic gift I'd ever had.

Kace watched with a concentrated intensity as I moved to pull it over my head.

"Skirt," he rasped.

My breathing was rapid as I did as he asked.

He grinned as it hit the floor. "Yeah, I'm the only one who gets to see what that looks like on you and on the floor." Then he moved his eyes back to me, where I was standing in drenched lace panties, spiked heels and nothing else.

Kace nodded toward my hips, his eyes hungry. "Panties."

I kept watching him as I pulled them from my hips then stepped out of them.

"Shoes are staying on," Kace informed me.

I swallowed roughly, nodding. All I wanted in the world was to go to him, to take charge and take what I wanted, but I stayed in my spot.

He was making it clear that he was in charge, and that's what made this so incredibly hot.

"Move to the bed. Hands on it. Feet splayed. Ass up for me."

I moved to do as he said, putting myself in a position that should've felt demeaning or vulnerable. Though it was neither. Not with him. It was powerful. Erotic.

There was silence for a long time. Too long. My body was crying out with need in a dull roar, yet Kace hadn't moved. He was watching me. I knew that. Feasting on my body with a reverence I trusted him to have.

First it was a palm on my ass. Gentle. Barely there. A stark juxtaposition to every other way he'd touched me tonight.

It moved slowly, caressing my skin, moving down to my thighs and then forward, toward the drenched area he'd abandoned earlier. But he didn't go in. He wasn't going to make it that easy.

Next it was his lips on my skin. Moving along my cheeks slowly, torturously. His actions left me feeling vulnerable, to say the least. But somehow empowering too.

Then his lips moved to the middle. He spread me open and ate me... there. In that place that felt so forbidden. So private. I should've been uncomfortable. But I fucking loved it. I fisted the sheets as I cried out, Kace moving his tongue like the expert he was.

"I'm gonna take your ass one day," he warned, moving his finger to tease at my entrance, not going inside. "Not tonight, though."

He moved away, standing to unbuckle his pants but keeping everything on. He didn't need to prime me, I was ready the second I'd laid eyes on him in the kitchen.

"Am I the only one who gets to fuck you like this?" he asked, hands tight on my hips, poised at my entrance.

"Yes," I ground out, my need for him making me near feral.

His grip tightened to the point of pain. The perfect kind of pain. "Am I the only one who gets to eat your ass?"

My stomach dipped. "Yes," I whispered.

"Fuckin' right," he growled.

Then he thrust inside me.

And fucked me all night long. Reminding me that my body may have belonged to me in the daylight when he wasn't around, but it was all his when the sun went down.

If you'd asked me Edmond's name that night, I wouldn't have been able to utter it. I hadn't been able to think about anything but Kace.

———

EDMOND HAD CALLED JUST like he'd said he would.

I watched his name light up on my phone screen the very next morning. Early, but not too early. Right after I'd gotten the kids to school and was settled on my laptop with a coffee, brainstorming jobs I could maybe get with a decade-long hole in my resume that would feed, clothe and house me and my children.

So far, I had stripper, cam girl and jewelry thief. The list was definitely depressing and unrealistic, so I would've grasped on to almost any reason to abandon it, eager to be distracted by anything, except talking to Edmond on the phone.

He'd be polite, ask questions. Thoughtful ones. Then he'd try to make a plan for our next date. He'd be insistent, not pushy, but in a way I'd feel uncomfortable rejecting him, forced to come up with a suitable excuse, then having to bump into him in the frozen food section.

Why had I gone on that date? I really hadn't thought this through.

No, I *had* thought it through. I couldn't become too close to Kace, getting tangled with another member of the Sons. I'd ruin my kid's lives if I didn't at least try to give them some other kind of life.

Not that I'd tried hard with Edmond. But the thought of going through another date, trying to be whatever version of myself I'd have to be to date a man like him, sounded less appetizing than a pap smear.

So I ignored the call. I was not ready to have a conversation with him. I'd only put it off until sometime tonight. Or maybe in the hours when he'd most likely be working. A voicemail would be so much easier. Sure, it'd be bitchier, too, but right now I didn't care much about whether it was or wasn't a bitch move, I just wanted the easy one. Every choice I made was based on ease now. It was trouble enough just getting through the day without screaming or necking a bottle of vodka.

Every decision was based on ease.

Except Kace.

That wasn't even a decision.

It was insanity.

I sighed and went back to my list. I could try and go back to the bookstore. I adored it there, but Evan was about to let his son take over, and I figured that his son would be able to handle the books. Even if they did employ me, it wouldn't pay enough to even cover our monthly grocery bill.

"Stripping? Not that you don't have the body for it, especially the ass, but I think that spells trouble for me." The voice came from right over my shoulder, breath hot on my neck.

I jumped in shock, spilling my coffee in the process. "Fuck!"

I snapped, slamming my laptop closed, storming toward the kitchen and putting it on the counter while I grabbed some paper towels.

Then I mopped up the spilled coffee, all the while not acknowledging Kace's presence. He stood there, watching me do all of this, not speaking or offering to help, even though the mess was his fault. To be fair, I would've damn near bitten his head off if he had offered to help, so maybe he was playing it smart. Or maybe he was just an asshole.

Once I'd cleaned up the mess and got myself in a condition where I could face him enough to speak evenly, I did.

"How did you get in here?" I asked calmly.

His eyes flickered over me as they always did. As if he hadn't just left my bed in the early hours of the morning. As if I didn't have marks on my ass and tits from the magnificent way he'd fucked me last night.

And my body responded accordingly, the traitorous bitch.

"You left the door unlocked," he nodded toward the front of the house. "You gotta stop doin' that shit."

Crossing my arms over my chest, I narrowed my eyes. "You've gotta stop thinking you can comment on what I do and don't do. You've also gotta stop walking into my house without permission. My kids could've been here."

"Your kids are at school," he countered.

"It could've been a teacher day, or someone could've been home sick."

"It's not and there wasn't. Can you stop throwing fuckin' sass at me and let me know what the fuck that list is?" He didn't sound pissed exactly. But definitely not as carefree as he usually did. It was last night. It had changed something. He'd claimed me in every way he could, and now he'd gone all alpha on me. Showing up like he had the right, talking to me like I was more than just a fuck.

"I'm not throwing sass," I snapped. "I'm acting like a normal, pissed off woman at some man who has walked into her house like he has the right too."

Kace was transitioning into pissed, his eyes narrowing into tiny slits. And why did I like seeing that side of him?

"I'm not just some fuckin' man. At least I wasn't last night. As much as you want this to be secret sex, it's not. I don't work that way. And it's my business if the woman I'm fucking has decided to go and strip at the place my club owns. Beyond that, it's on me and the club if someone who has sacrificed as much for the Sons as you have is at the point of needing to sell her fucking body in order to feed her goddamn kids."

Yeah. He was pissed off.

In the way any member would be if they knew the widow of a long-time member was doing this shit. Some maybe even a little more.

"I don't need to sell my body in order to feed my goddamn kids," I snapped. "I need to figure out how to stand without the club. I need to be my own person apart from all this. Be able to provide for my children."

Kace's eyes gentled, his body doing the same. "You want to be an island," he deduced.

"No, I want to be a peninsula," I corrected. "I want my friends, family, the club to be involved, to be accessible, but I want some version of my own life, my own identity. My own sense of security. I've spent most of my adult life as an Old Lady, wrapped up in the life of the MC. It's been a hard life. A beautiful one too. But that's over now. I'm not an Old Lady anymore. I know I will always have a place with the Sons. I know they will never abandon me or my kids. But I know I have to be something more than that. For my own sanity."

"And a jewelry thief is where you see yourself going?" Kace asked after a beat, amusement coating his words.

I was thankful he hadn't latched on to all the truths I hadn't meant to spill. Not calling me on them, not trying to talk me out of it. Not trying to make this deeper, more intense than it already was.

I folded my arms. "I'm just brainstorming. Not all ideas are great. This is a process. One that does not need your input, so you should leave."

I wanted to mean that. I really did. But after last night, with the tenderness between my legs, I wanted him to stay. I wanted him. Hopefully that didn't show in my voice or my face.

His lips curled . "I'm not saying your ideas aren't great. I'm definitely intrigued at what kind of moves you'd have for a lap dance."

My stomach dipped deliciously. "You don't get to flirt your way out of this."

He moved then. Quickly. Too quickly. He didn't give me time to retreat, to brace for impact. Kace obviously didn't want that. He wanted to catch me off guard. To have the upper hand.

One of his strong hands went to my ass, yanking me close to him, the other to the back of my neck, pressing our faces inches apart. "I don't need to flirt with you, Lizzie." His hand moved inside the waistband of my pants then underneath my panties, cupping my bare ass. "We're well past that." His lips moved to my neck, grazing the skin with his teeth. "Tell me I'm wrong."

I wanted to. More than anything. Wanted to push him away and at least show myself that I had some semblance of control over this.

Instead of speaking I stayed silent. Which was just as bad as admitting he was right.

"That's what I thought," he snickered, moving his hands from my panties and lifting me.

My legs wrapped around his hips on reflex, a hiss escaping me when I met the hardness of his crotch.

"Yeah, baby," he murmured, carrying me to the bedroom.

That's where he proved just how much control he had. How fucked I was. In many more ways than one.

———

"DON'T ANSWER IT," Kace murmured, hands tightening around me. Someone had just knocked at the door.

We were in the bed now.

There'd been no avoiding it. We'd fucking more and more often, the sex getting dirtier and more carnal. The words between the sex getting more personal. So it didn't much matter whether we were in the bed or not. It was just a mattress and set of sheets. It no longer smelled of my husband. It smelled of us now. Me and Kace.

His voice was thick and throaty and full of sex. As was the air in my bedroom.

It was the middle of the day. Someone could've stopped by for coffee. To haul me on some shopping trip. Call me to come and bail her and her boys from mall jail—that one was Mia. Or worse still, my kids could come home sick. I had become an addict. First it was just sex, the escape that he gave me. The awakening he made me feel. Like my body was something more than a collection of scars.

But it was starting to become more than just sex I was addicted to. It was Kace. The fact that he was easy to be with, gentle with me when we had our clothes on, but then was beautifully brutal in the bedroom. I needed to take charge of my life, feel like I had agency, make my kids think I had everything under control.

There was also a part of me that craved having someone else to control me. To take charge of me. Kace did that. And I fucking loved it.

Until reality came knocking at my door.

"I have to answer it," I said firmly, moving quickly from the bed. He let me, though, I knew he didn't want to. "You need to stay in here." I pointed at him sternly to make my point.

He moved to sit up in bed, not bothering to cover himself up with the sheet. Kace was not at all modest about his body, and he didn't need to be, he was nothing short of perfect.

Sure, there was a darkness about him. A damage to him that he'd told me about the first night me met. But I was careful not to delve into that side of him. I couldn't. As perfect as he was on the surface, I had managed to keep my distance from his soul. If I truly got to know his scars, his imperfections, I'd be in too deep. I'd want to know his pain. Want to wear his scars.

"Hiding me in the bedroom like I'm your mistress?" he taunted, his eyes twinkling with humor.

I scowled at him, not bothering to answer. The joke hit me somewhere deep inside. Ranger was dead. Long dead and gone. This wasn't cheating on him. This wasn't doing anything wrong. It was logical to think that. Gwen hadn't judged me, nor had Evie, but then again, that wasn't exactly their style. Despite the fact I knew that women and men were allowed to move on after their spouse died, that it was healthy, I didn't like it. I didn't want to be healthy. Didn't want to move on. But the man laying naked in my bed was proof I didn't want to stay where I was either.

I hurriedly threw on my clothes, forgetting my underwear in my rush. My hair definitely looked like I'd been well fucked, so I did my best to finger brush it on my way to the door. Hopefully I'd be able to convince Mia or whoever it was that I wasn't doing anything suspect. Which was a fool's hope, since she was totally going to notice all the signs of a woman who'd just been screwed.

What a hole I'd dug for myself.

I opened the door, already trying to find a suitable excuse for my friend, when I was faced with someone I hadn't expected.

"Edmond," I breathed out. "Um, hi."

His eyes flickered over me before settling on my eyes. He was, of course, in what looked like an expensive suit, no tie, his hair in order, holding two coffees.

"I know it's exceptionally bad form to show up the day after a date, especially when you haven't called me back yet, but I figured coffee from your favorite place and muffins may get me some points?" He held the bag up with a sheepish grin.

I gritted my teeth. Though I'd never agreed with her before, I found myself thinking like my mother. Being pissed like she would be at the audacity of someone—a male potential love interest no less—arriving on my doorstep without notice.

Even if I didn't have a naked biker in my bed, this would've pissed me off. No matter how nice and well-groomed Edmond seemed, it was out of line, taking the choice away from me. It was up to *me* whether I wanted to see him again. It was certainly up to me whether I invited him to my house. This felt oddly aggressive.

"I knew the kids would be at school," Edmond continued when I didn't answer. "So I figured it would be safe to come." He laughed, and there was a slight awkwardness to it. He felt uncomfortable. Good. He should.

"I don't think there's ever a *safe* time to come to my home unannounced, Edmond," I said, my voice icy. I'd planned on being polite, warm, hoping to push him into the friendzone. Maybe I was overreacting to this. But my home was my space. My safe place. My kid's safe place. Some man wanting to get laid because he'd bought me coffee and a fucking muffin had no right to come here.

That was the problem with men like Edmond with their

expensive suits, overpowering cologne and straight white teeth. They thought they had the right to do whatever they pleased.

Something moved across his face, rippling through the pleasantness like a stone on a lake. He was pissed at my response. Of course he was. He wasn't used to women speaking up. They were either charmed by him or too polite to set him straight.

"I don't mean anything by it. We had fun last night. I like you."

"So you think that coming here, despite me not answering the phone, is still acceptable?" I countered. "You're polite. You know good wines. You have a good job, and for all I know you could be the totally perfect man. But I just buried my husband a year ago. I have two kids who need to be my focus. What I don't need is a man on my doorstep without an invitation, no matter how polite he is. The date was nice. But I'm not ready. My kids are my main focus right now."

I delivered this with a little less ice than before, but made sure I was firm.

The mask flickered once more. He was pissed at this. At me holding firm. "This was a mistake. I was over eager. I apologize."

"Apology accepted."

"I can't even try to make my case over coffee?" he pushed.

This fucking guy.

"There's no case to make," I informed him. "I hope this hasn't disrupted your day too much. If you don't mind, I have a lot to do."

Despite my anger, I had the strong urge to add an apology in there somewhere, as women tended to do. It was something hardwired into us, that need to apologize for disappointing some guy. Hammered into us for years. We'd been convinced we must say sorry for speaking our minds, for occupying spaces men wanted to own. Even knowing that Edmond was in the wrong, I couldn't help but feel the need to protect his feelings ever so slightly by offering some sort of apology.

But I held firm.

I had nothing to be sorry for.

And you could bet your ass that men didn't apologize when they didn't have anything to be sorry for. Most of them found it hard enough to say sorry even when they were in the wrong.

Edmond was no different. "Of course. But I have to warn you, I'm not going to give up on you. I feel something between us. And I understand that a new relationship might be scary to you right now. You may not feel ready, but I'm willing to wait. Willing to prove you wrong."

Was he fucking for real?

No matter how gentle I had tried to be, he wasn't getting it. Apparently, I'd have to lay it out straight, I had no other choice, then his face would change, and he'd label me a bitch.

He was the type. I was seeing that now.

Lucky for me, I wasn't afraid of some lawyer in a suit. I'd spent far too much time around real badasses in leather to get scared by a man who spent more time on his hair than I did.

"Babe?" the voice sounded from behind me before I could start my well-deserved bitch tirade.

I was so shocked that I didn't fully process it as Kace managed to not only open the door but sling his arm around me. He was also shirtless.

I didn't fight this because I was so stunned. The look that Edmond was giving the both of us was pretty damn good too.

"We help you, bro?" Kace asked Edmond in a tone that communicated 'fuck off' in not so many words.

Edmond recovered quickly. I'd expected nothing less. Any pleasantness on his face was now gone, his expression curled into a scowl that could only be worn by a cocky, entitled man who'd been rejected by a woman.

"Ah. That's it. You weren't gonna let me in because you've already let someone else in. Once a biker slut always a biker slut." There was nothing polite in his tone. Just bitterness. Foul, rotten anger.

Now, I had definitely expected some kind of tantrum. Harsh words. But this surprised me. Interestingly, it didn't piss me off as much as it had when he was being nice.

Kace, on the other hand, was pissed off. His entire body tensed with fury. His jaw clenched and his eyes darkened. Basically, he transformed into a deadly biker not afraid to knife a guy. Or shoot him in the face.

"You better feel fucking glad I don't want to stain the doorstep of my woman's home with blood 'cause this is where her kids walk in," Kace said calmly. "You speak another fucking word, I'll forget that. Bleach ain't that expensive after all."

Edmond paled, and it was incredibly satisfying, if not juvenile, to feel the way I did as I watched fear overcome him. I moved my arms around Kace's hips. Not because I wanted to feel him or anything, but because I was worried he might make good on his word. He definitely seemed that pissed. And no one wearing a Sons' cut was about to let an Old Lady—widow or not—be called a slut in front of them without doing some serious harm.

Though I would say, it wasn't completely terrible having my arm around Kace.

Edmond's face turned cold, and his eyes filled with fury and hate. More than I'd suspected was hidden behind that handsome face. It unnerved me.

After the life I'd lived, people I'd spent time around, I considered myself to be a good judge of character. A good judge of what lay beneath the layers of civilians, able to see their true faces underneath the masks they wore.

But I'd missed it with Edmond. Hadn't listened to my

instincts telling me that there was something off, beyond the fact that he just wasn't my type.

"You touch me, I'll sue you for everything you're worth. I'll make sure you go to jail like the criminal you are," Edmond spat.

Kace grinned in the face of the threat like the joke it was. "Oh, you gonna hurt me with some fuckin' paper? Go right ahead. Try it." Despite Kace being younger than Edmond, much less groomed and put together, he sounded like he was talking to a child, something beneath him. His voice and demeanor shrank Edmond down into something small.

Edmond didn't like that. Not at all. But I could see that he was also scared of Kace. He was trying to hide it, but it was easier to hide ugliness than it was fear.

Instead of answering Kace, he focused on me. "You're making a huge mistake."

"You don't fuckin' talk to her," Kace fired back, moving me ever so slightly backward. I rolled my eyes at him trying to protect me from an asshole in a suit that even I could take down without much effort. Edmond was used to bringing people down with words, he was no match for the Sons of Templar, or anyone connected to them.

"You don't *think* about her. You don't look at her. You see her on the street, you turn around and walk the other way. That is, if you like the way you're walkin' right now. I'd be happy to change that for you. I'd take great fuckin' pleasure. The Sons own this town, and we'll be watching you. Every fucking move."

Kace meant it. Every word. He would hurt Edmond. End him. Just for talking to me like this.

"Change is coming," Edmond spat. "The town is growing. A thug, criminal biker gang can only stay in power for so long. It's not going to be a fist fight that brings you down. It'll be progress. And I'll glory in it."

Kace grinned. "Well, I'll be glorying in Lizzie's pussy."

On that note, he pulled me back and slammed the door in Edmond's face.

"You did not have to end it like that," I admonished.

"Yes I fuckin' did, babe," he replied, his voice still filled with anger. "That fucker is darker than he seems, and he wants what I've got. In a way that fuckin' worries me. He needs to know what'll come to him if he gets near you."

"I can take care of myself," I demanded, stepping back, folding my arms. "And I'm not yours. We fuck. That's all."

Kace moved forward, forcing me to retreat so my back hit the door. He didn't stop. Not until he caged me in.

"Very aware you can take care of yourself, Lizzie. I'm also very aware that you've got two kids who need their mom. You've been through enough shit. I've got the ability to make sure I'm between you and fucks like that, so I'm gonna do that. You can fight me on it as much as you want. Try to push me away, I'll take it. But I won't go nowhere. Because even though you're not ready to admit it, you are mine. The parts of you that can be."

"You need to leave," I gritted out.

He ran his eyes over me, and I hated the way that made me feel. "Sure thing, baby. But it's too late to really try and get rid of me. I'm under your skin."

I turned and walked away from him. Because I didn't have it in me to argue.

To lie.

Chapter 15

Someone had been in my house.

I knew that the second that I walked through the door. It wasn't locked. Something I forgot to do more often than not. Something that had irritated the ever-living fuck out of my husband. The cause of a lot of fights. Of course, I was extra careful in the bloodier days. I wasn't going to take any chances with my children. Now, I shouldn't have been as careless. Stupid. I was a woman alone in a house with the two most precious things in my entire world.

But there was a lot on my mind.

To say the least.

And the club was no longer attracting death and danger. Ranger's death was the result of a war that had been unavoidable. A war the club won. One that had made it so that all the criminals in the underworld stayed away.

None of that was an excuse for being so careless with my safety and my children's. I'd been stupid enough to think we were safe here. In Amber. Under the shade of the Sons of Templar MC.

Nothing was missing. I'd left some cash in a porcelain tray on a side table in the living room. It was still there. As were all of the expensive kitchen gadgets that Ranger had bought me and upgraded yearly. Not as gifts, mind you. He was partial to giving jewelry or first editions of my favorite books. Ranger was always a great gift giver. He was observant. Thoughtful. The Kitchen-Aid mixer and the espresso machine were more because he'd wanted to provide. He had wanted to be the father he'd never had. Maybe he had wanted to buy something beautiful to make up for the ugly ways in which we got that money.

It didn't matter now, did it?

I continued to move through the house, cautiously, moving first to my bedroom to retrieve my gun. Something told me there was no one in the house. The same kind of something that told me someone had been in here in the first place. Instinct. Intuition. Whatever you want to call it.

I checked the kids' rooms. Nothing out of place. Nothing stolen. Beds sloppily made, because that was one of their weekly chores, and neither of them loved doing them, they did them because they were good kids.

The laundry room was untouched, with piles of clothes that never really seemed to move with two children in the house.

Bathrooms the same.

Maybe I was going crazy. That wouldn't be out of the question. Everything inside me felt loose. Rattled. Broken. Resentful. Bitter.

Everything that Kace always chased away.

When he last left, self-guilt and confusion washed over me like a tsunami, all mingled with need for him despite still feeling his touch all over my body.

So yes, it could be entirely possible that I was going crazy. But I didn't think I was. There weren't many things in the world a woman could trust. A true girlfriend. The words of a good man. The fact that there were many bad men pretending to be good. And her intuition.

It wasn't something that lied. And I was pretty sure mine wasn't lying now.

Something creaked behind me. A footstep. A person. They were still here. Damn, I wished my intuition had been wrong this time.

I whirled, gun raised head level. Ranger always taught me to go for the kill. *"If you're at the point you have to point a gun at someone, don't fuck around trying to wound. You shoot to kill."*

Bex raised her hands, grinning ever so slightly. "I'm only here to raid your baby clothing supply, but if you're guarding it that fiercely, then I'll brave that god-awful baby store."

Horrified, I lowered the gun, turning the safety back on. Holy shit. I was going insane. I'd just pointed a gun at one of my closest friends. Who was a new mother. Jesus fucking Christ.

"Shit, Bex, I'm so sorry." I ran my hand across the back of my neck, tension now pulsing there.

She waved her hand in dismissal. "No harm, no fowl." She glanced downward then back up at me. "Why are you walking around the house with a gun?" Bex asked, tilting her head to the side.

I took a deep breath, my heart trying to settle at the familiar face. The safety in it. I surely didn't feel any safety in myself.

"I thought that someone had been in here, but I think I might just be going insane," I whispered.

"Babe, if you're not insane already, then you're way ahead of the rest of us," she replied with a grin.

I chuckled with only the faintest hint of hysteria.

"Beyond that, I know you. Don't think you'd be stalking around your house with a Glock without a reason. If you think someone was in here, then I believe you." She paused. "Should I make some tea?"

"Tea?" I repeated.

She shrugged. "That's what bitches offer other bitches in times of crisis. It's meant to be calming."

I laughed. "I think that whisky sounds better."

She grinned. "Me too. How about you put away the gun, and we'll have a chat over some whisky and cupcakes. Fair warning. I already ate one on the way in here." She winked and turned to walk toward the kitchen.

I moved slowly to our bedroom, emptying the clip, securing the gun. I was shaken. After a tragedy happens, it usually goes one of two ways. Some consider themselves somewhat immune from a repeat. Having had a huge blow dealt to you once was enough. There was also the belief that lighting didn't strike twice. A ridiculous kind of confidence. On the flipside, there was the certainty that more bad things could happen because you were living proof that bad things did happen. I was in the camp of the latter, if it wasn't already obvious.

Bex already had our drinks lined up and was chewing on a cupcake by the time I put myself together enough to enter the kitchen.

She didn't look at me any different, like I'd just pointed a gun at her a few minutes ago. That was Bex.

I took the drink she offered me, drained it in one go, then started to feel guilty about drinking in the afternoon and using alcohol to numb my emotions.

"Now, you know how much I hate to say thing like this, but we should call the club," she said.

My stomach dipped. Not just at the prospect of the club having to come to my rescue solely because I had some 'feeling' that someone had been in my house without any kind of proof. No one would make me feel crazy or paranoid. No one would say it out loud, but they'd think it.

Beyond that, Kace would get involved. And then the cycle

would begin. The woman in danger and the alpha male, coming out with the need to protect his woman, not letting her go anywhere alone, then the two end up in falling in love.

No. That wasn't happening.

"We should not call them," I replied, eyes meeting hers. "Seriously. I'm shaky. I'm not getting much sleep. I'm making too much of nothing."

Bex raised a brow. "You've been an Old Lady for over a decade. You are many things. Strong. Unflappable. Badass. You've been through shit that half of these men haven't. So I know for a goddamn fact that you're not making too much of anything."

Bex was not one for bullshit. I bit my lip. Dipped my finger in the frosting of a cupcake and licked it.

"Maybe, maybe not," I shrugged. "But right now, I don't need a bunch of guys coming in with guns to save the day. To rescue the poor woman without a man. You understand that?"

Bex's eyes turned dark, haunted, as they did from time to time. She'd been through some of the worst things a woman could go through. Her life had been hard and ugly. Full of wounds. Yet she managed to get through it. Not without carrying some things with her, though.

"Yeah, babe, I can totally understand that." She twirled her still full glass. I wondered if she was saving it or had just poured it to make me feel better about drinking. Or because she was careful about what substances she imbibed these days. She'd been clean ever since Lucky had saved her from a fate worse than death, but it hadn't been easy for her. She'd had to fight to get where she was. Less so since their daughter was born. But life would always be a battle for her.

For all of us.

"You're not sleeping well?" Bex asked.

Shit.

The way she'd said it showed she was worried. That I was spiraling. I could lie. Say I wasn't sleeping from the grief. The pain. It would've been much easier. But it would hurt my friend. She'd blame herself, thinking that she hadn't been there. Hadn't seen it. Hadn't been able to help.

I couldn't do that.

"Nights have had me kind of... preoccupied, if you know what I mean."

Bex sat up straighter in her chair, the worry instantly falling from her face. "I know exactly what you mean. You've been getting laid. Keeping it a secret, making it even more exciting."

I swallowed, picking up a cupcake for a distraction more than anything else. "Yeah it's really good. Scary good, because it was only meant to be just sex—"

"It's never just sex," she interrupted. "Not with someone wearing a Sons of Templar cut. He's a brother, isn't he? Not that asshole with the suit you went on a date with? Not that I'm going to judge you if it is, but I don't get the feeling he's got a good fucking in him."

I laughed. Bex not only said it how it was, but she saw it how it was.

"It's Kace," I admitted, feeling disturbingly comfortable letting my secret out to more of my friends. I was starting to feel less ashamed of it. The secret was too heavy. I was too tired and starting not to care like I should about all the promises I'd made myself before.

"Of course it is," she nodded, her smile even wider now. "And I'm guessing he's another reason why you don't want the club to know about what went on today? Because he would go all alpha 'you are mine, therefore I make all the decisions about your life now'?"

I grinned. She'd been through this, witnessed more of it. She knew the score. "Pretty much."

"Okay, I'm with you, sister. As long as you keep yourself safe. We don't need any more holes in us."

"Oh, don't worry, I am definitely going to be keeping myself safe," I said firmly, like I had any power over that.

Of course I didn't.

Bad things had happened to me once.

There was only more to come.

IT WAS pure luck that saved my children.

Luck and the fact I'd forgotten that Lily was supposed to bring food for her shared lunch to school. It was grocery day, and I had nothing but some mac and cheese and stale Doritos to offer. She'd dutifully reminded me of this by jumping on my bed at six in the morning. I was meant to have both kids at school by eight thirty and they still needed to get dressed, get showered and eat breakfast.

And I had to go to the grocery store twenty minutes away that opened at six thirty. Which meant my children would be alone for almost an hour. Despite Jack trying to convince me he was old enough to stay at home and look after his sister, that was something that wasn't going to happen.

It hit me again then. In the chest. Ranger's absence. Not just a longing for him. But the practical part of having another parent. A partner. Something like this wouldn't have been a big deal. Ranger would've kissed both me and Lily, rolled out of bed and gone to get what we need. I'd be here, taking care of the kids.

He'd be back in time. Everything would be fine.

But that's not how it was.

I couldn't leave them. Even though Jack techically was old enough. Something in the bottom of my stomach warned me against leaving my kids alone. Without someone to watch them. Protect them. But I just had to figure out who that would be. I couldn't call on one of my friends yet again. Olive was working the night shift, most likely on her way home from the hospital. She'd be dead on her feet by now. She'd come if I called. Without hesitation. But I couldn't do that.

My mother was out of the question because she was my mother and also because she'd lecture me about forgetting something like this and judge my parenting skills. I couldn't handle that without coffee and only a handful of hours of sleep. Kace had left just before the sun came up.

We'd been taking bigger risks. He was staying longer. Any night could be the one Lily had a nightmare and tried to get in the locked bedroom door. Kace would have to jump naked out the window. I'd have to explain to my daughter why the door was locked.

Fuck.

There was one option that was two minutes away.

While I was getting the kids ready, I texted him.

ARE YOU AWAKE?

HE TOOK LESS than a minute to reply.

WHAT DO YOU NEED, babe?

FUCK.

I quickly texted the information, and he was on my doorstep

five minutes later. He looked awake and alert. Not at all like he'd just rolled out of bed.

Which was exactly what I looked like.

I'd pulled on an old shirt of Ranger's, some jeans and worn sneakers. My hair was thrown into a messy bun. Not the chic, messy bun that Amy and Gwen perfected. No, the I haven't brushed and can't remember when I last washed my hair kind of bun.

So not cute.

Kace didn't seem overly disgusted, in fact, his eyes flared with an ember of heat.

"You got here quick," I observed.

He grinned. "Quick at some things, sweetheart. Take my time with others."

I swallowed roughly, my thighs pulsing with remembering.

"You weren't asleep?" I asked, trying to make my voice sound even.

He shook his head. "Was too buzzed. Worked out. Caught a few hours of the Asian stock market."

Who was this guy?

I decided to ignore that. "Okay, I wouldn't do this if it was any kind of emergency that didn't involve a PTA full of bitchy women judging me for forgetting something again," I said, snatching my keys and putting them in my purse.

"Babe, it's good. I like your kids," he reassured me.

My mind flashed back to the day after the migraine—the day that I had not mentioned to Kace since it happened because I didn't want to inspect what it had meant—and how both kids had raved about the time they'd spent with Kace. Jack had done so begrudgingly, as if it were something he was going to be punished for, but he did it, nonetheless. So it was safe to say the kids felt comfortable him, that they were happy to spend time with him. It only made me more reluctant to do this.

257

On cue, Lily entered the room. "Kace!" she yelled with glee. "You've come to hang out and have breakfast."

I'd already quickly briefed them on the situation, about Kace having breakfast with them while I went to get food. Lily had been over the moon. Jack had groaned about not needing a babysitter.

He was likely sulking in his room right now.

"Yep, breakfast is the most important meal of the day," Kace declared with a wink.

Lily's face sobered. "That's what I tell Mom, but she never listens to me, she never eats breakfast."

"Well, we're going to have to change that, aren't we?" Kace asked, eyes twinkling.

Lily nodded.

"Okay, I have no time for this." I kissed Lily on the head. "Be good for Kace. Don't try to trick him and say you're allowed ice cream for breakfast."

She folded her arms and pouted, since that was exactly what she'd been planning to do.

"Thank you," I muttered to Kace, still uneasy about this.

"Babe, we'll be fine. Go."

This was crossing a line now. Leaving Kace with my kids. Him being more than willing to do so. This was crossing to more than just sex. Or maybe that line had been destroyed a long time ago.

Nevertheless, I left.

―

I WAS SPEEDING. Because I was in a rush. Because I was distracted with my thoughts. Because the streets were quiet. I'd all but breezed through all of the traffic lights before getting outside of town. The local police weren't likely to touch me, even for blowing through stop lights. It's the way it was in Amber. The Sons and those connected to them were not bullet-proof, that much was clear, but they were definitely invisible to the law.

Edmond might be right, that might change one day, but not today.

So I was speeding when it happened. When a sharp corner came up ahead, when I was distracted enough to have to break at the last minute. But tapping on the break did nothing to slow me. I was fully paying attention now. My foot didn't tap the break this time. I slammed on it. Nothing happened.

Realization dawned.

Right about the second the turn came and there was a crash, crunching of metal, blinding pain, then not much else.

⌐══⌐

"LIZZIE, baby, you need to open your fucking eyes," a voice hissed.

I felt hands on me.

"Don't move her," another voice commanded. "We don't know what kind of damage has been done."

The hands on me tensed. "You want me to leave her in a *mangled fucking car?*" the voice, who I was now thinking belonged to Kace, clarified.

"I want you to lock it down for a second. Can hear the sirens and the ambulance minutes out," the other voice clipped. Bull. At least I thought so. A lot of these men had low, alpha male-type rasps. The pounding in my head and the ringing in my ears made it hard for me to differentiate.

"Lizzie?" Kace asked. "Can you open your eyes?"

He was worried. I could hear that in his voice. I could hear everything in his voice.

259

My vision was blurry at first. It was painful to blink. There was something wet and warm on my head. Blood, I deduced. A blinding headache, the fact that I'd been in a car wreck.

Kace was right in my face, hands on my neck, pale, terrified.

"I'm okay," I mumbled, trying to move.

His hands tightened. "No, baby. We're gonna wait for the paramedics before we do anythin' like that."

Sirens came closer, the pounding in my head getting worse.

"You need to tell me where it hurts," he demanded with urgency.

I wasn't sure how damaged my car was, but his voice told me it was bad. I could see shards of glass scattered around me.

"My head hurts," I groaned, taking stock of the rest of my body. Nothing seemed broken. I could feel my legs, wiggle my toes.

"Yeah, sweetheart, you're gonna have a headache for a spell," Kace said gently.

"I'm okay otherwise, I think." My stomach clenched. "The kids? Where are they?"

Kace's hands went to my cheek, gently cupping it. "They're fine. Mia is with them. She's making them ice cream for breakfast."

I smiled weakly. "Of course she is."

I didn't ask how Kace and Bull got here so quickly, how they'd known I'd crashed or how they'd gotten Mia to our place already. It was part of the alpha male magic.

Or maybe I was concussed.

The sirens were deafening now. Then they shut off. Bull came closer, eyes on me then Kace. "Brother, you need to step back, let them do their job."

Kace's eyes turned to granite. He didn't move. People in uniforms stood beside Bull. I recognized most of them. Not surprising. The town was small. Though I couldn't find their names right now.

"Kace, honey, you've got to move," I said gently. "I'm okay, promise."

His jaw turned hard. "You fucking better be."

Something in his voice caught me then.

It was the alpha male determination.

Somehow, I'd found myself in another Sons of Templar courtship.

Chapter 16

After being checked over at the hospital with Kace hovering—he refused to stay in the waiting room, the staff had done this dance many times before, so they just let him through—I was discharged a couple of hours after they brought me in.

A concussion, two stitches in my head. Apparently, I was lucky, considering the state of my car. Which I did not want to think about in that moment. I had insurance. It was good coverage. But I needed a car.

Ranger's truck was in the garage as it had been since he'd last driven it. I hadn't been able to bring myself to drive it. Definitely hadn't been able to bring myself to sell it.

Sometimes, in the darkest of times, I'd gotten out of bed in the middle of the night to sit in there. It still smelled of him. In amongst the musk and stale air. But only if I kept it closed up, didn't indulge in sitting in there often, only when the need was dire. It was the last thing I had of him.

If I opened it up and drove it around, it wouldn't smell of him anymore.

But I couldn't think about that. Not now. The drugs they

gave me were good at making the exterior and interior pain disappear.

Kace was always close. Always touching me. It was nice. I grateful for the pills since without them, I would've likely found a way to feel wrong about Kace. Being taken care of, protected, lusted after. It was meant to be a bad thing.

The drugs didn't make it feel bad. Not at all.

They made it feel normal. Natural. Easy.

They also made me feel like I'd just come from a spa and not a car wreck, so they weren't exactly to be trusted.

Olive had rushed over after I'd called her, calmly telling her what happened and trying to discourage her from getting in her car. I was obviously unsuccessful, presumably because Olive was a nurse who could care for someone on heavy drugs, and also because she'd lost her son and needed to see with her own eyes that I was okay.

What I didn't need her to see with her own eyes was Kace. Even in my drugged-up state, I knew that was wrong. I did my best trying to convince him to leave, but he did that hard-jawed thing and stayed put. It did help that Gage was there, too, watchful. Worried.

If Olive was surprised to see the two men from the Sons in my living room, she didn't show it. She didn't show much other than concern about the neat stitches on my head. She'd done her own examination, of course. She would've stayed for the entire day, I knew that for sure, but she had shift at the hospital which I convinced her not to miss. She'd be back tomorrow, I knew that. Olive was shaken from all of this, from how close she'd gotten to losing her remaining child, which was what I was to her.

I didn't tell my own mother, of course. The drugs made me feel foolish but not stupid.

Foolish enough to let Kace stay after Gage left.

———

THE DRUGS HAD WORN OFF. The kids had gone to bed, more than a little shaken that their only remaining parent had been in a car accident. Jack had been trying to stay staunch, as always, but he was visibly rattled. Lily hadn't left my side since I came home, then brought me a mug full of M&M'S to help me feel better. We called it 'M&M' tea, only to be brought out in the direst of emotional situations. Like when Lily liked her first boy and he'd called her 'weird'.

Once the pills had worn off, leaving me with my head throbbing, I felt overwhelming guilt for putting my kids through this again.

Kace had made dinner. Pasta bake. The kids had adored it. It didn't taste like much of anything to me, but he forced me to eat it. Just like he'd hovered all day to make sure that I didn't fall asleep and lapse into a coma.

I'd been getting texts and phone calls all day. Kace had apparently banned everyone from visiting, declaring that I needed time to rest.

SO THE ALPHA male bullshit has begun.

THAT TEXT WAS FROM BEX, and I could practically see her shit-eating grin through the screen.

It seemed the visitor ban did not extend to presidents of MCs since Cade arrived not long after we put the kids to bed.

Yes, *we*.

Lily wanted Kace to read the story while I lay beside her

until she fell asleep. It felt right and incredibly wrong at the same time.

Cade declined the offer of a beer, whisky or water. He was a man on a mission, it seemed. He had a family to get back to, so he didn't fuck around.

"Someone cut your brakes," Cade reported.

I blinked, pushing myself up from my position on the sofa. "What?"

Kace stood behind his president, body stiff, mouth straightened into a hard line. I'd never seen him like this. He'd kept it locked down throughout the day. He'd been intent on taking care of me, keeping me calm. Cooking. Distracting the kids from the stitches in their mother's head serving as evidence that she could not only get hurt but could die like their father.

"Towed your car, took it to the garage," Cade continued. "Something felt off, especially considering the crash. Brakes were cut. Clean. Definitely not an accident."

Though Cade spoke in his even, cold tone, I knew he was angry. Knew he somehow blamed himself. That's what these men did. They blamed themselves when something happened to people they were supposed to protect. The club was supposed to protect.

I was blindsided by this news. Although I had known something was wrong when I was driving. When nothing happened no matter how hard I stepped on the brakes. Ranger was religious about the upkeep of our vehicles. They were serviced every twelve months at the Sons of Templar garage. No way would someone have missed something like my brakes not working.

"Who would want to cut my brakes?" I wondered, more to myself than anyone else.

Cade's lips were a thin line. "That's what we're tryin' to figure out. Club doesn't have beef with anyone right now. And anyone who would be holding a grudge against us sure as shit wouldn't be targeting you."

Yes, it made no sense that I'd be a target even to the most ruthless of gangs. They'd want to go for maximum hurt, inflicting the deepest wounds. Sure, if I'd died, it would be a hit to the club. A small cut. But there was no one wearing a Sons cut who loved me to their core. Not anymore. No one who would use their pain and grief over losing me to make rash decisions and start a war, which was usually the goal when targeting Old Ladies.

It made no sense for the club to be connected with this. Someone was more focused on me, not the club.

"You have any kind of altercation with anyone? Anyone holding a grudge against you?" Cade questioned, obviously thinking the same thing.

I furrowed my brows, the expression painful. The most exciting and dangerous part of my life was my connection to the Sons of Templar. To be fair, the Sons pervaded most areas of my life. Or they had for over fifteen years.

They were still my family. They always would be. But a huge connection to them had been severed.

The majority of my life revolved around my kids. School runs. Laundry. Groceries. Going to sports games that bored me silly. Parent-teacher conferences. Suffering through dinners with my mother. I didn't have altercations with anyone. Mostly because even the mothers who disliked me did it privately because of my connection to the club. And almost all of my personal connections were within the club.

When it came down to it, I was a widowed mother who didn't do anything to require someone hating her enough to cut the brakes on her car.

"No," I told Cade. "Other than one mother at a bake sale who was pissed I didn't bake gluten free muffins, there's no one who would be willing to cut my brakes in order to get me out of the picture."

Cade nodded. There was guilt there. He felt responsibility for this. He already carried the responsibility for Ranger's death, wore it on his shoulders as a president did.

"That's not true."

Both Cade and I looked sideways to the person who spoke.

Kace wasn't looking at me. "A lawyer in town. Doesn't take rejection well."

I glared at him, anger bubbling up my throat. "Edmond is a toxic male who will do his best to cut with his words, but nothing else. He definitely wouldn't be someone who would cut my brakes just because I wouldn't go on a second date with him."

Kace acted like I hadn't spoken. "His interest in Lizzie is unhealthy. She backed him off in a way that made it clear he was never getting in."

Cade nodded. "We'll look into it."

"You will do no such thing," I snapped. "He didn't do this."

Cade's gaze was gentle, for him at least. "Regardless of whether he did or didn't, we're going to explore all avenues. We're not going to take any risks with you or the kids. Best case scenario, we scare off some asshole who doesn't understand the word no."

My mouth twitched with a sudden need to smile, envisioning Edmond flinching back while being confronted by someone like Cade and the rest of the Sons.

Despite my need to argue, I didn't. Not just because my head was pounding and my bed was beckoning. Because Cade was right. It would be reckless of me to think that there weren't people in this world who were capable of things like this. Everyone was capable of anything. It was stupid and deadly to think anything else. To have faith in humanity. To trust anyone who didn't share blood or wear a cut.

Shit.

If there really was someone out to get me, I had to tell them everything. Ideally, I would've liked to tell Cade without Kace in attendance, but there was no way would Kace move an inch right then. Maybe it would be better to not tell them about the incident at the house. It could also be infinitely stupid to keep that to myself.

"A few weeks ago, I had the feeling that someone had been in my house," I admitted in a small voice. I definitely didn't want to volunteer this information, mostly because of the reaction I expected—and the one I got—but also because I wasn't convinced that a 'feeling' was even worth mentioning. It seemed so alarmist. But I also knew that not mentioning this could be worse.

"What the fuck?" Kace hissed. "Why didn't you say shit about this?"

I should've told Cade in private. I did not need this response. Not in front of anyone, and not at all. His response demonstrating his belief that he was entitled to this information because he was fucking me. I hadn't said anything to Kace sooner because I did not want to awaken the alpha male protection curse.

I glanced to Kace, my eyes hard. "Because I thought I was just being paranoid. Nothing was taken, nothing was changed, no one jumped out of a closet. I figured I was just overreacting."

"You don't overreact to shit," Kace argued in a clipped tone.

There was too much ownership in that statement. Too much knowledge.

So I focused on Cade. "I don't know if anyone was even there, but if they were, they were only trying to scope things out."

Cade nodded. "We got you, Lizzie."

I smiled. "I know, Cade."

"We'll leave you to it," Cade said as he stood to leave. He leaned forward and brushed the back of his hand across my jaw. "We're gonna figure out who did this. And we're gonna make sure that no harm comes to you. Promise you that."

Here I was. Right where I hadn't wanted to be. Reliant on the club. On men. To protect me. Though I wasn't going to try and argue against it. I'd been in this life far too long, knowing it wouldn't do any good. Plus, there was real danger here. Danger that I surely couldn't handle on my own. Danger that the club knew how to handle. It was my responsibility as a mother to let them take care of it.

"I'm stayin'," Kace said, voice rough.

Cade glanced backward, his face not betraying a thing. His eyes found mine. "You okay with that?"

Of course I wasn't okay with that. I didn't want to be alone with Kace. Not now while I felt so vulnerable, so shaken. Especially not with him in protective, macho man mode. Things felt too raw. Too real.

But I knew far too well that arguing about this kind of shit, throwing sass, was a sure-fire way to shout from the rooftops that we were not only sleeping together but something else was going on too.

However Ashley kept her and Wire a secret for as long as she had, it was nothing short of a miracle. I made a mental note to pick her brain.

"Sure," I replied to Cade, glaring at Kace. "That's fine."

Something moved in Cade's eyes. Something I didn't at all like. He nodded once, did the whole chin lift with Kace and then left.

"You really had to be the one to volunteer for babysitting duty and do it in an intense, alpha male way that totally just spelled out we're sleeping together?" I snapped as soon as Cade left.

"Someone is after you," Kace ground out.

"Yes, I have a headache and the makings of a scar that prove that," I replied.

"So all bets are off now. I kept my distance, played by your rules 'cause I didn't really care about how I had you, it just mattered that I had you." He paced the room like a caged animal. "Could've lost you today. We all could've lost you. Your kids could've lost you."

His aim hit true, hitting me right in the heart.

"You can bet your beautiful ass I'll be acting alpha as fuck for as long as it takes us to figure out who the fuck was stupid enough to try to hurt you. Then you can steer us back in whichever direction you want."

Kace had stopped pacing now. He was staring at me, daring me to challenge him. There was so much aggression in his words. A fury. But I could see through it. He was scared. Because he cared about me. He hadn't ever hidden that. From the start, he'd made it clear that he'd wanted to know me. Then, that he wanted to fuck me. Then, after that, that he wanted more than fucking.

But he hadn't ever pressured me. Pushed me. He only dominated me when he was inside me, otherwise, I made the rules. But I guessed someone cutting the brakes in my car was the point where all of that stopped.

As much as I wanted to argue, just because I was scared about all of this, scared that I would get attached to another man taking care of me before I truly knew how to take care of myself, I didn't. I needed the club on this. My kids needed the club. And Kace.

"Whatever," I sighed, glancing toward the TV because I needed to escape his gaze. He'd put on *True Blood* because he loved vampires, something I'd recently discovered. That guy was always full of surprises. Then again, there were a lot of pretty graphic sex scenes that I was sure held his attention too.

It pissed me off that I was now addicted to the show. And the man who had turned me onto it.

Kace stared at me for a few beats more, then sat on the couch, lifting my legs and placing them so they were draped across his lap.

I didn't try to pull them back because I liked his warmth and his presence. Today had shaken me. Some faceless stranger creeping up to my home while my kids and I were sleeping, cutting my brakes? For what purpose? Were they going to try something again?

Yeah, I was scared. Not enough to cower, to hide away from the world. But enough to let Kace sit with me and watch TV and rub my feet, despite being scared by the casual intimacy of it all.

We didn't speak for a long time.

"I'm staying here tonight," he informed me.

"No you're not," I snapped.

"Beyond the fact that the doctor said someone needs to observe you, someone cut the brakes to your car. They didn't do it because you're a slow driver, babe. They did it 'cause they wanted to hurt you. End you. Neither of those things sit right with me. So I'm staying. You can argue with me all you like. It's happening."

"The kids—"

"The kids like me. The kids also know that their mother got hurt today. They know the patch I wear means something. That it will keep them safe. And I know this is a fucked-up way to do it, but they were gonna find out about us sooner or later. This stopped being about sex a long time ago, and you know it. We're not hashing this out right now because I can see by the way you're pinching your eyebrows together, you're hurting like a bitch, though, no way in fuck you'd admit it. So I'm going to run you a bath. You're gonna let me help you in and out of it. Then I'm putting you to bed. I'm gonna be in there with you too. 'Cause I need to sleep with your warm body next to mine. You're gonna try and fight that, too, out of instinct. But you want me there."

I bit my lip. Lying was a habit I was trying to curb. Or at least trying to reduce. Lying to Kace about my feelings seemed pointless; he saw everything. It felt wrong, too, in the face of all of the honesty he'd shown me.

"Fine," I gritted out.

He grinned, but chose not to gloat, which was definitely in his best interest.

He stayed the night.

And the next one too.

Three Weeks Later

Nothing had happened since the accident.

Well, a lot had happened. Just no one trying to kill me again. My scratches and bruises healed, like they'd never been there. Life returned to a semblance of normal.

A normal that included Kace in my bed every night. The first night after the accident, I'd let the kids wake up to him, but to the idea that he'd slept on the sofa. Neither of them seemed overly bothered, mostly because he made them waffles with whipped cream on them.

He stayed every night, but he crept out to his place as the sun rose. Having to wake before the sun and not sleep in his own bed didn't seem to bother Kace. Not in the slightest.

The fact that he was sleeping next to me every single night should've bothered me more. At least a little bit. It didn't.

I'd submitted to him physically from the first time we had sex. It took a lot longer for me to submit to him in other ways, though.

Especially two weeks after the accident. I'd woken up early and hadn't fallen back into an unsettled slumber like I normally did when Kace left. Instead, I got up, made coffee and sat out in the garden with my laptop. Writing.

I was doing that more these days. The days when I should've been looking for a job, finding a way to support my family. But I didn't do that. I continued to do all off the things that I'd done when Ranger was alive. And in my free time, I was on my laptop writing. There was a constant club presence, of course. Whether it be Kace or a prospect sitting on my sofa or outside my house.

Even though nothing had happened since the accident.

As stupid as it was, I'd all but forgotten about the fear I was supposed to be feeling, knowing that someone was out there wanting to do me harm. There wasn't room for it. And I did feel protected by Kace's presence. I felt confident in my ability to protect myself and my kids.

Whatever I was feeling poured out of me and onto my laptop. Into this... thing that I was creating. The thing without a title, without a name.

I'd been working on it almost every day after taking the kids to school, after putting in my first load of laundry or whatever the chore was that I knew not to postpone too long. Today, however, Kace had texted me and told me that he was taking me out for the day. He'd also said to wear something comfortable.

I didn't know what to make of that. Comfort for me was tight black jeans, studded boots, a tight black tank, a crapload of silver jewelry and a leather jacket, even though fall in California didn't really require it.

273

When Kace arrived, his eyes ran over me with a heat that hadn't dulled, despite the time we'd spent together. It reminded me of the kind of attraction Ranger and I'd had. Sure, through the years of marriage, our struggles, there had been peaks and valleys. But that passion had never gone away. Every time he'd kissed me. I got butterflies, sparks, fireworks, all of that.

It was cruel to both me and to Kace to continually compare the two men, my experiences with them, but it was also impossible not to. Though truthfully, there was no comparison. The only similarities they had were they wore the same cut and had those same, macho, alpha tendencies that men in those cuts usually had. Other than that, they were polar opposites. Kace was quick to smile, had a lightness around him, despite his past. Always ready to tease. Ranger was darkness. Once you learned to look at him close enough. He wasn't easy or laid back. He was tortured by his past. By his scars. He loved fiercely and forever. He smiled and laughed with our kids, but not without pain.

Two very different men. Two different seasons in my life.

"You look fuckin' beautiful, babe," Kace said, grabbing me and pressing our bodies together.

My stomach dipped when he did this, as he did every time he greeted me. "You're not so bad yourself," I murmured. "Future reference, comfortable as a dress code is not enough detail for a woman like me."

A line creased his forehead. A woman like you?"

I nodded. "A woman who likes to accessorize. Who likes to look good. Looking good isn't always mutually exclusive with comfort. I'm okay with that."

He smiled, kissing me. "So noted," he chuckled against my lips. "Just so you know, you look good no matter what. First thing in the morning, hair all crazy, still shaking off sleep, that's my favorite."

I raised a brow. "Bullshit."

He grinned. "Believe me or not, it's the truth."

I ached to fight him on that, but figured we could be here a while. "So, are we going somewhere, or is this some kind of elaborate ruse to get me into bed?" I questioned, totally fine with either one.

"Baby, I don't need an elaborate ruse to get you into bed," he smirked.

I scowled at him.

He just grinned back, stepping away slightly, intertwining our hands. Kace was all about touching. If I was within touching distance, he was there. When the kids were around, I made sure that didn't happen. But he took every single moment that they were distracted, reading, playing, to put his hands on me.

I liked it. His hunger for me. Bordering on desperation. Because I needed it too.

"We're going on a ride," he stated, leading me out the door.

His bike was parked in the driveway, next to a shiny SUV.

It was a 'loaner' from the garage. One that arrived the day after my accident. Cade had dropped it off without a word. He knew Ranger had a truck, and he knew it was still locked in the garage. Yet somehow, he knew how terrified I was to drive it.

So he'd made sure I had something to drive.

Because that was the kind of guy he was. Badass. Scary. Deadly. Kind. Protective. Emotionally considerate.

Kace had come on outings with me and the kids because he'd needed to. Of course, the kids didn't know someone might be trying to kill their mother, so they assumed he came along because he wanted to. Though that was probably true, he seemed to genuinely enjoy accompanying us.

He drove the SUV every time we went out.

We'd never gone on his bike.

I froze in the driveway, staring at it.

His hand was in mine. I could still taste his lips in my mouth, my thighs aching from what he'd done to me last night. Yet the prospect of getting on the back of his bike was too intimate.

It meant something in the MC world. I'd never been on the back of anyone's bike apart from Ranger's. No exceptions.

There was something pivotal about this moment. Kace knew it. He might've been younger, but he'd been in the MC all of his adult life. He knew the protocols when it came to this. Knew what me getting on the back of his bike would mean.

He didn't say anything as I just stood there, staring. He was patiently waiting. For me to either move forward or run back into the house. Run back into the past.

Every part of me wanted to do that. It was safer. Didn't come with all the internal dilemmas and real-life consequences.

Kace wouldn't say anything if I fled. Wouldn't judge me for it. Because that's the kind of person he was. This was the first time he'd pushed me toward something I hadn't guided us to first. Our secret was pretty much the worst kept secret in the Sons of Templar, although Ashley still held the title for the best.

Most of the women in my group knew, and were madly ecstatic about it, but refrained from talking about it since they knew how uncomfortable it made me. I assumed that they'd told their husbands, though, I'd promised them to secrecy. Not because they had big mouths or anything, but because that's what you did with your husband. You shared secrets knowing that they wouldn't go anywhere. You shared everything, and it was safe.

None of the men had said anything, of course. But Lucky grinned far too widely whenever Kace and I arrived somewhere together. I made sure not to act like we were in any way together, but that was for me and my delusions more than anyone else.

Getting on the back of his bike was a sure way to shatter those delusions.

I didn't make the conscious choice to move toward the bike, but it happened anyway.

Kace didn't say anything. But when I got to the bike, he grabbed the helmet that was sitting on the seat, snatched me by the back of my neck and kissed me hard. Branding me.

Then, I got on the back of his bike.

Chapter 17

Although Kace didn't like it, it had been almost a month of nothing, so I was no longer being tailed by the Sons of Templar. He did check my car daily now, before I drove it. Which I was totally fine with. I wasn't taking any risks with the kids and wasn't really in the mood for another concussion. Plus, I really didn't need my premiums to go up. Money was still somewhat of a worry even though my buffer had suddenly grown healthier these past two months. My monthly cut from the Sons of Templar was considerably more than I used to get.

I'd tried to take this up with Cade who shrugged, saying that the club was earning a lot more due to Kace and his investments.

Though I didn't doubt that Kace was bringing in a profit, I suspected that he had something to do with the increased size of the envelope I was getting. He'd said the exact same thing as Cade when I tried to talk to him about it, plus he hadn't mentioned my job search or my money situation. As much as it pissed me off and felt like charity, it helped. Gave me a little more breathing room.

Not that I was any closer to figuring out what I wanted to do with my life. Sure, I could've gone back to school, giving me some more options in the job market. But in addition to school being expensive and having two kids to look after, I didn't know what the fuck I'd even go to school for. Nothing interested me enough. I was in a luxurious position, being so picky about all of this instead of having to wait tables for nothing plus tips.

There was only so much time I could stay like this, though. I had kids to feed. Groceries to buy.

It was only a matter of time before I bumped into Edmond. In a town like Amber, there was no avoiding people. Though I had tried my best. Despite Kace's very real warning that he turn if he ever saw me on the street, I figured Edmond's arrogance would trump any sense of self-preservation he had. Beyond that, he probably didn't truly believe that Kace would really do anything.

He hadn't been in Amber long enough to truly understand the Sons of Templar. In his mind, they were low-life criminals, and he was a man with the expensive suit and haircut. The family money. Fancy degree. No doubt he thought all of those things worked as some kind of bulletproof vest to misfortune and violence.

So when I saw him while walking to my car in the grocery store parking lot, it wasn't surprising that he didn't walk the other way. Instead, when his eyes landed on me, he changed directions and walked directly toward me.

"Fuck," I muttered under my breath.

I was halfway through loading my groceries into the car. I wasn't about to leave any of it all; our finances weren't really conducive to me abandoning a week's worth of groceries just because of some asshole who didn't like to be rejected.

Plus, it took a lot more to scare me than a guy with a three-hundred-dollar haircut and shoes that cost more than my car payments.

I kept unloading my groceries from the cart when he stopped in front of me.

"I don't have anything to say to you," I proclaimed.

"I wanted to come over here and apologize," Edmond replied, sounding sensible, sheepish and nothing like the man on my doorstep weeks ago.

I sighed. Straightened. Looked at Edmond. "You don't need to apologize. Not because what you did and said aren't worth apologizing for, they sure as hell are, but I honestly don't want to be here while you try to trick yourself into thinking a few empty words make you a good man," I snapped.

His eyes flickered with that anger he'd kept so well locked down on our date. "My behavior was beyond atrocious."

I didn't say anything.

"It was completely out of character for me," he continued. "I was raised to respect women. To treat them with dignity and respect."

"Well, you sure as hell didn't do that," I told him.

He looked down at his shoes, doing very well at playing humble. Which was what he was doing. Playing. "Yeah, I didn't. My mother would be ashamed of me. I let my feelings get the best of me. And I do have feelings for you. Unlike I've had for any woman."

I put the last of the groceries in my trunk, pushing the cart to the return spot because people that didn't do that were assholes. I had the sneaking suspicion that Edmond was not a cart returning person.

Though he did follow me when I went.

"You don't know me well enough to have any of those kinds of feelings," I retorted while walking.

"I know enough about you," he countered. "And I want to

know more. Want another chance. I'm better for you, for your kids, than some... *biker*." He spat the word out like he was describing a serial killer.

Oh, no he didn't.

I whirled around, stopping in my tracks. "No, you are not better than him or any of them," I hissed. "You're much, *much* worse. Now do yourself a favor, and leave me alone."

I tried to turn back to my car, but a hand on my upper arm stopped me. Squeezing hard. To the point of pain.

"Please," he begged.

I looked down to his hand still gripping my arm. It was smooth. The nails manicured. Feminine somehow. But they were still going to leave a mark. Because he wanted to.

"Take your hand off me, right now," I instructed calmly.

"If you'll just listen to me."

Nope. I was done listening. I raised my hand and moved it fluidly, connecting with his nose, happy to hear the crunch. I hoped that meant a bone broke, so I'd ruin the perfect symmetry to his face.

The hand at my arm fell off as he doubled over to hold his nose, now bleeding.

"A little word to the wise, since they obviously didn't teach it to you in law school. You don't put your hands on a woman, and you definitely don't keep them on a woman when she asks you to let go. Now, you don't leave me alone, it won't be a biker that's teaching you a lesson, it'll be me. Biker sluts know how to hurt a lawyer just as good as the men in cuts."

I turned on my heel and walked away, smiling despite the dull ache in my fist from the impact on bone. It was the first time I'd had to punch someone in the face. My life was lived among violence, but enough people knew I belonged to Ranger, belonged to the club, they weren't near stupid enough to do anything that required me to punch them in the face.

But times had changed. I was the one who had to defend myself now. Sure it hurt, but all I was was pain these days. And I liked it.

———

THIS TIME, I didn't feel it when I came home. Didn't get the same feeling that had me going for the gun and almost shooting one of my closest friends.

Maybe I was distracted, still pissed off from the interaction with Edmond. Overwhelmed with what my life was now. Distracted by the knowledge that Kace would notice the swelling of my knuckles and the purplish bruising already blooming on my upper arm. As much as I'd love to have a front row seat to his visit with Edmond, I didn't need the drama. And I had the feeling that Kace going after him would only make things worse. Edmond would run with his tail between his legs, for a while to be sure. But this was a man used to getting everything he wanted. Used to the world bending to him. He definitely hadn't ever been punched in the face by a woman.

So he'd try something. I couldn't guess what, but it would be something sly, something shady. It wouldn't really hurt the club. Or maybe it would. I couldn't tell how fucked up this guy was. But I wasn't about to risk the club for my honor. That was long gone.

I'd showered, trying to get the echo of Edmond's hands off me.

No way had I led a sheltered life since Ranger patched in. I'd seen some of the worst humanity had to offer, losing one of my good friends in the most brutal of ways. My husband too. But I'd never been hurt physically before. Never had a man touched me without my permission. Edmond's casual violence, the possession in his touch, unnerved me. Left me more shaken than it should've.

Hence the shower. With all of the fancy, and I guessed very expensive bath and body products, thanks to Amy and Gwen. My plan was to put on my most expensive, sexiest lingerie—of which I had a lot, I loved it and Ranger appreciated the hell out of it—put on a badass outfit and make myself feel like the strong, confident woman I was pretending to be.

That plan went to shit when I opened my underwear drawer. There was no lace. Just cold, slithering, writhing snakes.

The blood curdling scream I let out kind of shot the strong, confident woman thing straight to hell.

———

"THAT'S THE LAST OF THEM," Lucky declared, shivering. "Fucking hate snakes."

He looked even paler than I was. Then again, I'd been sitting in the living room with a bottle of tequila and Evie and Ashley by my side whereas Lucky, Gage and Kace had been in charge of getting rid of the snakes that were residing in my underwear drawer, and looking for places where others might've been.

Luckily for all of us, there weren't any another cold-blooded creature of hell in my home. Nothing in the kid's bedrooms, which I'd made them check twice.

Kace had been stone faced since he'd arrived minutes after I'd called him. I was pretty proud of the fact I hadn't been as hysterical as I'd felt. Which was pretty fucking hysterical. I'd calmly told him about the situation, and he'd yelled at me to get out of the house and lock myself in the car until he got there.

He was likely afraid that whoever put the snakes in my underwear drawer was still in the house. But I wasn't exactly worried about that, since if someone had been in there waiting to kill me, they would've done it while I was in the shower. No one was more vulnerable than when they were naked.

So I didn't lock myself in the car. Didn't let whatever this was shut me out of my own home. My children's home. I'd poured myself a drink, sat on my couch—after I'd checked it for snakes with a broomstick—and waited. Granted, I didn't have to wait long for Kace to arrive, then half the club.

He'd been most unhappy to find me sitting on the sofa instead of locked up in the car like he'd told me to be.

"What the fuck, Lizzie?" he hissed, rushing toward me, eyes raking over my body, looking for signs of mortal injury. He didn't see the bruises on my arms because I'd managed to put on a big, fluffy robe since I couldn't exactly greet everyone terrified and naked in only a towel.

That wasn't Old Lady behavior. Well, Old Lady behavior would've been to get dressed in badass jeans, boots and a full face of makeup. But I wasn't that brave. I also was pretty sure at least one snake had escaped, and I had no idea whether they were poisonous or not. I figured if someone went to all the trouble of filling my drawer with snakes, they weren't going to do it with harmless ones.

"I told you to sit outside," he gritted out.

"You might not know this about me, sweetheart, but I don't do whatever a man commands me to do. I sure as shit don't lock myself in a car, terrified of some cold worms with long teeth," I snapped back.

"Tell him, sista," Lucky muttered. "Though, I'd definitely lock myself in the car. Snakes." He shivered. "Got any rubber gloves?"

"Get in the fucking bedroom," Cade barked.

Lucky obeyed his president, but he did not look happy about it.

Kace looked like he really wanted to say more about the whole situation, but luckily Cade was there to save the day, meaning that he was the first to verbally ask if I was okay—because that was the kind of guy that Cade was.

After that, it was a blur of activity.

Evie arrived first.

Then Ashley.

I was sure that other women would've come if not for the fact that there was a chance of something bad lurking somewhere. But their husbands probably banned them from coming. Not that that would stop them, mind you. I sent a group text telling everyone I was fine and that we would debrief over cocktails the next day.

Olive was picking the kids up from school, filling in for me after I'd told her I had something urgent come up. Rest assured, I wasn't going to tell her the details. She'd been happy over the years to know the bare minimum when it came to the club.

Evie and Ashley were here because they did not have men in cuts telling them what to do—though Wire shot Ashely a look when he entered the house.

Various men came through the house, checking for explosives, other creatures or recording devices.

They found none, thankfully.

But they also found that the snakes in my underwear drawer were highly venomous. This little tidbit had Kace checking me for bites once again. I was dressed by then, thankfully Evie had brought clothes with sleeves long enough to cover the marks on my arms.

Once all was declared safe, the men started to disperse. But not without promises of vengeance, expressing their determination in finding whoever this was and ending them. I trusted them to do so. I would not lose a single wink of sleep, knowing this person was going to die.

The watch was back on now. Kace was going to go DEFCON level alpha, no doubt.

Ashely and Evie eventually left. Evie had offered me and the kids to come and stay at her place, but I'd refused. Exactly like she had expected me too. Nothing was scaring me out of my home.

Olive was going to have the kids for dinner so I could get my shit under control. So I could do my own check of the house. So I could have a conversation with Kace. Or so he could have a conversation with me. The testosterone was almost leaking out his ears at this point.

He paced the kitchen while I made M&M tea.

"This is my shit. Coming to haunt me. Haunting you. It fucking has to be," he grated out, running a hand through his hair.

I frowned at him, pouring M&Ms into a mug. "How does this have anything to do with you?"

Kace stopped pacing to stare at me. "Because, the Sons are legit now. The Amber chapter doesn't have the kind of enemies who go after Old Ladies. Who'd do this fucked up shit. My old chapter... we did. Thought I'd cut ties. Thought I could come here to start a new life. But fuck!" he yelled the last word. I jumped, not expecting the outburst. The violence in it.

I was also jumpy because, well, there were fucking snakes in my underwear drawer this morning.

"You think that someone or something has not only followed you, but stalked you for long enough to see that you were in a relationship with me? And then stalked me for long enough to know my routines and then do cowardly things like cutting my brakes or putting fucking snakes in my underwear drawer?" I asked. "No, that's not exactly the style of any guy in the MC life."

Kace stared at me. I could tell he wanted to argue because

he wanted to take the blame for this, wanted to shoulder all of the responsibility, even if it didn't make sense. That's who Kace was. That's who all of these men were. They appreciated their women. They knew our strength, but they'd never want us to have to use it.

"Yeah, but you don't exactly live the life of someone who has secret enemies who like to torment them and attempt to murder them," he retorted.

He wasn't wrong.

"If this doesn't have anything to do with me or the club, and that's a big fucking if, babe, it was that lawyer fucker, I know it," he hissed.

The club had already sufficiently scared the shit out of Edmond. Lucky had given me the play-by-play in a tone that had told me Edmond had embarrassed the shit out of himself. Much like I'd expected him to.

Then again, he wasn't scared enough by the looks of our interaction today. But he also wasn't the one to put the snakes in my drawers, considering I was punching him in the face around the time someone was doing that.

But Cade had been convinced that he was not the one who cut my brakes, and on the slim chance he had, he had far too much self-preservation to try anything else.

Kace, on the other hand, had not let it go.

I rubbed my arms without thinking, trying to figure out how in the fuck I was going to hide the bruises—that would only grow darker—from him. The time was long passed where I could push him away. Where I could reject his touch. Ignore my need for him. Sure, if I really meant it, he wouldn't touch me.

The problem was, I could never mean it. Couldn't even pretend to mean it.

Kace noticed the way I rubbed my arms, the way my face looked when I did it.

"Baby," he said slowly. "Let me see your arms."

Fuck.

There was no way around it. Especially not now. If I had showed him right away, the bruises wouldn't be quite as dark.

"I don't want you to freak out," I responded, not moving.

"The fact you're saying that means that I've got something to be freaked out about," he snapped. "Now show me your fucking arms."

Though every feminist bone in my body told me to rebel against such a command uttered in that way, I slowly did as he said.

"It's going to look worse than it is," I warned, pulling my sleeves up. "You know better than anyone about how easily I bruise. But I saw Edmond at the grocery store today—which clears him of being the snake person. He made it clear he wanted to continue some kind of relationship with me. But I made it clear that most definitely wasn't happening. I tried to walk away. He tried to stop me."

That's when I showed him my arms.

Kace stilled completely. His eyes zeroed in on the reddish-purple marks on my upper arms. He didn't say a word. Not for a long time. But the energy that was radiating off him scared the shit out of me.

"He is fucking *dead*," he whispered.

My blood turned cold, and I gripped his arm firmly, scared he was going to run off and commit murder right then.

"No," I implored. "Kace, look at me."

His eyes stayed glued to my arms. "He put his fucking hands on you, Lizzie. He's made it clear he's got no sense, no respect and no will to live."

"You're not going to kill him," I repeated gently.

Kace's eyes finally met mine. They weren't full of fire or rage. No, they were cold and empty, the mask of the man who'd worn the same cut and a wedding ring for many years. Ranger wore that same expression when he came home covered in blood. When he tried to push me away. When he was preparing to do something that would stain his soul. He wore it on the night he died.

"He put his hands on you," Kace repeated. "He did that, there's a high fucking chance he's responsible for the other shit too."

"Honey," I beseeched. "Think about it. Edmond obviously thinks of me as some kind of conquest, something that he wants only because he can't have it. It makes no sense that he would want to try to kill me or torture me with snakes. It's not exactly his style."

"Men who want something special, want something precious and they know deep down that they never gonna get it, do shit that ain't got nothing to do with style. Beyond that, this fucker is bad. I see that in him. No matter what kind of suit he wears or car he drives. Even if he didn't do that shit, he put his hands on my Old Lady. He's going to fucking pay."

I wasn't surprised by this. This came with the life. Though many people on the outside thought that Old Ladies were thought of as property, possessions, that couldn't be further from the truth.

The men in the Sons of Templar cherished their women. Treasured them. Worshipped them. They took it as their personal responsibility to keep them safe. Happy. Unharmed. So when shit happened to put them in danger, hurt them, these men took it as a personal failure.

Losing Laurie had nearly killed Bull.

What happened to Bex had broken Lucky in a way that meant he'd never shine or smile quite the same.

Same with everything that had happened to Gwen, Amy, Lauren, Lily and Mia.

These men took the hits like they'd landed directly on them.

It was part of the MC code. Anyone who touched or harmed an Old Lady had to pay. I'd decided it was just the heat of the moment, Kace calling me that. That was something I could not handle right now.

"He will pay," I promised. "Eventually. You can go and threaten him, punch him once if you must, and do whatever you gotta do. But right now, I need you to say here. With me. With the kids. We've had enough violence and hurt to last us for a long while. So how about we just try our best not to go and seek more out? It'll find us soon enough."

Kace did not look happy about this, all of his alpha instincts screaming at him right now. There was anger in him that needed to be released.

I led Kace to the couch, and he thankfully let himself be led. I moved to climb on him, straddling him. "For now, I'm sure you've got some energy you need to release, and I suggest you direct it at me." I moved, grinding myself against him.

He hissed, his hands settling on my hips. Then his lips were on mine. And we channeled his anger into three orgasms.

Chapter 18

The kids came home after dinner. Kace was in my bedroom taking a shower when they arrived. Lucky, too, since Olive came in to chat, and I was not ready for her to meet him or know that he was in my life. The guilt of my deception settled heavily on my shoulders.

I didn't tell her about the snakes. Instead, I thanked her, hugged her and made plans for dinner the following week.

Luckily, both kids were tired from the food and the activities with their grandmother, so they were ready to go straight to bed.

Kace was reading Lily a story, Jack was indulging in his allotted one hour of TV time in bed, and I was outside, trying to decompress.

"What you doing out here?"

Something draped around my shoulders, despite there only being the faintest hint of winter in the air. I liked the chill. Something creeping into my bones, reminding me that I was alive.

But then there was the man who liked me, the one who

wanted to protect me from even the slightest chill in the air, despite him knowing that I'd survived well below zero in my past.

Kace sat down beside me, handing me a mug. It felt warm in my palms.

I glanced to him. "You made tea?"

He shrugged, his own mug in his hand.

Something warm moved over me, and it had nothing to do with the tea. "Bex is going to love that," I murmured.

Kace chuckled but didn't say anything else. He'd asked his question, giving me the option of answering or sitting in silence. It seemed to me he was over his earlier fury toward me.

I sipped my tea. "I like to sit out here sometimes," I answered finally. "Listening to the sounds of the neighbors. The crickets. The birds. Watching the sky. Listening in on people living normal, carefree lives. Even though I can't see them. I don't want to see them. I just like to hear them, be an audial voyeur for a while. It's nice. Gives me hope that normal is real. Normal can happen around me, even if it won't happen to me." I smiled. "I guess it's my version of meditation."

Kace wasn't smiling back at me. "You don't think normal is gonna happen to you?" he repeated.

I arched a brow at him. "Honey, I just had someone put a crap-ton of snakes in my underwear drawer, that's not exactly something that happens to Suzie Teller."

"Who the fuck is Suzie Teller?"

"I went to high school with her. We were friends. Kind of. She was a bit of a bitch. But in a teenage girl type of way. She grew up just fine. Married the boyfriend she met in college. He owns a construction business. They live on the other side of town. Our kids play sometimes. She brought over a lot of casseroles when Ranger died. But she made a point to keep her distance, you know? From me, from the club. Didn't want to cause any offense, of course, but she didn't want my lifestyle to rub off on her. Her husband didn't get shot to death. And I'm pretty sure if she got her brakes cut or found snakes in her underwear drawer, it would be a big fucking deal. For me it's just another Tuesday."

I didn't sound like I was feeling sorry for myself. At least I really hoped I didn't. Because I wasn't. This was the life I'd chosen. For whatever reason, someone wanted to hurt me, scare me. I fucking hated that because of what it might do to my kids, but I wasn't all that scared for me. Wasn't even all that surprised.

My mug was no longer in my hand.

Kace was no longer sitting beside me.

He was on his knees in front of me, clutching my neck.

"Is that what you think?" he hissed. "That all life has for you is death and violence? That you're never going to have normal, happy life?"

I let out a heavy sigh, surprised at how angry he'd gotten. "Look at my life. You see anything to prove me wrong?"

"I'm gonna prove you wrong," he declared. "This shit is gonna end, and when it does, we're gonna do normal shit. Go to Costco. Have brunch. Whatever the fuck normal people do. You'll get that. Until you get bored. And you will get bored, baby." His eyes flared, hands stroking my jaw. "Then we'll go back to fucking in the club bathroom. Riding down the coast. Living the outlaw life you were born for."

I blinked at Kace. Once. Twice. Then I looked around the backyard my husband had created for me.

"I can't fall in love again," I murmured, meeting his eyes, making my gaze cold and my voice indifferent.

He didn't blink at the look nor the words. Nothing showed on his face. "Okay," he replied.

"I'm serious," I snapped, somehow annoyed at the mild response even though that was supposedly what I'd wanted. "You need a young heart for love. One without scars and marks. Mine isn't young anymore. Not by a long shot." My voice hitched ever so slightly. "I'm not a person who can love now. You need to understand that moving forward, if we're going to be public with this. It can work for however long it works. But that's what this is. This is something that's always going to be this. I'm not going to fall in love with you."

He was quiet for a long time. Or what seemed like a long time for us. Seconds yawned into hours when conversations like this happened with Kace. When I let him through the cracks, letting him brush past all my broken pieces.

"I'm not arguing, babe," he tilted his head to the side.

"You're not?"

He shook his head. "We don't really have time to argue about this kind of shit when someone's trying to cause you harm. That's my focus right now. You can feel however you wanna feel. It's my goal to make sure that you're alive to feel it. I'm going hunting. First thing tomorrow."

Something moved in my chest. Something cold and painful. "You're not going hunting," I exclaimed.

"Someone's fuckin' with you. Right now, we don't know who they are, what their intentions are. What we do know is that they've entered your house. Where you sleep, where your children sleep. So I don't give a fuck what their intentions are. All I care about is making sure they forget your name at the least. Ideally that they forget to breathe."

I wasn't really focusing on his promises of death and murder. I was used to such things. In fact, I expected them. That was the way of this life. It was hard at first. To see death and violence used as currency. Giving us things and taking them away. Having violence be the first reaction. Retaliation. But like with everything else, I got used to it. Surrounded by enough of things, even the most horrible of things, they become normal. Beyond that, I wanted blood. Kace was right, whoever this was knew where I lived. Knew my routines. Knew about my kids. My conscience could handle this person being dealt with if it meant my children weren't in danger.

So none of that bothered me.

What needed further discussion was the first part.

"Old Lady?" I repeated. There was no hiding from it now.

Some of that alpha male fury left Kace's face. "Yeah, babe. In case you haven't noticed, we sleep together every night. We're no longer a secret. I have breakfast with your kids. I love your kids. You're on the back of my bike. Know you've been in this life long enough to know what that means. Also know that you've only been in this life belonging to someone else. Expecting to be theirs forever. So I know it fucks you up to hear me call you that. Know you got one hundred and one things to say about it too. All of them arguments. I hear them. I get you. I know you. If you don't want me to be your Old Man, I get it. But you *are* my Old Lady. So I'm going hunting. Now, I'm gonna let you sit out here. Stew. But not for long. I'll be in bed waiting for you."

He kissed me hard on the lips before turning and walking away, leaving no room for arguments.

———

WE ATTENDED our first club party together as a couple.

It was damn near impossible to hide it after the snake incident. And I didn't want to hide anymore. There was no point, really. Not with the kids knowing. I didn't want to create any kind of emotional bullshit with them, thinking they had to keep secrets about relationships. Didn't want to teach them that loss meant your life ended and that happiness wasn't possible.

At the same time, I didn't want them to think that their father was forgotten or that he hadn't meant the world to me. It was a thin fucking tightrope to walk, but that was life. That was motherhood.

I'd never been comfortable with PDA, plus I still wasn't uncomfortable in this new skin. With old memories merging always into the present. Ranger's ghost lurking. It felt strange but not wrong.

No one treated us like it was wrong, of course. There were plenty of grins. The men seemed to be happy about the pairing, but I was sure there were also warnings of death and dismemberment should Kace fuck with me. A punishment that he'd surely been well aware of before he'd started up with me.

The beers I'd drank before leaving home helped with my feelings of unease. Then the margaritas Amy made. Kace had one beer then switched to soda, since we were with the kids. He encouraged me to have fun. It was jarring, to be part of a couple again. A team. Where one could get a little tipsy knowing the other was sober enough to deal with any kind of scrapes or emergencies with the children, able to drive everyone home.

It scared me. A lot. Knowing what it was like to have that taken away, losing that half you'd learned to rely on. I wanted to push him away. Wanted to run from this. But I kept my feet on solid ground. Kace's hand sliding into mine, anchoring me.

"As much as I want to keep you here, getting tipsy so I can fuck my woman drunk later on, the kids are getting tired, and this party will become X-rated in another hour or so," Kace murmured in my ear.

A quick glance around told me he was right. Everyone who'd brought kids were rounding them up and piling them into various vehicles. The music was getting louder now, and the handful of members who were unattached—slightly more now due to the infusion of new patches after the war—getting drunker. The club girls would arrive shortly, of course, only after every child was gone. It wasn't dark yet, but it would be soon. It had been a long day. The kids had been running around, eating, enjoying the company of their extended family.

But they were getting that sleepy look that any parent could see. Apparently, Kace saw it too.

"Yes, we need to go," I agreed, leaning into him slightly because tequila made me forget I was supposed to be easing into this.

I caught Mia's eye, and she grinned stupidly, giving me two thumbs up. I couldn't help but grin stupidly back at her.

Because I was happy. Stupidly so.

WE GOT THE KIDS HOME, fed them a snack because they'd eaten junk at the barbeque all day. They went to bed easily, tired as they were. It was getting to the point that they were used to Kace being there. Being part of the nighttime routine. The morning routine too.

They knew nothing of the potential danger their mother was in. I planned to keep it that way. So it was better that they thought Kace was here because we were together—though I hadn't exactly had that talk with them—than he was protecting me from an unknown psychopath.

The club was on high alert. Kace had made his visit to Edmond. I hadn't tried to stop it. Knew I couldn't. Plus, Edmond deserved something, for thinking it was okay to put his hands on a woman. I thought I had reacted pretty well when

Lauren told me she'd seen him at the café with one hell of a shiner.

Kace had bruises on his knuckles after the visit. I hadn't asked about them.

Beyond Edmond, they had no leads on who might've been after me. There wasn't exactly a long list of people with active grudges against the Sons. Sure, we had enemies, but none stupid enough to pull this kind of shit. None cowardly enough either.

We had a brand-new security system installed. Top of the line, according to Wire. Kace, or whoever was with me at the time, did a walk-through of the house before we entered. A prospect on me whenever I left the house, when I went grocery shopping or did anything. I carried a gun in my purse too.

But I wasn't scared. Wasn't going to stop living my life. Stop moving forward. Over the years, I'd learned how to carry on, despite whatever was brewing with the club.

"You have fun today, babe?" Kace asked, opening the fridge for a beer.

I was leaning against the breakfast bar, a beer of my own in hand. I'd sobered, putting the kids to bed, but I really liked the idea of tipsy sex with Kace.

"I had a lot of fun today," I replied honestly.

Something moved in his face, something intense. A glimpse into the feelings he had for me maybe. Then again, he'd made never made qualms about hiding that. How much he wanted to be in my life. In my kids' lives.

"I'm glad, Lizzie," he said, voice quiet.

"We're public now," I proclaimed. Then I thought of my mother-in-law, my parents, still ignorant to my new relationship. My stomach lurched at that thought. "To the club, at least."

"You feel okay about that?" he cocked his head, waiting for my reply.

I nodded slowly. Sure, there were a lot of feelings I still had to wade through. And I still hadn't let him in, not fully, not yet. But I was trying. "I think I am."

"No less than five women have threatened to gut me 'medieval style' if I hurt you," he shared.

I raised my brow. "That didn't scare you off?"

"Oh, it scared me plenty. Since I knew that none of them were speaking in any kind of metaphorical way. But scare me off?" He shook his head. "I'm definitely brave enough to face the wrath of your protective friends. Mostly because I have no intention of hurting you."

"No one ever usually intends to hurt people," I countered. "Not in relationships, at least. But it tends to happen, one way or another. Romantic entanglements are nothing but pain and suffering with orgasms in between to distract you."

Kace made a choking sound, as I said that just as he'd taken a pull of his beer. He coughed and thumped on his chest before recovering. "Well, that's certainly one way of putting it. A little jaded."

I gave him a look. "Honey, I'm forty and already a widow with two kids and some unknown person trying to kill me. I think I'm entitled if not required to be a little jaded."

"I can't disagree with you there," he replied, stepping forward. My stomach dipped at his closeness. At the glint in his eyes. Something that I'd seen in passing since we'd been spending time together but not something he'd ever kept on his attractive face for long. Likely because he didn't want to push me, was being respectful or whatever. It looked like he had decided that he no longer wanted to be respectful.

I definitely wasn't mad about that, but I was terrified.

"But," he continued advancing. "There's one thing that comes out of romantic entanglements..."

My back found the wall as I realized I'd been retreating.

"Orgasms," he whispered, mouth inches from mine. His

hands settled on my hips, firm, burning through skin and bone to the core of me. "And I happen to be excellent at giving them."

———

THE ONE PLACE that Kace didn't come with me to were the dinners with Evie. I wasn't ready for that yet. That was something that was mine. Mine and the kids. I still needed that time with her. Still needed to talk to her about all of this shit.

I sensed she still needed it too. No matter how hard and strong she seemed on the outside, she was still a woman who'd lost the love of her life, who'd had to adjust to an entirely different life. There was pain there.

Misery.

And misery did love company.

"Do you blame them?" I asked her, watching the sun set. "The club? The life, for taking Steg?"

Evie chuckled. "Blame the club? No. Nothing took Steg but his choices. And my own. Made that same choice you did when Ranger got the patch. Was plenty young, but not stupid. I knew what I was getting myself into. Was fairly sure that I wouldn't get to grow old with my husband. I'm surprised we got the years we did. That he got to meet his grandchildren, got at least a taste of being an Old Man." She looked to me. "Do *you* blame the club?"

"I want to," I admitted. "It would be so much easier to blame the club. To hate everyone and everything connected to it. To hate the patch. It would've been the most rational thing to do. Sensible mothering would have had me moving out of Amber, taking my kids away from their father's legacy and settling into a safer kind of life."

I'd thought about it enough, hadn't I? Gone so far as

researching schools, rentals in other area, looking at our finances to figure out how far we could go, what we could get, where I'd have to work. It had almost happened so many times. But I hadn't had the spine. The heart.

Evie didn't say anything in response. She knew what was obvious. Had I been strong enough, smart enough, I would've done that already.

"But I can't do it," I continued. "Can't leave. We wouldn't fit in to any other kind of life. My kids have the gift of having this family. One where people die for each other. Ranger died for this club. It would be a disservice to his memory and his life if I blamed the club."

She reached over to squeeze my hand in an uncharacteristic sign of tenderness.

"He'd be proud of you, baby. Stepping up like this. I'm proud of you. For finding yourself. For finding a different life, with a different man."

"I'm not quite sure if I've found a different life with him," I argued. "We're still... figuring things out."

She chuckled. "Figure things out all you want, Lizzie. It'll surely take you another lifetime."

I really hoped it didn't.

That's what I told myself, at least.

Because part of me, a small part—growing larger by the day —really hoped I had another lifetime with Kace.

———

"IT'S TOO EARLY," I groaned.

Kace's lips were on my neck. Which I would've loved at any other time, even at the butt crack of dawn, but he was fully clothed, and that meant my chances at morning sex were slim to none.

"You know I wouldn't be leaving your warm body right now, especially since I've gotten used to wakin' up with it, unless it was vital. It's vital, baby. Club business," Kace explained.

Club business. I was no stranger to what that meant. I knew that there were no arguments, no delays and no promises about when he was coming home.

This was the life.

I let Kace kiss me, grope my boob and then walk out the door.

It was only after the front door closed and locked behind him that I realized how well and truly history was repeating itself. The men were different, in all ways that men could be different, but the club hadn't changed. Even without the gun running, the core of the MC had stayed the same. The day to day life was the same.

Sleep was well and truly lost to me with all of those thoughts swirling. I got up. Made the bed, inhaling the smell of Kace and I mingled. Then I moved to the closet, fingering Ranger's shirts, bringing them to my face. There was barely any scent now. So faint maybe I was imagining it.

I didn't dwell on that, though. I kept busy with laundry. With cleaning. With making breakfast for the kids.

Jack was up first. He was an early riser, kike his father. He loved to greet the day. He'd dressed in a Nirvana tee. Shorts. Chuck Taylors. His hair was messy, getting longer now. I made a mental note to book him in for a cut.

My world swayed, thinking about how quickly my little boy would turn into a little man. When he'd be wearing motorcycle boots and a cut. I wouldn't be making him breakfast for much longer, scheduling his haircuts.

"Sit down, honey," I encouraged, choking up ever so slightly at how quickly my boy was growing up.

He did as I said, climbing up to the breakfast bar. "Kace not here for breakfast?" he asked.

Normally, Kace would be sitting either where he was, with coffee and his laptop, or he'd be making something for breakfast.

"No, he had to work, sweetie," I answered.

Jack nodded, looking almost disappointed.

"What do you think of how things have changed lately?" I asked Jack, pushing a stack of pancakes toward him.

Jack eyed the pancakes as the bribe they were. I wasn't the mom who gave me kids refined sugar for breakfast on a weekday. My boy was smart enough to know that I had an ulterior motive. He was also smart enough to see what Kace and I really were. Or what we could be. There was no way we were going to be anything if my children were uncomfortable with it.

"Of you and Kace, you mean?" he clarified.

I blinked. Yeah, my boy was smart. Too smart. He was going to remember this time. Maybe not all of it, because time was kinder to children when it came to tragedy. It dulled the edges, gently removed memories, details.

He wouldn't remember all of it. But he'd remember enough. And even if he didn't remember, this would affect him and Lily in ways I couldn't even understand. My decisions were going to make all the differences in the adults they were going to become, how they'd behave in all of their future relationships.

No pressure or anything.

"Yes, sweetie, Kace and I," I replied, sipping my coffee.

He frowned, looking from me to the pancakes. He hadn't picked up his knife and fork yet, not a good sign. "I don't like seeing you with someone that isn't Dad," he said finally.

My stomach churned. "I know."

"But I like seeing you smile," he continued. "And you've been smiling a lot more lately. He makes you smile. He cooks good mac and cheese. He knows about baseball. He wears the same patch that Dad did." He paused, as if he were taking all of this into consideration. There were no quick, easy decisions for my boy. No, that wasn't his way. Even before all of this.

He picked up his knife and fork. "He must be good, if Cade let him into the club. They don't let in just anyone."

Despite the fact that this conversation was heartbreaking, I had to swallow a giggle at that statement.

"So, yeah, Mom, I'm okay with it," Jack mumbled through his first mouthful of pancakes. "I miss Dad, I know you do too. And Kace will never be my dad. But I think he's good."

Tears prickled at the backs of my eyes.

"What are you talking about?" Lily chirped as she sat down next to us. I turned to look at my daughter. She was still in her nightgown, a sleeping mask in the shape of a unicorn pushed up on her head. Lily was not an early riser. She liked to linger in her dreams.

"We're talking about Kace, and whether you two are okay with him being around more often. As mommy's..." I trailed off. No, I couldn't use the word *boyfriend*. That felt wrong. But I couldn't exactly use the word 'fuckbuddy' either.

"Special friend," I finished lamely.

Lily rolled her eyes. "Mom, I *know* what special friend means."

I blinked at her, hoping some little asshole on the playground hadn't been schooling her on sex so fucking early. I didn't want sex to be taboo or shameful in our house, but I also wanted my daughter to have a semblance of childhood innocence. "You do?"

She nodded with confidence. "It means he comes to sleepovers sometimes and that you might kiss and he thinks you're pretty."

The only reason I didn't chuckle was because I had enough

practice at not laughing at the adorable things that my children said. "And you're okay with that?"

"Of course," she answered. "You *are* pretty. And he makes you smile. You're even prettier when you smile. Plus he always gives me an extra scoop of ice cream, and he said we'd go riding on his motorcycle when I got taller."

Another punch in the chest.

Though my motherly instincts screamed at me at the thought of my daughter or son riding on a motorcycle, I knew that would almost inevitably happen at some point. I also knew that with Lily on the back of Kace's bike, he'd drive like an eighty-year-old.

That wasn't what the chest punch was from. It was from the fact that Ranger never got to do that. Lily wouldn't have a memory of that.

How long would Kace be here to give her those memories? Would he be the man she remembered who gave her ice cream and let her ride on his bike before he disappeared? Would he still be there when she was in high school? To threaten her first boyfriend?

Those were big thoughts. Scary thoughts. Ones that made me question everything. I couldn't fuck with my kids, take some man away from them again. But I also couldn't take away the possibility of having someone like Kace in their lives.

⊏===⊐

THIS MORNING WAS STILL heavy on my mind when Kace came in after work. My house was the first place he went when he was done at the garage. His clothes mingled with Ranger's in the closet now. I knew I had to get rid of them. Ranger's clothes. Especially now that they were hanging beside another man's.

Kace didn't say anything about them. Did nothing to push Ranger's presence out of the house.

That didn't make it better, though. Didn't make me feel any less confused. Especially since Kace was all but living here now.

It was too soon.

Much too soon.

Especially for the kids, who I watched like a hawk for any kind of emotional trauma stemming from Kace's presence. There was none. If anything, they seemed better than before.

But still, I felt off with all of the changes. Worried that new memories with Kace would erase the old ones they had with their father.

So all those thoughts were tumbling through my head, along with the whole 'someone's trying to kill me thing', when Kace got back.

Luckily, I was distracted with making dinner. With the kids talking during dinner. With bed time routines. I knew Kace saw the way I forced my smiles. The way I wouldn't meet his eye. But he waited. Waited until the kids were in bed. Waited for us to watch an episode of *True Blood*. Finished getting ready for bed. He didn't push. Eventually, he probably would, if I kept up the distant routine too long. But first, he was trusting me to work through it and talk to him when I was ready.

That made me like him even more. It made it so much harder to fight this. To keep my walls up.

"Why don't you want someone your own age?" I blurted, as we were getting into bed.

Kace didn't seem surprised or offended. "Why are you so focused on age?" he countered.

I frowned. "Well, how about the fact that the whole point of being young is to enjoy life being irresponsible, selfish and unattached. Not to hitch your wagon to a horse that has a bunch of problems not to mention two children," I replied.

"You're hot as shit. You chose this life because you wanted freedom. Getting into a relationship with me is the opposite of freedom."

"I didn't choose this life because I wanted to be free," Kace argued. "I chose it because I wanted family. Brotherhood. I grew up bouncing from one foster home to another. Some good. Most not. Aside from television sitcoms, I had no idea what family was, and even as a kid I was smart enough to know that was bullshit."

He paused, running his hands through his hair. "I knew that any kind of conventional family was lost to me. So I sought out the Sons. From the start, I haven't been after that kind of life, fucking whatever moves, answering to nobody. Sure, it was fun for a while, but it was meaningless. Empty. Had enough empty shit in my life. I wanted a family outside of the MC. An Old Lady." He stroked my face. "Got everything I want with you, baby."

My heart skipped at that. At what his eyes told me. The truth in them. It was beautiful, to be sure. If I had a younger, kinder heart, it would've been his long ago. And it would've melted at his words now. But it was old, wounded, scarred. My heart was harder to own. It definitely didn't melt anymore. It was in survival mode.

"I know that scares you right now," Kace continued, reading my mind. "Know that you're not ready to hear a lot of this, know that we've got a fuck of a long way to go. But I also know that you need to hear this. That I'm in this for the long haul. That this isn't some fucking phase or fling for me."

He moved to pull me into his chest, and I let him. He was warm, smelling of his body wash and the scent that was purely him. Safe. I felt safe in his arms. Mind and body.

"I know words don't mean shit. And we still don't know much about each other. Know there's a fuck of a lot more to you to know, and trust me, I'm looking forward to learning every new part of you. As for me, I'm an open book. When you're ready. For now, sleep."

I smiled. "Are you commanding me to sleep?"

"I sure am."

And fuck if I didn't obey him.

Chapter 19

One Month Later

"I've got something for you," Amy sang out, waltzing into my house.

She wasn't one to knock.

I wasn't alarmed at someone coming through my front door because of the prospect outside and because of the fact that I'd installed my fancy alarm, and only my family and friends knew the codes.

"Please tell me it's the answers to my son's math homework, because I'm meant to be helping him with this shit, yet I'm too dumb to even figure out how to Google it."

Amy frowned down at the various sheets I had laid over my dining room table. "He doesn't need math. He's going to be in the Sons. He's already been very vocal with both Cade and Brock that he thinks he should be able to patch in before eighteen."

I gave her a pointed look. "Well, I'm thinking on the off chance my now thirteen-year-old doesn't change his mind about his future in the next six years, he should have the option of going to college."

"Okay, well get your boyfriend to do it then. He's like *Rain Man* or whatever from what I can gather."

I blinked at her. "Kace?"

She nodded. "Apparently, he's been making the club a fortune on the stock market. Which Wire is totally jealous about because he had the title of hot resident nerd but now has to share the crown. I predict some kind of bitch fight coming."

"Kace knows about the stock market?" I clarified, remembering him mentioning something about that when I'd been too stressed and distant to take notice. "How can I not know that?"

She grinned. "Well, I'm thinking it's a good thing you don't know that because it means you two aren't spending your time talking about Wall Street."

No, we really weren't.

But it felt wrong, nonetheless. Because sure, we spent a lot of our time naked.

A lot.

But he also spent time with my kids. More and more now that I was running out of willpower to limit his time with us.

He listened to me complain about the fact that I had no clue what I wanted to do with my life. He knew how I liked my coffee. My history with my mother.

I'd made our whole relationship—if that's what this was—about me and had been too fucking selfish to want to know much about him. Maybe because I was scared of knowing more about him. Because it might make my feelings even stronger.

"Since that's sorted," Amy persisted, "now we can celebrate." She placed a bottle of what I now knew to be very expensive champagne—you become accustomed to the finer things in life with women like Gwen and Amy around—on top of Jack's math homework.

"Celebrate what exactly?" I asked, already getting up to get champagne flutes. Even though I wasn't about to spend two hundred dollars on a bottle of wine—especially now that I still hadn't found a job, and finances were starting to get a little scary—I was not going to turn it down.

Amy placed a large stack of papers on the table beside the champagne as I came back with the glasses.

"We're celebrating a very, very, lucrative offer from one of the top publishing houses in New York City!" she practically cheered, grinning wildly.

I stared at the paper. Back at her. "You got a publishing deal?" I replied, feeling extremely confused. Amy was someone who shared everything. So I found it hard to believe that she had been doing something like writing or getting herself a publishing deal without telling us all over cocktails.

"No, fuck no. Not me. Could you imagine?" She shook her head, opening the bottle.

A soft pop resounded through the dining room, then she started pouring.

"You, my talented friend. You've got yourself a deal."

I froze as my hand fastened around the stem of the glass. "Amy, there is no way that I could've gotten any kind of deal, since I haven't contacted any publishers or even told a soul about writing anything worth publishing."

"Okay, so I might've been a *little* nosy." She held her thumb and finger together.

I just gaped at her.

She sighed, rolling her eyes. "Okay, a lot nosy. I caught a peek at what you were tapping away at a few months ago. Liked what I saw. A whole lot. Now, my upbringing means I've been forced to read all sorts of bullshit written by long dead fancy English people. It's okay. Whatever. But I don't really care about all that. I like romance. Smut. Dirty stuff, you know?" She winked at me. "Brock likes it too. He takes it as a personal challenge to recreate every scene from my books."

Sharing. That was Amy.

"Anyway. I've read everything there is to read, especially when you've got a baby on your tit for the first year of their life. So I was hooked by the snippet I glanced at on your laptop. So when you were getting ready, I emailed myself the file. Got even more hooked. Then totally pissed the book wasn't finished. I also knew I couldn't ask you to finish it and send it to me because you were all secretive about it in the first place."

She sipped her champagne.

I continued gaping at her.

"I knew you wouldn't take my praise without thinking I was just a friend blowing smoke up your ass," she continued. "I also knew you've been pulling your hair out, trying to find a job that pays decent and doesn't make you want to blow your brains out. Pretty slim pickings. I also know you wouldn't take a job from me or Gwen or Mia or any of us gals. So I took it upon myself to contact some agents and publishers, sending them the first half of your book. They bit. Hard."

Her eyes were alight with excitement.

"We've been in a fucking bidding war. I wasn't going to bring this to you until I had a number that you deserved. That might prove to you that you are seriously talented."

She tapped a red tipped finger on the stack of papers in front of me. "That is a pretty great number. Not what you deserve, because in my eyes, you are priceless, but it's pretty fucking great. So we're celebrating tonight. I'm getting you drunk. Then you can have hot, drunk sex with Kace, wake up tomorrow and have hot hungover sex, then open your laptop and write the rest of the story. If you haven't finished it already. I suspect Kace has been a *total* muse."

She was right.

He had been.

At first, misery and pain were my muse. Longing for Ranger. Memories. With Kace in the picture, I still had all of those things, but something else too.

Which only pissed me off even more.

"Okay, so you're telling me that you invaded my privacy, read something that I did not want anyone reading, then, without my permission, negotiated some kind of deal?" I recounted, voice quiet.

Amy caught the fury in it. The girl wasn't stupid. "Not some kind of deal. *The* deal. I knew you'd be pissed. Okay, I thought the champagne at the really big number might help with that, but—"

"No buts," I hissed at her, slamming my glass down so the liquid sloshed all over the papers. "You had no right to go behind my back like that. To take something from me that was personal. That I hadn't told you about because I didn't want to tell you about it. That I didn't want the fucking world to know about. I don't need you coming in here with your two-hundred-dollar champagne trying to fix me. Or whatever the fuck it is you're doing because you feel sorry for me. Or feel guilty about the fact that you have a husband and a life that's still whole. Just because you didn't have to bury Brock does not mean you get to come and do this shit." I waved my hand at the table.

"Lizzie," Amy croaked, red tinging her cheeks.

I glared at her. "No," I roared. "I don't want to talk about this anymore. I want you to leave."

She flinched like I'd struck her. I felt guilty, but still angry enough to keep my glare in place.

Her emerald eyes measured me, likely trying to figure out if she could talk me down. Reading me correctly, she picked up her purse from the table.

"Fine, I'll leave. I'm not going to apologize for doing this, though. Even though you're right, I did invade your privacy. I should've told you. But I can guarantee what would've happened if I had tried to talk to you about this. Nothing. You would've shut down. Retreated back. Just when you were finally venturing out. Living again. There's something that makes you push away happiness. The future."

She sucked in a breath. "I get it. You're trying so hard to hold on to the past, to hold on to him, you can't grip anything else. You certainly can't build any kind of life other than the one you'd had with him. You can't grow into someone different than you were when you were with him. Because then he's further away. I get that, honey. Not in the same way, I'm sure. But I do understand. So I'm not going to be sorry for this. For fighting for my friend. For trying to show her that she has a future."

She left after that.

Luckily, she left the champagne too.

I WAS PRETTY much drunk by the time the door opened then closed quietly. We hadn't come to any kind of verbal agreement, but every night Kace came. Sometimes early enough to have dinner with Jack and Lily. To read Lily a story. To talk to Jack about plans for the car.

Other times it was so late he woke me up with his lips between my legs.

But he always came.

I never slept alone.

He still snuck out before the sun came up, before the kids woke up. Then he strolled in again around breakfast time, acting like he hadn't just left a few hours before. No way was I ready to have them knowing Kace slept over, though.

It was bad enough I was becoming used to him being there. Relying on it.

Though tonight, I wasn't. Tonight was a bad night for him to come. I should've called and told him that. But I got distracted. By Amy's words. With the deal in front of me. Then with the champagne.

His footsteps echoed through the quiet house.

I didn't look up when he entered the room. I kept staring at the number on the page. Amy was right. It was a big number. Now, I might not know a lot about the current state of the publishing industry, but I knew first-time authors were not getting deals like this every day.

Amy had to have pulled strings. She had many to tug on. Her family name carried weight.

It couldn't have been me. My story. My pain.

"The door wasn't locked," Kace growled.

Not a good growl.

A pissed one. I rarely saw Kace really pissed. Nor heard it. He was an easy-going guy, outside of the bedroom at least.

I blinked, looking at the clock, at the darkness that had engulfed the twilight in what seemed liked minutes, then at the empty bottle of champagne.

"I forgot," I answered lamely.

"You forgot?" Kace repeated.

I nodded. "Yes, I've got a lot on my mind tonight."

"I should fuckin' think so, in order to forget that some asshole in a suit is borderline obsessed with you and that you're alone with the fuckin' kids after downin' what I'm guessing is an entire bottle of booze."

I snapped my head up. He was really pissed. And that made me pissed. Mostly because he was right. I'd been sitting here, wallowing and drinking while night fell, my kids asleep, thinking their mother was going to keep them safe when instead, she was too self-absorbed to lock the fucking door.

"I had a fight with Amy," I muttered.

Kace looked taken aback, still pissed, but surprised. He'd most likely been expecting me to argue with him, since that was what I did about almost everything.

"Okay, that sucks, babe. But you still need to lock the fuckin' door when you're in here." He grabbed a hold of me so I was standing, supporting most of my weight. Which was good, since I was pretty sure I might've fallen over if I'd been forced to stand on my own.

His lips went to my forehead. "You're precious," he murmured. "All of you. And this world is full of assholes who like to steal and tarnish precious things. So I'm gonna need you to set the alarm and lock the fuckin' door. 'Kay?"

I nodded, although I should've been pissed that he was ordering me around. He wasn't wrong, though.

"What did you and Amy fight about, baby?" he asked after a beat, all anger gone from his voice.

That was Kace. He had been pissed. Really pissed. Now he wasn't. He wasn't going to hold it against me, act like an asshole all night. He said what he'd had to say, and we were moving on.

On to a topic I really, really did not want to talk about.

"Are you a math genius?" I asked instead of answering.

He blinked in surprise again. "A math genius?" he repeated.

I nodded. "Like *Rain Man*."

He smiled now. "*Rain Man* was not a math genius, he was an all-around genius. But I'm not any kind of genius. Just good with numbers. Shit with words. Always get them jumbled up. Now I know it's dyslexia, but shitty public schools and foster parents who didn't give a shit just thought I was stupid or a trou-blemaker. Which I was, since I got too frustrated, embarrassed that I couldn't do the work. No one wanted to help me. Fuck, even if they did, there were too many kids that needed help, and just one underpaid, exhausted teacher to try and stretch herself across them."

I thought of my childhood. Of the small classrooms in our small town. Mostly caring teachers. Very few speed bumps. Reading came easy. Math didn't, but I had a father who sat with me after dinner and talked me through all of my homework, rewarding me with ice cream my mother only let me have on weekends.

I'd had plenty of people around me who cared, who had wanted to help when I was struggling, pick me up when I stumbled.

Then I thought of my kids, who had the same thing. Or had up until a year ago. Since then, there were nothing but speed bumps. But even then, they were surrounded by people who loved them.

My heart broke for young Kace, without parents, extended family, with adults all around him who ignored him at best and mistreated him at worst. Then I marveled at the man he'd become.

"Math was the one thing that came easy to me. That felt steady." He shrugged. "I liked being good at something. And, like any kid who came from nothing, I quickly figured out the best ways to make money out of it. When I patched in to the club, I shared this ability that I'd honed. Figured out ways to make money in legit ways. Not legal by any means, but criminals wearing ten thousand-dollar suits commit those same crimes in broad daylight, so the world has figured out a way to palette that shit more."

"And you're making our club money?" I clarified, my champagne drunk brain having trouble following on with all of this information. Realizing that Kace was so much more than he seemed. So much more than a hot guy who was great in bed.

Kace shrugged again. "You could say that."

I stared at him, really stared. "You're amazing," I whispered. "What you've come from. What you've made of yourself. You're truly amazing."

Something moved across his face, something serious. Intense. "Babe, I survived foster care, most kids do that. Patched in to an outlaw motorcycle club. Wouldn't call any of that amazing."

There was something about the way he said that. Not humility. Vulnerability. He truly didn't believe me. Why would he? He'd had a lifetime of people treating him like he wasn't worth something. That he wasn't somebody. I'd been sleeping with him for months now, yet I'd been too deep in my own head to realize that he needed things. That he wasn't as strong as he appeared to be. That I'd been fucking selfish in my bid to protect my heart.

I'd left his out in the cold.

I stepped forward, clutching his neck. "No, you listen to me Kace..." I trailed off. "Oh, my God. I don't even know your last name. We've been getting all heartfelt and intense, fucked in every way people can fuck and you eat breakfast with my kids. You need to tell me your last name."

Kace chuckled, not at all horrified or offended about this. "Renyolds, babe. Not a big deal."

I scowled. "It is a big deal. If we are really doing this, if I'm really your Old Lady—"

"You are," he interrupted.

I rolled my eyes. "Okay, whatever. I need to know things like your last name. And if you're Rain Man of the stock market. And I need you to believe that I think you're amazing"

Kace's eyes were soft. Liquid gold. "Okay, Lizzie."

"I'm serious," I snapped. "Let me show you you're amazing."

My hands moved from his neck, down his torso, cupping him on the outside of his jeans.

"Oh, you can totally fucking show me in any way you'd like," Kace rasped.

So I did.

Then he showed me he thought I was pretty amazing too.

◁▭▷

"WHAT DID you and Amy fight about?" Kace asked me again later.

I was halfway asleep, the alcohol and orgasms helping me drift off within seconds of Kace finishing and cleaning me up. Not something he did normally, it felt too intimate and weird. I'd preferred the separation that came from going to the bathroom, closing the door and taking care of myself after sex.

It took the intimacy out of it. Which was the most important thing with Kace.

The champagne and orgasms made me forget about that. And they'd also made the idea of getting up and walking to the bathroom far too tiring.

Kace had immediately brought me into his arms when he finished. I'd tried to fight the cuddling. Again, too intimate. It worked at the start. Kace was still being careful around me. Still figuring out just how fucked up I was. How breakable.

But then I got lax. Or maybe Kace had finally figured me out. Whatever the reason, he took charge. Gave me not much of a chance for escape. Sure, he would've let me go if I'd asked, but tonight I wasn't strong enough to ask.

And no matter what I tried to tell myself, I liked being held by him. Even if I had moments of pure panic and guilt. Moments I'd tense up, roll out of bed and cry in the bathroom for ten minutes.

"She invaded my privacy," I murmured. "Made decisions for me that weren't hers to make." I hadn't planned on telling him the specifics of the fight. Or even anything vague. But I was feeling sleepy, warm, safe.

Kace squeezed me a little harder. "So, I'm new here and definitely don't pretend to be any kind of expert on female friendships, but from what I can see, all the Old Ladies seem to be solid. Fucking insane of course. But willing to cut off a limb for their friends. Who they consider their family."

I pursed my lips because I couldn't argue with him. Even though I wanted to.

"I also know Amy. Who, if you get on the wrong side of, is scarier than Bull and Gage combined. But, if you get into her heart, she'll do anything for you. You're in everyone's hearts, babe. Not knowing the specifics, I can't say much for sure, but I will bet whatever she did, she did out of love. She did it because she thought she was doing something right for you, good for you."

"Why is it that you're younger yet so fucking wise?" I snapped, pissed that he was being so reasonable, making so much sense. I was also pissed that we were laying here after sex, talking about something like this. It was a different kind of intimacy, a more dangerous kind.

⸺

"I'M STILL MAD," I grumbled when Amy opened the door.

She grinned. "I'd be disappointed if you weren't."

The door closed behind me, and I went straight for the living room. The house was decorated in an impeccable, impossibly expensive way, but also in a way that didn't make you scared to sit on her sofa.

"Do you want wine?" she offered.

"It's eleven in the morning," I pointed out.

"I'll put some orange juice in it."

I really wanted to grin, but I had a hangover to nurse, so instead I just nodded with pursed lips. She smiled and disappeared.

I looked at the photos spaced expertly between very expensive looking prints and pieces of art. There were many of her and Gwen from their time before Amber, looking amazing, laughing, smiling, cocktails in hand. A couple of her, Gwen and Ian. I stared at those the hardest, wondering when I might feel like I could have photos of Ranger mixed in with old and new memories. Of course, we had many photos of him around the house, but I'd made an art out of never actually looking at them.

All I wanted was to take them down, so I wasn't faced with the fact that he only lived in photographs now. But my kids needed to see their dad. Remember him, know that he was still a part of their home and their hearts.

"Mimosas!" Amy announced, thankfully jerking me from my melancholic wonderings.

I took the flute thankfully.

She sat across from me, eyes meeting mine. "So, you want to start in with the bitch fight or have a drink first?" she quipped. "Then again, it's most likely going to be a one-sided bitch fight since I'm not mad at you, and I'm not the bitch fighter I used to be in my younger days."

"I fear my bitch fighting days are behind me too," I replied, although I'd never really had any bitch fighting days. "I'm just here to talk. To apologize. I shouldn't have come at you like I did."

Amy raised a perfectly manicured brow. "Girl, yes you had a total right to. I was way out of line. I should've talked to you first. But I knew talking to you wouldn't have made you believe me. Believe in yourself. So I made a choice. One that I don't regret. "

I chewed my lip. I'd been doing a lot of thinking this morning. Had gone over the publishing deal after Kace and the kids left. Not that I knew a whole lot about such things, but I knew that number was fucking big. I also knew that Amy was smart. She most likely had a very fancy and expensive lawyer look over the deal before she brought it to me. Kace's words had followed me throughout the morning too. He was right. She had done this out of love. Goodness.

Still, I was pissed.

"Let's get one thing straight. I'm not happy about what you did," I pinned her with my stare. "This was something private. Something I hadn't told anyone about, something that you should've waited for me to reveal instead of invading my privacy."

"Yes, yes, you're right, I'm sorry. Let's get to the part where you talk about how you'll forgive me, and we'll get on a jet and head to New York," she chirped.

I blinked. "Jet. New York?"

"Uh, duh," she rolled her eyes. "They're waiting for you to get back to them so we can organize a meeting. I'll be coming as your stylist and friend and also because I am in serious need of a Fifth Avenue fix."

"We can't go to New York," I countered. "Someone is trying to kill me."

"It's the perfect time to go then," she argued. "I highly doubt that your would-be killer is going to find themselves on a jet or be able to afford a room at The Ritz. We're going."

"I haven't agreed."

She grinned. "You're going to."

She was right.

I was going to.

Not just because of the number and what it would mean for my kids and their future. What I could give them with just that number.

It was mostly because what it would mean to me. Something more. Something different. A dream I hadn't let myself have. Even though it scared the shit out of me. Even more than the person potentially trying to kill me.

"Kace isn't going to be happy," I frowned.

"Another plus!" Amy exclaimed. "Pissing off the alpha male is all part of the process. Plus, makeup sex. We'll call him from the jet."

"Wait," I demanded, holding up my hand as Amy tapped on her phone. "We can't go today."

She glanced up. "Why not?"

Holy crap, she was serious. "First, we both have kids. Second, I can't just have my kids coming home from school and me not be there. Third, I'm pretty sure that a big publishing company won't take a meeting at such short notice. Fourth, I have nothing to wear to such an important meeting. So there, four reasons."

Amy grinned wider. "We both have men to look after said kids. And if you don't want your man to look after them, you've got a mother-in-law, Evie and about six other women who would happily let them stay, and who your kids would love to stay with. We'll book the jet for later this afternoon so you can pick up the kids and give them the lowdown. The publishing company will move shit around for me, rather for you, so we'll do it tomorrow morning. A breakfast meeting. I know the woman at Chanel. She'll keep it open for us. All problems solved."

"Chanel?" I repeated. "I cannot afford Chanel."

Amy raised her brow. "Honey, did you not see that number? You can totally afford Chanel. Beyond that, any woman walking into a meeting that is going to change the course of her life is like... obligated to wear Chanel."

"This is too crazy," I whispered.

"Which is exactly why we're doing it. You need crazy."

I should've argued harder. Stayed in my safe zone. Told her I'd take a phone meeting. Or something a little less spontaneous.

But I didn't.

Instead, I told the kids about the situation. Both were absolutely fucking elated. Well, in their own ways. Beyond that, they were more than happy to stay with Evie.

I hugged them close, inhaled their smells and left them, though, it felt wrong and hurtful. I called Kace from the plane.

He was not happy.

Like, at all.

But he couldn't do anything about it.

Amy and I shopped at Chanel. I got the most kickass outfit that made me feel like someone who belonged in a fancy meeting in downtown Manhattan. Amy used her credit card when I wasn't looking and waved me off when I tried to fight to give her cash. She informed that the only reimbursement she wanted was to meet Chris Hemsworth when he played my male main character in the movie version.

We stayed at the Ritz. It was the most opulent place I'd ever been. We ate at Per Se, which served food that had to have some kind of drugs in it, it was that good. We drank incredible cocktails.

Then, the next morning, we meet with serious publishers. Who were totally fucking serious about giving me a book deal. An agent who was serious about representing me.

Then we flew home. Amy on the jet. Me on cloud nine.

Kace was totally fucking pissed when we got back.

And Amy was right, the makeup sex was amazing.

Out of this fucking world.

Chapter 20

"Lizzie! What a wonderful surprise," Olive said, hugging me. We'd already had a champagne dinner together, celebrating my publishing deal. One of many dinners and parties thrown for me. Kace was beyond proud of me, but I'd banned him from acting like it because I still felt weird about it. He, of course, did not heed my ban and continued to buy my flowers and cook me dinners to celebrate.

I relaxed into Olive's embrace, soothed by the warmth of it, grateful she still wore the same perfume she'd had on the day I met her. It comforted me that some things stayed the same, even though everything else was different.

Different meaning completely and utterly fucked.

"What do I owe the pleasure?" Olive asked.

"I was just in the neighborhood," I lied.

"The kids at school?"

I nodded. I'd been tempted to wait till they got home so I could use them as some kind of buffer. But that would've made me feel like an even bigger fuck up. My stomach had been churning since Kace and I had gone public with our relationship. I'd been putting off this conversation, even though it was like a ticking time bomb. Olive may not move in the Sons of Templar circles, but she was around my kids, who were likely to talk about Kace at some point. It was hard to get Lily to stop talking about Kace. Fate had stepped in and Olive had had to work extra shifts at the hospital because of staffing issues, so we hadn't seen her in almost three weeks. The kids missed her. I missed her. My worst fear was that the truth would create a chasm between us, and I'd lose her forever.

"Well, come in. I'll make some tea," she offered, moving back to let me in. "I'd offer tequila, but I'm on shift tonight."

"Tea sounds great," I replied weakly.

The house was similar to how it had been when her and Ranger had first moved here. Feminine but not in a way that would make a teenage boy feel ashamed to be living there. It was warm. A plush green sofa with patterned pillows and soft throws on it. Vintage rugs covering the hardwood floors.

Olive had a boyfriend, Bob. He was widowed ten years, owned the hardware store in town. They'd been together for almost five years but still had their own places and seemed perfectly content with that. Ranger had done his whole macho man, protective son thing at the beginning, but Bob was just too nice and genuine for my badass biker to continue his intimidation tactics.

I was glad that Olive had that. Especially now.

Framed photos of Ranger were displayed throughout the house. Pictures of our wedding. Each kid's birth. All of our milestones collected over the years. These were all she'd ever have. There'd be no more photos of her son.

Would his absence hit me the same every time I walked in here? Or would I figure out a way to deal with it? Get stronger so it didn't hurt so bad. That was the cliché that everyone spouted about grief. That it didn't change but you got better at being able to handle it.

Honestly, that sounded like bullshit to me, because I'd never felt weaker than I did right then.

I sat down at the small dining table while Olive made the tea, talking while she did so. The same scenario with my mother would've transpired in stilted silence. She would be judging my outfit (tight black jeans, spiked heel boots, a black silk blouse and silver jewelry on both wrists, all my fingers and around my neck), trying to set me up with some guy from her church whose mother still did his laundry.

I felt guilty. Ashamed. Olive was sitting here, pouring me tea, chatting about how big the kids had gotten and helping me with ideas for Lily's birthday. Doing it all with a smile that was pretty close to genuine, but not all the way there. As close to happiness as someone who had buried their only son would ever get.

"I met someone," I blurted, unable to sit there with my wonderful mother-in-law who treated me like I was her own daughter, keeping her oblivious to the fact that I was betraying her dead son.

Olive stopped talking, blinked a couple of times, her smile still in place, mostly out of shock I guessed since I didn't think she'd be happy about this.

"I mean, it's not serious or anything. The kids know him, but only because he transferred in to the club about a year and a half ago. They don't know that he's... anything more than that. I don't even know what he is."

The words came out quickly, awkward and jumbled. I was trying to rip off the Band-Aid, doing it quickly, as if that would make her hate me any less.

My body was taut, ready for the inevitable coldness that had to creep in to her gaze. The judgement. Disappointment.

But none of it came.

Olive reached over and squeezed my hand. "I think this is good," she mused, voice soft and the same it had been moments before. No hatred or even veiled dislike.

I stared at her. "You don't hate me?"

She laughed, the sound easy and kind. "Of course not, honey." She squeezed my hand once more before she let it go. "I never expected you to stay single forever, young and beautiful as you are. In fact, it would've broken my heart if you didn't try another version of happiness for yourself. You deserve it." She paused. "In an ideal world, you would've stayed with my son forever. Whatever bumps in the road that came along, you'd overcome them together like you have before. You'd watch your kids grow up, Cody would walk Lily down the aisle." She wiped a single tear from her eye. "And my son would outlive me. The way it's meant to be. But, sweetie, we both know that this world isn't ideal. It can be cruel. Horribly so. But I still have you. My grandchildren. Bob. There are plenty of reasons to continue living. Not merely surviving. Allowing yourself to live doesn't mean you've forgotten about Cody. Doesn't mean you love him any less."

Her words sunk in to saturate all of my emotional wounds, like salt and salve at the same time. "Man, I really lucked out in the mother-in-law department," I choked out.

She grinned. "You totally did."

A WEIGHT HAD BEEN LIFTED off my shoulders telling Olive. It also let me give myself permission to actually feel happy about this. Content. My kids were, with Jack trying his best to act like he wasn't.

Everyone at the club was happy, to say the least. Every single person there was a hopeless romantic, whether closeted or out in the open. I didn't have any kind of hope for this becoming anything more than a relationship that didn't make me hate myself. But I wasn't about to burst anyone's bubble.

Not yet.

Also, that was my mother's job.

With everyone else I was worried about, I'd forgotten about my mother and her unyielding disdain. Which was no mean feat. But my mother was, for the most part, out of my orbit. Sure, I made sure that the kids saw her at least once a month, occasionally joining them for dinners I gritted my teeth through. I sometimes ran into her in town and made painful conversation. But for the most part, when it came to my mother, my mind was on the quickest form of escape without some kind of bloodshed.

So I was unprepared when she turned up at my house late on a Tuesday morning. As a rule, my mother did not go anywhere unannounced. She considered it to be the upmost form of rudeness. And she certainly did not turn up at my home unannounced when her grandchildren were not around.

We didn't do well without some kind of buffer, my mother and I. Kids worked best. My father. Any kind of strong booze in a pinch.

But she'd definitely frown on me opening the vodka at ten in the morning. And I couldn't exactly bar my own mother from entry, despite how bad things had gotten.

I shouldn't have called it bad, really. There were plenty of women in this world who didn't have mothers. Whose mothers didn't look after their children, who didn't come to their home after their husband died, cleaning everything top to bottom daily because they didn't know how else to show support.

My mother was not a bad person. She just wasn't proud of the person I was. The choices I had made. Sure, we weren't the best of friends in high school, but there wasn't this chasm between us that erupted as soon as Ranger decided to patch in, and I decided to marry him.

I was at peace with the fact that this was our relationship. It sucked, but I had Olive. I had the opportunity to make sure I had a beautiful relationship with my daughter.

But still, having a bone crushing sense of panic when your mother showed up at your home was not a good sign.

At least she brought muffins. If I could say one good thing about my mother, the woman could bake. Especially her white chocolate and raspberry muffins.

And she certainly was not a woman to show up empty handed.

I let her in, mostly because of the muffins, partly because I had no other choice.

Though she declined my offer of coffee, tea, juice or a bottle of water, which left me standing in the middle of the kitchen without anything to do with my hands.

Luckily, my mother wasn't one to beat around the bush and definitely not one to linger in her disappointing daughter's home for longer than she needed to.

"The kids have been telling me about a man," my mother proclaimed, picking up the throw on my sofa and re-folding it. Her disproving gaze moved to the pillows. If she was here long enough, my entire house would be redecorated.

That was not going to happen.

"Yes, and?" I pressed, folding my arms and leaning against the breakfast bar. Sitting would give her the impression that I wanted her to stay a while.

My tone helped move my mother's attention from the cushions. "And, they've given me the impression that this man is around the house. Often. That he was in the same club as their

330

father was." Her voice was pure ice. "Elizabeth, please don't tell me you're that stupid."

I blinked. "Stupid?"

"Yes. Stupid enough not only to bring some man you've been... sleeping with around your children. Not just that, but he's also in that *gang*?"

I took a deep breath. "You've lived in Amber your entire life. You spent Christmas with Ranger, however reluctantly. He is the father of your grandchildren. You can't possibly be stupid enough to call them a gang when you know that's not what they are."

The vein in my mother's forehead started pulsing now. "I know that they are the reason that my grandchildren will grow up without a father. That they are the reason why you never lived up to your potential, never left this town. Yet after all of that, you're still bewitched. You're still willing to subject your children and yourself to more of that."

"What would you suggest I do, mom?" I hissed. "What? Should I cut all ties with the only family I've had the past ten years? The only family other than Olive. And dad, when he can escape from you. They don't judge. They don't offer their love or support with strings. They will come whenever I call, without questions. Every single one of the people in that club would die for me and my kids. So no. I'm not going to let you poison this."

I pushed away from the breakfast bar, walking toward the front door.

"You're always going to be my mother. My children's grandmother. You will always have a place at my table, be welcome in my home. But only on the condition that your figure out how to keep your opinions to yourself. I know it's hard. I know you might even mean well, in your own way. And I know you love the kids. Kids who have had something horrific tear apart their childhoods. So I won't cut you out of their lives. They've lost enough already. You can continue to be nasty, but I won't take it. I promise, you'll lose my respect. That if you continue this way, our relationship will break. It's up to you."

Then I walked away, hating that I wished for Olive instead of my mother. Hating that she might be right, just like she had been about Ranger leaving me.

———

MY MOTHER DIDN'T CALL for a week. I hadn't expected her to. She was far too proud to make contact any earlier. I half expected her not to make contact at all. It wouldn't have surprised me.

But she called, inviting herself to dinner the upcoming Saturday. "If that suits the kids and you and... your male companion."

I had stifled a giggle at my mother calling Kace a 'male companion' like I was eighty years old and had some widower courting me.

But I told my mother that it would be 'lovely', even though that was not a word to describe what it would be. It was her extending an olive branch. Even if afterward, she counseled me on what to cook and urged me not to try anything new.

I tried to give Kace a way out. Even offered to break a limb for him so he could end up in the hospital.

"Babe," he said, pulling me to him. "I'm not going to fight anything that brings us closer together, that stitches me tighter into your life. That's your job. I'm gonna have dinner with your mother. You can try and get out of it if you want, but I'll be here Saturday, suited up and ready for battle."

And he was.

Wearing a black shirt, dark jeans. Motorcycle boots. Looking absolutely delicious.

My mother looked at him like he was going to steal her jewelry right off her hands. Kace wasn't fazed. He shook my father's hand. Met his eye, answered all of his questions. He expertly handled my mother's jabs, which hadn't been too sharp since the kids were present.

I wasn't sure if my mother was charmed by the end of the night. She was trying too hard to hate him. Not because she was a terrible mother. Because she was trying to protect me in her own way. Because she'd seen how Ranger's death had broken me. How the MC life had changed me. She wanted to spare me from all pain. Much like I wanted for Lily.

It was what any mother wanted for their child.

But it was too late for me. The world had cut me, marked me. There was no other path for me. Kace had been right. I was my own kind of outlaw. This was the only life I knew and the only life I wanted.

My father tried his best to accept Kace. To support me. I knew it was hard for him too. He didn't want this danger, this pain either. Nor did he want to change me.

They left with air kisses—my mother—real kisses and hand-shakes—my father. There were no more dinner plans made. My mother had fulfilled her obligation and had formed her judgement.

The kids didn't seem to find it weird that Kace was now present at dinners with their grandparents or that he participated in the movie nights afterwards. He was cemented into their world now. He and Jack were almost done with the car.

They were ready for a future with Kace.

It was me who was fighting it.

"We should break up," I said.

Kace kept drying the dishes, his eyebrows raising ever so slightly. "Break up?"

I nodded. "My mother has accepted you, and that is too scary. That must mean there's something wrong with you."

Kace grinned. "Babe, your mom didn't look at me the entire night, and every time she said my name it sounded like she was trying to spit out something she really, really didn't like the taste of."

"Yes, and that is my mother's version of acceptance."

Kace kissed me on the mouth. "Well, I'll take it. Plus, I'm planning on having plenty of time to win her over."

His words scared me.

Terrified me.

But I held fast.

Held on to him.

KACE HAD SURVIVED dinner with my mother.

Olive had hesitantly asked whether she could meet him. She'd done it in a way that made me feel comfortable. That made it seem like it wasn't a betrayal to her and Ranger.

The dinner between Olive and Kace and the one with my parents were night and day. Olive hugged him the second he crossed the threshold to her house. It was a long hug too. She smiled at him wide without caution. Without falsity.

She asked questions about his background, not even blinking at his history with foster care, not shying away from the subject either.

When he asked questions about her life, she answered freely, speaking about Ranger with that same glint of heartbreak in her eye that she'd always have but in a way that didn't make it uncomfortable.

That was Olive. That was her magic.

She'd pulled me aside while Kace was doing the dishes. "I

like him," she whispered. "Really like him. He's good for you. For the kids. You deserve this, sweetheart." She squeezed my hand, and I did my best not to burst into tears.

We'd had various couples' dinners with everyone in the Sons of Templar family. Since the warnings had already been distributed, none of the women treated Kace any different. They welcomed him. Teased him. It was becoming more real. More normal. And that was the danger. The normality of it all. That we were settling in to each other. Creating a new kind of life together.

Which freaked me the fuck out.

Luckily, I had a night with Evie scheduled. Kace was at home with the kids, something he didn't do often. Not because I didn't trust him with them, because the threat of... whatever or whoever was still out there, and he didn't like me traveling anywhere without him. Evie's house was little more than a fortress, and there were two prospects outside. I was safe. As safe as I could be.

"It's more than fucking now, isn't it?" Evie suggested as we sat in the backyard. "He's your Old Man."

No judgement. Never any judgement.

I bit my lip. "He's young," I frowned. "Too young."

Evie shrugged. "No one would be sayin' that if you were a man and he was a woman."

I raised my brow at her. "You know better than anyone that gender equality doesn't really exist in *this* world, of all places."

She raised her brow back at me. "And you know better than anyone that this world has no rules or judgment when it comes to fucking. As long as everyone's a consenting adult."

"I have children. I'm a mother." I didn't even know why I was fighting her on this anymore. The fighting was done. I'd lost. Or won. Depending on how you looked at it.

"You're also a woman," Evie acknowledged. "One who

needs to and deserves to get fucked well and right." She paused. "He do that?"

Heat crept up my neck at the mere memory. I nodded once.

She grinned. "Well then, baby. Age is really just a number. And put it this way, younger men tend to die on you less."

I stared at Evie. Should I really be surprised that she was saying shit like this? Evie was not one to pull punches nor be delicate. But I found myself relieved. As fragile as I felt, people treating me with care made me feel close to truly breaking down than anything else.

I smiled, something I hadn't thought I'd do when someone was joking about my dead husband and my new... Old Man? It was fucked up, but it was a smile, nonetheless.

"You and I both know when it comes to death and sex, age is just a number, baby."

I pursed my lips.

"You love him," she said, sucking on her cigarette.

Her words hit me in the throat. Because she hadn't structured them as a question. She was saying it as if it were some kind of forgone conclusion. It scared me. That she could think such a thing. See such a thing.

"Of course I don't," I choked out.

Her eyes narrowed, and her face changed to an expression usually reserved for club girls who didn't know their place. Cold. Calculating. Terrifying.

She stood, jabbing out her cigarette in the ash tray on the table.

"Where are you going?" I asked, slightly panicked to be without her company and to be on the receiving end of such a look.

"I don't drink with liars, honey," she admonished, showing her pack of smokes in her back pocket. "And you're lying to us both."

"I'm not meant to love anyone," I blurted as she walked away.

She paused, back turned before she turned and made her way back to the table.

"What? You're meant to sew up your pussy and your heart because you lost your Old Man?" she countered. "You're too smart to think that shit," she continued without waiting for me to answer. "You've been in this life long enough to know the ugly truths of this world. We're not people who get fed bullshit about things like happily ever afters, one true loves and the American fucking dream. You forfeit your ignorance the second you made the decision to stick by your man. To become part of this club. You also accepted the fact that you might lose him one day. Whether it be to him thinking with his dick and working out his problems on club girls instead of talking through his shit or dying to protect the club."

She poured us two more drinks before she sat down again. "It hurts in a way you can't even put into words because we love differently here. We live differently. So our grief is deeper, more violent, it can eat you from the inside out. But we don't try to mask it and get on with our lives. " She leaned back, sipping her drink. "You're too good of a mom to let this shit eat up you up entirely. You'll grit your teeth and get through it for those kids. But you're really gonna try to keep yourself the grieving widow for life?"

I sipped my own drink, needing the burn of the booze to take away the sting of the truth. "I'm betraying him some-how," I confessed, voice quiet. "I know it doesn't make sense. Maybe I feel this way because I don't want to let him go. I don't want him to be dead. Because if he isn't really dead, in my mind, being with someone else, feeling anything for someone else, is cheating." I looked at her. "In order to be with Kace, I first have to bury my husband, truly put him to rest. I have to feel all of that pain. I'm not strong enough for that."

"No, baby. You're not weak enough to believe that," Evie countered. "We both know you buried your husband almost two years ago now. He's gone."

She was right. Ranger was gone.

It was well past time for me to understand that.

Chapter 21

"Did you have a good time with Evie, baby?" Kace murmured.

We were in bed. He'd waited up for me, because he was Kace. Also, I guessed, because he felt the threat wasn't gone. Though I doubted whoever was doing this would wait this long between... attacks? If someone really wanted me dead, they would've tried a lot harder. Maybe they'd been scared off. Decided I wasn't worth the effort.

Of course neither Kace nor the club were going to be taking any risks. So the two prospects had followed me home and walked me to my front door, which Kace had opened before we even got to it.

He'd left the porch light on.

The house was dark and quiet inside when I arrived, the kids asleep, Kace's laptop on the coffee table, a glass of tequila beside it. Kace wasn't a huge drinker, he enjoyed having a few beers with me, but never in excess. I'd never seen him drunk. Or tipsy. He occasionally had one glass of tequila at home. Maybe two. No more. Especially when he had the kids to look after. I wondered if it was because he always wanted to be prepared to jump on his bike at the sign of trouble or drama.

Surely, he was expecting it, surely his brothers had updated him on all of the chaos that befell the club in previous years.

Someone cutting my brakes and putting a bunch of snakes in my underwear drawer was slightly chaotic, sure. But it was small potatoes compared to what the Sons of Templar had been through.

As soon as the door was closed, locked and the alarm was set, I was in Kace's arms. His mouth on mine, his violent need palpable. He carried me to the bedroom, where he did glorious things to me. Things that made me forget my own name.

It was only after I got my breathing under control, managed to stumble to the bathroom to clean up and brush my teeth, did Kace ask the question about my night.

"Yeah, it was... reassuring, I guess," I replied, voice husky.

"Reassuring?" he repeated. His hand was drawing lazy circles on my back.

"Yeah, with everything going on."

"I'm guessing you mean me and you, not the faceless killer looking to end you?" he questioned dryly.

It was a point of contention between us, that I wasn't taking the threat seriously. Or that's how he saw it. I saw it as carrying on with my life and not letting some nameless, faceless asshole ruin a life that I was just figuring out how to put back together.

"What did you need reassuring with about us?" he asked. I knew Kace wasn't pissed about me talking to someone else about us. About the fact I needed reassuring. He accepted that I couldn't dive into this with the same confidence he had.

"You're young," I answered honestly.

He grinned, in that wicked way that he had. "Noticed that, did you?"

I pursed my lips against the effect that grin had on my

thighs, and in between them. "I did. Noticed that you're young. That you're good with kids. That you are great with them. And you don't have any kids."

"Not that I know of."

I scowled at him. "Do you want them?"

His eyes darkened ever so slightly. He understood what I meant. And he didn't answer straight away. No more quick quips, no more teasing tone. "I mean... yeah. My lifestyle doesn't really accommodate kids. But I figured I'd meet the right woman, it would all fit into place and I'd become a dad."

I bit my lip in order to keep my expression neutral.

Not that it helped. He knew me far too well to be fooled by my forced expression.

"But," he continued, moving me so I was laying right on top of him. "I've met the right woman. Fallen in love with her and her beautiful children. I never want to replace their dad, but I'd like to think he'd approve, that I'll do things for them that he'd want. If you'll let me, stop holding me at arm's length, I'll be happy with that. More than that. My cup runneth the fuck over with all of that, baby."

We didn't say anything after that.

Even I didn't have an argument for that.

━━━

"MOM?"

I glanced up from my computer screen to see my son standing in front of me looking hesitant. Tentative. Two words that I'd never used to describe my son. He was confident, ready to try anything, do anything, say anything. He'd always felt comfortable in his own skin, and I was so proud of that fact. That Ranger and I had given him enough room and love to feel like he could fit into this world however he wanted to.

Lily was the same. But she was quieter about it. Still discovering. I loved that curiosity.

It unnerved me to see my son like this. And, of course, my first instinct was panic. To get hysterical. But whatever this was, it wasn't life and death. He wasn't bleeding from anywhere. Nothing was broken. Therefore me panicking would only make him feel worse.

I forced my face to neutral. "Hey, dude. What's up?"

Jack looked to the ground. Fidgeted a little. Then his eyes found mine. "Is Kace going to die?"

It was only through pure determination that I didn't flinch at the question. At the even, almost jaded way he asked that.

"Everyone dies, sweetheart," I explained, forcing myself to give him the true, realistic answer instead of placating him with a lie that everything was going to be fine. "But most everyone lives to be old, gray, wrinkled. Kace has many, many years to wait for that to happen. He's young and healthy. It is definitely not something that's going to happen soon. Surely not something that you need to worry about." He was worried, that much was clear. "What makes you ask that?"

He sighed, looking out the window. "Because Dad died."

The blow was immediate. Paralyzing. There would always be these moments. When I thought my kids might've healed. Might've somehow figured out a way to get through life without this shadow over them.

But, of course, that wasn't how life worked.

Although I sure wished it did.

I took a deep breath. All I wanted to do was grab hold of my son, pull him into my lap and hug him tight enough to protect him. But he was too old for that now. For the hugs. For the protection.

"And you feel that because Kace wears the same patch, does the same stuff that dad did that he might die too?" I asked.

Jack shook his head. "No, because sometimes people die. Not because of anything else, they just do. It can happen to anyone. Dad was strong. He was kind of old, I guess, but not like grandpa. And he still died. The same with Grandpa Steg. He was old like grandad, too, but strong like Dad. But they both died."

Another blow.

This one deeper. Harder.

Because he wasn't just thinking about death on the surface. Specific to the Sons of Templar. He was thinking of it like it was really. Cruel. Unyielding. He was losing his innocence, and there was not a damn thing I could do about it.

"Yes, baby. Sometimes people die," I answered. "No matter how strong they are. No matter how good they are. Sometimes the world is cruel, and it hurts us when we don't deserve it. It's natural to be a little afraid of something happening to people around you. But you're afraid because you like Kace, right?"

Jack frowned ever so slightly at that. It almost made me want to smile, despite the subject matter. He was so stubborn and concerned with breaking his 'cool guy' façade that he was trying so hard to maintain. Admitting he cared about Kace, in his eyes, at least, would damage said façade. But my son was not a liar.

So he nodded, still frowning.

"Sweetheart, that unfortunately is the thing about caring about people. Loving people. We give them a part of ourselves to take care of. And even the best of people—Kace is one of those, by the way—the people who will take care of that part of us, they can't control the big things. Like death. It's scary. It makes you not want to care about people because you don't want to get hurt."

Jack's eyes darted to his shoes, then back up to me.

"I'm gonna be honest with you, kiddo, there's always a chance of getting hurt," I told him softly. "Of something bad happening. But I promise you, caring about people, loving people. It's worth the risk, okay? We were unlucky enough to have someone we loved very much leave us. Even though he didn't want to. I need you to remember that doesn't happen all the time. That isn't normal, okay? I can't promise you nothing bad is ever going to happen, even though I wish I could. I promise you right now, though. You're going to be so glad you were brave enough to care about people. It's going to make you into a better man. You're already one of the best I know. Right up there with your father, who would be so darn proud of you."

I reached out to ruffle his hair because it was straight up impossible not to touch my son in some kind of way in that moment.

He screwed up his face in that way boys did, but he didn't pull away.

"I love you, kid," I whispered, holding tears in through sheer choice of will.

"I love you too, Mom," he said back, eyes glancing away. "I want you to be happy. I'm glad Kace makes you happy. I think Dad might've liked him."

I smiled. Jack was totally wrong on that one. Ranger most definitely wouldn't have liked the man who was sleeping with his wife, making her and her children fall in love with him. He'd kick his fucking ass. Maybe kill him.

But he wasn't here for that. Which was the whole point.

"Yeah, baby. He would," I lied.

―――

"YOU OKAY, BABE?" Kace asked, handing me another beer.

I was sitting at the breakfast bar with my laptop. Writing.

This book was almost done. That's what it was now. A *book*. At this point, I could no longer trick myself thinking it was anything else. Then there was the fact that I had a publishing deal, signed and everything.

It felt weird. To have something like this happening. To be creating. To call myself an author. It made me feel vulnerable too. Because this book was full of my demons and grief. And, of course, I was surrounded by supportive and loving women who wanted to read it. Amy was the only one who had so far, but no doubt I'd get harassed if I didn't let the rest of the women soon.

Not to mention Olive.

My mother was proud of me in her own way, which was demanding she get the first copy to read to make sure it was suitable for her church group (it totally wasn't), squeezing my hand in hers for a second.

I hadn't wanted to tell anyone about this, of course. Even when it became apparent I was going to get the publishing deal. I wanted it kept secret. Separate from my life. I was worried it might change who I was. Further still from the woman that Ranger had married.

Then again, she was changed irrevocably the second he died.

But still, I clung to the illusion of thinking that if I didn't change too much, I was somehow closer to him.

It was Kace and Amy who gently—Kace was gentle, Amy didn't know how to be—urged me to tell people. To be proud of myself. To feel entitled to shed the skin that didn't serve me anymore.

So I did that. People responded with love, excitement, various alcoholic drinks. My advance was already in the bank, a hefty enough buffer that I wasn't becoming a thief or stripper anytime soon.

I was waiting for the other shoe to drop. Things couldn't just happen this way. Tragedy had to strike again. It had my address, after all.

Kace had just finished doing the dishes. And he'd made dinner. Forced me to sit and write while he cleaned up. It wasn't a terrible view. Not at all. I would've been completely content with it, now being comfortable with Kace being in our space, had this afternoon not still been weighing heavily on me.

I was so powerless to the situation, yet I still second guessed every choice I'd made since Ranger died. Everything I'd done. That's what motherhood was, questioning yourself, wondering if you had done different, done better, could you have saved your child from hurt?

I'd done my best to cover up all of this throughout the night, which was made easier by the fact that Jack seemed back to his old self, warmer with Kace, if anything. The two of them had even been throwing a baseball outside before dinner.

It helped a little. But not enough.

And Kace was far too perceptive for his own good.

"I know you've been stewin' on somethin' all night," he continued when I didn't answer straight away. "And I'm not going to pressure you to talk about it if you're still working through it. If you're not ready. But something's eatin' you. Might not be able to help. But it might be nice to get it to stop doing laps in that beautiful head of yours."

Seriously. Where did this man come from? Had they colonized the moon in the future, developing emotionally intelligent, super-hot, kind and caring men then sent them back in time to test them out on unsuspecting women?

If so, how in the fuck did I get two in the same lifetime?

I closed my laptop, since I'd only been tapping at the keys, pretending to write anyway.

"Jack likes you," I said by explanation.

He smiled. "Yeah, getting that. Makes me happy as fuck. Weird thing to say, but it's made me happier than anything I've ever done... so how's that bad?"

Kace was happy, beaming over the fact that my son accepted him. Was most likely falling a little bit in love with him. Kace was falling a little bit in love with my son. I was falling in a little bit in love with Kace, too, despite my best efforts.

"He *really* likes you," I reiterated, slightly freaked out at this realization.

"Again, babe, fail to see why that's got you twisted up."

I pursed my lips. "He likes you, but he's afraid you're going to die," I clarified, wondering even as I said it if it was right to have told him. To steal the joy he was feeling.

Kace's expression sobered, and I instantly regretted saying anything. "Ah, I get it. Thinks that getting too close to people, especially male type figures, may end up with him alone, confused, hurt."

I nodded.

"And him saying that to you would've broken your fuckin' heart," he continued softly.

I nodded again, trying to hold my tears back.

Kace dried his hands and moved around the breakfast bar, twirling me in my chair so he was standing in between my legs. He grasped either side of my neck. "Wish I could protect you from this. From any kind of fuckin' pain. You've had enough. If you let me, I'll love you every day of my life. Do everything to make sure it's a long one. I'll love your kids too. I won't ask you to love me. Not right now. But I'll wear you down. eventually"

I stared at him.

I'd known Kace loved me for some time now. He wasn't exactly hiding it. He'd been saying it with everything but words. But I was well practiced at denial. An expert in it, some would say. So I'd chosen not to think about what I knew deep down.

Now I had no choice

And I did already love him. Evie had called me out on that. Something else I'd been denying.

No way I could say it out loud, though. Not even now.

It felt like it would be a curse. Among other things, it felt too soon. Too permanent.

So I didn't say it back. Though large parts of me really wanted to.

"Why did you choose this?" I mused. "This complicated, arduous, hard version of love. Of life. Why did you walk over to me that night? Why did you mow my lawn? Why did you choose to love me?"

"The night at the club wasn't the first time I saw you," he answered. "I was running on the beach early in the morning. My first morning here. My mind was rushing. Moving. Questioning my decisions, my actions, haunting me with things I've done. Something that happens a lot. Can't get out of this lifestyle, this world unscathed. Even if you were born for it. Even if you love it."

Kace's hands moved up and down my arms.

"The things that you love scar you the most, after all," he murmured. "So I don't sleep well, when that scar tissue hurts. And I run. No one was on the beach. No one but you. You were just standing there. At the edge of the water. You were wearing PJs. And a jacket. An old one. Much too big for you."

I remembered that. It was after one of our nights at Evie's. We had stayed the night. Because of whisky. Because I'd been using any excuse not to sleep in the bed that didn't smell of my husband anymore.

The kids liked it. Being around family. They probably also liked being away from their beds, ones their father had tucked them into for their entire lives up until then.

I'd woken from a nightmare. Or I guess you could call it a good dream, since Ranger was still alive in it. We were sitting by the ocean, my back to his front. His hands were wrapped around me, and I felt safe. Warm.

The nightmare began when I woke up. Cold, because I'd kicked off all the covers. Because I was alone.

It hit me then, much harder than it had up until that moment. That my husband would only ever exist in my dreams. That I would never smell him, feel him again.

It was as if a scalding hot knife had ripped through my belly. I didn't think then, I'd just grabbed my keys and left, knowing that the kids were safe, sleeping, had Evie there if I wasn't there when they woke up.

I didn't remember the drive to the beach. Which was a bad thing when you were the only remaining parent of two beautiful children. Luckily, it was too early for anyone in Amber to be awake, and I made it there without incident.

The ocean was the wrong place to go. As soon as I set foot on the sand, I knew that. Recreating my dream wasn't going to make him magically appear. But maybe that had been what I'd needed then. To know there was no way out of this. That there weren't going to be any miracles. I needed to be comfortable in my nightmare.

I didn't remember anyone else being on the beach with me. I did remember feeling more alone than I ever had in my entire life. I was far too occupied by the pain I was in to notice any other living thing. Too focused on one dead man.

"You stopped me in my tracks," Kace recalled. "Literally. It was like I ran into a wall. Something about you. The way you fucking stood. I watched you for a long time. You didn't move. Didn't make a sound. But something about you told me all you wanted to do was scream. Open yourself up. Sink to your knees and break. But you didn't. You just stood there. I didn't know anything about you then. Didn't know who you were other than you were a woman in unimaginable pain. Yet you were still standing."

His eyes moved across my face. "When I saw you at the

party, you had that same look. I couldn't help myself. I had to know you. And I know that you don't feel the same way, fuck, I know it's impossible for you to feel the same way after what you've been through. But I loved you already. Love at first sight sounds cheesy as fuck, and it also sounds like a line, but I swear to fuck it's not. There was a magic about you. In your pain. Your brokenness. I didn't want to fix you. I just wanted to fuckin' know you. See if I could possibly create a miracle and make you fall in love with me."

"You can't say things like that," I choked out. "All of these romantic, crazy, heartfelt things. Not all in one go. I can't, I'm not... ready for all that."

Kace smiled then leaned in to kiss me hard and quick. "That's fine, baby. I'm a patient man. Plus, you can write about all the romantic, heartfelt things I say." He nodded to my laptop screen which he knew better than to look at directly.

Despite myself and all the intense, serious things I was feeling right then, I laughed. "Yeah right, no one would believe a real-life man would say things like that."

He chuckled. "Don't need anyone to believe the things I'm saying but you." He paused. "Do you believe me, Lizzie?" he questioned, voice quiet.

I didn't move my eyes from his. "Yes," I admitted, my heart on my sleeve. "Yeah, I'm starting to believe you, Kace."

And there it was. The beginning of the end.

Chapter 22

I should've known better.

I'd been around for enough Sons of Templar courtships to know the drill.

Then again, I wasn't exactly thinking of this as a Sons of Templar courtship. I'd spent a lot of time in denial, thinking this was little more than sex. Denial born out of fear. Fear that I could feel this way so quickly. Fear of what my choices might me doing to my kids. Fear at what kind of mother and person people would think me to be.

Mostly terror at the prospect of loving someone again.

Of losing them.

But Kace managed to cut through every layer of fear and land himself under my skin. Among my scars.

It took me by surprise that I wasn't prepared for more. I'd lapsed into some false sense that there was a quota on how much pain and drama the world can serve you.

When it comes to love and the Sons of Templar, it was a fucking buffet.

It was only lucky that the kids were with Kace. He'd decided to take them fishing. Lily, my little princess who wore dresses and plastic heels agreed to *fishing*. Then again, it shouldn't have surprised me, since her dad had always managed to get her to do all of the things that she would've turned up her nose at had anyone else suggested them.

Kace was under her skin too.

So it was good that none of them where there when I got home to a woman in my kitchen pointing a gun at me.

I didn't recognize her, though she definitely seemed to be aligned with the MC crowd. She was dressed in biker babe chic, without the chic.

Her frayed denim mini was on the wrong side of short, even for the MC crowd. It showed off skinny, blotchy legs. Her boots were cheap and scuffed, her bra showing through the stained white tank she was wearing. Her arms and chest were covered in a mishmash of tattoos, her neck as well. Though her bleached blonde hair had about an inch of roots and hadn't seen a brush in a while, it looked like she'd put a lot of makeup on for the occasion, a smear of bright pink lipstick and heavy black liner around her eyes.

"Who are you?" I asked calmly, not moving, but calculating the distance I was from the hall, where I would be covered for hopefully long enough to run into the bedroom, lock the door and retrieve a gun of my own.

It was a risky move, and her finger was on the trigger of the gun, meaning she was not here to fuck around. She could be a crappy shot. Might be clumsy. But I wasn't going to risk making my kids orphans on coulds and mights.

It was also risky to stay where I was since she could've just shot me and been done with it. But she was the woman who had been fucking with me. I knew it. She wasn't going to shoot me now. Why go to all that trouble to torture me for a quick kill?

"I'm the Old Lady of the man your husband fucking killed!"

she snapped, spittle flying from her mouth. Her eyes were wide, her movements jerky. She was either high or just insane. Both equally dangerous when combined with a gun.

If I could get the gun off her, I had a good chance. She was skinny, weak looking. Ranger had trained me in fighting, self-defense. We'd sparred at the gym once a week right up until he died.

Plus there was the fact I had a whole lot to fight for. But you couldn't discount the crazy biker bitch with a gun.

"My husband is dead," I told her flatly.

"Don't I fucking know that?" she yelled, shaking the gun at me. "Fucker died before I could even get my revenge. Been planning it for a long time too. Watching you fucks."

Something unnerved me a lot about that. This woman was not crazy. She was heartbroken. She'd lost someone she loved. She'd let in the ugliness that came with that. Let in the evil, the fury, and she'd decided to lay ruin to the world that had ruined her.

Not only that, she was smart... in there somewhere. She obviously had known about the Sons—I was guessing her husband was part of a rival MC—and knew that going in half-cocked with no plan wasn't going to serve her. She'd been patient enough to wait. To learn. Her revenge was being served cold.

"Your club is full of fucking pretty boy pussies and their stupid cunt wives. Their kids. My Old Man's club is still too fucking scared to retaliate. Like they're full of pimply eighteen-year olds instead of men. No surprise a woman needs to do it all. Surely you know that, being an Old Lady and all."

Though she was clearly emotional, clearly out of her right mind, she kept her finger on the trigger, keeping the gun pointed squarely at me. If I moved, she'd pull it. I knew that. It might miss me. Might clip me. Might hit me straight in the head.

I thought of the bullet holes in Ranger's body the night he died.

That couldn't be both of us.

Our children couldn't bury two parents full of lead and hate.

"I know that being an Old Lady is accepting the fact your Old Man goes out every day with a goal of staying alive. He also knows that there's a chance he won't get to come home that night. That's the commitment he makes when he puts on a cut. That's the commitment we make when we stay by their sides," I said, keeping my eyes on her. I was furious at her for coming into my home, ruining what I'd built.

But I made sure that my fury didn't leech into my voice. This was not the time to lose it. This bitch wanted to talk. She would've shot me otherwise. So I'd keep her talking until my moment came.

"You don't get to play the victim or the villain here," I continued. "You think you're special because your Old Man died? That it gives you the right to take something away from my family, my kids? That's not going to change shit except you're gonna be on the run for the rest of your life, which will be short because no matter what you think of my club, they will end you for this."

"Shut up, bitch!" she screamed, shaking the gun.

"I won't," I stated calmly. "Because you know I'm right. You know that if you pull that trigger on me you may as well turn it right on yourself. It'll be quicker. More humane. The Sons might've gone legit, but the second you cross them in a way like this, the law doesn't mean shit. They'll rip you apart."

Her eyes flared with fear at this. She knew I was telling the truth. I didn't know what club she used to be with, but they probably weren't on the straight and narrow like the Sons. And they probably didn't fiercely protect their women like the Sons.

They'd hang her out to dry or deliver her personally to the Sons if she did this.

"I know that the pain of losing someone you love makes you want to die. Makes you want to kill," I continued. "But you don't really want to die. And if you kill me, that's what will happen."

"Fuck," she hissed. Uncertainty clouded her face. The gun moved as she ran her fingers through her hair, as if she was momentarily forgetting that she was holding a gun.

I didn't hesitate. This was the moment. To make sure I tucked my kids in tonight. That I went to sleep beside Kace.

I charged.

My body hit hers with a thump. We both landed on the floor, hard. The impact jarred me, but my hands were already on hers, yanking for the gun.

A shot resounded through my house only seconds later.

———

I WAS SITTING on the porch when Kace arrived. The police had arrived first. Because I'd called them first. I'd been an Old Lady for a long time. Lived in this town my entire life. I knew that back in the day, the police were on the Son's payroll. As long as there wasn't any blowback on Amber, they didn't bother them. Certainly didn't arrest them.

Things had changed, though. There was a new sheriff in town. Not Luke. Who definitely never would've been on the Sons' payroll. But he was in love with Rosie, the daughter of the president, so he'd never hurt the club. Because he knew that hurting the club and hurting Rosie was one in the same.

So he gave up his badge for Rosie. Moved to L.A. to work at Greenstone Security. Did his best to rein her in.

Rosie wasn't one to be reined in. Only a few months ago,

she'd gotten involved with a movie star turned murder witness turned target of an organized crime boss. Things would never be boring with them.

Or me, as it seemed.

The new sheriff knew the score with the Sons. She was young, for a sheriff. Pretty too. In a hard way. She had a kid, slightly younger than Lily; I'd seen her at school drop-off sometimes. No husband. She had become acquainted with the Sons when she first arrived. They seemed to be on good terms. She'd looked the other way during the war that had been impossible to ignore. The one that stole my husband from me.

But I was erring on the side of caution now. I wasn't going to have Kace at the scene before the cops.

I'd planned on calling him after I made my statement. But I should've known better. We had Wire, who was likely listening in on all 911 calls, especially ones that were being called to my house and involved the word 'death'.

The roar of the bike sounded just after I'd given my initial statement. The sheriff said it was obvious self-defense, but I'd need to come down to the station anyway.

I'd expected this.

And the look on Kace's face when he leapt off his motorcycle.

Cade, Brock, Gage, Asher, Bull and Gage rolled up behind him.

"What the fuck, Lizzie?" Kace seethed, hauling me up, eyes wide as he took in the blood staining my shirt.

"It's not mine," I reassured him.

"I know it's not fucking yours," he clipped. "What I need to know is why you're covered in blood, why the cops are here and why I didn't get a fucking phone call."

His hands were tight on my upper arms.

"Easy, brother," Gage commanded from behind him.

The men were all hanging behind, Cade on the phone, likely making plans, getting lawyers prepared should I need them. Instructing his wife to take care of the kids.

Kace didn't acknowledge that Gage had even spoken. His furious glare remained focused on me. I saw past that, though. Saw the fear.

"Honey, I called the police first because they needed to arrive first," I explained calmly. "You know that."

"I know my woman is covered in blood, white as a sheet, sitting on her fucking own and I'm not clued in as to what's going on," he snapped.

Gage stepped closer. My eyes found his, and I gave him a look to show it was okay. He stopped moving but stayed close.

"It was an Old Lady," I announced. "Of another club. She was the one doing this. Not Edmond. Not anyone from your past. Ranger had been involved in her Old Man's death. Who knows how long ago? She wanted to punish me. She wanted to kill me. I didn't let that happen."

Kace stared at me, fury melting off his face. He yanked me into his arms. "Fuck, baby," he murmured into my hair.

He didn't let me go for a long time.

Not until the police came back and needed more statements.

Kace let me go then. But he wouldn't let go of my hand. Straight up refused to let me go anywhere without him. Normally, that wasn't something that police would be down with. But this was Amber. Kace was wearing a Sons of Templar cut.

We found out much later who she was. Nicole Felix. Her Old Man had been a member of the Hell's Renegades. Years ago, they'd tried to steal business from the Sons. The Sons hit back. There was blood. A lot of it.

It was likely I had washed the blood of her Old Man off my husband's clothes.

There had been a peace treaty between the two clubs, only after the Sons made it clear they would exterminate them if they didn't back down.

It seemed that she had held on to this for a long time. Let everything inside her fester and turn rotten. The Sons made a visit to the Hell's Renegades and had been convinced Nicole was acting on their own. There was still a healthy fear for the Sons of Templar MC across the country.

As for me?

I survived.

Which was all that mattered.

Two Months Later

I was staring at my laptop when the knock came at the door.

It was done. I had absolutely no words left inside me. Not for this story, at least. I had plenty of other words, a mess that didn't yet make sense on another document in my computer. But neither had this until now. Until it was done.

It was confronting to be done with the book. Just like it had been confronting to hear Kace say he loved me. While I was writing this, fuck, even when I got the publishing deal and was sitting in that fancy New York office, it hadn't felt real yet. The book had been unfinished, I was still in its clutches. Still swept up in the world I was creating.

What did I do now? Send it off to some stranger? Send it out into the world?

The mere thought terrified me.

Luckily, the knock delayed me from thinking about all of this too hard. Once I looked through the peephole, I disarmed the alarm.

It was always armed when I was in the house alone. Though the kids and I were barely alone in the house these days. There were always after school events. Playdates. One or more of the women in our group coming over here or inviting us over there. Then Kace came straight home. To our home. Where he stayed every night. Where the kids now woke up to him being there, knowing he'd slept over. It didn't seem to bother them whatsoever that he was all but living with us. He still had his place. Him and Jack were still rebuilding the car. Sometimes he'd work over there, though not very often, not with everything going on. It was not because the club was orchestrating things to make sure I was never alone. That's just was life was like. That's what life had been like before Ranger too. Busy. Full.

Everyone had been watching me, waiting. For the break-down that they thought would come after me ending someone's life. Having to clean up the blood of my would-be killer from my kitchen.

The police don't do that. I hadn't known that. Fortunately, Evie had. She'd arrived with a mop and bucket and a bottle of whisky. She'd helped me clean up the blood of the woman I killed.

Kace wanted to help too. But the biker queen had turned to him and cupped his cheek. "Baby, some things a woman needs to do herself. I got her."

Kace didn't want to leave me. That much was clear. It was burning inside of him. But he respected Evie. Every man did. On reflex. It was also reflex not to leave their woman with a pool of blood to clean up after she killed someone.

He nodded once, and Evie release him.

Kace then turned to me, kissing me hard and quick. "I love you, baby," he murmured.

I didn't say it back. Not with words at least.

He left and Evie and I got to cleaning.

When he came back that night with the kids, the house

smelled of bleach and lemon, with only a hint of death. Though I think that I was the only one who smelled that.

We watched movies and ate pizza until the kids fell asleep. Then Kace carried them to bed.

Then he carried me to bed and made fierce, intense love to me.

Throughout the next few weeks, he made it clear he was there to talk to. That I was safe. He treated me like I was made of glass, expecting me to shatter. The women didn't do that because they knew that we were diamonds. It took a lot more to break us.

But that was something I had to communicate to Kace. I got frustrated with the edge in the air, the way he was waiting for me to crumble.

"You want to protect me," I acknowledged.

"Of course I want to fuckin' protect you," he barked.

"That's the problem," I replied, voice even. *"Every single other one of the courtships I've watched over the years have been different. Because the men and women are so incredibly different. But there are some things the same, at their cores. You men. You big, biker men who are used to strong-arming your way through situations. You live a life where you have to be strong, violent and willing to do whatever it takes to protect the club. It's who you are. You love fiercely. The patch. Your brothers. Your women. So it stands to reason you want to protect them too. But the thing is, you're all attracted to different women, sure. But these extraordinary women who can survive this life do not want or need a man to protect them. They don't need shields. They need swords. And to be fair, a lot—okay, all—of the Sons of Templar courtships have involved kidnappings, drive-bys, bombs, poison, gunshots. All things in your wheelhouse. All things you men know how to fight back. But what you want to protect me from is nothing that your experience, that your strength, that your willingness to get bloody is going to beat. I'm not going to have some extraordinary situation with car chases, gunfire or explosions. You're not going to ride in to save the day or my life. You can't*

protect me from what's coming. What's already hit me. You can't protect me from myself."

"I can't do what you're asking."

"You have to," I implored. "If you want me. This. Us. You have to trust that I know this life. That I can look after myself. I can't do this otherwise."

Kace gritted his teeth. "I trust you, baby," he scowled. "I just don't trust the rest of the world."

"Makes the two of us," I agreed. "I'm always going to worry that saying goodbye to you means I'm never going to see you again. I'm going to see your death twenty different ways before you come home each night. I'm going to imagine all kinds of horrors. Going to see twenty different versions of what life would be like without you."

Kace sighed, his eyes troubled and dark. "Fuck, Lizzie," he murmured.

"You want to back out of this yet?" I joked.

His hands went to my hips. Firm. Bordering on painful. "I never want out of this. Ever."

So that was that.

Kind of.

This was the first day I'd had alone at my house for more than a couple of hours at a time since Nicole. And Kace texted me at least every hour to make sure I was alive and not bound and gagged in a cheap motel room.

Or trapped in a mansion in another state.

That had happened.

And worse.

I figured Gage was knocking on my door because Kace had bribed or convinced him to come and check on me in a way that seemed organic.

"Gage, what a surprise," I smirked slyly. "Can I get you anything?" I asked once I'd let him inside.

"Nah, I'm only here to drop something off then I've got to get home. Lauren needs to paint, so I'm taking over."

I smiled, thinking of their dynamic. Of their happily ever after. Even though the first half of his life had been broken. He gave me hope.

"You're here to drop something off or to make sure I'm not rocking in a ball on my kitchen floor?" I teased.

Gage's mouth twitched. "Seeing you upright and sane is a bonus, but I didn't expect anything less," he proclaimed.

Gage was one of the only men who didn't look at me like I was going to lose it. We had a connection. He'd seen parts of me, raw and open. He'd watched me heal too. So he knew this wasn't going to break me.

He opened his cut to retrieve something from an inner pocket. "You know the club better than anyone. Know that we're all at peace with the fact we might die by the club. Sure as shit fight against it, considering all the things we've got to live for. But it's not somethin' we ignore. Not a responsibility we take lightly. We've got things in place. In case of the worst."

I stared at the thing he was holding in his hands.

"He made me promise not to give this to you until you were living," Gage continued, handing me an envelope. "Really living, not going through the motions like you have been for the past year."

I stared at the envelope now laying in my palm. It didn't weigh anything, but my palm ached from the mere act of holding it.

"I'm sure many of the women have already said something along the same lines as this, but moving on isn't betrayal," he explained, voice soft. "Living is the greatest gift you can give his memory." He leaned in to gently kiss my head and then left.

I didn't read the letter right away.

Maybe months ago I would've. I probably would've torn at the paper with a desperation to devour any words my husband had for me. Ranger had really thought this through. Giving it to me when the grief and death were so close to the surface, it wouldn't have done anything.

So now that they were deeper, I was managing to breathe around it all. I set the letter on the counter while I opened a bottle of wine and poured it into a glass. I stared at it as I drank the first glass.

Then, with a steady hand, I opened it.

LIZZIE.

Baby. You're probably mad as fuck to be reading this right now. Maybe at me. Maybe at the club. Or maybe not at all. I can honestly say, even after us being married all these years, I can't say what you'll do. How you'll react to my dying. I just know one thing that never changes. The way you love.

I've written many versions of this letter over the years. And every time I get to tear up the one that came before, I'm happy. Reminding myself what a lucky bastard I am to continue life with you.

Fuck. I've put you through a lot. The fact that I'm writing this knowing everything I've done to you and the fact you're still sleeping in our bed, yeah, I'm lucky.

Not many women are strong enough to go through what we've gone through. I wasn't strong enough half the time. But you carried us through.

You carried me through loss I didn't know how to handle. You carried our children, your own pain. You made me feel like I was something. That my past didn't define me. You saved me, baby.

I fucking hate to think there is any kind of possibility that you're reading this. When we're finally at a good place. The club is straight. The kids are growing. We're stronger than ever.

I've broken my promise to you. If you're reading this. I've broken the promise I made to grow old with you. I hate myself for it. Maybe if I was a fucking contractor, I wouldn't have to write these letters every few years. You'd get what you wanted. What you deserved. But I'm not that. There's no changing who or what I am.

I hate that I've left the kids. That I don't get to do all the things a father should do.

THERE WAS a harsh mark in the paper. A smudge. Something to show that the mere thought of leaving his children had pained him. I took a painful breath and a large sip before I continued.

FUCK I HOPE I get to rip this letter up. As soon as I do, I'm coming home, gonna tuck in the kids, tell them how much I love them, then I'm going to spend the whole night worshipping you. Tasting you. Imprinting my utter fucking devotion to you on all of your skin.

But it's because of that devotion that I'm writing this. I'd be a coward not to. To stick my head in the sand and try to forget the fact there is a chance you'll have to go through this alone. And I know the club has your back. Those crazy fucking women have your back. I also know you'll be alone. In our bed. At midnight. When you make coffee in the morning. When you watch the kids at the recitals and sports games you hate. You have to do all of that shit alone. It hurts my very soul. So I'm asking you to make sure that's not forever. That you don't sentence yourself to a life alone. Now this is hard as fuck for me think about let alone put on paper. I hate the thought of any other man near you. But what I hate more is you waking up alone every morning for the rest of your life.

I won't let you do that.

If you're reading this, then it's time. Get your shit together, baby. Give someone the gift of your love. And know I died fighting, because I didn't want to let go of it. Kiss our kids for me. Never let them forget how much I loved them.

THE LETTER WAS in shreds at my feet before I realized exactly what was going on. My hands had worked of their own accord, ruining the words before I could try to preserve them. Wasting hours, poring over them. Losing myself in it.

I'd read the letter once. That's all I needed. It wasn't like I was about to forget a single fucking letter.

Slowly, purposefully, I walked to the sink. got a lighter out of our kitchen junk drawer and set the pieces on fire. Then I washed the ashes away.

Then I called Gwen to request an emergency girlfriend meeting.

Chapter 23

"Wait," Gwen interrupted, holding up her hand. "They've all got *letters?*"

As I expected, every single woman in our circle had joined us.

I nodded. "Apparently they've all made some kind of deal."

"A deal?" Amy repeated, rifling through her purse. My heart hurt for her. She'd had a letter from a dead love before. I was pretty sure she wasn't too hot on the idea that there was a chance of reading another one in the future.

"So they've all been writing death letters like Nicholas mother effing Sparks?" Mia asked, though it was clear she didn't need an answer. "Do they not realize this is not a romantic comedy and such letters are *not at all cute?*"

"That's insane," Bex snapped, her eyes narrowed, likely thinking of all the ways she was going to tell off her husband later.

"It's kind of sweet," Lily added quietly. Of course, the softest of all of us, found the romance in this, though she got more than a few eye rolls.

"Sweet my tight ass," Amy muttered, snatching her phone from the table and pressing angrily at the buttons. She put it to her ear. "Hi, honey," she said in a tone that Brock likely picked up as a warning. "Oh, no, I'm fine," she said after a beat. "I'm just sitting here with all the gals, having cocktails, talking about the death letters you've written all of us."

She paused, presumably while Brock tried to say something to make up for it. Making an excuse. "Oh, I don't need you to try to bullshit your way out of this," she stated, most likely interrupting what Brock had to say, if he'd even had time to say anything. "I just need you to know that I know about the letters. And I swear to fucking God, if I ever read one, I'll take up necromancy in order to bring you back from the goddamn grave in order to accurately punish you for not only writing the letter but for dying in the first place." She sipped her drink. "And if you haven't figured it out already, you're sleeping in the guest room tonight." She hung up the phone.

"Was it a mistake telling you?" I asked, feeling very responsible for the tongue lashings that most of the Sons of Templar would be getting at various points throughout the day.

"No fucking way," Amy huffed.

"What she said," Gwen put in.

Mia nodded.

As did Bex.

Lily bit her lip with what I could only guess was unease.

Lauren had a relatively even look on her face compared to the rest of the women. Gage had given her a lot of darkness, all of his scars, so she probably wasn't surprised by this. Wasn't hurt by it.

"Are you okay, sweetie?" Ashley inquired, leaning forward to squeeze my hand.

"Yes," I answered automatically and honestly.

Amy raised a brow. "I've gotten one of those mother fucking letters, so I call bullshit."

I smiled sadly at her. At the morbid connection we'd share forever. Receiving letters from dead men.

"Maybe if it had been sooner," I explained. "If I'd read that when everything was raw and open. When the world didn't make sense, and I hated it almost as much as I hated myself. If I didn't have someone like Kace. If I didn't have friends who pried me out of my own shell of grief." I looked around at the women who meant everything to me. The cornerstones of my life.

"I'm sure there's still going to be moments when I want to sink onto the floor or float down the shower drain," I continued. "But I'm different now. The letter hurt. But I'm used to being hurt now. I recover quicker. I'm at peace with my pain now."

All of the woman looked at me with glassy love in their eyes. They hurt when I hurt, wanted to fix me. If they couldn't do that, they'd always be there with a drink, a kind ear and a fuckload of curse words.

"Love that for you, honey, but I am not at fucking peace with shit," Amy said, lips thinned. "And I'm planning on punishing my husband in many different ways later on tonight, none of them ending in an orgasm... for him, at least."

"Cheers to that, bitch," Gwen chuckled, holding up her glass.

Everyone clinked, laughing. Because that's what these women did, they turned their lemons into margaritas.

———

I DIDN'T SEE Kace for three days after the letter.

He obviously knew about it. Though the guys didn't look like the kind of men who would gossip over cosmopolitans, they definitely spilled secrets over beers, whiskies or the dead bodies of their enemies.

They were honestly worse than us, which was kind of saying something since our group had no secrets.

I thought about Ashley and Wire. Her being expert at evading any and all conversations about her love life.

So maybe *almost* no secrets.

I was also pretty sure Wire kept tight lipped on the whole thing too. Something very interesting was going to play out there, hopefully sooner rather than later.

But what was happening right now was at the forefront of my mind. Or rather, what wasn't happening right now.

Had Kace heard about the letter and come to his own conclusions about what it would mean? Deciding to cut things off without so much as a word?

No. That wasn't him.

That was just one of the many possible explanations I'd gone through over the past three days.

I'd had to lie to the kids and say Kace was away on club business because even three days of his absence created a hole in our lives. In our home. It was terrifying. It pissed me off too. How hard was it to fucking text?

It was safe to say I was going through about a thousand different emotions. The most prevalent of which was need. For Kace. To tell him the truth Ranger had given me permission to tell.

He'd given me permission to feel it all.

It wasn't simple. I was going to struggle with this. With my feelings for Kace and my longing for my husband. I suspected it was going to be a long journey. But I wasn't about to let it end here.

No fucking way.

Which was why I was at the garage. Wearing my best outfit.

369

Not that his feelings for me could be swayed by an outfit, but it sure did help. A floral sundress that wasn't exactly 'biker chic' but when paired with chunky heeled black boots, a wide black belt and a buttery black leather jacket, it totally worked. The sun, beach days with my kids and Kace had kissed my skin so my legs were bronzed. I showed off a lot of them since the dress ended well above my knee. If the wind blew, you'd see the white lace panties I'd put on for Kace, too, with the hope that things would get that far.

My hair was in wild ringlets around my face. I'd finger brushed some of them softer, but Kace had always commented on my 'lioness hair' when I wore it this way.

My makeup was soft, in contrast with everything else harsh about my outfit. A lot of blush to make my cheeks extra rosy. Clear lip-gloss. The kind that was designed by witches because it didn't smear through even the most intense of make out sessions. My friends had all done the research. A little perfume, but not much.

I looked good. Hopefully not like I was trying too hard.

Of course, there was an audience for my arrival. There was no such thing as privacy in this place. The various garage bays were filled with cars and mechanics working on them. Most of the mechanics working there were patched in to the club, but there were also a handful that weren't. The Sons kept up their reputation around town, protecting the residents, making sure drugs weren't dealt or cooked within town limits, helping out with pretty much anything that veered slightly outside the law.

And they also employed talented young men and women who hadn't had a chance anywhere else.

So the ones without the patches paid little attention to me, beyond the respectful chin lifts reserved for Old Ladies.

But the men in patches, yeah, they paid attention.

Lucky helpfully pointed to the last bay with a wink. I gave

him a weak smile. I'd gotten over the fear that these men would somehow respect me less for taking up with another member. They had done everything but throw a damn party since Kace and I'd gone public. In fact, Lucky *had* suggested a party, but I'd bugged out my eyes, and Bex had quickly taken care of that.

Having an audience was uncomfortable even in a best-case scenario. It could be humiliating in the worst case.

The Rolling Stones played softly over the sound system Cade had installed throughout the garage. There was a chart on the wall by the office with shifts of who was in control of the music throughout the day. Before that, there'd been fistfights.

Kace was closing the hood on the car he was working on when I made it to the end bay. His eyes found mine immediately. Something moved in them, something slight, but the rest of his usually expressive face stayed blank.

My blood chilled, but I continued forward.

Kace wiped his hands on a rag as I approached.

I stopped a few feet away from him, feeling awkward with the space between us. The second we became... a thing, he was not about space. He was about touch. Presence. Always.

He made no attempt to cross the distance I'd put between us, and that made things even worse.

"Hey," I said in a small voice.

"Hey," he replied evenly.

I swallowed. Hadn't I rehearsed what I was going to say in my mind? Where was all of that now?

"I've missed you," I said.

Kace jerked. Ever so slightly, but it was a change. Whatever mask he had been clinging to fell.

"You did?"

There was something different about the way he spoke. More vulnerability.

It clicked then. The mask. The radio silence.

371

He was scared. Afraid that the letter had changed something in me. Changed my feelings for him.

Once again, I'd been so caught up in my own feelings, so convinced that Kace was this take charge, alpha kind of guy, that I'd forgotten he was human. He was scared.

So instead of waiting for him to cross the distance, to make a move, I did it. He stayed in place as I approached him, as I wrapped my hands around his neck and yanked my mouth to his. Then he moved, and the kiss was everything. Filled with all the words I'd been afraid to say.

Kace's hands went to my ass, slipping under my dress to squeeze my bare ass. He let out a hiss at the same time I moaned into his mouth.

If he hadn't stopped the kiss, I would've let him fuck me on the hood of the car, regardless of our audience.

"As much as I want to be inside you right now, Lizzie, not gonna let anyone else have the privilege of seeing your face when you're full of my cock," he growled, his hand giving my ass one last squeeze before he righted my dress. He didn't let me go, though.

"I love you," I said in response, my voice breathy.

He froze then, his eyes on me, hands flexing around me. "What did you just say?"

I smiled. Warmth spread through my bones. "I know you heard me, being much younger and having that superior hearing. But I'll repeat it. I love you, Kace. I've been too scared to admit it. Too scared to let you in. But you got in anyway. And now I can't escape you. What I feel for you." I stroked his cheek. "I don't want to. I don't ever want to escape you."

His mouth was on mine again. Quick, hard. "In case you hadn't caught on, being *much* older and all, I love you too, baby." His eyes met mine. "I'm so in awe of your bravery."

I tilted my head. "My bravery? What, because I shot that bitch that was about to kill me? No. That was survival."

His eyes clouded over as they did with any memory or mention of that day. No matter how it all ended, I knew he was haunted by how it could've been different. How he could've lost me. I knew that he was haunted by the fact I'd had to kill someone. I knew this because he'd told me. Kace was a communicator. If he was pissed about something, he told me immediately. Didn't brew on it. Didn't create a storm cloud over the house. He laid it out. Same with the things that made him happy. He wore it on his face. He spread it around the house. He shared it with me.

So yeah, I knew that the situation with Nicole haunted him still. He'd killed before. And he carried it with him in different ways. In dark ways. I knew that he hated how I had to carry it with me too. Or how he thought I carried it with me.

But honestly? I didn't carry it with me in a way that haunted me. I guess I should've. Something in me should've been broken or ruined after taking a human life. Should've sickened me. Sure, there were a few nights I woke up in a cold sweat. Moments in the day when I walked past the spot where she'd died and something moved inside of me. Something cold, slithery, reptilian.

But nothing lasting. I'd saved myself so I could continue being a mother, friend, and whatever I was to Kace. I slept next to him every night. Had breakfast with my kids every morning. Saw my friends for coffee, cocktails.

No. Being alive didn't haunt me. We were all killers in different ways. Whether we killed those out to harm us or killed parts of ourselves.

"No," Kace stated in answer to my question. "Though that was fuckin' brave, you defending yourself so I could be here right now with you." His hands rubbed down the sides of my body, as if he needed reminding I was real flesh and blood. "The bravest thing you've done is to let yourself love me after what you've lost. It's a gift you've given me, Lizzie. One I intend to treasure and nurture for a lifetime. Nothing less."

Though something cold hit me at the thought of how short that lifetime could be, Kace's warmth chased it away.

MY BOOK ARRIVED the day after I told Kace I loved him. The day after I decided that I was ready to move on with him. To start a life beyond my fear. Felt a bit too much to be a coincidence.

I was glad that no one was around when the box arrived.

It gave me a moment. Or a lot of moments. I needed all of them. It felt heavy in my hands. And it was. In more ways than one. Most of the time I'd spent writing it, I hadn't let myself consider it an actual book. I didn't even know what I'd considered it. Something to keep me sane. Keep me connected to Ranger. That's what it was, when it came down to it. It was our story. All of the good, all of the bad, all of the love.

I'd left one part out though.

A big part.

Ranger's death.

I'd written how the rest of our lives could've been. Should've been. Wrote a gritty, raw, romantic saga. One that I wanted to read. For a while, one I wanted to live.

It was all here. Four hundred pages.

My publishers and editors had mentioned the length, it being unusually long, especially for a romance debut. But I'd been firm on nothing being taken out. I was aware that 'killing your darlings' was a common practice. Maybe I was making a mistake. Maybe I'd look back on this after many more books—

hopefully many, at least—and regret it. But for now, I wanted it all in there. Needed it all in there. Our happy ever after had to live somewhere.

And it did. Right here. In the book in my hands. One that would be on bookshelves for the rest of our lives. I liked that. We'd get more time together. Even if it wasn't in reality.

Chapter 24

Three Months Later

Happiness was a funny thing.

It chased away terrors and pains that at one time had seemed so permanent. Dulled the pain of scars that would always at the very least itch.

It left you unaware that the world did not have a limit on horror.

Which was what I got on a Wednesday evening.

Horror.

Of course, I didn't know it at first.

"What a surprise!" I exclaimed, smiling at Gage and Lauren. I was so happy that I didn't notice the looks on their faces. Yeah, even though I knew better, even though I had all of the monstrous experiences to show me what a trap happiness was, I was stupid enough, human enough to think my tragedy insulated me from further horror.

But life didn't work like that.

There was no ceiling on how many times life could destroy you.

"Kace would not shut up about lasagna," I continued, ignorant to the fact that this would be the last few moments of happiness I'd have for a while. "So I made lasagna. I might've gone a little overboard, because I was taking into account that he's got all those muscles to feed, and now my son has decided he's going through a 'growth spurt' so he eats almost as much as Kace. Anyway, that's my long way of saying I actually have enough for two macho men, one mini-man, three and a half women and a toddler." I peered around. "Where's David? There's plenty for him too."

"I'm going to go to the kids," Lauren remarked, something odd about the way her voice sounded. She moved past me, but not before grabbing my hand and giving it a squeeze.

My blood went cold. This was all far too familiar. I knew what that voice was, what that squeeze meant.

I squared in on Gage. "What is going on?"

"Honey, I need you to brace yourself," Gage instructed, his voice as gentle as I'd ever heard it.

And it scared the ever-loving fuck out of me. If I didn't know my kids were in the backyard playing, I would've collapsed right there, thinking that something had happened to them.

But since they were in the backyard, and Gage had that soft look, was calling me honey, I knew there was only one person he was here to talk to me about.

"Is he alive?" I choked out. "Is Kace alive?"

"Why don't we sit," he invited, trying to move inside. I barred the doorway.

"No. We're not fucking sitting. You're telling me right now, *is he alive?*" My voice bordered on shrill, my patched-up heart already bracing for another break. Scars from the last time I'd gotten news like this were as fresh as if they'd been inflicted yesterday. The tissue knew. Emotional muscle memory.

Gage was silent for a beat, most likely trying to figure out what would be gained from trying to force me inside to give the news versus doing it right here. As if it made any kind of difference. As if my fucking sofa would soften any kind of blow he was about to give me. I could be wrapped in ten tons of cotton wool, and it wouldn't make a damn difference.

"He's alive."

There was no relief that came from that statement. No. The way he said it was not meant to comfort me. It was a fact. One that seemed tenuous. I could feel it.

"It's bad," he continued. "We need to go."

"The kids," I choked out, thinking of the two children who'd so recently recovered from the loss of their father. Who had welcomed a new man with the same cut into their lives. Who had fallen in love with that man. A lot in love. They'd done it without fear or hesitation, because the scar on their hearts was alone. They thought their father's death was a fluke. They had no reason to think that life would give them another wound so soon after they'd healed.

I'd done that too. I'd been foolish with my own heart. But that was fine. It was whatever. The biggest sin was being foolish with my children.

"Lauren's got them," Gage replied. "We're goin' to the hospital."

There was an urgency in his voice, something that told me he didn't know how much time we had. How much time Kace had.

The bottom fell out of my life then. For the second time. And I didn't know how I was going to survive it.

I DIDN'T SPEAK on the way to the hospital.

I must've breathed, because I was still alive when we got there. But everything inside me was frozen, on pause. My mind was blank. Empty. I couldn't think anything right now. Wouldn't let myself think anything.

The second Gage rolled to a stop, I jumped out of the car. Cade met me at the entrance of the hospital. I still didn't say a word. But I didn't need to.

"Semi clipped him," Cade explained, his voice grim. He held my eyes because that's the kind of guy that Cade was. It was hard for him. Painful, too, because despite what first impressions might communicate, this was a man who cared about people. About his club. So this was hurting him too. A lesser man would've looked away.

Cade did not look away. That's why he wore the president patch.

"Bastard was eating a fuckin' sandwich. Fat fuck." He shook his head. "We're taking care of him."

I nodded. I probably should care about the fate of the trucker who'd done nothing wrong aside from driving carelessly. But I really didn't. In fact, in that moment, I really hoped they made him suffer.

"Hospital staff won't tell us much, but they've told everything they can, thanks to Lily," Cade continued. "He's in surgery. Didn't look good at the start. Looks slightly better now, but I don't think that's saying much. I'm not going to give you false hope, Lizzie. I respect you too much for that. I wish to fuck I could lie to you." He ran a hand through his hair.

He was preparing for another funeral. I saw it in his face.

———

I DIDN'T KNOW how long I'd been sitting there when Lauren

arrived. It must've been awhile because it had gotten dark outside.

It was dark on the inside of me, so I liked that, at least.

I hadn't taken much notice of anything or anyone, blocking out the world as I sat in limbo. But a mother had a sense when her kid was near, so I jerked myself out of my oblivion to see my son standing beside Lauren, looking pale and scared but doing his best to look brave.

"What is he doing here?" I snapped at Lauren in a tone she did not deserve.

"He said he'd break out of our house and walk here if I didn't drive him," she replied in a kind tone that I, too, did not deserve. She smiled sadly. "Lily is sleeping."

I frowned at my son, hating what he'd see on my face. On my entire body.

Defeat.

"Mom, you're not going through this alone," he informed me in a tone too strong for a boy his age.

"Oh, sweetie, I'm not alone." I nodded around the waiting room, which was wall to wall with Sons of Templar patches and various wives.

Jack didn't look at them. Instead, he sat down beside me and took my hand in his. "You're not alone now," he corrected. "Kace is my friend. You love him. We love him too. I know you think I'm too young to be here, I know you want to protect me, but it's too late. I'm too smart." He smiled weakly. "So you can ground me when this is all over, but no matter what, I'm staying here until we get the news that Kace is okay."

Lauren wiped her eyes, giving me a look and blowing me a kiss before leaving.

There were no tears for me. Not even with Jack breaking my heart and soul. I couldn't cry right now. That was for after.

As much as I wanted to lie to Jack, and myself, I couldn't.

"Honey, you need to know. Kace might not be okay. We need to be prepared for that."

Jack frowned, jutting his chin up in that stubborn way his father used to do. "He's going to be okay," he repeated firmly. As if the stronger he spoke the statement, the more likely it was to be true.

I didn't have the heart to try and argue. Instead, I tried to believe it with the same strength that my son had. Tried to hope that the world couldn't possibly be so cruel as to take away my only other chance at love. Life.

⸺

THE DOCTOR CAME EVENTUALLY. They said a lot of things. Though I didn't absorb most of it, mostly holding on to the fact that he was still alive. I chose not to let the words like 'critical' and 'no guarantees' get through. No, alive was all I needed. The rest couldn't sink in. Because he couldn't die.

Wouldn't.

Jack's small hand was tight in mine. Suddenly, my son became so much larger. So much more mature. Yet another tragedy unfolding, molding him into the man he was meant to be much too soon.

Though I wanted to clutch on to my son and benefit from all of the strength he was holding in his body, the strength he was sharing with me, I urged him to go home. Be with his sister. Look after her. That was the only way to convince him. He was a protector, my boy. It was a struggle for him to leave me, even now. Even with all of the men sitting in the waiting room. He reminded me so much of his father in that moment, the pain almost crippled me. The memory of my dead husband in his son, already preparing to grieve the second man who had entered his life. Who I'd given him permission to love. Who I'd given myself permission to love because there was no way I'd bury two men in Sons of Templar cuts.

People survived things like this, surely. They had to. Mothers had no choice but to survive anything and everything.

Mothers had to put on false faces to assure their sons that they would be okay in the hospital without them. That's what I would do if alive stopped being the word used to describe Kace.

I would be nothing but a museum of pain. But I would not let my children see that. I would be a woman in a mask.

But I couldn't think of that right now.

Instead, I kissed my son and murmured that everything was going to be okay. Told him I loved him. Watched him leave, watching my heart and strength go with him.

People approached me. Women took turns sitting next to me, holding my hand, handing me coffee, sometimes speaking, though I couldn't remember what they said.

At some point the doctor came out again. My heart crawled up my throat as I watched her slow walk toward our encampment. There was nothing on her face. Of course there wasn't. Doctor's couldn't wear their news on their faces. Couldn't carry their heart on their sleeve. Being human amongst all of this sickness and death was the quickest way to go insane.

I knew that because we'd all clutched on to our humanity with bloody fingertips in the midst of the worst years. After Laurie.

She was coming to tell me he was dead. However long it took her to get here was my remaining time to clutch on to that singular word.

Alive.

Three seconds.

Two.

One.

None.

The doctor stood directly in front of me.

Bex was beside me now, not holding my hand, because that wasn't exactly her style. Which I was grateful for. I didn't want to be touched. She was close enough that I could feel her body tense, waiting for impact. Everyone was. No one thought he was going to make it. It became clear to me now. They'd been listening better before, when the doctor had explained his injuries.

They were ready for death. They were waiting to watch me hear about it. So they could try to do something. Save the human in me.

But there was no saving me.

After this moment, I'd be human for my children. I'd fuse my mask to my face, but I'd be empty inside.

"You can see him now," the doctor said.

The words didn't penetrate at first because I'd been trying to block out words of death. I blinked rapidly.

"He's not awake," she continued. "We've got him in an induced coma. There is some brain swelling that needs to go down before he can wake up. Once that happens, we will be able to gage the full extent of his injuries. For now, he's stable. Serious, but stable. You won't be able to see him for long, but I'm sure he'd love to hear your voice."

She said the last part with kindness. With a humanness about her. Her eyes smiled ever so slightly, but there was still a detachment there that I understood and envied.

Serious but stable.

Not dead.

I still got to hold on to the word alive. But now came the complexities of what that meant. Alive but... what? Brain dead? Paralyzed? Unable to remember my name?

If he could open his eyes and breathe on his own, it would be a victory. Surely, I could handle anything else.

I didn't want to see him. To see him hooked up to things. To see him in a hospital bed without his cut, without his smile, without his ease.

But I had to.

That was my job.

I'd made the decision to become and Old Lady again. I'd known the risks. Known that this life could steal him from me at any moment. All the while, I'd been worried about gunshots and explosions when it was a semi-truck that might steal my second chance. My second life.

Strength was required here. The club was all around me. I couldn't disrespect Kace with my fear. With all of my ugly worries. So I stood, my knees thankfully holding me.

I followed the doctor in silence. Sterile smells invaded my senses as we walked past rooms. I didn't want to get to Kace's room. Be faced with him while fragile.

But I eventually reached his room, because there was no room for wants in times like these.

He looked worse than I'd imagined. Which had been pretty bad. One of his legs was in a cast, with scary looking metal prongs going through the plaster and presumably into his skin and bone. His body still looked big, crowding the small hospital bed, though the tube down his throat and the machines he was attached to looked bigger still. White bandages covered his head. Had they done brain surgery? Had someone cut into his skull?

"I know it's overwhelming to see him like this," the doctor conveyed softly. I hadn't caught her name. I hadn't wanted to know it. If there was still a chance that she was going to tell me that Kace was dead, I didn't want to know her name.

"He has gotten through the worst of it," she continued. "The next few days will be critical, but he's young. He is healthy, and strong, which are all of the ingredients needed to get through this." Her eyes found mine. "And he has a life to fight for, and obviously, a whole lot of love. I know I'm a doctor and supposed to speak purely on the science of things, but sometimes, love can be what brings people back from accidents this."

She left on that, though her words hadn't made me feel particularly warm or hopeful. Ranger had also many reasons to live. He was strong. He was loved. If there had been a way he could've fought his way back to us, he would've done it.

I stood in the doorway, just staring at Kace. I wanted to hover there, maybe forever. Because in this doorway, he was alive, none of the realities of what his life might be—what my life might be—could catch me in this doorway.

My boot moved. Then the other. He looked even was worse when I got to his bedside. The side of his face was swollen, covered with scratches and scrapes. From his face being scraped across the road, I guessed. My stomach lurched at the vision of his injuries. How something simple like a driver's error, a distracted moment, could end so many things.

It wasn't as quiet in here as I'd expected. I had imagined without Kace's presence, without his smile, his easy words, his hard words, without any of his words really, that there would be nothing but a cruel silence filling the room. The same one that was there when I was cleaning my husband's bloody body two years ago.

But there was the beep of the monitors he was strapped to. A low hum. Sounds of nurses, patients and doctors moving around in the hallways. My heart thumping between my ears.

My fingers moved to trail his. They were slightly scraped up too. The rings he usually wore were gone. I wondered what happened to them. Had the doctors taken them off? What about the necklace Lily made him that he wore every day, even in the shower?

I checked his neck. That was gone too.

I was thankful for his tattoos. For the permanence of them. His identity, his personality, stamped on his skin so he didn't seem so anonymous laying in this bed. He was somebody. He was ours.

"I don't think you can actually hear me right now," I rasped, my voice a hoarse whisper. "I think maybe that's something doctor's say to people to try to make them feel better. To soften all the hard edges of this. Or maybe because the talking thing isn't even for you. Maybe it's for me. Being able to talk to you is a reminder you're not gone." My fingers interlaced with his. He was still warm.

"I know I'm meant to sit here and tell you I know you're going to make it through. Know you'd never leave us. But that's not how it works. You are not in control of this. Something else is. That makes it so much harder, doesn't it? That neither of us are in control of what life will look like. I've gotta say, I can't even think of a life that doesn't have you in it. You managed to find your way into our lives, and it just isn't fair for you to leave us yet." I paused, tears prickling the backs of my eyes.

I took a deep breath and looked at the ceiling, doing my best to hold them back. I couldn't let them fall. Not yet. I'd either cry with joy when he opened his eyes and said my name, or I'd fall apart in the shower after burying the second man I'd loved.

Either way, I had to hold it together for now.

"We'll be waiting for you," I whispered. "To come back to us."

Six Months Later

"Okay, babe, I'm not a snob, not by any stretch of the imagination. But I'm afraid I'm not doing my job as your Old Man if I let you walk in there, let alone catch whatever STD is living on the sheets in those rooms."

I smiled, watching Kace screw up his face at the exterior of the motel. He was still leaning on a cane that he was expected to need for another few weeks. He'd tried to tell me he didn't, but that hadn't worked. Not with me. Not with Lily. Or Jack. Or even any of the macho men of the Sons of Templar. Sure, they were mens' men, alpha males to the max, but they also weren't about to let their brother jeopardize his health for any kind of dumb masculinity bullshit.

It hurt me to see him need to use it. The slight hardness in his eyes illustrating that he was in pain. But he was alive to feel pain. And as much as I hated for him to suffer, that was all that mattered. And the doctors had assured us—me, many times— that he was going to heal completely as long as he used the cane, did his rehab and took it easy.

He did most of those things.

Except when it came to sex and his bike. Two things he did not ever do easy. I should've fought harder, but I was a weak, selfish woman. I liked being fucked hard by my Old Man. Liked being on the back of his bike.

We'd just gotten off it and were standing in front of a familiar motel.

It had definitely fallen into disrepair since the last time I was here. Which was saying something, since it wasn't that long ago since I'd last been here. Even though it seemed like eons had passed.

Where it used to only look somewhat questionable but functional for a road trip traveler who was tired, hungry and didn't have many other choices, the motel was now a place even the most desperate of long haulers wouldn't likely venture into. They'd get another large coffee from the gas station up the road and take their chances.

I liked that it had slowly started to decay since the day I came here. That it was crumbling to ruin. Because one day it

387

wouldn't be here anymore. One day, I wouldn't need it to be here.

And it wasn't meant to be anything but ugly. If someone had bought it, redid it, tried to make it something desirable, comfortable, pretty, I would've hated it. This was right.

I reached out to squeeze Kace's hand. "The first time I came here, I'd just lost my baby."

There was a sharp intake of breath beside me. I didn't look at him. I found solace in the crumbling paint and a crooked sign.

"It was after Jack," I continued. "Another boy. Four months along. There was no reason for it. Nothing we did wrong. The doctor's said it just... happens sometimes. They can't explain why. Other than death is all around us. Death doesn't always make sense, doesn't target the evil, the deserving. It just... is."

I sighed, thinking of the hell I'd gone through six months ago, waiting for Kace to wake up, terrified he never would or that he'd be changed forever. Then seeing him struggle with the most basic of things, seeing him grit his teeth through the most basic of things, trying to hide the extent of his pain because he didn't want me to feel any.

Those six months had been hard. On me. On Kace. On the kids. But they'd also been... something else entirely. We'd created something.

"It was the first time I'd really experienced it, death," I continued. "And in the most brutal and horrific way. My baby died inside me. No matter what the doctor said, no matter what Ranger said, I knew it was my fault. I was the reason for it. There was no way to breathe under that weight. Not with the most understanding, loving husband. Or kind, supportive friends. There was only escape. So that's what I did. I stopped here because I was tired. Because I needed somewhere to hide. To tend to my wounds. And because I liked its ugliness. Liked that the sheets were scratchy, the bathroom dirty. It's what I needed at the time. Eventually, someone came to get me."

"Ranger?" Kace guessed.

I realized then it was the first time I'd heard Kace say his name. Surely, that couldn't have been right. It wasn't as if Kace was afraid of my husband's ghost. Wasn't like he was living in fear of my dead husband. He hadn't ever made me feel guilty or uncomfortable for still mentioning him. Still grieving. There was no forcing me to forget him, to move on. Kace was perfectly comfortable with sharing me with my dead husband.

Yet I hadn't ever heard him say his name out loud.

Was that on purpose? Had he waited for me to bring him up because he didn't want to push me? Hurt me? I made a mental note to go back to that thought later.

"No, not Ranger," I answered.

My mind went back to those memories. Before all of this, before Kace, the recollections coming back in crisp detail. Stark color. As if they had just happened yesterday.

But now they were blurrier. My pain couldn't get through as easily. Like my body had some kind of protective shell around it. Or maybe I was finally starting to heal.

"It was Gage," I clarified. "I'm sure that Ranger fought him hard on being the one to come and get me. No one mentioned it, but I know it was most likely not pretty. He wasn't exactly the kind of man who would sit back and let anyone else be with his wife when she was in pain. Especially his best friend. But he was also a man who knew when to step back, even if it hurt him. Which I know it did. But he knew me well enough to understand I couldn't face him, not then. And he loved me enough to put every one of his instincts and needs aside. Because he'd just lost a baby too. He was bleeding too. But he wanted to tend to my wounds first. Like always."

I smiled. It was easier to remember these things about him

now. It still hurt, I figured it always would, at least a little. But now I could see Ranger more clearly. His death didn't permeate every thought of him.

"Gage didn't seem like the right person, before all of that happening. You wouldn't look at him and think that he was. But these Sons of Templar men all tend to surprise you."

I glanced back from the motel to look at Kace.

"I thought I was going to be finished then. I'd survive, of course, because I had Jack at home. I had Ranger. There was a whole life beyond my pain. My plan was to leave it all here. Like a time capsule of suffering. Suspended, yet still connected to me somehow. My pain did stay here, yet it was also still inside of me. Gage helped me understand I wasn't finished. Some things would just be different. Life did carry on. I'd drive by here sometimes, though. With an almost kind of cockiness. That I'd been dealt my pain and I'd survived it. Then Ranger died. I didn't come here immediately. No, there wasn't time. Wasn't space for that. There were two children to care for. There were things to do. There were lies to tell myself. It came much later, that visit. But it came. And like last time, Gage brought me back again. But I left a lot here. Almost all of me. Left it to die."

I paused, sucked in the air that smelled faintly of the fast food place across the street. "Then I met you. You grew new things inside of me. You changed me. And I want to show you this, the last of my pain. Maybe I want to show myself I don't need it anymore. To go to this place for a different reason."

I sucked in another breath. Deeper this time.

"I'll always love two men," I said. "One dead. One alive. He is buried, but what I have for him, it's eternal. It doesn't go away. I don't work that way." I looked up, but I found myself afraid, and that was unfamiliar. When was the last time I'd felt afraid for myself? To see the look on a man's face, to see if it was painted with rejection.

He didn't give me anything. The master of the poker face.

It was torture.

"If you want me, you have to know that," I continued. "That I'll always love him. He will always live for me. I can't change that."

"Baby," he murmured, lifting his hands to cup my face. "There's not a single thing I want to change about you, sure as fuck not the way you love. I can handle you loving your dead husband. As fucked up as it is, I'll only love you more for it. I'll make it my personal mission to stay alive longer than you do so you don't ever have to feel the pain of that loss ever again."

"Don't ever leave me," I whispered.

"Not a worldly or other worldly thing can take me from you," he promised, having proved this six months ago. The doctor had told us—after he'd woken up—that his recovery was nothing short of miraculous.

So Kace had kept the promise he'd made all that time ago. About preforming miracles.

———

"WHAT DO you think about us getting married?" I asked, sitting in front of the empty pool on a rickety sun lounger.

"I think you need to not suggest things like that when I'm staring at what is quite possibly a dead rat being consumed by one of its own kind. I need a little romance, please," Kace replied from his own sun lounger.

I smiled. "What? The dead rats aren't doing it for you?"

"They do it for my plenty. But I have an ego. I like control. As you well know." His gaze went dark, and my stomach dipped in a delightful way.

"So because of all of this, and because I do only plan on proposing once and plan on you only being proposed to once,

I'm gonna need to take the lead on this. But if you want, when I do mine—at an undisclosed place and time when I catch you by surprise—if you aren't enchanted, we can tell everyone the dead rat story instead of mine. That okay?"

Warmth bloomed in my stomach. An unfamiliar feeling in this place. This place reserved for my wounds and scars, my sorrows.

I put my drink down, moving from my chair to straddle him on his. My hands framed his face. "That is more than okay with me."

Then I kissed him.

He kissed me back for a while.

When things started to heat up, he pulled away. I made a sound of protest and glared at him.

"As much as I want to continue this, and I really fucking do," he adjusted himself to communicate just how much he wanted to continue, "I can't with a good conscience fuck you in one of those rooms." He titled his head, regarding me. "We make enough good memories here, baby?"

"Yeah," I whispered.

He stood, taking me with him. "Good, then we're going to that fancy as fuck hotel an hour away."

"An entire hour?" I whined.

He grinned wickedly. "Don't worry, babe. I'll make it worth the wait."

And he totally did.

Three times.

Then, two months later, he proposed to me.

That was worth the wait too.

Epilogue

We had lived hard.

Both of us.

Life gave us pockets of easy. Of love. Happiness.

But we also had hard times. Ugly, traumatic times. Blows that were meant to kill but only scarred us. Even together, there were more wounds. More scars from yesterdays coming back to hurt us.

So our epilogue, our ending, whatever you want to call it, needed to be soft. Gentle.

Of course there were things we couldn't control. Both Kace and I had chosen a hard road in life. Choosing to love is harder still.

But things were softer now.

Things were quieter.

We'd both healed from the wounds that we'd obtained, each of them joining all of our other scars. Now memories.

There were no babies for us, although I had thought after our wedding that maybe that was going to happen for us. I'd wanted to give that to Kace, despite not being sure if I wanted

ANNE MALCOM

more kids myself. More than anything, I wanted to give him the gift of fatherhood. Wanted to see a child who was a mix of the two of us. He would be patient with my pregnancy. He'd hold my hand while giving birth. Cut the cord. He'd get up in the middle of the night with me. Change diapers.

In short, he'd love that child an unimaginable amount. Because that's who Kace was. Because he already loved my children that much. Loved them like he had watched them grow inside me, like he'd known them forever. Like they were his blood.

And they loved him back. Hesitantly at first. Well, not Lily. She was not one to love with hesitation, which was going to spell trouble for us in her teenage years. Jack, on the other hand, had been more guarded. Which was entirely to do with losing his father. It created borders, boundaries to his love. A fear of loss that broke my heart.

Beyond that, he idolized his father. Adored him. And he considered it his job to protect me. One he took more and more seriously with every passing year. So even though the child inside of him wanted to love Kace for teaching him about cars, about guns—that one got me—about all the things his father had started to teach him, there was also the fact that the ghost of his father lingered. He was also old enough to feel guilt for wanting to love Kace. Like it was somehow dishonoring his father.

So it had taken him longer.

But not that much longer.

Because that was the magic of Kace.

You couldn't not fall in love with him.

Especially when we'd all been faced with the possibility of losing him. And when we didn't lose him, we'd had to see him weak. Injured.

And my son stepped up. He was there every step of the way.

And they were steps. Kace had had to learn how to walk again. Had to go through months of intense rehab. Had to weather constant pain. It could've done something to him. It could've made him depressed. Negative. Angry. It sure made me all of those things.

But not Kace. Through everything, he smiled, even if he was gritting his teeth while doing so. Regardless of his physical condition, he always found enough energy to be kind to me. To the kids. He was magic.

Jack certainly viewed him that way. He respected Kace's strength. His dedication. When Kace got out of the hospital, it was Jack's insistence that he move in with us. That he drive him and Lily to school when he could drive again. That he should sell his house down the street because he 'didn't need it anymore'.

He also helped Kace pick out my ring. Lily helped with the proposal. Kace made sure they were involved in such a big change in their lives. A bookend to their life with their father. Kace was so sensitive and knew that they didn't have control or agency over losing their father. Over having their mother move on. He wanted them to feel like this wasn't happening 'to' them, but like they were involved in everything.

Jack was his best man at the wedding.

Things got... softer from there. Easier.

Problems arose, to be sure. There were two growing kids around with scars of their own. There were more Sons of Templar courtships, Ashley and Wire of the most surprising. Well, not to me.

But for us, at least, things seemed to settle.

Then the baby thing slowly started. He didn't pressure me. Didn't mention it. But still, I felt it there. With his youth, with the fact it might just be an insult to science and the human race not to carry on his magical genes.

But I just felt... done.

Life was soft now. The loss of my baby and my husband after haunted me. Was I tempting fate by bringing yet another soft, pure, unmarked piece of happiness into the world?

It was surely a selfish way to think. But I couldn't help it.

And it had to come to a head eventually. Kace knew me too well, was far too in tune with me for me to be able to hide my thoughts on this.

I feared telling him. That he'd think less of me. That it would put a wedge in our beautiful marriage. But I had to. So I did, with a shaking voice and a fearful soul.

"Baby, I have you," Kace affirmed the moment I spoke, pulling me to him.

"Got two children that need a second father, one here on earth to do their first one proud. It's a responsibility. A big one. A beautiful one. In addition to being your husband, being their father fills me up. There is not one part of me that feels like my life is lacking without a kid. If you truly want one with your heart and soul, I'd be down. Only because I want to go on any adventure with you. But you don't truly want one. And you're torturing yourself thinking that is taking something away from me, when in reality, baby, you've already given me everything."

So there it was.

Our soft ending.

For now, at least.

Sure there would be bumps in the road. There would be things that cut us further. Wounded us still. But for the most part, we were content. Happy. We had made peace with all the scars of all of our yesterdays. We had the beauty of today.

Acknowledgments

Ah, it's so hard to write this.

For those of you who don't know, I wrote this book when I was pregnant. I started around the exact same time I found out. I wrote this book in the middle of the chaos that came with finding out this beautiful news and making preparations to go home to New Zealand so I could have the baby there.

Not long after I sent this book to the editor, at three months pregnant, I lost the baby.

It was (and still is) the hardest time of my life. I'm still going through the pain and emotions that too many women know all too well. This loss has battered me. Scarred me. Having to go through edits for this book while I was still suffering cut me all over again.

Lizzie's miscarriage at the beginning of the book was my way of acknowledging my own fears, thinking that if I wrote them into a book they wouldn't happen to me. But it did happen to me. The pain and loss in these pages is my own.

It's even more important to me now, even while still going through this, that I share this book. I share some of my story with you. Maybe I might make you feel less alone. I shared what happened to us with my readers on Facebook and I was overwhelmed with the strength and bravery of women willing to share their stories with me.

You made me feel so much less alone. You gave me so much hope. Thank you.

There are so many people all over the world who made this book possible. Who helped me feel strong enough to publish this.

Taylor. My soulmate. My best friend. My protector. You worked so very hard for us. For our daughter. You carried me through when I couldn't hold myself up. Held me when I was falling apart. Showed me love when I felt alone. I am so lucky to have you by my side for the rest of my life.

Mum. It has been so very hard being a world away from you throughout all of this. But I am so lucky that you answer every single one of my calls, that you let me cry, let me talk, let me do whatever I need to do. I'm so lucky that you have supported all my dreams and helped me through this nightmare. I can't wait to get home.

Dad. You're not here, I'd like to think you're somewhere with Ember, watching over me. I am the woman I am today because my dad taught me to never give up, to believe in myself and fight for what I want.

Jessica Gadziala. My #sisterqueen. My rock. You are such a wonderful person and talented author. You've been there for me throughout all of this and continue to be such an amazing human being. I'm so so lucky to have you as my friend.

Annette Brignac. You are always there for me. Always a message away, and I've needed that so much lately. You are steadfast friend, sister, superhero. Thank you for being there for me. And for being there for this book.

Michelle Clay. I'm so lucky that my books brought us

together. That my family is bigger and more beautiful than ever because of our relationship. The light you bring into it. You are such an extraordinary woman, mother, wife and friend and I cannot wait to see how you kick ass in the future.

Amo Jones. My ride or die bitch. Soul sisters forever. I love you so so much, am in awe of your talent and your all around badassery. Forever.

Polly. You have been there for me so much during this horrific time, even though you're on the other side of the world, I couldn't have gotten through any of this without you.

Emma. My beautiful friend. I miss you so very much and I cannot wait until we're reunited. Thank you for loving and supporting me across a world.

Harriet. I miss you so much, girlfriend. Especially now. Miss our shopping trips, spending too much money on food and wine and having adventures together. Love you so so much.

Kim. Thank you for doing such beautiful edits on this book and being a generally beautiful person.

And most importantly, **you, the reader**. Without you, this life of mine wouldn't be possible. This life where I get to write stories for a living. Daydream about bikers, vampires, witches, rockstars and call it a job. You've made my dreams come true.

About the Author

ANNE MALCOM has been an avid reader since before she can remember, her mother responsible for her love of reading. It started with magical journeys into the world of Hogwarts and Middle Earth, then as she grew up her reading tastes grew with her. Her love of reading doesn't discriminate, she reads across many genres, although classics like Little Women and Gone with the Wind will hold special places in her heart. She also can't get enough romance, especially when some possessive alpha males throw their weight around.

One day, in a reading slump, Cade and Gwen's story came to her and started taking up space in her head until she put their story into words. Now that she has started, it doesn't look like she's going to stop anytime soon, with many more characters demanding their story be told as well.

Raised in small town New Zealand, Anne had a truly special childhood, growing up in one of the most beautiful countries in the world. She has backpacked across Europe, ridden camels in the Sahara and eaten her way through Italy, loving every moment. She has settled down with her fiancé, their dogs and happy to be in one place…for a while at least.

Want to get in touch with Anne? She loves to hear from her readers.

You can email her: annemalcomauthor@hotmail.com
Or join her reader group on Facebook.

Also by Anne Malcom

The Sons of Templar Series

Making the Cut

Firestorm

Outside the Lines

Out of the Ashes

Beyond the Horizon

Dauntless

Battles of the Broken

Hollow Hearts

Deadline to Damnation

The Unquiet Mind Series

Echoes of Silence

Skeletons of Us

Broken Shelves

Mistake's Melody

Censored Soul

Greenstone Security

Still Waters

Shield

The Problem With Peace

The Vein Chronicles

Fatal Harmony

Deathless

Faults in Fate

Eternity's Awakening

Buried Destiny

Standalones

Birds of Paradise

Doyenne

Printed in Great Britain
by Amazon

83720463R00236